Sign up for our newsletter to hear
about new and upcoming releases.

www.ylva-publishing.com

Tales of the GRIMOIRE

book one

EDITED BY
ASTRID OHLETZ
AND
GILL MCKNIGHT

Ylva

Table of Contents

Introduction

Tingles. When we read something that gives us tingles, it may be a scary, frightening read, or perhaps something sensuous and erotic. In this anthology we hope to give you a little bit of both. We have sexy, scary, and the downright unsettling. These stories go bump in the night in all manner of ways.

It is a pleasure to work with such gifted authors. Some names will be familiar and well-loved, and some are new and exciting. We looked long and hard and collected the eclectic mix our anthologies have come to represent. *Tales from the Grimoire* will give you chills whatever way you want them. Enjoy.

Astrid Ohletz & Gill McKnight

Return Visit

BY CHERI FULLER

THERE'S A SOFT KNOCK ON the door and Dr. Clements comes in, looking at my chart as he walks.

"Susan, back's not better, huh?"

"No, and I noticed a mass about a week ago. It's gotten considerably bigger. Oh, and the stretches you had me do aren't helping at all."

"OK, lie on your right side and let's have a look."

I do as he asks, and I hear him wash his hands and pull a paper towel from the dispenser. I close my eyes and feel his chilled fingers as he locates the spot and very gently prods the mass.

"I feel what you're talking about. This wasn't here the last time you were in. You noticed it about a week ago?" I can feel him start to manipulate various spots, and when he gets to what feels like the base of my spine, the pain is so strong and sharp that I can't help but call out.

"Sorry about that. I just need a few more seconds." He continues, and the pain intensifies.

"Is it moving?! I think I can feel it moving!" I don't know how much longer I can lie still. It's getting very hard to control my breathing.

Suddenly it feels as though something has punched through my back. I hear him gasp and curse and the stool he was sitting on clatters over on its side. I feel light-headed from shock and pain.

My hand automatically goes back and I feel hot, sticky wetness. I move my fingers a little higher and can feel where my skin has been torn. I hear a gurgling yelp just before I feel something bite into my index finger. I yank my hand back and stare at where my finger used to be.

Before I can react, I feel it rip itself from my body. I can't help the scream that rushes forth. I double over and fall from the exam table just in time to see the creature skitter across the floor and jump onto the doctor's chest. Its spider-like legs, still heavy with blood and bits of my tissue, have small pincers on the ends, and they're holding tightly to Dr. Clements' white coat. I scream again and I can hear the nurse pounding and shoving on the door but the doctor is pressed against it, trying to get the thing off of him.

I hear a loud crunch and a large portion of the thing's body disappears into the doctor, who shudders and goes still. I sit up but can't bring myself to move. I'm mesmerized by the sight of this thing feeding on my doctor.

It's quiet except for the sounds of the pincers tearing at flesh and organs; the nurse must have gone to call for help. Slowly, the creature backs out of its meal and turns toward me. Its face is human-like with blue eyes and round, chubby cheeks. It moves a little closer, opens its mouth, and says "Mama."

Rise & Shine

BY JOVE BELLE

THE THING ABOUT ZOMBIES? PRETTY fucking hysterical on TV. In real life? Not funny at all. They should be. Seriously, when you see a person so fucked up he can barely stand and moaning "ehehehe," that shit *should* be funny. Hell, if it were a frat party, I'd treat somebody in that bad of shape to a game of cow tippin', featuring the staggering drunk bastard as the cow. But zombies are like Weebles. They wobble, but they just won't fucking fall down. Never mind that if you get close enough to put your hand on them, they'll eat your arm off.

There are a lot of urban myths about zombies, and some of them are true. Most are just asinine, like the idea that zombies are mindless shells doomed to wander aimlessly. Shit's not like that at all. They're not mindless. They have singular focus. Like a dedicated lover, they think of one thing only—food.

Sucks for us, because they're not too picky about what they eat. If it has a heartbeat, it's fair game. Field mouse? Yep. Ally cat? Absolutely. Bleating goat? No problem. Screaming human? That's just more to share with all their undead friends.

And zombies don't mess around. They are relentless. If you get into a barroom brawl with a human, you can yell, "Look over there!" And the dumbass will look away long enough for you to clobber him upside the head with a pool cue. If you try that shit with a zombie, you're going to die. It doesn't give a shit what's over there, and it'll use the time it took you to say the words to move closer to its goal—eating your face off. So your best—and only—bet is to run like your shoes are on fire.

Zombies don't give up, so you better be faster than they are.

Unfortunately, there's *always* another one waiting to take up the chase. Which is how I ended up here, sliding around corners on a fucking 50cc scooter while my best bud, Rise, blasts the shit out of the hoard following us with her shotgun. And here's the thing. One shotgun against a hundred zombies? Does a lot of damage to an individual zombie, but doesn't do a damn thing to a hoard. One falls down, another pops up. And firing a shotgun off the back of a scooter? *Never* a good idea. Every time she pulls the trigger, the ass end of the scooter slides sideways, and it's only through some physics-defying miracle that we've managed to stay upright.

"We need to go faster!" Rise yells, then chambers another round. She uses them sparingly, but frequently enough that I've a developed a Pavlovian response to the snick-click sound that precedes a blast. One shot is enough to teach even a stupid person to brace for impact next time around.

"No shit!" The scooter wasn't my idea in the first place. If we'd run right instead of left, we'd be in a big-ass Bronco tearing it up right now. I twist the accelerator harder. We're almost back to base and just need a little bit of good luck to get us through the door. If we show up with the army from hell bearing down on us, they'll barricade the gates and ignore our screams. If we're really lucky, whoever is on watchtower duty will spare the bullets and end it quickly.

I swerve around a corner, circling away from base. We need more space between us and the mob. Up ahead there's a building that's more rubble than structure.

"Grenade?" I shout. I've lost count of how many Rise has used, but I really hope she has at least one. We need more damage than a shotgun or a grenade can generate alone. Errant bricks always fly nicely with a well-placed explosive device.

"On it." Rise digs through her backpack. When the world first went to shit, we carried more clothes and food, fewer weapons. Took about two weeks for that to go all topsy-turvy. A person can wear dirty clothes providing she's still alive. And hungry is unpleasant, but it beats the shit out of being zombie kibble. "I have two left."

Rise pulls the pin on both and drops 'em easy-peasy on the ground. They bounce and roll right on target to intersect the horde as they reach the middle of the block. At the same time, we bounce and roll around the next corner. The grenades blow, and we're far enough away that the concussion wave doesn't throw the scooter off the road. Maybe that luck I've been hoping for just kicked in. Debris flies through the intersection behind us. The zombie moans decrease notably.

With a loud whoop, Rise twists around to face forward and wraps her free arm around my waist. She keeps the shotgun at the ready in her other hand. "Let's get back to base before they dig themselves out."

For a while, we referred to wherever we were holed up as home. It didn't take long to learn that nothing is permanent. It doesn't hurt as much to lose a base as it does a home.

When we pull through the gates, we're greeted with a howling mixture of laughter and cheers. People spill down the ladders from the guard tower, binoculars in hand. They'd watched our run through the streets. Fucking great.

"Shine!" Beastie, my surrogate baby sister, throws herself at me in a full-body hug before I get the kickstand down on the scooter. We just about topple to the ground. Rise saves us by planting her feet and holding tight to my waist.

"Whoa! Hold up, Beast, let me get this thing under control." I hold Beastie with one arm and kill the engine with the other, then drop the kickstand. Rise slides off the back and heads to the armory to refill her bag of tricks. I hope she finds something suitable. Last I checked, we were just about out of grenades and shotgun shells—Rise's two favorite toys.

Beastie climbs on my back and hugs me around the neck hard enough to choke. I pry her fingers away. "Ease up, kid."

"It was awful." Beastie buries her head in my neck. Wet tears coat my skin.

"Which one of you fucktards let her watch?" I yell at the guys. They were great in a fight, but useless at things like making sure Beastie doesn't end up more emotionally fucked up than she already is. Life in zombie-land sucks. It's hard and scary, and every single thing a person tries to believe in ends up dead. Or worse—turned. Beastie watched her parents die. Then, she beat her own dog off with her Little League bat. She survived in her school for weeks. Alone. She's a tough little shit, but she's seen enough. There's no way I can stop going on missions, and odds are I won't come back at some point. But she doesn't need a front row seat when that day comes.

"Chill, Shine. We kicked her off the tower when we realized." Braden is our leader, the guy with the maps and the radio and the plan. "She snuck back up there. Nobody *let* her."

I pull Beastie around to my front and hug her tight. "I'm here. I'm okay."

She squeezes me tighter for a long beat then drops to the ground. "Okay." She wipes her nose on the back of her sleeve. "Can I have the scooter?"

At eight, she's the only one of us who actually fits on such a small vehicle. It's a fucking miracle it moved at all with Rise and I both hanging off it. "All yours." I pass her the keys.

"Debrief," Braden yells from across the yard. He's impatient and halfway to the war room.

I lay my hand on Beastie's head and look her in the eye. Neither of us says it aloud, but I try my damnedest to make sure she knows I love her even though I'm an idiot who sucks with words. I like to think that, in our shared silence, she tells me the same. I give her a pat then jog after Braden. He's probably pissed that Rise went to the armory first, so it's better if I hustle to make up for it.

"Did you find it?" Braden asks before I even make it fully inside. The war room is really just a fancy name for a storage room where we set up a table, and Braden hung some maps on the wall. He stares at them all the time, marking them with Xs and Os and arrows in a pattern that nobody else understands. There's also an old CB radio that I yanked out of an abandoned semi on the highway. It works and someone monitors it all the time. Today, Braden's son, Rich, is at the controls. He gives me a wry smile and rolls his eyes a little. That's his way of saying, "Don't take it personally." He knows his dad's a pain in the ass, but that's okay. We all respect Braden anyway. And, really, whether we completed our mission is more important than manners right now.

"I think so." I close the door and sit at the table before elaborating. I get that this is life and death—especially since it was my ass depending on a freaking scooter to deliver Rise and me to safety—but I totally earned the right to sit. Granted, we are constantly being sent on these crazy missions with low odds for success, so Braden probably thinks I'm used to almost dying regularly. I'm not. It's not like I'm going to refuse his orders or anything, but a little consideration would be nice. And if he refuses to give it—mostly because he doesn't even think about it— then I'm not above extracting it from him in subtle ways. Like making him wait for the rest of my answer. "We couldn't get inside. It was locked up tight."

"Traditional or electronic?"

"Electronic." Rise enters through the side door. The war room and armory are connected. "But we'll take this next time." She holds up a length of primer cord. We have a shit-ton of the stuff but don't use it very often. Zombies won't stand still long enough for us to wrap them in it, and that's about the only way it would do any damage. Without anything stronger to detonate, it's easy to forget we even have it. In this case, however, it'll totally do the trick. So long as the door isn't too heavily reinforced. That's a chance we have to take.

Braden nods and asks Rise about the armory since my answer is useless. "Is it the right place?"

She nods. Rise is the navigator. I'm the driver. I turn left when she says, and she trusts me to keep us on the road. So far our arrangement has worked just fine. Besides, she has more interest in the target than I do. Braden thinks he's found a National Guard armory. An entire building full of weapons is straight up nirvana to Rise. She really likes things that go boom.

If Braden sent us out scouting for a Hostess factory, better believe I'd be all over that shit. Can't eat a box of 20-guage shells. Well, you can, but it'd be hell on your dental work. Still, our own armory is dangerously depleted. We have a sweet set up here. The zombies can't get in, and we can stay on the watchtower and pick 'em off all day long. So long as we don't run out of ammo.

I hate watchtower duty. Everyone has to take a turn at it, along with every other job that keeps the base functioning. Braden set up a rotation months ago, and we all slot in as we're told. I remember what it's like trying to survive outside of this compound. I'll sit on a watchtower—or any other crap job—every day of the week, as long as I get to stay here where I know Rise and Beastie are safe. Well, as safe as possible.

Still, I prefer my weapons more…tactile. Give me a baseball bat or a broad sword over a rifle every time. I trust my muscles and my swing. And zombies aren't big on ducking. That's why Rise and I make such a great team. She keeps 'em at a distance, and I deal with the fuckers if they breach her perimeter.

"You'll go back tomorrow." Braden stands, our future decided. "And try to bring back something bigger than the Barbie-mobile."

I'm surprised he doesn't say more about the scooter. I doubt they were able to see the moment when we went the wrong way. A badass bone-crushing vehicle waited for us one direction, and we took a wrong goddamned turn. It happens. It's easy to get mixed up when you're rushing and ready to piss yourself out of fear. Still, I kick Rise under the table. Navigation is her job, after all.

She salutes and says, "Sure thing, boss." Sure, she salutes him, but she smirks while she's doing it. And Braden gets it. This isn't the army. We fight because we have to. The only other choice is to die. We follow Braden because, so far, he's the only one with a plan. It may even be a good plan, but we don't have anything to compare it to, so it's impossible to know for sure.

Braden turns, the open door in his hand. "One last thing. Rise, Shine." He regards us respectively. "We're all glad you made it back."

In case it isn't obvious, those aren't our real names. Braden gave them to us not long after we joined his group. We are always together and way too happy early in the morning. Not particularly original, but we were so damn grateful to find a place where we could rest safely, he could have called us anything. We didn't care. Besides, Rise and Shine are terms of endearment. Not everyone gets a nickname, and we're special because of it.

"C'mon." Rise snakes the primer cord around my neck and tugs me toward the door. "I heard there's hot water, and Beastie is busy with the scooter."

"Hot water? No fucking way." I press Rise up against the door and kiss hard enough to let her know I'm interested, but not hard enough to make her think about anything too kinky. Rich is still in the corner playing with that radio. He doesn't need to see Rise tie me to the table with the primer cord and then fuck me with the detonator. That's totally something she would do. She's twisted like that, and I'm not much better.

She relaxes into the kiss, and I let all the tension and fear from our trek through zombie-land drain with each stroke of her tongue inside my mouth. Rise pulls away, biting my bottom lip. I follow after the snag-pull of her teeth and kiss her again. She laughs and ducks away, and I chase her out the door. "Bye Rich," I call over my shoulder without looking back.

The cool thing about an apocalypse is no one really gives a shit about the morality of the situation. Your only priority is to stay alive. If you can find a little pleasure in between near-death experiences, no one is going to judge. We could run naked through the compound yelling "We're going to fuck now!" and people would cheer. A few might ask to come along. Nobody would threaten us with eternal damnation. It's the one refreshing thing in this world made of rotting flesh that refuses to die.

Before, when the dead stayed dead and we were just normal kids in a small town, Rise's daddy was a preacher. The two did *not* see eye to eye. He thought she was an abomination because she likes pussy. I thought he was an asshole for not seeing how perfect she is. Rise cried a lot. He'd catch us together and beat the crap out of her. She's always been tough; that didn't happen because the world turned upside down. Her daddy, by trying to knock the fight out of her, ensured that she's always watching for the next attack. She's unpredictable and fearless.

With her old man, though, she'd just curl up in a ball and let him wail on her. I caught him once, quoting scripture—fucked up stuff from the Old Testament that must've been out of context—and bringing his wide, leather belt down against her back, over and over. She just lay there, whimpering and flinching every time the leather ripped across her skin. Her back was a mess of crisscrossed, raw, flay marks, and her blood was fucking everywhere.

He had this weird sweaty sheen on his face, and his eyes... Jesus, his eyes were fucked up. They were wild and unfocused, and I knew if I didn't stop him, he'd kill her right there in the middle of their kitchen. I busted a chair over his back, and when he fell to the ground, I kicked him in the ribs as hard as I could. And, just for good measure, I kicked him in the face. I didn't care if the fucker ever got back up. I never told Rise, but in my heart, I hoped he'd lay there and choke to death on his hatred. She didn't deserve the shit he spewed at her.

After that, I kept her at my place for six days. I smeared this nasty-smelling ointment on her back. The pharmacist said it would help her heal, and I guess he was right. She barely has any scars now. She cried a lot during that time, and I held her. That wasn't easy because, everywhere I touched, she was raw and wounded. I had to be really careful to not hurt her more than I helped.

To this day, I've never seen her cry again. Not even when I smashed my Louisville Slugger into her daddy's skull to stop his zombified ass from chewing her to pieces. That's the thing, I think, that made the difference. No matter how self-righteous somebody was, it didn't change a thing. The God they threw around like their heavy-weight savior died right along with everyone else when the wave of zombie death swept over us. All those years of looking down on everyone, bragging how their God would protect them, and they all died just as easily as anyone else. Or they turned. A zombie carrying a bible is enough to make most people pause a moment.

Anyway, when a person works as hard to stay alive as we all do, the thought of two girls fucking isn't all that scandalous. At least we're alive to fuck. And after what we went through to find that damn armory today, they should clear the way for us. We have some excess adrenaline to burn, and there's really only one good way to do that.

Rise and I make it to our room in record time. It's crazy small, and reminds me of the dorm room we shared during our first year of college. Only it's not filled with textbooks and illegally purchased liquor. Instead, we have a collection of machetes and spiked metal bats. That's my hobby. When I was a kid, my uncle taught me how to weld in his auto-body shop. So, every time I find a bat—or a good length of metal pipe—I bring it home and badass it up with some killer spikes. As soon as others figured out I can do this, they started bringing them to me, too. I get us some cool stuff in trade for the work, like candy bars for Beastie, or cigarettes for Rise.

One time, a dude gave me a full ounce of pot. In exchange, I did up three bats for him and also added spikes to this crazy metal glove he had. Personally, I never want to get close enough to punch a zombie, but he was way into it. Before the world went insane and the dead started eating the living, that much weed was worth a few hundred bucks.

Now, it all comes down to what a person can do to stay alive for another day. That glove was worth way more than the weed, but I'm not looking to rip people off. I want everyone to live through this shit storm. Besides, nothing takes the hard edge off reality like a tightly rolled blunt. And Rise rolls a great joint.

Anyway, our room is small, with a twin bed that Rise and I share, and another mattress on the floor for Beastie. There was a time, when this room would have felt claustrophobic. Now, it works really well. I like knowing that I can reach out and touch the two people I actually give a shit about. If Beastie wakes up in the middle of the night from a bad dream, we're right there. I think I'd go bat-shit crazy if it were any bigger.

Next to the bed, we have a crooked, busted up chest of drawers. Today, as soon as we clear the door, Rise shoves me up against the dresser, and I brace myself for the whole thing to crash to the ground. It doesn't. Last time, she pushed me into the weapons cabinet and the doors collapsed. We almost got skewered on those damn spikes I love so much. So, even if the dresser falls apart, it's better than the other hard surface in the room. And for some reason, Rise never aims for the soft.

"Hurry." Rise tugs my T-shirt out of the waistband of my cargo pants and moans when she finds skin. Her knuckles graze over my ribs, and I moan right along with her. "I'm so fucking glad you didn't die," she whispers a moment before she thrusts her tongue into my mouth.

"I'm glad you didn't die, too." We say those words to one another a lot, generally during sex. And often in place of *I love you*. I can't remember a time when we didn't love one another, but it's not something we really ever say. Rise is just as fucked up and emotionally repressed as I am, so it works.

I remove the primer from around my neck as discretely as possible. There's no telling what she'll do if it catches her attention again. She's crazy enough to try to incorporate it in our lovemaking. I prefer for the explosions we share to take the form of orgasm, not detonation.

The cord slips through my fingers and drops silently to the floor. Rise is distracted by the heavy buckle holding my pants up and doesn't notice at all. The buckle is usefully utilitarian on missions but utterly frustrating during foreplay.

I pull her shirt over her head and suck on the skin where her throat turns to shoulder. She tastes of sweat and gun powder. "Shower," I remind her. We haven't had hot water in so long. I want to feel her naked skin next to mine as glorious, beautiful, perfectly heated water sluices over us.

"Huh?" Rise grows impatient with the buckle and runs her hands along the edge of my pants, then dips inside to grip the rounded curve of my ass. She squeezes, her fingers digging into my road-sore flesh.

I pull away but stay close enough to kiss her chin. "You promised me a shower."

"Right." Rise pushes her hands deeper, holding me firm as she grinds her hips into mine. "Later," she murmurs into my ear the moment before she sucks the lobe into her mouth and worries it between her teeth. I moan, partially from disappointment, because I know the hot water will be gone long before Rise finishes with me, but mostly because of the sharp bolt of lust that pulses low in my belly.

Rise nips at my neck, her teeth sharp and quick, then she smooths a kiss over the spot before the sting fully registers. This woman, this perfect, deadly, soft and sensitive woman, manipulates my body in all the right ways. She draws me up, and pulls moan after moan from deep inside me. She does it with such ease, a light touch, a heated look, a gentle kiss. Sometimes, though, like now, she pounces, forcing my arousal to build through sheer brutal power. Her grip is just a little too strong, bordering on painful in exactly the way I need. Her teeth close along my neck as she sucks hard to bring my pulse hot and heavy into her mouth.

She breathes out her approval, her adoration as she squeezes and pushes and pulls my body. She's restless and devoted at the same time.

When she says my name, soft and pleading, I pull her mouth back to mine. I try not to grip too hard, one hand on her chin, but I can't judge the press of my fingers as I hold her and curl my tongue into her mouth.

Rise breaks away with a gasp. She reverses our position until she's leaning against the dresser and gently pushes me away. The heat in her gaze promises she's not done, just changing strategies. And then, in a low, dangerous voice, she says, "Strip."

She watches as I easily unfasten the buckle she'd given up on, and slip my pants down. They get caught up at my feet. The hitch in my sexy-soldier striptease is always the goddamn combat boots. They are fucking awesome to wear when we venture outside the compound, but totally wreck the seductive groove I'm rockin'. I shuffle over to our bed and sit down with a heavy "Oomph."

Rise laughs but doesn't move away from the dresser. The tightly wound tension in her shoulders and abdomen tell me she's not nearly as amused as she is horny, but the laughter lets her bleed some energy off while making me wait for her to fuck me. That's her thing. She makes me wait. Makes me beg. And just when I'm about to give up, she fucks me hard and fast while whispering the nastiest, most depraved shit in my ear.

She's not always like that, of course. Sometimes, she's so gentle, so soft, that I'm not even sure she's touching me until my orgasm rises up and turns me inside out. I've been with other people—sometimes with Rise there too—but nobody has ever affected me the way she does. She says the same about me.

The upside to my complete lack of grace while removing my boots is that Rise ends up with an unobstructed view of my pussy. My pants and underwear are already down as far as they'll go and I'm not about to pull them back up while I fuss with my damn boots. The longer I struggle with the laces, the more likely it is that she'll stop watching and fuck me already. *That* would be nice. Really nice.

I finally get both boots off and sit on the edge of the bed, legs spread and hands on my knees. And I wait. I want a shower, but I want Rise so much more.

She licks her lips. "You're wet enough for both of us."

Of course I am. That's what happens when we almost die screaming. I debate saying something sassy, but instead, I simply spread my legs a little wider. And I wait.

Rise isn't known for her self-control. I brace myself for impact, expecting her to full-body tackle me to the bed and bury her tongue in my cunt. Several long moments crawl by, and Rise doesn't move. Her eyes grow darker with every rise and fall of her chest, and I grow wetter by the second.

"Rise…" It's barely a whisper, and my voice fades off and builds again as a moan. When she looks at me like this…I melt. Liquid fire churns through me and pulses in my cunt, and if she doesn't touch me soon, I'm going to come anyway just from thinking about it.

Life continues in the hall outside our room. I hear people talking, walking past, and Rise stays perfectly still just staring at me. A shiver runs through me, and Rise smiles in a predatory, secretive way that makes me moan and shiver even harder. When she finally moves, she doesn't come to me as I expect. She quickly strips away the rest of her clothes and *finally* makes her way to the bed. She holds out her hand, and I take it, unsure if I can stand even with her help. My pussy throbs and my knees don't work quite right. Still, she draws me up until I'm standing with my arms around her neck for support.

She slips her hand between us and holds me with the other arm around my waist. She snugs me close and moves her fingers directly to my clit. She slides against it and then twists it between her knuckles.

"Oh God." I gasp and push my face into her neck. Rise slaps my ass.

"Who said you could talk?" Her warning bursts hot in my ear, and I barely keep myself from crying out when she moves her hand away from my cunt. Rise is often a demanding and greedy lover, but she rarely gives me orders. When she does, I listen. I know not to apologize even though I think about it for a moment, curious what her punishment might be. It's impossible to know with her until the moment she acts.

As though she senses my hesitation, she reaches between us and grips my nipple between her thumb and forefinger. She doesn't hesitate, doesn't tease. She twists hard and fast, and pushes me past the point of feels-good, right up to oh-my-god-stop-that-hurts. I gasp, and she bites my ear. I didn't speak, but I made a noise. And apparently that's against the rules today. She slaps my ass again, her fingers still pinching hard at my nipple. "I said quiet."

I don't respond. She establishes the rules with the warning salvo—the easy slap against my ass, followed by the second, much sharper one. I won't make a mistake again. So far she's been fairly gentle. That all ends if I don't follow her lead. Tonight she wants me quiet and obedient. I drop my head, averting my gaze in the process.

"Good girl." She releases my nipple. Blood rushes into the sensitive area, and I stifle a whimper. Rise is all lean muscle and bad intentions. She likes to make things explode, and I live at the top of her list. My head is still down when Rise pushes against my shoulder. Not so hard that I fall to my knees, but hard enough I know that's what she wants. I give in easily. It's always so easy with her.

She smooths her hands over my hair. Her fingers massage my scalp for a moment before she fists my hair in her hands and jerks hard until I look up at her. She smiles, but it's not the sweet smile that makes my heart fill with love. No, her grin is feral and wild, and it makes my heart gallop in my chest and rips the breath from my lungs. As she holds me in place, she adjusts herself until one foot is propped on the bed behind me and her cunt is spread before me.

My body tenses, at war with my mind. I know to stay put, but my muscles ache with the desire to touch, to taste. She grips my hair a little harder, holding me firmly with my mouth perfectly in line with her pussy. She tugs me closer, but still not close enough to touch.

I want to ask if this is her revenge for me spreading myself open on the bed earlier, but before I can form the words, she dips her other hand between her legs. She holds herself open, her fingers sliding easily through the contours of her labia to outline her clit. She frames it between her fingers and squeezes. She gasps as the tight knot pokes out of its hood. She's teasing me.

I lick my lips.

"You like this?"

I nod. Speaking isn't allowed, but so far Rise hasn't banned gestures. I hope. My thoughts are a little clouded and singular. I want—no need—to touch her clit with my tongue.

She jerks my face even closer, close enough I could taste her if I dared to try. "You want this?"

I nod again. Sharp pinpricks of pain pull at my scalp where she holds my hair. I moan and dare to say, "Please." It's a risk, speaking. There's a chance she will slap me again, but there's also a chance that she'll give in and let me have what I want—her cunt in my mouth.

Rise draws me in abruptly until my nose is buried in her curls, and I'm finally able to lap at her clit with my tongue. She drops her foot to the ground and spreads her legs, making it that much harder to get my tongue where I want it, and it takes all my willpower not to grab her around her thighs and pull her even closer. I desperately want to use my fingers.

"Tongue only." She grips my head on either side of my ears and holds me in place while she thrusts against my face. I hold out my tongue, willing to let her use me. Rise could masturbate and make me watch, which is hot as fuck, but instead, she lets me taste her. It's a gift, and I am grateful.

Desire drips between my legs. I reach for my own clit, testing if her tongue-only rule applies to me as well. Rise thrusts harder than normal, battering into my teeth and knocking me off balance. At the same time, she pulls my hair, sharp and quick. No touching at all. I moan into her cunt.

Rise fucks her hips rhythmically against me, smearing her arousal over my mouth and chin. "Fuck, Shine." She tenses, curses again, then vibrates against me. Her grip in my hair eases, but she doesn't let go entirely.

I wait, crouched on the cold tile floor. Finally, after a moment so short there's no way she's fully recovered, Rise pulls me up. She kisses me gently, reverently, lips parted, and her breath hot inside my mouth. And still I wait, throbbing and ready to beg.

She eases me onto the bed, and her mouth never leaves mine. As my back hits the mattress, she presses her tongue inside. I suck her in, grounded by the weight of her body above me and her tongue sliding against mine.

She touches me. Her movements are rushed and callused one moment, then slow and easy the next. She takes her time on the bits

18

that make me gasp and completely skips the parts that make me scream. I desperately want to speak, to beg her to fuck me. Instead I lie perfectly still and let her have her way.

Rise presses her lips to my ear and stays there. I listen to her stilted breath, labored and shallow. She's ready again, and I'm not sure what that means. She could easily climb the length of my body and lower her cunt to my mouth, riding my face to another orgasm. I wouldn't mind that at all. Or the look in her eyes and the hitch in her breathing might mean she's about to fuck me. Hard and fast the way I like. Maybe she'll let me touch her at the same time. My fingers itch to feel how hot and wet she is. How long will it take her to come a second time if I fuck my fingers into her?

She moves her leg between mine and rocks her thigh against me hard. "You're so wet. God, Shine, you're so fucking hot. I can't get enough." She slips her hand between her thigh and my pussy, then eases her fingers between my folds.

I whimper. She's so close to giving me what I want. And I'm so very bad at holding back. My embarrassing lack of self-control is the main reason she likes to give me impossible commands and then tease me. It turns both of us on beyond reason.

Finally, Rise thrusts inside me and, at the same time, bites down on the fleshy part of my shoulder right above my collarbone.

"Yes," I hiss. She's committed. Once she penetrates me, she never stops until I come. She might punish me for speaking without her express permission later, but I'm willing to pay the price. How can she expect me to be responsible for the words that issue from deep inside me when she's *so* hot, so relentless? "So good."

Rise thrusts slow but hard, pressing deep and holding. She flutters her fingers inside me, and my eyes roll back. God, I need this. She pulls out and thrusts again, her pace methodical. Steady. Torturous.

"Please." I claw at the blanket, trying to be a good girl and keep my hands off her body like she wants, but I need *something* to grasp.

"More?" Rise licks over the bite mark, then bites down again.

She pushes in with another finger and stretches me even wider. I shudder with the early tremors of orgasm.

"Not yet, baby, I'm not done with you." It's not a command, just a casual statement. She's letting me know I can come if I want, but she's not going to stop.

My body trembles, and I fight to hold back. She fucks me faster, increasing her tempo slightly, but still pausing long enough to wiggle her fingers inside. She's stretching me, preparing me for something larger, but in my pre-orgasm haze, I can't think of what.

"One more, Shine, can you take it?" She doesn't wait for me to answer before she thrusts in with all four fingers. Again, she moves a little quicker, but her pace is still moderated. She's very much in control, and I'm very much a sloppy mess on the verge of breaking.

I nod frantically into her neck. I can take it. I want to take it. Anything she has to give, I want every last bit. She wiggles her fingers and twists them in tight half-circles, drilling her way deeper into my cunt.

"Rise," I pant, a benediction to a god that no longer exists. Rise is the only religion I've ever really known anyway. "Please."

"Okay? Shine?" For the first time tonight, Rise asks me for permission. She isn't sure what I want, and she's holding back. For all our games, she would never truly hurt me.

"Yes." I nod, pleading. "Yes...yes. All of you."

She pushes into me, slowly, reverently. I stretch and hurt and burn and feel so fucking good all at the same time.

"Don't stop." I grit my teeth, pushing my body onto her hand. We don't do this very often, because it's just too intense, but, God, when we do... Rise owns me as her hand finally slips past the tight ring of resistance. I exhale sharply.

Rise smiles, but still manages to look serious as she wiggles her fingers again. I feel it everywhere, through my entire body. Inside my cunt, in the tips of my toes, tripping over my scalp. Rise is everywhere. My pussy contracts, and the tremors bring Rise to her knees.

She holds herself still and watches me closely. "I'm going to fuck you now."

She brushes a fleeting kiss over my lips, and she rocks her fist inside me. I scream—that good kind of scream that starts low and builds along with the pleasure inside. The heat in my core threatens to consume me, and I need her mouth cool against mine as counterpoint. I pull her into a frantic kiss.

"Shush, I've got you," she whispers between kisses, her breath hot on my face, but not as hot at the fire she's dragging through my body. She barely moves her hand, but it feels as if I'm being torn apart and plowed open to make room for new growth.

She rotates her knuckles, touching every part of me. I want more. "Please...Rise..." I can't find the words to tell her what I need. My lungs stop working with each teasing, twisting thrust of her fist inside my cunt. My mouth falls open in a breathless, soundless scream.

Rise stops being gentle and works her fist harder. Pushing in, then pulling back until I feel the intense pressure of her hand trying to exit. I gasp, and she pushes in again. Over and over until I can no longer see. I tense and shudder and curse as I come. The orgasm hits me hard and fast, then keeps coming wave after wave. It lasts a millennia until, finally, everything goes dark.

I come to when Rise pulls her hand from me. I'm lost, bereft without the intimacy of her inside. I moan.

"You okay?" She smooths my hair and kisses my face. "I didn't hurt you?"

I laugh, but it's weak and thready. "God no. You're perfect."

I don't tell her that my hips feel as if they've been pulled apart in a modified version of being drawn and quartered. She wouldn't believe that's a good thing no matter how much I reassure her, so it's best left unsaid. She presses a light kiss to the corner of my mouth and curls her body around mine. Tremors—aftershocks from the orgasm—work their way from my cunt out through the rest of my body in waves, and I close my eyes to enjoy the residual feeling rolling through me.

"God, Braden wants us to go out again tomorrow." I moan as I remember the reason Rise was so worked up in the first place. "If I can't walk, you're going to have to explain it to him."

"Happily." Rise grins rakishly. The devil in her loves what she's done and can't wait to brag about it.

"Don't look so pleased with yourself." I slap her arm, but it's a weak, uncontrolled movement. Sadly, it takes all my energy to do even that.

She laughs and kisses me. "I have bad news."

The look in her eyes is mischievous, not troubled as her words imply. I smile, uncertain. "What's that?"

"I'm pretty sure the hot water's gone by now."

I tug her closer to me. Hot water isn't as important as her arms around me. Eventually, we'll have to get up and check on Beastie. For now, though, I just want her as close to me as possible. Everything else can wait. I know we won't sleep, but this part, the cooling off after the firestorm, is just as important as the blaze itself.

We go on runs together because she won't let me go without her, and I won't let her go without me. It's hard to see her risk her life, but if she ever actually dies, I want to be right there with her. Everyone knows, without Rise, there is no Shine.

Glitter Hill on Fur Tor

BY CHERI CRYSTAL

RAIN OR SHINE, SLEET OR snow, Roseland went walking on the moors, ready for anything. For beating the winter blues, nothing compared to a strenuous trek over hill and dale. In her youth, she'd avoided sports as she would an infectious disease. One of those people who never had an issue with her weight, diet and exercise hadn't ever even entered her stream of consciousness. Why work out if she didn't have to, she had reasoned. Spending precious time engaged in intellectual pursuits far outweighed physical activity on her priority scale. But the combination of time, age, and bad genes could easily land her immobile in a dribble chair, like Gramma, and she didn't want to end up like dear old dad either. One minute he was finalizing his dream vacation plans that he'd "…spent the best years of my life saving for and as a surprise for your mother," he had confided, and the next, he was dead of a massive coronary at only three years older than she was now. Finding him that way, slumped over in a kitchen chair, had been a major wake-up call. Her dad liked an occasional whiskey for celebratory purposes, and he didn't smoke or eat too many puddings, but look what had happened to him anyway. The shock had spurred her into action. She had vowed to get out there and move her body while she still could.

Roseland had begun her fitness regimen because she didn't want to leave Mum the way her father had. What began as just parking a distance away from the entrance to her job led to walking to and from work, three miles there and back. Eventually she found herself looking forward to hiking on the moors and coastal paths, and even walking the six to eight miles into town. Roseland was fitter and genuinely happier at fifty-two than she had been in her entire life. It was funny that the girl who had invented excuses to get out of gym class in order to spend extra time in the library would now be practicing physical fitness on purpose. No use in having a sharp mind in a sluggish body.

Roseland opened the *Ordinance Survey of Dartmoor* and spread it over a large space on the floor. She had to move the coffee table for additional room, knocking off a few books and journals as she did. Last night's half full teapot fell off also, but luckily the pot survived the fall and the tea was the same colour as the carpet. She read the words *Clitter Hill*, then laughed herself silly. It figured that the closest she would get to anything that conjured up images of that neglected part of her anatomy in decades would be charting a path to Clitter Hill. The good laugh lifted her spirits. Then she spotted *Fur Tor*. Whoever had named these landmasses was a pint short of pissed.

Wiping an errant tear, she Googled Fur Tor. The pictorials on the web painted a picture of a desolate area. Still, whenever possible, she liked to judge people, places, and things for herself, not relying on the evaluation of others. As a scientist, she was loath to believe things she couldn't prove through her own devices. The day God—Him, Her, or Itself—came to visit for afternoon tea was the day she would know, without a shadow of a doubt, that there was indeed a Supreme Being. Failing that certainty, she insisted on hard evidence and absolute facts. Until then, Roseland didn't buy into any of this blind faith bunk. It seemed to her that it was primarily a strategy for controlling the masses or lining the pockets of the clergy.

She jotted down notes as she mapped out her route, starting at Postbridge. From there she would continue towards Fur Tor, despite the foreboding weather forecast that threatened to make the trip across the most northerly part of Dartmoor difficult and unpleasant. Wind and rain always seemed harsher on high, open spaces. Regardless of all that, she was looking forward to staking her claim, so to speak, on Clitter Hill, and planned to snap a selfie for her album to record the accomplishment. It amused her every time she thought about the personage who had first called a collection of boulders and stones the "clitters," and subsequently named the tors "Mis" and "Fur."

Through the years, she'd hiked most of the coastal paths from Devon to Cornwall. Roseland rated the South West Coast Path National Trails as her favourite route, followed by the Thames Path and Hadrian's Wall. She still had much of Dartmoor and The Lake District to explore. Someday she hoped to plan a proper trip that would include the centremost part of the northern moor, which was surrounded by treacherous terrain and ensured the penultimate isolation. Today's hike was a lot less ambitious, but would be satisfying both for scenic reasons and exercise potential. First she had to eat breakfast and pack a lunch.

Preferring hard copy to electronic versions, Roseland read the morning paper while chewing on a toasted tea cake with a sprinkle of chopped walnuts. She'd added walnuts to her diet, after she'd read a study done by an institute she trusted about the heart benefits of consuming walnuts. It was an added bonus that she quite enjoyed the nutty flavour, as it complemented the sweet cinnamon tea cake.

Since she'd lost her dad, she'd made other changes as well—reducing her consumption of fish and chips, crisps, and her favorite puddings. The latest recommendations by nutrition experts no longer designated the simplest form of high quality protein, the egg, as a taboo food based on fear of increasing blood cholesterol. This was an adequately referenced study that Roseland was excited to accept. She enjoyed eggs. After reading about the importance of high quality protein in warding off sarcopenia, especially as one aged, Roseland ate a hard cooked egg at least three times a week. She wished the experts would stop changing their minds about whether eggs were good or bad for you, and conduct a definitive study once and for all. She popped the last bit of yolk into her mouth, then followed it with a last swallow of tea. She'd be damned if she was going to allow a decrease in *her* muscle protein synthesis without a fight.

Periodically glancing out the window as she washed the breakfast dishes, Roseland envisioned the walk ahead. It was a dress rehearsal of sorts. She often found that when she was utterly absorbed in thought, such as when rehashing complicated theorems and hypotheses, she often lost track of time and place. Losing track of the "where" and "when" was not something Roseland welcomed, but rather something she endured. It also sucked to have a poor sense of direction, another thing she had inherited from her dad. She shrugged off the thought and turned her attention back to the small TV set on the counter by the table.

BBC News droned on in the background. BBC was her constant breakfast and dinner companion when she wasn't watching Sky News for their spin, Eggheads to test her trivia recall abilities, or some documentary. In tandem with the paid commentator, Roseland voiced her opinions as if the newscaster could hear her as she shredded a nice portion of Tickler vintage cheddar onto thick slices of multigrain seeded bloomer. Savoury cheese sandwiches and sweet biscuits were indulgences she only allowed herself when she was out hiking, as she'd need extra fat to keep her fuelled over the long haul. Even using care, Roseland still managed to get some cheese and crumbs on the floor. *That never used to be a problem*, she thought with a heavy heart.

It had been hard, but she had finally donated Trixie's bed and bowls to a co-worker who had adopted a puppy. It was too painful to see them both sitting empty. Not one to dwell on sadness, she decided her sandwich needed relish. She spread Lurpak butter on one side of the bread and Branston pickle on the other, added diced spring onions and peppery rocket leaves, and closed her sandwich. She then washed red seedless grapes, fixed carrot and celery sticks, and, as a special treat, threw in a few Jammie Dodgers. The luscious jam-filled biscuits always hit the spot. No sense in avoiding treats, as long as she didn't eat them to the exclusion of more nourishing foods.

"That should do it," she said aloud, clapping the crumbs off her hands.

BBC repeated the weather forecast. The newscaster painted an awfully bleak picture. The southwest of England was usually spared the brunt of winter weather as long as winds came predominantly from the westerly or south westerly direction. Apparently a mid-Atlantic chill was sweeping down from the north.

She stepped out onto the backyard terrace. As if in testament to truth in forecasting, a brisk wind whipped her shoulder-length bob right off her face. Roseland glanced toward the grey skies thick with clouds and their threat of rain, sleet, or hail, but the idea of staying in with a good book and a box of chocolates, while it sounded heavenly, was just not an option for the new her that thrived on her love of the outdoors.

In her youth, she'd had no idea what she was missing while she read volumes indoors. Now when she planned a walk, there was no changing her mind. She assured herself she wasn't fussed about a bit of weather. She would bundle up, pack a lunch, head out, and be just fine—a brave soldier marching off to battle.

As she ran up the stairs two at a time, Rosalind smiled at her seemingly boundless energy. Flinging open the door of the antique wardrobe that belonged first to Gramma at the farmhouse and then to Mum, Roseland paused. She missed them, and wished they were both still alive, but there was no use shedding more tears. Loss was inevitable. Homo sapiens, animals, all living creatures were born to die. It was a fact of life that could not be escaped, but still Roseland couldn't help feeling more alone in the world, especially since she had also lost her beloved pet—dear, sweet Trixie.

Dwelling on sadness was an indulgent and wasteful pursuit, and she quickly redirected her thoughts to concentrating on gearing up. She knew exactly what she'd wear. The dire weather prediction was nothing that couldn't be countered by a good set of thermals, lined hiking trousers, two layers of heavy gauge socks, and four layers on top—thermals, cotton shirt, fleece, and body warmer. Weighing the pros and cons of wearing a down insulated ski-jacket for extra warmth or the shell jacket for more breathable protection against wind and rain, Roseland couldn't wait to get out on the moor.

She glanced at the wall clock. Ten past nine. She was ahead of schedule. According to her plan, she would park at the Moor Sheep and Dartmoor Pony Inn and pop in for a quick hot chocolate, hike starting at ten-thirty, the latest, and pack it in around three that afternoon in order to get back to her car before dark.

Roseland checked and rechecked her backpack, filled the water reservoir about three quarters, hoping it wouldn't freeze, and decided against the heavier down-filled jacket for something less bulky. She'd be walking at a brisk pace and doubted she'd need extra warmth. Next she slipped into hiking boots and laced them up snug but not too tight.

The driving route from Princetown towards Crazy Well Pool should be uncrowded this time of year. There was a weather-beaten, barren farmhouse at Nun's Cross she planned to find, so that she could tick off another landmark she wanted to see. By half nine, she was on the road, arriving at her destination at precisely ten-thirty. There was already one other car parked in the area she had chosen to leave her car. She cut the engine and pocketed her keys. At first she wondered whether the pub was closed, but as she drew closer to the inn, she spotted signs of life within.

The bartender took a fiver and handed her a few quid change as he signalled a waitress to make a hot chocolate. She collected her drink from the bar and sat at a table by the window. As soon as the chocolate was cool enough to not scald her tongue, Roseland drank up. The creamy, steamy mixture was oh so thick and chocolatey, but not sickeningly sweet. It was just what she needed to warm her up and fuel her fire for a brisk walk. She loved it when the moors were virtually empty, as she preferred to enjoy the solitude in peace.

A bitter wind blew right through her the moment she stepped out of the toasty inn. It was bloody cold outside. With each step, staying indoors by a cozy fire grew increasingly more enticing. Only the bright rays of sunshine when they managed to poke through the clouds for more than a few minutes at a time cheered her up. Having lived in England all her life, she never took the sun for granted and wasn't bothered in the least about having to squint against the intense light, but it was a shame the winter sun wasn't effective at warming her. Even on the short walk to the car for her woollen scarf, she hurried along, just to warm up. It was a good day to go at a quick, steady pace.

Roseland shut the boot and glanced up in time to spot a middle-aged couple headed back down the mountain with an ambitious stride. They must have set out at first light to be finished this early. Two Scottish terriers caught her eye as they ran to join their owners. One white and the other black, they were both wearing plaid coats. Roseland felt a sharp pang in her chest. She wished her beloved golden brown labradoodle hadn't succumbed to Addison's disease just three short months before. When the symptoms became more than Trixie and Roseland could bear, Roseland held her best girl in her arms, sobbing when Trixie took her last breath. At the recollection, a tear escaped the corner of Roseland's eye, but fond memories helped push aside some of the pain—Trixie wagging her tail exuberantly, always trying hard to please, and splashing around in the water as Roseland walked along the rivers Dart, Avon, or Thames. Her beloved pet was no longer suffering. Still, life was much lonelier without Trixie. Sure, Roseland had her job at the chemical research plant, but she didn't work seven days a week. She used weekend hikes to fill the off hours, but winters seemed longer and drearier without her trusted four-legged-friend. She should probably get another furry child, but it was too soon. Her heart wasn't in it. She knew that whoever she adopted would one day leave her. Better to relive the precious memories rather than risk another broken heart.

Checking her cell phone pedometer app, Roseland noted the number of steps she had done puttering around the house getting ready so that she could subtract them from the steps she would accomplish on her walk. At the beginning of the hike she could key in the starting place, which would show the exact time she began. The pedometer app would then allow her to calculate the total miles walked later that night. In four or four-and-a-half hours, she could easily walk a looped circuit of eight to ten miles, stop at Nun's Cross to eat her picnic lunch, and get back to the carpark before nightfall.

Spence preferred working weekends and packed out holiday seasons to working on ordinary days when business was steady but much slower. She liked to keep busy, the busier the better. She grew restless and bored if she became too idle. In addition to her studies, she tended bar at a popular inn with a pub and restaurant that had accommodations for holidaymakers. The luxury bedrooms had remodelled en suites and were in high demand on Dartmoor. Spence had been hired as bar staff, but she soon was filling in as a hostess, waitress, and in a pinch she wasn't above stock work, reception, and getting rooms ready for guests.

"Hey, Spence, we need a hot chocolate."

"Sure thing, Colin. One sec."

Spence had just cleaned out the expensive, commercial hot chocolate machine and had to run clear water through once more before filling the requested order. She was meticulous with the equipment. It was well worth its cost, as it ensured repeat customers and high scores on Trip Advisor. Some people remembered their beer, coffee, and even hot chocolate better than they did the food. How many times had she heard "Moor Sheep and Dartmoor Pony Inn has an excellent selection of locally brewed Dartmoor ales, their specialty coffees are memorable, and they make a hot chocolate you'll never forget"? Too many to count. Spence was very proud of the way she did her job, and went to great lengths to insure customer satisfaction. She had enrolled in a course on Hotel Management, as she knew she would someday own the place. As soon as it was hers, she would change the name. At the moment, it was more than a mouthful.

Had she not been busy in the kitchen, Spence would have seen more of the woman who'd ordered the hot chocolate. She made a point to ask guests how they were and if everything was satisfactory, but the blonde-bobbed woman had finished her hot chocolate and was out the door so fast, Spence only got a glimpse of her as she exited the pub. She was pulling on a woolly cap beneath what looked like a double layer, or perhaps even a triple.

Returning to the kitchen, Spence swiped mist off the window with her sleeve and turned on the taps. While she scoured baking trays, her gaze followed the lone woman out to the carpark. Spence could make out a thick vapour trail in the woman's wake as she dashed to her car. Her clear view didn't last long, as the ovens were on full whack, crisping up sausage rolls for the staff's mid-morning snack. The window repeatedly fogged, and when Spence wiped it clear, she could see that the woman had added a thick scarf as well. It seemed like overkill, especially in addition to the hoodie she has already been wearing, but it was raw out. The blonde shut the boot, and then headed straight for the path. Seldom did a woman venture out on the moors alone. Even rarer was finding one who was apparently planning a hike when inclement weather was on the way.

The food orders were coming in at a faster pace as more hikers were showing up after turning back. Why would this crazy woman be heading out instead of staying put?

Spence figured the woman must know what she was doing. Maybe she wasn't going very far. Serious hikers just couldn't pass up any opportunity to get outside. Maybe she was a hiking fanatic. She looked fit, so that must be it. Spence sized her up. Her gear didn't scream sport enthusiast, but she had a nice figure under all that outdoor clothing. If Spence had had her binoculars handy, she would have loved to get a closer look at her features. From a distance, all she could tell for sure was that the hiker was an unusual woman, and that made her interesting.

Colin called out, "A pot of English Breakfast, two cappuccinos with extra chocolate sprinkles, a treacle tart with clotted cream, and two scones with butter and jam, Spence."

"Sure thing, Col." Spence lost track of the hiker, but not before she saw that the only car left in the lot was a purple Picasso Citroen.

Roseland strode on. Blood pumped through her veins, warming her core, but her extremities were still a bit chilled so she picked up her pace. Long walks in complete solitude were excellent for both physical and mental exercises in soul-searching, but they also left room for ruminating on things that might have been. The cows weren't the only ones chewing their cud, she often mused when introspection carried her off into oblivion or regret. What did she have to regret, exactly? Nothing too earth shattering. Perhaps that she had moved around so much for work...

Research demanded funding and without it she'd have been unemployed for long stretches of time, waiting for her next job, so she gave up the sponsored variety of cutting edge clinical trials and settled in the Southwest for a permanent position. While the work was not as challenging, the money was reliable.

She credited her dad for her thirst for knowledge, inquisitive mind, and perseverance in uncovering truths. Back when she should have been in the market to find someone, she was totally engrossed in her work and had few interests aside from discovering something important like designing less toxic drugs to treat Cancer, AIDS, or any number of diseases, drugs which would be as effective but with fewer side effects. Any advances in chemical toxicology would surely make a difference in patients' lives, especially those with compromised immune systems. Now even small accomplishments were enough to keep her excited and fulfilled.

CHERI CRYSTAL

Had she been more social, perhaps she might have had a deep and meaningful relationship by now. Prospects had dwindled as the decades whizzed by at an accelerating rate, but Roseland had always thought she would have plenty of time for love. So why did she suddenly feel being single in her fifties meant she'd be alone for life, and honestly, did she really care? At her age, she was too set in her ways to adapt to being accountable to another human being. If being single was meant to be, she'd get on with it, as she had always done with things beyond her control. She couldn't dictate the outcome of her research studies without fail either.

She was not the type to hang out in pubs hoping to meet a girl with similar interests, and gay-friendly pubs weren't exactly abundant. Well-versed in technology, she could at least find like-minded women with the help of the internet at her fingertips. If she wanted to join a lesbian hiking group, no problem. Do a search and voila — walks popped up within a ten to twenty mile radius.

Whatever the case, Roseland wasn't completely disillusioned with the way her life turned out thus far. Nope, it wasn't her lack of romantic attachments or stagnant professional aspirations in exchange for steady work that were eating at her gut. Then what was it? Midlife crisis?

Her musings were interrupted by the appearance of a hiking group on another track. As they were wearing red, yellow, blue, or green winter jackets, they were hard to miss. A sprightly bunch of seniors with lots more spring in their step than one would expect at their age, they swung their walking sticks in time to a longer than average, steady stride.

Roseland found satisfaction in observing older adults engaged in athletic activities. It gave her profound hope. Perhaps if her father had exercised more and eaten better, he might still be around, enjoying old age. A quick glance through her binoculars showed that the eldest had to be in her nineties, at the very least. Either that or she was prematurely wrinkled, possibly due to years of exposure to the elements. They marched on, heading in the direction that would take them back to the main road. In forty or so years, Roseland hoped she would be as fit as they seemed, and vowed to never slow down if she could help it.

After an hour or so, the moors were more desolate and devoid of human life than Roseland had ever seen them. Even the sheep not herded and holed up by their owners were lying huddled together on the ground in an effort to keep warm. When the moors were empty, it was as if they belonged to her alone. The last vestiges of warmth from the open fire and steamy hot chocolate at the inn dissipated as a sudden shift in the weather nipped at her nose and chin. The only positive element was how the swift rush of air at her back pushed her up the gradient.

The ground wasn't muddy, but walking along the uneven terrain was no picnic either. Sometimes the path narrowed, presenting a challenge to not twist an ankle or get a boot caught in a deep crevice, but mostly it was manageable. When it was time to turn back, she would be walking against the wind. It would be a bitch with the bitter cold directly in her face. As if proving her point, a powerful gust of air instantly made her eyes water and her nose run. She dabbed at both with a tissue which was soon too damp to absorb more. Stopping to take a clean Kleenex out of her pocket, she noted that the storm clouds were headed her way at a brisk pace. One thing about the moors, the weather could turn on a sixpence.

Tired and peckish, she realized she would have to stop for lunch soon. Surprised by how quickly she had developed an appetite, she searched around for suitable protection from the elements. Some of the sizable masses of granite had natural overhangs that were large enough to sit under to get out of the rain and wind. It was amazing what a difference four or five degrees made to the perception of temperature on the moors as compared to Teignmouth, for instance. Not surprising with elevations at Princetown at 417 metres compared with 35 metres in Teignmouth.

Roseland sat on a plastic grocery bag while she ate. Something about enjoying a picnic made the slim pickings delightful, despite the miserable weather. She lingered too long and had to force herself back to her feet. The moment she stood, the orange plastic—leave it to Sainsbury's to select a shopping bag that stood out—took off towards the sky like a kite off its string. It shot up so quickly, there was nothing she could do but watch it fly away.

She sucked in a breath of extremely cold air and turned to face the direction from which she'd come. She could turn back now or keep going in hopes that the conditions would improve so she could finish her hike. She chose to keep going. A short while later, snow, sleet, and rain were pelting her so hard, unforgiving actually, that she couldn't see a millimetre in front of her. One thing she knew for sure from sheer exertion alone, she was heading toward higher ground. The other thing she knew was that she was hopelessly lost.

She didn't bother digging in her bag for her cell phone. It was unlikely that there'd be phone service on Dartmoor. She knew she'd already walked over 30,000 steps, and now the path was totally obliterated. Strong winds blew copious amounts of snow around her, while the clouds continued to drop enough of the fluffy stuff to cover the frozen ground in a blinding white. Roseland had never in her life had a greater longing to be sitting on her settee, wrapped in a warm blanket. She pulled the straps of her rucksack tighter, which somehow lent a false sense of security. Panic shook her when she could not get her bearings. If she became even more disoriented as to her direction, she could go down with hypothermia before she found her way back to the inn. Cursing her stubborn resolve to hike under such conditions, she vowed to join a gym rather than hiking on the moors for her exercise if she made it back alive.

Despite the bitter cold, not being able to see, and the weariness that accompanies worry, Roseland toiled on until she'd expended her last ounce of energy. Her muscles simply would not take one more step. She had no idea where she was, but she had to stop and find shelter. It would be dark in a couple of hours, and if it kept snowing, she wouldn't be able to see the North Hessary Tor BBC transmitter located in the centre of Dartmoor, not far from the prison. It was already impossible to see the satellite aerial—a landmark which helped even the most directionally challenged find their way if they had any sense at all. What a welcome sight it would be! She could walk towards it and know for certain that she wasn't heading off to the ends of the Earth. Of course she was entirely aware that the Earth was round and it was utter nonsense to think about falling off the "edge." Maybe delirium had already clouded her judgement.

She drank the last drop of water. Why hadn't she filled the water reservoir in her backpack to capacity? Or had she drunk her fill whist she wasn't paying attention? Why hadn't she brought more high-calorie snacks? The Jammie Dodgers were long gone, a sweet memory, already metabolized. Never mind. "No worries" became her mantra until she felt like kicking the stupid useless words to the curb, had there been a curb. There was always melted snow to drink, so she wouldn't readily dehydrate. Her teeth chattered at the thought. Roseland forced her legs onward, fearing that if she found a semi-secluded spot to sit and wait out the storm, she might not be able to get up again. As much as she'd welcome a rest, she was too fearful of falling asleep in a blizzard and risking being buried alive.

Glad for the business, she had a stake in it after all, Spence readied the rooms for the elderly hiking group. As luck would have it, some of the guests from the previous night had checked out early, making room for the senior hikers. They were a spry bunch, who knew how to get the most out of life, and as they registered, their stories had made her laugh. They were glad they turned back when they did, and just as happy that there were vacancies at the inn so they could stay the night, as they were parked a fair distance away.

Spence scrubbed the last countertop, wiped the fog off the kitchen window for the third time that day, and glanced out. She had been so busy with unexpected guests, she had not noticed before now that the purple Citroen was still parked in the lot. Spence frowned. The hiker who owned that car should have been back long before now.

"Hey, Colin, have you seen the lady from this morning?"

"Who do you mean?"

"The blonde who ordered hot chocolate. Hers was the only one this morning."

"Oh, yeah. She was an odd one—very quiet, a serious type, not adventurous like you'd expect for someone who hikes alone."

"Well?"

"Well what?"

"Have you seen her?"

"No." He scratched his bald head. "As far as I know, she hasn't been back here."

Spence threw her rag on the counter and removed her apron.

Colin tilted his head in confusion. "Where are you going?"

"To look for her."

"You don't even know if she's still out there. She could be holed up in another pub, miles from here. Even if she is still out in the storm, you'll never find her in this weather."

"Maybe not, but nobody knows the moors better than I do. If something bad happens and I haven't at least tried to find her, I'll never forgive myself."

Regret flooded over her with a gripping vengeance. She forced the painful thoughts from her mind.

He nodded, wiping the sad expression off his face. "You go on then. I'll finish up here."

"Thanks, Col. I hope I'm back in an hour."

"If you're not, I'll send Forensics."

"Very funny, but it won't come to that."

"Be careful."

"Cheers," she said. "And bloody behave yourself."

He laughed at her remark, and she let him get away with it this once as she was in a hurry to collect her gear from her room. As a teen, Spence had joined the rescue unit, where she learned respect for Moorland and developed a deep appreciation for hiking. Her disaster bag was always packed. She had lived in the inn for six years. If she found this woman, it wouldn't be the first time she had saved some unsuspecting holidaymaker who found him or herself waist high in a bog, suffering from overexposure or sheer exhaustion. People tended to overestimate their capabilities, but they should never underestimate Mother Nature. Moorland was notorious for conditions turning treacherous with little warning.

Using her sleeve, she rubbed snow off the driver's window of the Citroen so she could peep inside. She had to confirm the owner wasn't inside, snoozing or worse. It was empty. Stickers affixed to the windscreen told Spence that the woman was a member of the National Trust and English Heritage organizations. Neither membership made her either an avid or brilliant hiker. Spence couldn't imagine how she could be making any headway in this awful wind without getting blown off the hills.

She set off in the direction she had seen the woman take. Although snow-covered, the gorse and brambles outlined a route she knew by heart, and Spence followed the well-travelled path. Three miles out, there was still no sign of the missing blonde. Determination made her trudge on. After another mile or so, Spence sighted a wobbly entity, seemingly on the brink of falling over. Spence blinked to see through the frost clinging to her eyelashes and, sure enough, the form took on the shape of a human. It had to be the person she was looking for. All the other hikers had turned back. The woman staggered, her body bent over into the wind but barely moving.

Spence ran toward her, calling out, "Hey there. You all right?" But her words were ripped away by the storm.

No answer.

Spence didn't want to startle her, but she had to reach out and grab her sleeve to get her attention. The woman's lips looked as if they'd crack if she spoke. *How did the elements get to her so quickly?* she wondered. She knew she'd have to get her into shelter quickly. If she didn't, she'd end up carrying her, and that wouldn't be easy.

She looped her arm around the woman's waist and hoisted her up on her hip. "We must warm you up. Try not to bend your knees." She tightened her grip. "I'll help, but you have to do your part."

If Spence hadn't known it was extremely unlikely, she would have thought the woman's vocal cords were frozen, because she didn't so much as grunt. Surely there were colder places on the planet, but right then Spence couldn't think about those. She continued with the monologue.

"I know of a place nearby. It's boarded up at the minute, but I can get us inside. We'll make a nice fire to defrost your frozen hands and feet. Are you okay?"

When there was still no answer, Spence filled the quiet. "Forget the cottage, I have a better idea." Her main concern was to get them indoors before the woman's legs gave out. Spence kept her voice even, reassuring, like a proper paramedic encouraging a patient. "Twenty minutes more. Go on, you can make it. We're almost there."

Spence supported her until they were up on the porch. She sat the weary traveller on the step and propped her up against the building. "Wait here. I'll go in through a window and be right back."

Spence was only gone two minutes, but when she opened the door the woman looked to be suffering shock, and Spence literally had to drag her inside. She needed to start a fire, but first she had to get the hiker out of her cold, wet clothes and wrap her in blankets. She removed the outerwear, thankful to find that the clothing beneath was mostly dry. The woman murmured a weak "thanks" as Spence wrapped her up in a woollen blanket which smelled of sheep, dust, and smoke. It would have to do.

When the kindling flared into flickering flames, Spence added logs and soon had the sitting room aglow, and infinitely warmer than the vast outdoors. She found a kettle and wiped it out with a tea towel as there was no running water. The house hadn't been plumbed. There probably wasn't a need, as the most likely visitors would just be there to spend a night before continuing their trek.

She filled the kettle with snow to melt for tea. In addition to tea bags, her food ration bag was filled with Digestive biscuits, energy drinks and bars, nuts, seeds and dried fruit, coffee granules, and dried milk. As the water heated, she did a brief inspection and found that the last group to use it had left a bag of crisps that were well within the "use by" date. They must have left in a hurry, because they had left a few bottles of ale behind. *Those will come in handy*, Spence thought. Although she didn't really like to leave Colin on his own overnight, she knew he and his wife Jean could manage without her. She just liked to think they couldn't.

Spence took two mugs from the cupboard and cleaned them out as best as she could without running water or Fairy dishwashing liquid. The antique gas stove was only good for show, so she made do with the fire. When the tea was steeped, Spence raised the steamy brew up to the hiker's mouth. Her lips parted eagerly. The woman appeared to be thawing nicely. "Careful, it's hot."

"Thank you." She tentatively accepted a sip and then reached out to take the mug into her own hands. Their eyes met and held while Roseland took tiny sips. "Thank you, this is wonderful."

Spence offered a few Digestives. They ate and drank in silence. Once finished, Spence held out her hand. The woman's fingers were like ice, but her smile was warm.

"I'm Spence, and I have to say that you're looking much better than when I first found you."

"Thanks to you, I'm feeling much better. I'm Roseland by the way. Very nice to meet you, Spence."

"What possessed you to go hiking alone in this weather?"

"Well, I could bore you with my life story, but it was all down to stubborn pride as much as me not wanting to miss out on my walk. I suppose I thought I could weather any storm."

"You probably could, but the moors can also be an unforgiving adversary."

"How ever did you find me?"

"I used to volunteer with Dartmoor Search and Rescue. I followed a hunch, and lucky for you I was right."

"Lucky for me, indeed. I don't know what happened, really. One minute I was fine, and the next I had lost my bearings. Dizziness hit me quite quickly, my vision blurred, and I found it impossible to concentrate. I was cold and hungry. My blood sugar plummeted at the worst possible time, making me feel colder. And to top it off, I had a hot flash, which heated me up, but the resultant sweat cooled me down fast." Roseland flushed deep red. "Oops, I apologize. Too much information."

"No worries. I'm getting them too. Symptoms started in my late forties and weren't too bothersome, but now I'm fifty-six and they give me quite a start at night. It's a nightmare waking up soaked. I hope it's gone long before I turn sixty."

"Tell me about it. I'm fifty-three and hoping it ends much sooner than sixty. Are there any more Digestives please?"

"Plenty." Spence handed her a package of biscuits.

"Did you know Digestives were first developed by two Scottish doctors in 1839 to aid in digestion?"

"No, I didn't." Spence smiled as she chewed, listening to more facts about the UK's most popular biscuit than she'd ever cared about knowing. "You are a walking, talking encyclopaedia."

Roseland blushed again. "You've caught me out for being a bore."

Spence was captivated by the fact that Roseland's flawless light skin made it impossible for her to hide her embarrassment. Captivated by how lovely a blush looked in contrast to the blonde hair, Spence found it impossible to imagine that Roseland could ever be a bore.

"Stop me before I really get carried away," Roseland teased.

"No need. I'm enjoying these biscuits a lot more now that I have this wealth of fascinating facts at my disposal. Thank you for that." She deliberately chose "fascinating" instead of "useless" to describe the information, as she did not want to offend her companion. Spence typically didn't care about things such as tact, but Roseland made her want to keep her curt remarks to herself.

"Had I planned ahead," Roseland said, "I'd have brought more food, but I didn't expect to be gone quite so long. It's like I ate my sandwich and snacks hours ago."

"You did, unless it was dark when you had lunch."

"No, it was still light out, but... Wait, what time is it now?"

"It's gone seven. Been dark since half-four at least."

"No wonder I was knackered and famished."

"Amazing you weren't unconscious."

"You just barely saved me before that happened."

"Someone left beer and crisps. We could share."

"Goody. The sodium chloride, er...salt in the crisps will help. Can't say the same for alcohol, but hops come from plants and are sometimes used in medications. Sugar is fortifying too."

"Who says 'goody'?"

Roseland blushed again. "I guess I do."

They ate and drank, and merriment rising from relief filled the room. Drinking alcohol on a nearly empty stomach combined with swapping stories and jokes soon had Roseland yawning, unable to stop. Yawning was contagious. Spence and Roseland were soon in a fit of giggles whilst having a yawning competition. It was no contest; Roseland proved to be far sleepier.

Spence added more logs to the fire, thankful that there was a healthy supply, and then she joined Roseland, who was lying on her side, barely able to keep her eyes open but obviously trying her best. The sound of crackling flames and the way it made Roseland's eyes glisten as the fire slowly turned the logs to ash just moments before she fell fast asleep touched a romantic chord in Spence. She was not usually a mush, but

40

Roseland had that power over her for reasons Spence tried to ignore. The first rule of rescue was to not take advantage of a damsel in distress.

She laughed at herself for comparing Roseland to a damsel, as well as knowing bloody well she herself wasn't exactly the knight in shining armour. In this particular situation, anyone would have done the same. The salacious thoughts had to be the result of the beer, and the close proximity to a woman who, under ordinary circumstances would intrigue her. There was a secret part of Roseland that Spence could easily infiltrate, given the opportunity. But Spence held little hope of that. Besides, she had to finish her BSc in hotel management and concentrate on the inn rather than putting her energy into a relationship.

Spence knelt on the blanketed floor, surprised to find that Roseland had drawn her knees up close to her chest in the perfect spooning position, as if they had done this a million times before. At first Spence felt awkward about it, but in no time at all it seemed natural that they share the woollen blanket, lying bum to tummy for warmth—two strangers doing what was needed to survive the long, cold night. The last sound Spence heard before succumbing to sleep was the unrelenting howling of the wind.

When Spence woke, she gazed down at Roseland, taking in her features as she slept. She fought the urge to smooth the tangles of her blonde bob and touch her wind-burnt cheeks and red-tipped nose. It was lucky she had found the woman in time. Had hypothermia set in, there was no telling whether she could have been saved.

Spence didn't have the heart to wake Roseland, who clearly needed her sleep. Roseland's chest rose and fell peacefully, her breathing rhythmic, and Spence soon found her own breathing slowing to match. It would have been nice to wait with her until she woke, but Spence had to get back to the inn. She couldn't leave Colin and Jean with all those stranded hikers depending on them for breakfast. She started a small fire, figuring it should burn for a while. After the breakfast rush, she would come back to collect Roseland.

The next morning, Roseland woke with a start. She had a vague recollection of eerie images that had flickered in the fire light on the

paint-chipped walls, but not for long. Her lids had been too heavy to remain open. Now that she was awake, she became painfully aware of her pounding headache, and that she had no idea where she was or how she had gotten there. She didn't even know what day it was. The embers of the fire smouldered, close to extinction. She saw a stack of logs and rose to fetch one, shivering when the blanket fell to the floor. She hefted two small logs, placed them in the hearth, and fanned the embers. The flame quickly caught on the dry bark, and soon the fire was blazing. Her memory came back like a light coming on. There was a woman, Spence, and she had saved her from frostbite...and worse. And it was the woman's comforting embrace that had sent her off to dreamland.

"Spence?" she called. When there was no answer, Roseland went to look for her. She checked out the kitchen and two bedrooms, each of which was outfitted with Army issue style bunk beds. Spence was not in the house. Perhaps she had gone outside to fetch more snow for the kettle. Roseland heaved open the solid oak front door and peered out. Blinding sunshine reflected off the snow, and she squinted until her pupils could adjust. In the distance, she saw a farmer.

"Hello. You there, hello." Her warm breath condensed in the cold air.

He turned to face her. His scruffy white beard and weathered face resembled those that appeared in photos in news clippings from days gone by.

"Have you seen a woman about my height, medium build, with dark hair and eyeglasses pass by? She's wearing a dark jacket, navy, I think, and her name is Spence."

"Nope. Nobody here but me and the sheep." He turned and continued checking his stock that had spent the night outside.

Belatedly, Roseland thought it very odd that there weren't any prints in the snow, not even the marks of sheep hooves. *Weird that.* She turned to go back into the house, then stole one last glance at the farmer. A shiver ran along her spine. Standing as still as a stone, she blinked. He was nowhere in sight. It was as if he had vanished, just like Spence.

Why didn't Spence leave a note, or wake her up to say goodbye? That was downright rude. Why had the woman rescued her only to leave her there alone? It didn't make sense, and Roseland liked things to make sense.

Back inside, the house felt cold despite the fire. She dreaded going back outside, but she needed to gather more snow if she was going to have a cup of tea before she tried to hike back to her car. Luckily there was one tea bag remaining. She polished off the rest of the Digestives and drank her tea, knowing that before long, she would have to relieve herself. Outdoors. She shivered at the thought. The farmhouse wouldn't have a working indoor toilet with the main water supply shut off.

She washed out her mouth with snow and yelped at the pain it caused her sensitive teeth, another badge of honour of aging. Then she rinsed out the mug, threw the empty biscuit and crisps wrappers in her bag to dispose of later, folded the blanket, snuffed out the fire as thoroughly as she could, and left the farmhouse as close as she could to how they'd found it. Only the smell of smoke lingered. The sun had melted some of the snow that had obscured her pathway back to the car. She could have used sunglasses, but didn't have any with her. She rarely thought about that when hiking on the moors, since it was more often than not cloudy, foggy, or raining.

The path was now detectable, but still she found it odd that there were no footprints in the pristine snow. Roseland trudged towards the carpark, recalling how much better she had felt once she'd thawed out. Talking with Spence had been the highlight of the adventure. The woman had an infectious smile and a carefree attitude, and seemed capable of performing miracles. It was a shame she took off before Roseland got to thank her properly. A different type of loneliness descended upon Roseland. It was as if her heart swelled at the mere thought of Spence, but then that buoyancy was closely followed by a suffocating sensation. Something wasn't right. She had to stop to catch her breath. Roseland didn't remember the last time she had longed for or needed companionship, certainly not the company of another woman, but Spence had sparked an interest she had long ignored.

By the time Roseland dug out her keys to unlock her Citroen, the carpark was chock-o-block. Moor Sheep and Dartmoor Pony Inn was heaving with patrons, and they were spilling out onto the snow-covered lawn adjacent to the carpark. It wasn't until she noticed a blushing bride shivering by the gazebo that she realized a wedding reception was underway. The unfortunate bride had bright red cheeks from the cold, but she looked radiant. Roseland decided against stopping in for a quick meal, or even a hot drink. Truth be told, she wasn't in the mood for being surrounded by a party of revellers while she was all alone, feeling deflated over not seeing Spence. All she wanted was the comfort of her own home, a hot bath, and a long sleep in her own bed.

Roseland toyed with the idea of taking some time off. It had been a year since she had been on holiday. Weekend excursions were usually enough to rejuvenate her, but quite unexpectedly, Roseland found herself suffering from an overwhelming weariness. She blamed her sudden fatigue on a drastic reduction in the stress hormones that had kept her going during her overexposure. She needed a break. She would go home, regroup, and then come back to find Spence. The least she could do was to appropriately thank the woman who had saved her life. She would not be deterred by the fact that she had no idea where to find Spence. Roseland didn't know anything about her other than her first name, and that stirrings rose in her intimate places just envisioning her hero, Spence. Medium length dark hair, dreamy dark eyes behind fashionable glasses, strong jaw and angular features all combined with a strong personality and potent sex appeal to make for an unforgettable woman. Her most alluring attribute of all was her seductive lips. Kissable lips...capable hands...sharp wit...

Stop it, right now, Roseland, or I shall have to spank you, she scolded herself.

First thing Monday morning, she requested a private moment with her line manager.

"Hiya. You asked to see me?" Becks looked up and waved her inside. "Come in, and do sit down."

Roseland sat next to her boss. She appreciated the fact that Becks trusted her staff to do the right thing and only interfered when necessary for the benefit of the team.

"I know it's short notice, but I was hoping to take some paid leave."

"Well, it's about time Roseland. You are looking a bit rough around the edges. I dare say you could do with a rest. When do you want?"

"As soon as possible, please."

"Not a problem." She took out the annual leave binder and opened to Roseland's blank sheet. As Becks shuffled through the pages, she briefly glanced over at Roseland, who immediately sat up straighter. "Can you wait a fortnight, okay?"

"Yes, that will be perfect. Thank you."

Roseland's spirits lifted. She was going to find Spence.

When her vacation began, Roseland spent three days on the trot, driving to Princetown. She was repeatedly disappointed to find that nobody had heard of Spence, and when she'd finally come upon the farmhouse where they had stayed, it was still locked up. Roseland vowed she would never quit searching. Maybe she could find something helpful at the local library. Why hadn't she thought of that before? There was bound to be some information about the farmhouse that she hadn't already learned off the Web. It made sense that the farmhouse was rented out to visitors, mostly teen tours, as a place to stay along designated hiking routes. That explained the ready supply of logs, matches, and simple amenities including unopened beer, no doubt left by hikers lightening their loads before resuming their walk. There were bits and pieces of the house's history to be learned online, but it would be helpful to check the local library for more in-depth, perhaps even insider information.

During the week, Roseland stopped at a reputable hiking shop for thermal underwear, a new pair of hiking boots, heavy gauge socks, hand-warmers, and a spare pair of waterproof, lined trousers. The following weekend, she filled her backpack to full capacity. When she found Spence, she would impress her with how well-equipped and ready for a hike she was as compared to the day they met.

She could not stop thinking about Spence, wondering what she was doing at that moment. Was Spence thinking about her, too? Would she ever see Spence again? Of course she would. She was on a mission to find the mysterious woman who had saved her life and captivated her mind, and possibly her heart. Surely somebody knew who Spence was. But whom?

Dartmoor was much less travelled in the winter, especially on weekdays. The weather was milder, but some snow still lingered and there was a damp chill in the air. Each season featured a diverse assortment of vegetation with Gorse the only constant, its vibrant yellow flowers forever in bloom. She enjoyed the drive to Princetown when it was unspoilt by traffic. While it was a photo opportunity to occasionally find cows or sheep lounging on the tarmac, the novelty quickly wore off when it proved difficult to get them to move out of the way.

Driving conditions were less ideal when she shared the road with tractors, caravans, SUVs, lorries and hesitant drivers unused to the winding and narrow lanes. Oversized vehicles, bikers and hikers made traveling along single-track country lanes frustrating and dangerous. It was unusual for the roads to be as empty as they were on this trip, but she didn't want to jinx it by being too grateful.

Roseland arrived at her destination sooner than she'd expected and parked along the road outside a local convenience shop. Inside, it was overcrowded with aisles of food, sundries, beer and wine. There was a small post office in the back, but the clerk was nowhere in sight, so Roseland asked the young man at the till if he knew a local woman named Spence, and where she might find the library. It was odd, but he had no idea about either, so she purchased a bottle of J2O orange and passion fruit juice and returned to the car. There was a couple having a drink and a fag at a picnic table. She stopped to see if they could help her.

"Excuse me, but do you happen to live around here?"

"Not far. Why do you ask?"

"I'm looking for a woman named Spence. Do you know her?"

"Can't say that we do. Sorry."

"That's okay. By any chance, do you know where the local library is?"

They shook their heads, and Roseland thanked them for their time and moved on.

After speaking to a third person who hadn't a clue whether there was a library and had never heard of anyone named Spence, Roseland began to believe that no one knew where the library was, or how to give her directions that she could easily follow. She had begun to doubt its existence when she stumbled upon a dated building that looked like an old house but functioned as the public library, town hall, and meeting centre all in one.

The librarian could have been a throwback to the last century, and the books were rife with mold, dust, and mildew. Roseland sneezed a few times, but soon her immune system quieted down.

"Hello. I'm interested in the history of the farmhouse not far from Nun's Cross Farm."

The man looked at her over the rim of his spectacles, eyeing Roseland suspiciously at first and then letting down his guard a notch. He cleared his throat, but when he spoke, Roseland wondered whether he had sandpaper for vocal cords.

"I'm George Hariford. What is it you'd like to know?" he asked.

"Hello, Mr Hariford. I'm Roseland. Pleasure to meet you, sir. I'm after general information, mostly about the local inhabitants. Who owned the farmhouse, when it changed hands and ended up a lodge for hikers, that sort of thing."

"I can tell you the Nun's Cross Farm is the last remaining structure of a property that was farmed…in the 1950s, I believe. The Royal Navy later took it over for training purposes, but it now belongs to the Duchy of Cornwall, which leases it out to private organizations. But that's not what you're after, is it?"

"No. I read about that on-line. It was dark when I first saw the farm, but actually I'm thinking I may have come upon another house in the vicinity, maybe not this one. Is there more than one farmhouse nearby?"

The man's thoughts appeared to retreat to some faraway place. It seemed ages before he returned to continue their conversation.

"You say it was dark when you walked past it?"

Roseland didn't want to admit that she had spent the night in case she and Spence would be considered intruders. "Yes."

"It's possible that the place you mean is the old warren house. It was owned by a woman named Spencer."

47

Roseland couldn't believe her luck, finally a mention of someone named Spencer. "Do you know where I can find her?"

"In the old graveyard by—"

"Pardon?" Roseland sputtered. "What do you mean, graveyard?"

"She died of injuries and exposure six years ago. She was lost in a storm, and Search and Rescue failed to find her in time." He shook his head. "Tragic. Such a shame, really. She was very well liked and is sorely missed."

Roseland gasped. She collected her emotions, and when she could trust her voice, she said, "How sad. What happened to the house after that?"

"The house is rented out, much like the Duchy's but not as often. It's leased to private adventure type groups as an alternative to Nun's. There's hearsay from those who have stayed there that it's haunted, if you believe in such things. Myself, I have my doubts, but Dartmoor is rife with legends."

All this time, Roseland had thought she had spent the night at Nun's Cross Farm, but actually she had stayed somewhere nearly three kilometres away. No wonder she hadn't been having any luck finding Spence. She had been searching in the wrong area.

It was a long shot, but she had to ask. "Would you happen to have any articles or maybe the local newspaper report of the circumstances surrounding Ms Spencer's death?"

"As a matter of fact, we keep archives dating back to the eighteen hundreds. Most of the local newspapers are stored on microfilm, but those were sent off to Exeter to be uploaded using modern computer programs. We've kept the original newspapers. They aren't in the best of condition, mind, but you're welcome to have a look. This way, Miss, please. Watch your step."

Roseland followed him to an overstocked storage room underneath a set of stairs. Roseland's heart sank. She couldn't imagine finding anything in all of the mess. Mr. Hariford hadn't exactly employed a suitable filing system and his care of the archives was less than impeccable, a lot less. Thick dust wafted up as they walked, which started a new sneezing fit until her eyes and nose were running faster than she could wipe them with a tissue. She mostly ignored the nuisance as she anticipated what she was about to discover, *if* he could locate what he was looking for. She was determined to remain hopeful.

Using an old woollen cloth that was lying on the table, he wiped off the cover of an old scrapbook that held clippings, some tattered and others in better condition. After a while, when Roseland was beginning to think that she'd die of impatience, he produced a torn clipping of the obituary of Olivia Elizabeth Victoria Spencer, 8 April 1959 to 31 January 2009. As the person was reportedly well thought of, it was strange they hadn't protected the copy.

Roseland examined it closely. The paper had yellowed, but thankfully hadn't faded beyond readability. Unfortunately, all that was left of the original obituary was a photo, the deceased's name, and the years of her birth and death. There in black and white was a picture of Spence—the spitting image, only younger. She hadn't changed that much. Only now she was just a little sadder around the eyes. Roseland glanced at the dates again. Had Olivia Spencer survived, she would have been fifty-six, the same age as Spence.

Chills ran down Roseland's spine. The woman in the photo and the woman she had met in the warren had similar names—at least if the Spence she met went by a shortened version of her surname, and they shared a likeness, plus, they were the same age. This was too many similarities to be coincidence. If Olivia Spencer was dead, then who was Spence? Of course she could be a relative. But then why, other than looking in the wrong location, was Roseland having such a job of tracking Spence down? If she was still alive, then unquestionably somebody would have known her. And people claimed the house was haunted...

Surely this train of thought was preposterous! Then she remembered the eerie noises she'd heard before she fell asleep that night in the warren, and a shiver ran through her.

"Thank you so much for your trouble." She handed back the clipping and then hastily climbed the stairs.

Roseland couldn't bring herself to believe the unbelievable. Reviewing the facts once more in her mind, she sorted through them, intent on finding a reasonable solution. A fool proof explanation. A scientific deduction.

Spence had saved her. They had spent the night together but, come morning, Spence had vanished without a word or even a note. Why would she leave without at least saying goodbye? That made no sense at all. There was another explanation, but surely a scientifically minded person would be hard pressed to even entertain the remotest possibility that she had actually imagined the entire thing, or, even more improbable, that Spence had been a ghost.

Roseland knew she had been suffering from dehydration and possibly a touch of hypothermia that day, definite hypoglycaemia, and a bothersome hot flash, but surely she hadn't been hallucinating. Conjuring up an alluring, entertaining and unforgettable woman sounded wonderful, but fantasies were something she rarely, if ever, engaged in. Besides, she was lucid that night, once she'd gotten warmed up and had food and drink in her belly. Which was all thanks to Spence.

A ludicrous thought insistently pushed its way through her native practicality and clamoured for consideration: What if the warren house *was* indeed haunted? Plenty of observers had reported such sightings. Had she been saved by a ghost?

Suddenly spooked, she tried to shake away the notion, casting about for a rational explanation as to how she had ended up in that safe harbour and why her saviour was now proving difficult to find. Maybe it was because she *was* dead.

Roseland made her way out of the library in a daze, tripping over her own feet on the bottom step. She had to locate the right house this time, had to see if she could have gotten inside on her own. Wishful thinking also had her imagining that Spence would be there. It was another silly thought, but there was no harm in trying to establish facts. She had to prove to herself there was no such thing as ghosts, but it wasn't like she could conduct a controlled study on the matter that would definitively say there were or weren't spirits. That would be like trying to prove the existence of God.

There was a chance, whether she cared to believe it or not, that she had been so delirious she had hallucinated being rescued by a fetching woman who made her blush. It wasn't the sort of thing that happened to her, ever. She would go home and do another search in the Ordinance survey to find the Spencer house. She would start at the Moor Sheep and Dartmoor Pony Inn.

The next morning Roseland parked in the same exact spot where she had parked before beginning her hike that fateful day. She gathered up her fully loaded Osprey backpack and set off. The weather was pleasant, and the ramble was a lot less difficult than the last time she had ventured there.

When she arrived at her destination, she was truly amazed. The house was similar to Nun's Cross Farm, but in the light of day, now that she was paying attention, there were noticeable differences. The morning she had trekked back to the parking lot, she hadn't registered the details of the warren, as her mind had been focused on why Spence had left her without a word, and on getting back to her car.

Performing a thorough inspection, Roseland checked every possible entry point into the building. There was no hidden key that she could find, no way she could have entered the Spencer house without someone's help. She would have had to break a window to get in, and there was no sign of damage. Also, she clearly remembered going inside through the front door.

After many unsuccessful tries, she came to the inescapable conclusion that she could not break in if her life depended on it. That much was certain, but many unanswered questions remained.

She still hadn't washed the clothes she had been wearing on that hike. Her outer clothes and hair had smelled distinctly musty, with lingering hints of smoke from the open fire, and the garments underneath held hints of Spence's cologne from sleeping in her embrace. If Spence hadn't rescued her, then how had she survived the storm? How had she ended up with Digestive crumbs in her bra when she was positive she had taken along Jammie Dodgers? It wasn't unusual to find crumbs in her shirt or bra. She laughed, ashamed to admit that she could be a bit untidy when she ate, especially after a few drinks. Once she had found half a crisp in her bra after suffering half the night with a scratchy, low cut blouse.

Roseland wished she could get inside the warren, but she wouldn't break in. She sat on the front step and ate her apple while devising her next move. Finally, she shrugged. There was only one course of action for her—she would keep coming back, on the off chance that one day Spence, living or dead, would be there when she returned.

Roseland labelled the path she ritually took "the Nun's Cross hike" to avoid confusing it with the "Warren House Inn hike" she often took starting at Bennet's Cross. Time and time again, she would have a picnic on the porch of the house, and then venture beyond, to check out the tors, until she knew the area like the back of her hand. Each outing resulted in the same outcome—there was no sign of Spence, not even a ghost sighting.

By that time, Roseland would have happily entertained any indication that she had, in fact, met an otherworldly being, but there was none. Occasionally she saw the sheep farmer, who offered nothing more than a quick nod before he skittered off as if he was hiding from the authorities. He wasn't a chatty type, and if he minded her traipsing past his herd, he never said. It was a public right of way, after all; he didn't have to like it. But still, he was polite enough.

Disappointment caused Roseland to use her spare time for reading everything she could find on the subject of ghosts. There were too many accounts to study them all, but the consistent thread of what she read was that meeting a ghost was not an impossibility. Convinced it was only a matter of time until she saw the object of her fantasies and thoughts, Roseland vowed that she would never stop searching. She opened her heart and mind to belief, hoping beyond hope that if she was completely receptive, she'd see Spence again.

The Dartmoor Sheep and Pony Inn was filled to capacity. In the midst of a Sunday carvery roast dinner rush, Spence was calmly going about seeing that each diner was happy with their meal.

"Spence, call for you," Colin hollered above the din.

Assessing the loud buzz of conversation, clinking of silver on plates, crackling of the fire, and the groaning of a dishwasher on the fritz, Spence went into her office and closed the door.

"Spence here."

"Miss Spencer? It's Rachel."

Spence swallowed the lump that formed in her throat and forced herself to ask the question to which she did not want an answer. "What's up, Rachel?"

"It's your mum."

Her mum had been in a nursing care facility, receiving physical therapy after a bad fall. Her hip had mended, and she just needed to regain her strength. She was supposed to be home in a few weeks' time. Nobody, least of all Spence, had expected the otherwise healthy woman to go downhill so quickly. Spence visited her as often as she could and had seen her just last week. Now she knew the news couldn't be good. Why else would the senior sister be calling her from the rehab unit of the nursing home? "Is she...?"

"She's asking for you. You need to get here as soon as you can. Her kidneys are failing, and it won't be long before she suffers multi-organ failure as well."

"I can be there in a few hours. Please tell her I'm on my way, will you?"

"Of course."

Spence put the phone back on the cradle with exaggerated care, as if to not shatter the plastic receiver by slamming it down. She would not allow herself to succumb to the fear of losing her mother, her last remaining relative. She told Colin the news, and he ushered her towards the staircase.

"Go to her, Spence, and stay with her. Jean and I will hold down the fort."

"Promise?"

"Yes, now go. Just don't go speeding. And keep your head about you."

When Spence arrived, she found that her mother had been transferred to hospital. Stepping into her mother's room full of life-prolonging machines that beeped maddening brought home the reality of having death on one's doorstep. But Spence refused to let go of her mum. She plastered on a bright outlook and breezed over to her bedside, clasping the cold metal railing to hold herself up.

A drastic change had taken place in Silvia. She wore terminal pallor and had a skeletal appearance, except for her distended abdomen. Spence wanted to look away. She wanted to cling to the vision of her mother all strong, and stoic, and indomitable, even in the face of this tragedy. Spence had never even seen her mother cry. Until now.

There were tears in her mum's eyes, and they spilled over onto her cheeks. The paper thin skin showed the tiny veins just beneath the surface, and it looked as if her mum's tears were following little tributaries towards the gorge that was her full mouth—the only feature Spence had inherited from her mother besides her will of steel.

Spence held it together as long as she could, but the anguish of seeing her mother cry was more than she could bear. Spence broke down and, quite extraordinarily, Silvia didn't tell her to butch up and stop blubbering. They both had a limitless store of unshed tears to expend.

Spence visited every day, spending hours by her mum's side. They allowed her to be at her mother's bedside in the intensive care unit well past normal visiting hours.

Spence spent the rest of the winter and into early spring in her childhood home with all its memories, and its familiar scents. Her mum had not tried to persuade Spence to move back; rather she asked her daughter to sell the house and use the proceeds as she wished. Unfortunately, the building was in a state of disrepair, so, per her mother's last wishes, she stuck around to do such renovations as she could. Spence found herself immersed in the project of getting the house and property into better shape so that it was marketable, perhaps even lucrative. The money would help Spence purchase the inn from Colin and Jean when they were ready to retire. Her mum would surely approve.

Halloween was near, and Roseland decided that the day that was notable for entertaining ghosts and goblins, even if they were fabricated using convincing costumes, was as good a time as any for her habitual hike to Nun's Cross. Trick-or-treating on Halloween was gaining popularity in Britain. The last few years she had even bought sweeties for the children who rang the bell. Leaving an ample stash of goodies by the front door, Roseland greeted a couple of convincing "ghosts" on her way out. The twins from next door were wearing stark white sheets with holes cut out for eyes, nose, and mouth.

But she had not yet encountered her own personal ghost. It had been almost a year with no sign of Spence. While Roseland still held on to hope, she mostly continued to go just to enjoy the walks as she ventured further and further, until one day she had actually made it to Clitter Hill on Fur Tor.

She longed to share that experience. How wonderful it would be to view the incredible landscape with Spence. If only she would come back, even if it was only to haunt her. If ghosts existed, there seemed no better day to discover one than on Halloween.

As she walked the well-known route, Roseland found herself constantly talking out loud, as if carrying on a monologue with the woman who had saved her and who seemed to be with her at all times, watching over her, keeping her safe. It was irrational, she knew that, and yet she could not help believing she would see Spence again one day. Busy admiring the fungi and what a good year they were having, Roseland was surprised to look up and see the now-familiar house in the distance.

"That was quick," she said aloud.

The sheep nearby ran away as she approached. Little lambs bleated in response to their mums' warnings, but like naughty children, they ran off in the opposite direction.

"I'm getting fitter, I can feel it," she told a sheep that was too busy eating grass to look up.

When Roseland was only a few feet away from the house, she stopped dead. She blinked several times, even closed her eyes for a moment to be sure her vision was clear. When she looked again, there was Spence in all her glory, busily putting in new windows. Before her mind could fully register what she was seeing, her legs took off at a trot. Her thoughts tumbled: *She's dead. I saw her picture in the paper. They don't print obituaries about the living.*

But her eyes told a different story. This woman in the house was indeed the woman who had saved her, and she was either there in the flesh or a ghost after all. *Otherwise how would I have found this shelter in the first place? She brought me here*, Roseland assured herself. "Imagine that!"

Roseland was not fussed. She would take Spence any way she could get her—in the flesh or in spirit.

"Spence," she called.

Spence stopped hammering and turned to face her. She waved a greeting. Soon they were standing face-to-face. Spence was every bit as handsome as Roseland remembered. Perhaps there was a sadness around her eyes that was more pronounced than before, but she appeared to be very happy to see her.

An awkward moment ensued, as if neither knew what to say, but then Spence smiled. "Hello, Roseland."

Roseland was dumbstruck. Spence looked very real, but maybe the sun was blinding her perception of reality, because honestly, how on Earth could she be talking to a ghost? She had to get a grip. This just wasn't happening. She suddenly felt foolish, not only for believing in ghosts, but for thinking she was actually seeing one.

So, she did the only thing that made sense; she poked Spence. Shocked when her finger met flesh and bone, Roseland poked her again.

"What are you doing?" Spence's tone was more amused than annoyed.

"But...you're dead. I saw it for myself. There's an obituary with your picture in the local paper. You died six years ago." Roseland shook her head, hope warring with disbelief. "I've wanted to believe in ghosts, but now I just think that I'm losing my mind." Roseland poked Spence one more time, just to be sure.

"Stop doing that. I'm not a ghost, Roseland. Come here, you're shaking." Spence gently clasped her trembling arms. "Look at me."

Roseland opened her eyes and stared, waiting for an explanation. It wasn't long in coming.

"What you saw was a photo of Olivia, my sister."

"The clipping had *your* picture," Roseland insisted.

"My identical twin. Olivia died six years ago. I'm Leila. I tried to save her, the entire team did, but..."

Roseland shook off her shock in order to comfort Spence. She pulled the distraught woman to her, and they hugged for a long while.

When Spence had finished telling her the entire story, both women were sobbing. Her heart breaking for Spence, Roseland cried over Spence's grief at being unable to save her sister and for the recent passing of her mum, but she also cried over the loss of her own parents and grandparents, and Trixie, too.

When the catharsis subsided, Roseland and Spence went into the house. Compared to the first time she had first seen it, Roseland thought that the little house looked more lived in. It needed a lot more work, but it was clearly looking homier.

"Care for a cup of tea and some Digestives?"

"Yes, please. I dare say I've become a bit of a Digestives fan." Roseland was grateful to engage in such a normal activity to relieve the tension. There was nothing a cuppa couldn't cure.

The two talked and talked over a pot of tea and a packet of biscuits.

"I'm sorry I didn't stay to say goodbye that morning, but I needed to get back to the inn to help with the breakfast rush," Spence said regretfully.

"But you didn't even wake me. Why?"

"You were sleeping so peacefully, and after all you'd been through, I decided it was best to let you sleep." Spence's eyes held a faraway look, the corners of her mouth turning up subtly, but visibly, as if recalling a pleasant memory. "I planned to come back to collect you after helping my boss with breakfast. I should have figured you wouldn't wait for me."

"After that night, I tried tirelessly to find you, but nobody out this way knew you. How stupid of me. Now I could kick myself for not going inside that inn with the ridiculously long name."

They both laughed.

"Don't be hard on yourself. By the time I finished work, your car was no longer in the lot. There was no point looking for you then. I wondered if you'd come back for another hot chocolate, but you never did. A month or so later, I got a call about my mum, and left straight away to be with her. I never thought I'd be gone as long as I was, but I was happy to be with Mum until the end. I never had that with Livvy."

Roseland frowned and forced herself to take another sip of her tea. "Why are you here now?"

"I sold Mum's house, which was worth a lot more than I expected. Part of the money will cover renovating this place as a permanent residence. Mum received a fair bit of trade with hikers, but Nun's Cross Farm gets the majority of lodgers, without question, so I may as well use a perfectly good dwelling that holds many fond memories, including the night I found you."

Roseland was touched to her very core. "That's very sweet. It was a great night for me, too. So, you work at the inn."

"Yes, it's what inspired me to study hotel management and get my licence. I want to own Moor Sheep and Dartmoor Pony Inn—"

"Crickey. Pardon me for saying so, but honestly, that name's a mouthful," Roseland interjected.

"Exactly. After I purchase the property and business, you can bet I'll change the name straight away. I'm just waiting until Colin and Jean are ready to sell. In the meantime, it's ideal to work and live there while I finish my course work. I can always rent this place out to friends and family rather than hiking groups."

"What a brilliant idea."

"I'm mostly doing this in Mum and Sis' memory. They would have wanted me to keep the place in the family."

"It's a wonderful tribute. And will be a lovely home."

"I have to have it plumbed. It's not habitable for long term use without toilets, running water, and a cooker. I'm doing most of the renovations myself, but the major plumbing, electrical and roofing I'm leaving to professionals."

"Isn't it dear to get hooked up to a water supply up here?"

"Yes, but even though it will cost a bundle, getting planning permission was a bigger undertaking. I was lucky. The council granted permission as long as I leave the exterior as a proper warren house and keep the grounds unspoilt. That's not a problem. I hope you'll holiday here with me once it's sorted."

Roseland clapped her hands like a young girl whose dreams had just come true. "I would love that." Quite spontaneously, she leaned in and placed a firm kiss on Spence's tantalising lips.

Spence lifted Roseland right off the chair, wrapped her in a tight embrace, and deepened their kiss in a way that could only be described as "out-of-this-world amazing."

At last Roseland said, "After you left that morning, I met an old farmer hanging around the sheep out there." She pointed past the front gate. "I inquired, but he was adamant that he hadn't seen you. Something peculiar, though. When I started my walk back to the car park, I noticed that there weren't any footprints, or hoof prints, in the snow out there in the field. It was creepy. I thought I was hallucinating. I hope not."

Spence raised a quizzical eyebrow. "Can you describe him?"

Roseland did the best she could with what she could dredge up from her memory, then Spence pulled an old almanac from the bookcase in the sitting room.

"Is this him?" She showed Roseland a photo.

"Yes! That's definitely him."

"Read the date, please."

Roseland gasped. The farmer had been dead nearly two hundred years. "Did he have a twin brother?"

A gruff voice forestalled Spence's reply, and Roseland jumped. Sure enough, there by the hearth stood the farmer, as clear as day. Spence grasped her hand and held it tightly, and they stood as if turned to granite.

"Nope, no twin, just me!" Then the farmer disappeared the way he had appeared—instantly, soundlessly.

Spence cracked a smile. "He's been haunting my family for as long as I can remember. Harmless, though."

"I'm a scientist. I do not believe in ghosts, but perhaps I can conduct a study on this one. I'll have a think on it."

"You do that."

Spence smiled and Roseland melted all over again. "What happened to him?"

"We believe he suffered critical injuries after an altercation with a nasty cow. Farmers get killed by cows more often than people think."

"I've heard that. But why would he be haunting your family home?"

"Apparently he worked for my great-great-great-great— Aw, you get the idea. One day he got too close to a cow protecting her calf. They did all they could to nurse him back to health, but pneumonia got him in the end."

59

Roseland was fascinated. If she hadn't seen and heard the old farmer with her own eyes and ears, she would have remained sceptical about the existence of ghosts, but this was just too surreal not to be true. "Having him around would give us endless conversation topics. How often does he drop by?" she asked, quite seriously, allowing that it was indeed possible to see a ghost.

"Honestly, I can't say."

"Does he ever stay long enough for a chat?" Roseland asked.

Spence shrugged. "He's a man of very few words."

"I bet if he were chatty, he'd have some interesting stories to tell," Roseland mused. "Have you seen him anywhere else?"

"I've seen him hanging around Clitter Hill, particularly near Fur Tor. Maybe he's fond of solitude."

Roseland sucked in a breath with such speed, she sputtered, "Clitter Hill? Honestly?"

This couldn't be a coincidence. The object of her desire, a woman she at first suspected was a ghost—no, not suspected, but believed to be a ghost—was not only living, breathing, and breathtakingly alluring in every way, but she had been on Clitter Hill!

Roseland, cleared her throat and said, "I've been dying to explore Clitter Hill with you. Please say you'll come with me."

Spence smiled so broadly, Roseland could have counted her back teeth, if she hadn't been too busy becoming more smitten by the moment. She smiled back.

"Of course I will."

Spence was too good to be true! Roseland began ticking boxes of what her ideal love interest would be, and so far Spence possessed most of the qualities she was looking for in a partner.

"I hike every chance I get, and Clitter Hill is a favourite," Spence added. Once I finish the house, I'm adopting a puppy. I always planned to do that as soon as I had my own place. A puppy would be the perfect hiking companion...next to someone like you, of course."

Spence wanted a dog too. Another box ticked off.

Roseland grabbed Spence and pulled her close, holding her tight while she snogged the air right out of her lungs. She took a brief pause from the kissing to announce, "I'm so thankful that you're flesh and blood! I plan to do so much more than kiss you here, there, and everywhere."

"And I plan to let you."

An uncustomary smile creased the weathered face of the old man peering in the window. The house was going to be filled with love again. He nodded his approval, then left them alone together, his departure leaving no footprints in the damp ground.

Sugar and Allspice

BY TIANA TATANOV

CARMEN BLEW A STRAND OF hair away from her face and wiped her forehead with the back of her hand. It was 9 a.m., and the coffee shop was crowded. It was getting a bit too much to manage on her own; she really needed to start thinking about hiring a barista.

She pumped milk foam into a macchiato and gave the customer in front of her the once-over. It was a woman in her thirties, looking harassed despite her impeccable make-up. Carmen opened up her perception – just a bit, she didn't want to be flooded by the collective emotions of everyone in the coffee shop – and winced in sympathy. The woman's mother was severely ill with an aggressive form of breast cancer. Carmen reached for her special shelf: valerian for anxiety, cinnamon for courage, and some yarrow for strength. She added the ground plants to the coffee and stirred them in, sincerely hoping for the woman's mother to recover her health. Sometimes she wished she could do more – be really powerful, like some of the witches whose blogs she followed religiously, and who could have actually helped this woman's mother instead of fiddling with the palliative effects of basic herbs and potions. She'd always been rubbish at spells or any kind of higher magic. Well, she was doing the best she could, wasn't she? With an encouraging smile, she handed the cup to the woman.

She turned to the next customer in line, and froze. Fuck, she was pretty. And really tall. Carmen estimated she could probably fit underneath the woman's chin. With a head of riotous, fiery ginger curls and a smattering of adorable freckles on her nose, she looked like she'd walked straight out of a fairy tale. Given the customer's appearance, she was the one who should be a witch, not Carmen, with her dumpy frame and her loose curls pulled back in a practical ponytail.

"Hi." Carmen tugged self-consciously at her ponytail and smiled at the woman. "How can I help you?" The woman smiled back, and Carmen swooned internally.

"A tall cappuccino, please."

As she fixed the woman's drink, Carmen's hand hovered over the shaker that contained allspice, for attraction. Appalled at herself, she quickly drew it back. Helping along a couple on a first date who obviously fancied each other was one thing. Using magic for her own purposes by tricking someone into feeling attracted to her was quite another. Somehow it felt intrusive to even peek into the woman's psychic vibes to figure out what plant could be more specifically helpful. She limited her additive to the very generic clover, for luck.

Carmen held out the cup, and the blinding smile she got in response made her weak in the knees. What a pity she didn't ascribe to the Starbucks policy of asking a client's name to write on their cup. At least she'd have known something about the woman. As it was, she'd probably never see her again.

But the next day, she was back. Carmen noticed her as soon as she walked through the door, and her heart started thumping in her chest. She could barely muster the concentration to add the special something to the drinks of the clients who were in line ahead of her new favourite customer. Luckily, they were easy cases: vanilla, cinnamon, and peppermint for a young starry-eyed couple; sandalwood and bergamot for a harassed businessman; and pecan and chamomile for a young woman on her way to a job interview. Too soon, or not soon enough, the object of her fascination was standing on the other side of the counter.

She smiled. "A tall cappuccino, please."

Carmen wiped her clammy hands on the front of her apron and got to work. As she filled the paper cup, she inhaled deeply. The smell of coffee never failed to calm her.

"I'm annoyed at you, you know."

Carmen looked up too fast, almost spilling scalding milk all over herself.

"A-at me? Why?" she stammered.

"Because I was trying to cut down on drinking coffee, but now that I've discovered your shop, there's no way I can ever be expected to restrain myself." She winked.

Was that a wink? Carmen was pretty sure that was a wink. Her cheeks grew hot.

"Thank you? I'm sorry?"

The woman laughed, and Carmen mentally nixed the witch comparison she'd thought of the previous day. This woman was more like a fairy. No human being had any right to have a laugh that pretty. Tinkling and clear, it radiated spontaneous joy.

"It's a compliment, you know." The woman bent over and rested her arms on the counter. "This place is really cozy, and your coffee is delicious. What's your secret?"

"If I told you, it wouldn't be a secret anymore, now would it?" Carmen was reasonably sure the woman was flirting with her, and the thought gave her confidence. She added some clover to the coffee and placed the cup on the counter.

"Fair point." Her grin was crooked as she took her coffee and handed Carmen the money for it.

Carmen was certain she didn't imagine those long fingers purposely brushing against her own.

The woman threw Carmen a last look over her shoulder and was halfway out the door when Carmen called, "What's your name?"

She turned around with a broad smile. "I'm Ruth."

Carmen was adding fresh coffee beans to the bags on the shelf behind the counter. She had less than five minutes before she opened for the day, and this was a favourite ritual of hers. She let the beans stream through her fingers, then pushed her hands into the bags, reveling in the feeling of the beans rolling against her skin.

Suddenly there was a knock against the glass in the front door. She turned around to yell, "We're not open yet!" but stopped, mouth open, when she saw that it was Ruth standing outside. Carmen hurried over to open the door. "You're a bit early. I'm still closed."

"I know. I wanted to be sure to catch you alone."

"Oh. Why?" Carmen had an inkling, but she didn't dare hope she was right.

Ruth ran a hand through her hair and shuffled uncomfortably. "You're a witch, right?"

Carmen gaped. She had *not* expected that. Most people didn't even believe witches existed, let alone recognize one when they met them. That would teach her to think pretty women were flirting with her. Apparently that was even less likely than someone discovering she mixed potions into the coffee she sold.

"No– I– What...what gave you that idea?" she stuttered.

"Don't bother denying it, I know you are."

Ruth's face was unreadable. Carmen made herself as tall as possible and took a step into Ruth's personal space. She wasn't going to let herself be intimidated. "Are you *threatening* me?"

Ruth looked down at Carmen, eyes wide. "Oh no, no, not at all. Please don't think that!" Her tone was sincerely apologetic. "It's just that, well, my stepsister is a witch too, and I kind of work for her – personal assistant, more or less." Her smile was self-depreciating.

"She wants to start a coven in the city, and she felt there was something special about your coffee shop, so she sent me to investigate. At first I thought she'd made a mistake – your shop looks quite typical, though I wasn't lying when I said it was cozy – but yesterday I noticed your little shelf. Those are all magical plants and herbs." Ruth shrugged. "I don't know a lot about magic, but I can recognize those."

Carmen was baffled. "You're saying your stepsister wants me to join a coven? Why would she want to start a coven here? Who *is* she even?"

"Uhm..." Ruth ran a nervous hand through her hair. "Esther Simmons."

Carmen's mouth fell open. "Your stepsister is Esther Simmons."

"Yes?"

Ruth's response was almost apologetic. She must have been quite aware of the effect her stepsister's name had on most people "in the know."

"And she wants me to join her coven."

"Yes." This time, Ruth sounded more assured.

It couldn't be. Carmen knew maybe five witches in the entire city, and none of them were powerful enough to be part of Esther Simmons' circle. "Just so we're clear, we *are* talking about Esther Simmons, the witch who single-handedly revolutionized glamour spells?"

An amused smile tugged at the corners of Ruth's lips. "That would be her, yes."

"Wow!" Carmen shook her head in disbelief. "Why me?"

"She needs a Potion Master. The person she originally had in mind has moved to Croatia or something. There was a lot of talk about mushrooms."

Croatia was, indeed, known for its magical mushrooms, so that made sense.

Carmen nodded slowly. "Oh, okay. That...that's great."

"And yet you seem a bit disappointed," Ruth commented. "Or am I reading that wrong?"

"No– I– Ugh. It's silly." Carmen stared at the tips of her black ballet flats. "You're going to laugh at me."

Ruth put a hand on her shoulder. "I promise I won't laugh."

Carmen shivered at the touch. "It's just that, uhm, I thought maybe you were flirting with me. And that was why you were interested in me." She laughed uncomfortably, not quite looking Ruth in the eye.

"Of course I was flirting with you. How could I help it? You put something in my coffee to make me interested in you, didn't you? I saw you do it!" Ruth didn't actually sound angry, although her arms were crossed in a rather stern posture.

"I did not!" Carmen vehemently shook her head, and her ponytail danced across her shoulders. "Well, I did put something in your drink, but it was just clover. It helps with general luck." She blushed. "I did think about using allspice, but I swear I didn't do it. That would have just been wrong. Making you want something isn't any better than forcing you to do something you don't want."

"So, it's wrong when it's me, but not when it's all those other people you sneak your potions to?" Ruth raised an eyebrow. "Am I supposed to believe that?"

"With those other people, I can...well, not read their thoughts exactly, but get a feeling of what they're experiencing at that moment." God, Ruth was going to think she was a freak. Or a scam artist. Or both. Carmen tried to explain. "Busy, stressed, in love, angry, sad...I never force them to do anything; I just help them along a bit. Figure out what they need, then try to give it to them insomuch as I am able."

"And why couldn't you do that with me?" Ruth seemed genuinely intrigued. She had uncrossed her arms, and one hand curled against her jaw in a pensive pose.

"It's not that I couldn't, it's that I didn't want to."

"Why not?"

Carmen had spent a lot of time thinking about that very question. "It would be cheating, obviously. Helping others is one thing, doing things just for myself is something else entirely."

"That's...actually quite noble." Ruth looked down at her, frowning slightly. "Just clover, nothing dodgy? You promise?"

"I swear." Carmen stared directly into Ruth's eyes, trying to convey her sincerity.

Ruth looked back at her for a few very, very long seconds, then she smiled. "Okay, I believe you."

Carmen breathed a sigh of relief and smiled back. "Thank you."

Ruth's smile turned into a grin. "That does, however, mean that I actually like you. All on my own. Without any influence from creepy magic plants." She cocked her head and looked at Carmen through her lashes. "Whatever shall we do about that?"

Carmen did some eyelash fluttering of her own. "You could ask me out."

Ruth burst into laughter. "Yup, I definitely like you. When do you close the shop?"

"At six p.m."

"Can I pick you up then? Dinner and a movie, how does that sound?"

Carmen had to restrain herself, lest she end up hopping up and down giddily like an excited seven-year-old. "Sounds brilliant." Suddenly she noticed the growing queue outside the door. She threw a look at her watch. Five past eight already!

"God, I'm so sorry," she said to Ruth, "but I really have to open the shop now." She pointed to the people on the street. "See you tonight?"

"Yes, absolutely." Ruth leaned down and dropped a kiss on her cheek before strolling toward the door, stopping briefly to send a wink at Carmen over her shoulder.

Hands pressed against her blushing face, Carmen stared after Ruth until she disappeared around the corner, then she hurried to greet her customers

Carmen usually kept the shop open until a bit after six, but this time she made it a point to be punctual with her closing. It was barely five past six when she finished loading the cups and plates into the industrial-sized dishwasher, and she had just pressed start when she heard a knock on the front door. She hurried out into the shop, pulling the apron over her head.

"Sorry I'm late," Ruth said as soon as Carmen opened the door. "The Tube was crowded."

"It's seven past. That hardly qualifies as late." Carmen smiled at her. "Besides, I've only just finished cleaning up. Just give me a second to put this away." She gestured with the apron in her hand, and then rose on tiptoes to hang it on its hook. Suddenly there was a warm presence behind her. Carmen turned around, deliberately slowly, and found herself mere inches from Ruth.

They stared at each other for a moment, before Ruth broke the awkwardness by saying, "Tell me about the potions."

Carmen smiled delightedly. Beyond exchanging recipes with other witches on the internet, she so rarely got to talk about her craft. People in Real Life tended to look at you strangely if you started talking about magic potions. She eagerly led Ruth over to her little shelf behind the counter.

"These are the herbs I use the most often. Valerian calms anxiety. I generally have to put a lot of it into someone's cup in order to counteract the stressing effect of the caffeine. It's easy when I don't have to be careful with the proportions, but some herbs are much trickier and can have negative effects if I use the wrong dosage. Poppy seeds, for example, work as an anti-depressant, but having too many of them becomes addictive, so I have to be very careful. That's where those come in handy." She pointed at the electric scales on the counter. "Extremely precise, they weigh down to the milligram."

Her eyes went back to the herbs. "Chamomile is good for the nerves too, and it tastes better than valerian." She reached into the little pot and crushed a leaf between her fingers, then held it underneath Ruth's nose.

Ruth breathed in its scent. "Wow, that's different from bagged tea."

"I hope it is!"

Carmen ran her hand along the shelf, occasionally tapping a porcelain lid. "Bergamot for money and financial success. Pecan. I use a lot of it, because it's good for job security and stimulates a flourishing career. Most of my clients come here before work, you see. Neroli and anise enhance happiness. Clover, for general luck. That's what I gave you."

Ruth winked. "It seemed to have worked,"

"You flirt." Carmen shook her head with a fond smile. She ran her fingers over Ruth's upper arm. "And of course there are herbs for romantic love, since a coffee shop is an ideal place for a date. I'm very careful with those, though. The idea is not to create artificial feelings, but to help bring feelings that are already there to the surface. It's a very fine line. There's cardamom, for faithful love, and vanilla, for young, passionate love, and allspice, for attraction."

She looked up at Ruth with a sheepish smile. "That's the one I thought about using on you."

"Turns out you didn't need it, did you?" Ruth arched an eyebrow. "And you're even prettier when you talk about things that you're passionate about."

"Oh you." Carmen blushed. She suddenly realised she'd barely have to stand on the tips of her toes to be able to kiss Ruth right on the mouth. So she did.

For a second, Ruth seemed shocked, staring at Carmen in a comically cross-eyed way, but then she kissed her back.

And God, she knew how to kiss. She coaxed Carmen's lips open and licked into her mouth, her tongue soft and slick against Carmen's.

Carmen's fingers tangled into Ruth's curls and she pulled her down, kissing her more deeply, pressing their bodies together.

They broke apart, both of them panting with desire.

Carmen sighed. "Whoa."

"What you said." Ruth grinned, then her look turned to consideration for a second before she looked Carmen straight in the eyes. "How do you feel about sex on the first date?"

Carmen's stomach swooped and then soared. *Fuck yes.* She tilted her head. "How do you feel about sex *before* the first date?"

"*Fuck yes.*"

Ruth's response echoed her earlier thoughts. Carmen's giggle was cut short when Ruth's mouth covered her own in a bruising kiss. Her hands slid down Carmen's back to cup her arse, and Carmen moaned.

"Up. On the counter," Ruth told her, ineffectively trying to lift her up.

"O-oh, bossy," Carmen said in a singsong voice. She disentangled herself from Ruth's grasp just long enough to hop onto the counter, then grabbed her by the hips and pulled her close again. "I like bossy."

She kissed Ruth again. The counter was quite low, so Ruth was still taller than her. When she ran her fingernails over the sensitive skin of Ruth's neck, Ruth moaned into her mouth.

Carmen smirked against Ruth's lips. "And you like a bit of pain, it seems."

"Shut up, you."

Ruth grabbed her free hand and pinned it to the counter. It was Carmen's turn to moan. She liked being restrained.

As if reading her thoughts – but no, that was Carmen's thing, though she was doing her best to keep it reined in – Ruth looked at her intently. "If you like bossy. Does that mean I can tie you up?"

Carmen smiled broadly. "Oh, yes please!"

"What with?"

Carmen pointed to the row of hooks on the wall. "Apron ties."

"Aren't you the creative one." Ruth grabbed the apron off its hook and untied the bow at the waist. She drew Carmen's hands behind her back and tied her wrists together, slipping a finger beneath the bonds to make sure they were not too tight. "Good?"

Carmen nodded. "Great."

Ruth pressed a kiss against her jaw. Her fingers deftly undid the buttons of Carmen's shirt, and then pushed it over her shoulders so it bunched against the ties around Carmen's wrists. Jeans and knickers – already slightly wet – came next.

Carmen wriggled her hips to help Ruth get the clothes off quicker. She wanted to reach out and touch Ruth, pull her closer, slide her fingers underneath her shirt, but she couldn't. Not with her hands tied. So she waited.

Ruth stepped between Carmen's spread legs and rested warm hands on her hips, then ran them up her sides, fingers tickling her ribs. Carmen's skin broke out in goosebumps. Ruth pushed her fingers under the cups of Carmen's bra – that couldn't have been comfortable, with the underwire biting into her hands like that – and found a nipple. Carmen yelped and arched her back. Ruth pulled one hand away. She brought it to her mouth and licked her fingers, and Carmen whimpered at the sight. Then, Ruth's hand was back on her breast. It felt *lovely*.

Carmen whined in disappointment at the loss of sensation as Ruth's long fingers travelled downwards. They brushed against the swell of her stomach, then down, over her hipbones, to her sensitive inner thighs. It felt nice, but that wasn't where Carmen wanted Ruth's touch.

"Touch me?" she asked. "Please?"

Ruth apparently liked her begging, because her hand moved from Carmen's thigh to press against her clit. Carmen gasped. Ruth kissed her, wet and open-mouthed. With her free hand, she played with Carmen's hair.

Ruth tugged playfully at the tie holding Carmen's ponytail. "May I?"

"Sure." The word ended in a needy moan as Ruth rubbed the pad of a finger against her clit.

Ruth pulled the tie off Carmen's ponytail, and Carmen shook her hair out. It felt nice, caressing the skin of her back and shoulders.

"You have gorgeous hair."

Ruth's fingers combed through her curls, and Carmen's neck arched in pleasure. Ruth caressed her back, stopping on her hip, and then pulled Carmen forward until she was sitting at the very edge of the counter, her legs dangling, just short of reaching the floor.

Ruth straddled her right thigh and gently rocked her hips, panting as she rubbed her clit against Carmen's leg. The wool of her stockings burned a bit on Carmen's skin, but the added friction must have felt wonderful to Ruth.

Ruth pushed two fingers into Carmen's wet cunt and this time, Carmen didn't moan; she *shouted.* Ruth's body was pressing against her, just enough room between them for the hand doing those delicious things. Carmen dropped her forehead onto Ruth's shoulder, but Ruth curled her fingers *just right* and Carmen only managed not to shriek because she bit down hard on Ruth's collarbone. It was Ruth who shouted instead. Apparently she really did like pain.

Carmen left a trail of bites along Ruth's neck and shoulders, pushing the fabric of her knit dress out of the way with her nose. Each time she bit down just that tad bit harder, the rhythm of Ruth's cunt on her thigh accelerated, as did the movement of Ruth's fingers inside Carmen's cunt. She was grinding her palm against Carmen's clit, too, and there was a familiar heat coiling in Carmen's groin.

Her barriers against her psychic perception were starting to erode, and Ruth appeared to be as blissed-out and incoherent as she was. Carmen's hands clenched into fists behind her back, nails digging into the skin of her palms.

Ruth's fingers rubbed against Carmen's sweet spot, and Carmen cried, "There. Oh God, right there! Don't stop!"

Ruth stroked again and again, and suddenly Carmen was coming, the world exploding behind her closed eyelids.

When things swam back into focus, Ruth was panting broken little moans into her ear, her breath tickling flyaway hairs. It wouldn't be long before she came. She pulled her hand away from Carmen's cunt and gripped her hips, hard, her fingers slick against Carmen's skin. She ground down harder against Carmen's thigh and threw her head back, panting.

"Oh God!"

Carmen dipped her head and sank her teeth into the line of muscle along Ruth's throat. Ruth went rigid and shouted wordlessly, fingers digging into Carmen's hips. There would be bruises tomorrow.

After a moment, Ruth relaxed and brought her arms up to encircle Carmen's shoulders.

"Whoa." Her smile was blinding.

Carmen couldn't resist kissing her. "Exactly, yes. Let's do this again."

"Now?" Ruth raised an eyebrow.

Oh, Carmen decidedly liked this girl. "If you want."

"I do want." Ruth took a step backwards, away from the counter. She hooked her thumbs in the waist of her stockings and took them off in one fluid movement, together with her purple cotton knickers. Bunching up her skirt above her hips, she set her feet wide apart. "Come here, then."

Carmen grinned. "O-oh, yes Ma'am."

She hopped off the counter and went to her knees. Her face was mere inches from Ruth's cunt, so close she could smell her. She looked up teasingly, conveying a silent challenge.

Ruth understood. She grabbed a handful of Carmen's hair and pulled her face between her legs, mashing her mouth against her cunt.

She was wet and tangy, a taste that made Carmen's own cunt even more slippery. With her hands bound behind her back, Carmen only had her mouth to work with. She didn't need anything else. She kissed Ruth's inner thigh, dragging her teeth against the soft, pale skin. Above her, Ruth inhaled sharply.

With a self-satisfied smile, Carmen moved to the other thigh, nipping and nibbling, followed by soothing little licks. She kept licking, along the crease of Ruth's groin, until her tongue brushed against springy ginger curls.

"Come on, Carmen." Ruth's voice sounded a bit strangled. "Stop teasing."

There she was. Carmen kissed Ruth's cunt, then sucked gently on one labium. Ruth sighed in pleasure.

Carmen dipped her tongue into Ruth's cunt and pushed deeper, curling the tip back towards herself. Her nose brushed against Ruth's clit and Ruth screamed, tightening her grip on Carmen's hair.

Taking the hint, Carmen moved up, dragging her tongue gently over Ruth's cunt and pointing it when she reached her clit. Wetness dripped into her mouth and trickled down her chin.

Carmen licked small circles around Ruth's clit, slowly, insistently.

"Bit– uh! Bit faster," Ruth gasped.

Carmen obeyed, quickening her motions, and Ruth's hips bucked so hard, she almost hit Carmen's nose.

"Fuck." She moaned. "Oh my–"

Her grasp on Carmen's hair tightened almost painfully as she rode out her orgasm, uttering little gasping sounds that made Carmen's stomach flutter.

Ruth's legs hadn't even stopped trembling against Carmen's shoulders when she dragged Carmen up by her hair and spun her around to bend her over the counter. Carmen grunted as the air was forced out of her lungs, and she spread her legs a bit wider to keep her balance, the height of the counter forcing her to put all her weight on the tips of her toes. Fuck, being woman-handled like this was hot.

There was a dull thud behind her. Carmen looked over her shoulder and swallowed heavily. Ruth was on her knees, staring at her cunt with an intensity that made Carmen blush.

When Ruth put her hands on Carmen's thighs and pushed them just a tad wider apart, Carmen rested her head on her forearm, her other hand gripping the edge of the counter in anticipation.

The first touch of Ruth's tongue wasn't gentle or timid. She pressed deep into Carmen's cunt, her lower lip smearing wetly against Carmen's clit. Carmen groaned deeply, the sound muffled against the skin of her arm. But when Ruth pulled back to press her tongue hard against her clit, Carmen threw her head back, her loud moan echoing in the emptiness of the room.

Outside the plate glass window, the street was dark, illuminated only by a few streetlamps. If one of the passersby looked inside, they might see her getting eaten out over her own counter, even if they'd have to peer hard, since the counter didn't face the window. Someone might even have seen them already, while Carmen wasn't looking.

The thought shot a jolt of pleasure down Carmen's spine, and her mental barriers lowered further. Oh. Ruth seemed to be enjoying herself at least as much as Carmen was. That was good. That was brilliant. Unexpectedly, Ruth's happy mental vibes were abruptly cut off.

"Fuck!" Her voice was muffled by Carmen's cunt.

Carmen looked back and couldn't help but snorting out loud. The shirt that was still dangling from her bound wrists had flopped downwards, covering Ruth's fiery curls. The sight was incongruous, to say the least.

"Don't laugh at me, you minx." Ruth took a hand off Carmen's thigh to disentangle herself from the offending piece of clothing.

"I wouldn't dare," Carmen assured her. She managed to gather the shirt between her fingers and clutched it tightly to make sure it wouldn't interrupt them again. "Please, go on."

"Since you ask so nicely."

Ruth buried her face back between Carmen's legs. She licked broad, firm stripes over Carmen's cunt, her hands on Carmen's thighs, spreading her open. Heat pooled in Carmen's stomach and slid down to her cunt. Ruth tilted her head, changing the angle, and the heat uncoiled as Carmen's orgasm hit. She shouted, arching her back, thankful for the counter and Ruth's strong hands holding her up. Her legs felt so wobbly, she was sure she'd have crumpled to the floor without the support.

Carmen panted softly into the crook of her elbow, trying to regain her breath.

"Still up for that movie, then?" Ruth sounded entirely too pleased with herself.

Carmen threw a disbelieving look over her shoulder. "Do you even need to ask? We might need to clean up a bit first though. Lucky there's a sink in the kitchen, hm?"

"Great." Ruth smiled broadly, but her tone grew less secure. "Uhm, and..." She wiped a hand over her sticky mouth and looked up at Carmen with hopeful eyes. "Stay at my place after?"

"I've got you hooked this quickly, do I?" Carmen teased as she wiggled her hands out of their apron-tie bonds and shrugged her shirt back on. "And without the allspice!"

Ruth pressed a sweet kiss against Carmen's inner thigh. "You can save your allspice for people who really need it."

Carmen tucked a stray curl behind Ruth's ear and smiled down at her. "Well, no allspice for me, then." She reached for her jeans and knickers that were lying on the floor. "Come on. Let's cuddle at the movies, and then you can take me home."

A lawyer, a succubus, and a blonde walk into a bar…

BY LILA BRUCE

ONCE YOU MAKE A DEAL with the devil, there's no going back.

Mercy O'Brien threw her best fake smile at the brunette sitting across the table and silently cursed her cousin Katie. *Well, maybe devil is a bit harsh.* When an apartment fire had left Mercy in housing limbo, Katie offered up the use of her spare bedroom without hesitation. Mercy had been more than happy to return "the favor" when Katie called her earlier in the week. Of course, had she known that favor was a blind date with Katie's old friend from nursing school—her obnoxiously loud old friend—Mercy might not have been so keen.

After listening to the brunette drone on now for the better part of an hour, Mercy wished that she'd stayed home and worked on unpacking her new apartment. She'd had a bad feeling about tonight, but, feeling obligated to honor the favor to Katie, had gone out anyway. *Next time I have a bad feeling, I'm listening to it.*

She picked up a glass from the table and slowly sipped at her cocktail as she let her gaze drift across the bar. Located just off River Street, The Blue Siren was one of Mercy's favorite spots to unwind after a busy week at work. She and the brunette—*oh God, what was her name?*—pretty much had the place to themselves, which was unusual for a Saturday night in Savannah. It was only a little past ten o'clock and typically the bar would be teeming with people at that time of night. Outside of the two of them, there was just Max the bartender and one other customer, who was sitting quietly at a table in the corner. Mercy couldn't help but wonder if her date's insufferably loud voice had something to do with the bar's patrons jumping ship well before closing time.

"So, have you?"

Mercy realized then that the woman had apparently stopped talking about her Chihuahuas and was asking a question.

"I'm sorry, have I what?"

"Ever have to shoot anyone?" She lowered her voice. "Or kill anyone?"

Frowning, Mercy shook her head. "What are you talking about?"

"You know, while you were over there. Katie told me that you were in the military." She leaned forward so her breasts rested on the table. "Although I do have to say you're awfully pretty to have been in the military."

Unbefuckinglieveable. Well, actually considering the source, it wasn't. Telling herself that she needed to be nice for Katie's sake, Mercy forced a smile. "You know, if I had a dime for every time somebody has asked me that stupid-ass question, I'd be a rich woman." *Well, relatively nice.* "I was in the JAG Corps, so I never served directly on the front line the way you're thinking."

"Oh, like on that old television show?"

"Yes, but no. As a general rule, the Navy doesn't allow its lawyers to fly combat missions."

"God, I loved that show," the brunette gushed. "You know the best part was that Marine JAG. You know, the one…" She leered at Mercy as she continued. "…Sally or Sarah or something; the one with the… ahem…endowments. She was on some other show not too long ago, what was it called…"

Exhaling loudly, Mercy turned her attention away. The customer in corner looked on in open amusement. An attractive redhead dressed casually in jeans and a black t-shirt; she caught Mercy's gaze and lifted her wine glass in a mock toast. *Great. I'm glad someone's enjoying this.*

"Excuse me," Mercy said, interrupting the brunette, who had gone back to talking about her dogs. "I need to go get a refill on my drink."

"But, it's not even half-empty."

Nodding, she rose from the table. "Yeah, but if we sit here for much longer, I'm going to need something with a lot more alcohol in it." Not waiting to hear a reply Mercy turned and went over to the bar. She found Max playing on his cell phone, one elbow propped up on the counter.

"Gotcha live one tonight, huh, Mercy?" The stocky man with short, charcoal gray hair asked, glancing up from his phone but otherwise not moving.

"Stow it, Max," she quipped. "I'm doing a favor for my cousin." *A damn big favor.* "What do you have that might help to drown out the sound of her voice?"

Straightening, the bartender scratched the day-old stubble on his chin. "Well, lemme see." He nodded to himself and then snapped. "Tell you what. I've wanted to try out some of the new cocktails before the big Halloween party next week. How about an Afterbirth?"

Mercy wrinkled her nose. "That just sounds gross."

"A Lobotomy shot?"

"I think I'm having one of those already tonight."

"A Headless Horseman?"

"Nah."

"How about a Black Witch?"

Mercy bobbed her head. "What's in that?"

"Rum, apricot brandy, more rum, pineapple juice."

"Okay, I'll try that." She leaned against the bar and watched as Max began to pour dark rum into a shaker. "Quiet in here tonight."

"Yeah," he said. "Supposed to be a storm rolling through, according to what they were saying on the news earlier. I guess that's kept most people at home." He strained the dark amber cocktail into a glass and then slid it across the counter to Mercy.

"I should be one of those people," she muttered, turning away from the counter. Mercy was halfway to the table when she stopped abruptly, realizing that the brunette was no longer there. An amused redhead sat in her place. *What the hell?*

"Please, have a seat," the woman who had been sitting on the other side of the bar said, motioning to the empty chair opposite hers.

Darting her eyes around the bar, Mercy found the brunette was nowhere to be seen. "I'm sorry, where did—?"

"Your friend go?" The woman smiled as she swirled the wine around in her glass. "She had to leave rather suddenly. Something about a dog."

Mercy frowned. "Strange, I didn't see her leave." To be honest, she wasn't going to complain too loudly. Still, it was odd that the brunette would have left without at least saying something.

"I did say it was rather sudden," the redhead drawled. She motioned again to the empty chair. "Please, sit. I promise I don't bite."

"Well…" Mercy chewed on her bottom lip as she considered her options. There wasn't a whole lot waiting for her at home. She'd only just moved out of Katie's house and into her new apartment. She supposed she could unpack the last of the moving boxes that littered the one-bedroom apartment. *Please, you know you'd just go home, watch Netflix and eat a pint of ice cream.* Ignoring the overwhelming feeling that she should just turn and run away, Mercy nodded and then slid into the empty chair. "Why not? I'm Mercy, by the way."

The redhead ran a slow tongue over pink lips. "A pleasure to meet you, Mercy. I'm Eris."

The sound of crashing thunder and a slamming door made Mercy jump. She turned to see a tall, blonde woman standing in the doorway of the bar. Her white button-down shirt and khaki pants dripped with water as she pounded her feet on the black mat by the entrance. She cast a disparaging look in Mercy's direction and then grumbled, "It's pouring down rain out there."

Watching the blonde trudge to the counter and take a barstool at the far end, Mercy suppressed a grin. *Guess I made the right decision to stay inside, then.* She turned back to the redhead. "Eris? That's an unusual name."

The woman shrugged. "It's an old family name."

Reclining in the chair, Mercy regarded her new companion. *Italian maybe, or Greek*, she thought, noticing a trace of an accent accompanying the other woman's olive complexion and aquiline features. Although the red hair was unusual for someone of Mediterranean descent. Assuming, of course, she was a natural redhead. Mercy took a sip of her drink and instantly winced.

"Are you okay?"

"Yeah," Mercy coughed. "Just a tad stronger than I expected it to be."

"I see," Eris nodded. "So, you are a jack?"

Mercy frowned. "I'm sorry, what?"

"I couldn't help but overhear your conversation with that..." Eris swirled the wine again and gave a slight smile. "...distasteful woman. She said you were a jack? I haven't heard that term before, but then English is not my language."

Laughing, Mercy returned the smile. "No, she said JAG. It's short for Judge Advocate General." When Eris raised an eyebrow, she continued. "A military lawyer."

"Aha. So you are a—"

"Soul-sucking attorney?" Mercy said, remembering the phrase her late grandfather would sometimes jokingly use. "That's right."

"Mm." Eris leaned forward in her chair and ran her eyes over Mercy. "I knew there was something about you I liked."

Mercy shifted in her seat, feeling surprisingly uncomfortable. *What the hell?* She'd stared down two hundred pound men aboard ship without so much as a second thought and suddenly this redhead had her squirming in her seat. Sure, she was attractive, but Mercy had met her fair share of exotically beautiful women. Hell, she'd even dated a few. "So," she said, clearing her throat and trying to shake off whatever it was that was about this woman that affected her so. "What are you?"

Eris seemed to stiffen at the question. "How do you mean?"

"Lord, I don't mean to sound like an inbred hick. I'm sorry." She picked up the glass and motioned with it. "I couldn't help but notice your accent. And, you said that English is not your language."

Relaxing back into the chair, Eris smiled. "Ah. I'm Greek." She pushed a wayward strand of hair away from her face. "More or less."

Thought so. She sipped gingerly at the cocktail. "So what brings you to Savannah?"

"Just passing through," Eris answered, shrugging one shoulder. "I enjoy traveling. And you, Mercy? As that bland woman with the loud voice asked earlier, is it unusual to find someone as tempting as yourself serving in the military?"

A shiver ran down her spine at Eris' sultry tone. Mercy took another drink. She realized she had never fully understood just what a sultry tone meant. It was like the hot, oppressive air that builds up just before a thunderstorm hits. Mercy glanced up to meet Eris' heavy gaze and was not sure if she was ready to risk getting struck by lightning just yet.

"Not really," she said, surprised by the gravelly sound of her own voice. "I served for six years. You see a fair cross-section as a JAG and I can honestly say that there really is no one 'type' in the military."

"Interesting. And what made you decide to become one of these, what did you say? A soul-sucking attorney."

"Well, that's kind of a long story."

"I have nowhere else to be," Eris said, running the edge of one thumbnail across her bottom lip.

Transfixed by the movement, Mercy found herself wondering what those pink lips tasted like. Red wine, certainly. Although, now that she thought about it, Mercy realized she'd yet to see Eris actually drink from the wine glass. She stared at the exotic woman sitting across from her for a long moment. That little voice in the back of her head was telling her to get up and walk away now. Most of the time she listened to it, and, as a general rule, the little voice of reason was right about such things. Right now, however, it was being drowned out by the buzz of rum and apricot brandy. The buzz reminded her—rather loudly—of all the bad luck she'd had over last year, most recently the apartment fire that had claimed the bulk of her worldly possessions. She was long overdue for a break. Smiling at Eris, Mercy leaned forward in the chair.

"Okay," Mercy said, rolling the flavor of rum off her tongue, "if you insist. To be honest, it's not that much of a story. Really, rather plain."

Eris' eyes glinted as she spoke. "I assure you, I find you to be far from plain."

Zahra Mahzarin al-Jinn sat on a stool at the end of the bar, sipping her warm beer and trying to ignore the not-so-subtle glances she was receiving from the bartender. Had she known it was going to come to a torrential downpour, she wouldn't have chosen a white shirt. She'd seen more rain in the past year than she'd seen in the past seven hundred and was honestly rather sick of it. Of course, the rain was a welcome change from the oppressive humidity that'd she had to endure over the summer. And the pollen. *Gods, the pollen.* At times, it had gotten so thick that it coated the ground—and the windows, and the cars, and the park benches, and anyone walking down the street—in a heavy yellow dust. Indubitably, there would be those who would say that Zahra was exaggerating and that Jinn were immune to such as things as pollen. To those people, Zahra would say, "Fuck you, come to Georgia and see how you like sneezing for two months straight."

Shifting in her seat so that she could get a better view of Mercy and the *shaytan*, Zahra shook her head. She could hear her father now... *You had one job, Zahra, one job!* And it was a job she was screwing up royally, Zahra thought with a sigh. As a daughter of the seventh Prince of Djinnestan, Zahra's place in the royal family had been decided long before her birth.

Prince Bahadur was charged with overseeing the King's personal guard and, as an extension of that, all his seventy-seven children served as *muhafiz* in some form or fashion. Prior to this particular assignment, Zahra had always been quite good at her job. Watching over the daughters and concubines of Caliphs and Wazirs through the ages, Zahra had never lost a charge. Not once. Of course, none of those daughters or concubines had been Mercy O'Brien.

"Well," Zahra heard Mercy say, "I'm from a military family."

"Ah, so you followed in the family tradition?"

"Hardly," Mercy answered, shaking her head. "It was actually the last thing I ever wanted or planned to do."

"And yet..." The *shaytan* darted her eyes in Zahra's direction. She was sure the demon suspected that she was no more human than it was pretending to be.

From the *shaytan*'s aura, Zahra recognized it as one of the black-hearted creatures that seduced the innocent and fed off their soul until there was nothing left. The demons went by many names—*qarinah*, succubus, temptress. Zahra shook her head. Whatever the *shaytan* called itself, it now had Mercy in its sights.

"And yet," Mercy repeated with a faint smile. "No, my brother was the one to do that. After he was killed..."

Zahra tensed at the sound of heartache in Mercy's voice. She'd been with Mercy long enough to recognize that her brother's death was a subject that she rarely spoke about, and never with strangers. That she was doing so now was an indication that the *shaytan* was successfully working its sorcery on Mercy. It was the creature's calling card to marinate its victim with emotion before devouring them.

She grimaced at the thought of Mercy's brother. After all, it was that dying wish of a hero, to keep his family safe, that was the reason Zahra found herself in her current predicament.

For the first seven years, Zahra's brother Dareh had successfully completed that task of guarding Mercy, the sister. Then, as was the custom, assignments were rotated and the job of safeguarding Mercy O'Brien fell to Zahra. At first, Zahra had no reason to believe it would be different from any other assignment she had been given. Of course, that had been before she laid eyes on the quiet human female with honey-brown hair and fallen totally, hopelessly in love with her.

Seeing the shaytan smile at Mercy, Zahra felt a shiver of anger run through her. She took another swig of beer, trying to keep an eye on Mercy and the demon without being obvious. She frowned, thinking there was nothing more that she would like to do than drive a sword through the demon's black heart. Of course, it would take more than that to slay a *shaytan*. Luckily, as a *muhafiz*, Zahra was equipped to contend with forces natural and supernatural in the protection of those under her charge. That said, Jinn law forbade direct intervention if a charge freely and of their own accord put themselves in harm's way. A Jinn could whisper suggestions, act indirectly upon outside elements, or even "give the willies", as one of her former charges used to say. All of this to warn that danger was imminent, but that's where her involvement ended.

If a human, of their own free will, chose to endanger themselves, there was nothing that Zahra could do about it.

Get it together, O'Brien. What the hell had her so emotional tonight? Maybe it was the drink stirring up painful memories that hadn't come calling in years. Blinking back the tears that suddenly threatened, she took a long haul of her cocktail, ignoring the burn of alcohol as it washed down her throat. With a grimace, she sat the now half-empty drink back on the table and pushed the glass away. Mercy looked up to see Eris staring at her, an unfathomable expression on her face. "I'm sorry." Mercy shook her head apologetically.

"There's no need. Your remorse over his loss is obvious." Eris held her gaze steady. "You should embrace your feelings, not hide from them." Eris reached a slender hand across the table and place it over Mercy's. The touch sparked a tiny shiver that ran up her arm, stirring a warmth in her chest. Mercy stared wordlessly at Eris' hand on hers. "Humanity's greatest gift is the one that it denies itself the most. All those emotions that swirl around inside of you like wine in a bottle. So many layers—anger, fear, grief, love…" Mercy met Eris' eyes as she paused, "…lust. And like the wine, if you keep those emotions bottled up, the soul will become flat, sour." She began to rub tantalizing circles on the soft part of Mercy's wrist with her thumb. "But open a fine wine to the air, allow it to breathe, and its flavor will be exquisite."

Between the delicate caress on her wrist and the soft, sultry tone of Eris' voice, Mercy felt bewitched by her gaze. Her eyes were unusual—a smoky black that left Mercy enthralled and craving for something that felt just out of reach. She wondered just how ferocious this exotic Greek woman would be in bed.

"You need to be careful there."

Mercy tore her gaze away from the dark abyss. She jerked her head toward the blonde woman standing beside the table with a disturbed look on her face. "Excuse me?" She felt disorientated and clumsy.

"Your drink," the blonde said, motioning at the cocktail glass teetering on the edge of the table. "It looks like it's about to fall off the table." As she moved, a strand of hair, still partially wet from the rain, drifted down across her face. It struck Mercy that the woman's hair wasn't truly blonde-blonde, but more of a strawberry blonde. It was a peculiar color but complimented the woman's apricot skin and violet eyes. Looking from Eris to the blonde, Mercy wondered for a moment if there was a supermodel convention in town that no one had bothered to tell her about.

"Um, thanks." Mercy pulled the glass away back towards the center of the table and watched as the blonde nodded and then made her way to a table by the window. Drawing away from Eris' grasp, she sat back in the chair and rolled her shoulders in an attempt to relieve the sudden stiffness she felt in her neck. "Let's see, where was I? Oh, yeah…so anyway, after my brother's death I decided the best way to honor his memory was to continue the—what did you call it?—family tradition, but in my own way."

"I see," Eris said quietly and tossed a not-so-subtle glare in the direction of the blonde woman.

As Eris directed her gaze back to her, Mercy noticed the air between them no longer felt charged. She shifted uncomfortably in the hard chair. "Mm, but I'm sure you didn't go out tonight to have some random woman in a bar bare her soul to you."

Seemingly amused by the comment, Eris grinned. "Oh, you'd be surprised. There's nothing I'd like more."

Zahra wondered if throwing the half-empty bottle of beer at the *shaytan*'s head constituted direct intervention and then had the thought interrupted by a loud clap of thunder. *Apparently it does.*

"You know, I think we've talked enough about me," she heard Mercy drawl. "What do you do, Eris?"

Watching the rain slash against the window before trickling slowly down the plate glass, Zahra blew out a breath. This was a disaster of her own making. She should have begged out of this assignment as soon as she realized that her objectivity was compromised. Any one of her brothers or sisters would have sensed the *shaytan* before it even got close to Mercy. They would have made sure that she had never stepped foot in the bar in the first place. Unlike Zahra, who was so caught up in her feelings for the alluring human that, at times, everything else in the world ceased to exist.

"What I do? I don't understand your question," Zahra heard the *shaytan* say.

"You know, for a living. I'm a soul-sucking attorney and you are…" Mercy's voice trailed off. She couldn't see her clearly in the window's reflection, but Zahra knew from the soft lilt in Mercy's voice that she was smiling. The first time she'd seen Mercy's soft pink lips turn up gently at the corners, Zahra had almost come undone.

In fifteen hundred years, she'd never been in love. Of course, Zahra understood the concept and had witnessed acts—both noble and otherwise—committed in its name. She'd seen wars started over it, read poetry inspired by it. All of that had been as a spectator. None of those things had even remotely prepared Zahra for the reality of what love really was. The feeling of euphoria that swept over her whenever Mercy walked into a room. The anxiousness that came whenever they were apart. And the enigmatic clumsiness that took over Zahra at the most random of times. *Well, maybe not so random.* She'd probably never live down the apartment fire that she'd started when Mercy ran naked from the shower to answer a phone call, causing Zahra to trip over her own feet and knock over a scented candle.

"Ah," the *shaytan* said. "I am…a collector."

"A collector? Well, that's certainly, um, different. Like for a museum or something? What do you collect?"

"The essence of man. I hunger for it. I seek it out and devour it wherever I can find it."

Zahra snapped her head around at the *shaytan*'s words. She never imagined it would be so bold as to proclaim who and what it was to Mercy. For her part, Mercy looked just as shocked. Using every fiber of her being to will Mercy to stand up and flee from the demon, Zahra felt her stomach fall when a small grin crept across Mercy's face.

"Okay, I get it. You're a photographer," she said with a nod. "Capture the essence of man, I like that. Very poetic."

"If that's how you would like to think of it, then yes," the demon answered.

Mercy drummed her fingers on the table and seemed to be considering something. Fearful of what that something might be, Zahra shifted in her seat. "So tell me," Mercy said after a moment, confirming Zahra's worst fear, "are you hungry right now?"

Oh no, Mercy. Please, no.

With an evil smile, the *shaytan* nodded. "Starved."

Caught up in Eris' dark, hypnotic gaze, Mercy felt a subconscious desire to be possessed rise up within her. How long had it been since she'd allowed herself to be totally controlled, utterly consumed, by her own base needs? Hell, she hadn't even been able to have more than two dates with any one woman in the past year. Something about the women she'd been seeing since settling back in Savannah had just felt wrong. Eris stretched out a slender hand and turned it palm up, silently beckoning. Mercy flushed with fever. She heard the voice of reason give one last, feeble attempt to tell her that this was wrong. Random one-night stands with strangers was not who she was—no matter how damn deliciously sexy they were. The buzz of shameless desire drowned out that voice as, almost afraid to breathe lest she lose her nerve, Mercy reached out to claim Eris' hand and all that went with it.

"Then what do you say we go get a bite to eat?"

"I thought you'd never ask," Eris said, her sultry tone eroding any vestige of doubt that Mercy may have had left.

Mercy rose from the table. Eris tightened the grasp on her hand, eliciting a smile from Mercy. "Don't worry," she murmured, flexing an arm to draw Eris in close. "I'm all yours tonight." Mercy gestured with a nod of her head. "My place is not far from here. It's a little more private than this bar."

"Mm," Eris breathed, extending her free hand to drape it over Mercy's shoulder. "I would love nothing more." Mercy trembled with suppressed desire as she felt Eris trace a fingernail along the back of her neck. "I intend to feast on you all night."

Mercy licked her suddenly dry lips. "Then what are we waiting for?" She turned to lead them toward the exit but came to a jarring stop. Max, the bartender, barreled into her. The opened, oversized jar of maraschino cherries he was carrying spilled out onto her clothing.

"Dammit, Mercy, I'm sorry." Max looked from Mercy to the jar of cherries and then back toward the bar. "I don't know what the hell just happened. I swear I was just at the bar experimenting with the new drinks." Looking dazed, Max shook his head. "It's like magic. One second I was there and the next I'm knocking into you. Here, let me help you get cleaned up."

Crap, this is going to stain. Mercy frowned at the red splotch covering the front of her blouse before pushing away Max's offer of a bar towel. "No, that's okay, Max. It was an accident." Mercy looked over her shoulder at Eris. "Give me just a minute to go clean up and then we can continue our...conversation."

Eris' dark eyes glinted sharply in the flustered bartender's direction as she nodded. "Of course."

Mercy ignored the stare from the blonde woman as she passed by her table and made her way to the restroom. She turned on the faucet and allowed cool water to fill up the sink. Soaking a handful of paper towels in the water, she began to dab at her blouse. *At least it's not a new shirt.* She gave a disgusted sigh and then glanced up, catching her reflection in the mirror. The juice from the maraschino cherries looked like blood against the creamy white blouse. Splashes of red dotted her chin and neck. It was a jarring image and one that brought Mercy plummeting back down to earth.

"What the hell am I doing?" she asked her reflection. What was she thinking? Had she really been about to take some random woman she'd just met in a bar home with her? Mercy shook her head. It had to be the alcohol. She wondered if Max had a back door that she could sneak out of, when Eris' face appeared in the mirror behind her. She froze.

"I hope you don't mind," Eris said quietly. "You were gone so long that I thought I had better make sure you hadn't escaped." Mercy fell mute as Eris stepped up behind her. Feeling Eris' soft body press against hers, the woman's breath warm against her neck, Mercy moaned. The sound brought a smile to Eris' lips. "I'm eager to pick up where we left off."

Any reservation Mercy had about Eris melted away as the woman dipped her head and, pulling away on the stained blouse, began to graze the bared skin of her nape with her teeth. Fire followed the path of Eris' tongue as she ran it along the sweet spot on Mercy's neck. Her knees threatened to buckle. Mercy grabbed the edge of the sink and allowed her head to fall back, surrendering as Eris nipped and kissed at her neck ravenously.

"Mm, you taste sweeter than I imagined," Eris purred, her hands moving forward to encircle Mercy, turning her towards her. "It looks like you missed a spot. Let me help you with that." Pulling Mercy tight, Eris lowered her hot mouth to lap up the splash of juice staining Mercy's chin. Unable to do anything, Mercy's lips fell open and were quickly claimed by Eris'. Tasting the sweetness of the cherries on Eris' tongue as it laced across her own, Mercy groaned. "So succulent," Eris murmured.

Mercy arched as Eris delved her hands under the damp blouse, slowly teasing their way up Mercy's ribs, tracing the skin just beneath her breasts. When slender fingers pushed away the flimsy fabric holding them and brushed over nipples aching to be touched, Mercy whimpered. The sound normally would have surprised her, but the pleasure Eris was drawing with her fingertips was too potent, too intense to make Mercy care. The sensation of Eris' touch on her breasts, kneading, caressing, pinching, was too much, but somehow she wanted more. A fire deep from deep in Mercy's core had been stoked and it threatened to consume her. Eris hummed as Mercy began to rock her hips in a sensual rhythm, silently pleading for Eris to bring her tantalizing touch lower.

Gliding a palm across Mercy's fevered stomach, Eris nipped again at the edge of her neck. "You are more delicious than I could have ever imagined you would be," Eris said, her breath scalding as it met Mercy's skin. "I'm afraid the craving is too great. I must have all of you right now."

Mercy struggled for breath against the relentless burn of passion sweeping her body. Nothing else existed but the feel of Eris' lips and tongue and hands, all fueling the inferno that pulsed in time with her heartbeat. "Yes," she murmured, needing to be consumed by it.

The slam of the restroom door hit Mercy like a bucket of ice. She broke from Eris' embrace, and turned to see the blonde woman standing in the doorway.

"I'm sorry," the blonde said with a crooked smile. "I didn't realize anyone was in here."

Zahra heart froze as she walked into the room and saw Mercy helpless within the *shaytan's* grasp. She kicked the door closed behind her, thankful when Mercy took a startled jump back, the creature's thrall on her broken by the sound.

"I'm sorry," Zahra said, her eyes fixed on the *shaytan*. "I didn't realize anyone was in here."

Mercy's gaze darted from Zahra to the creature. She had a green-tinged queasy look. Without a backward glance she turned and rushed past Zahra and left the restroom. The *shaytan* moved to follow but Zahra threw a hand against the door.

"Not so fast, *shaytan*. That one is not for you."

The demon took a step back and glared at Zahra, her eyes glowing red in the dark light of the restroom. "Lost are you, little genie?" Zahra felt the heat rise in her cheeks at the derogatory term. "If you're looking for a new bottle, I'm sure there's a nice selection at the front of the bar for you to choose from."

"I'm not that kind of Jinn," Zahra said, refusing to let the demon bait her.

"Well, I'm the kind of succubus that just saw her dinner run out of the room, so if you'll be so kind as to remove yourself from—"

Zahra squared her shoulders and stepped forward in an aggressive stance. "I said, that one is not for you."

"Oh?" The *shaytan* arched an eyebrow. "And who is she for, then? You, perhaps?"

"I am charged with her protection. You will need to find another soul to feast on tonight." From the look on the demon's face, Zahra knew that she'd hesitated a second too long before answering.

"Ah, you're in love with the human."

"Don't be ridiculous. I'm *muhafiz*."

"You may be her protector, but that doesn't change the fact that you are in love with her. Or at least, in lust." The demon gave a scornful smile. "You can't lie to me, little genie. Lust is my business."

Ignoring the words that she knew to be true, Zahra shook her head. "Your business is of little importance to me. I am charged with safeguarding Mercy O'Brien and that's what I intend on doing."

"Tsk, tsk, little genie." The *shaytan* leaned back against the porcelain sink, smirking as she folded her arms. "It may have been a few hundred years since I've encountered one of your kind, but I know your laws. You can't intervene if your 'charge' gives herself to me willingly, and we both know that I have been nothing but straightforward in what I am..." The demon crossed the distance between them in a blur of motion. She leaned in so that her words were a hot whisper in Zahra's ear. "...and what I am intending to do with her. There is nothing you can do. So mouthwatering, that one is. Having sampled of her sweet essence, I can understand your attraction."

Anger flaring in her once again, Zahra pushed the demon away with a sneer. "Enough."

"That word means nothing to me."

"Then maybe this will, *shaytan*." With a wave of her hand, the Zahra drew a curved dagger out of the air and brought it to the demon's throat.

"I'm unimpressed by your threats, little genie." The demon held her gaze steady. "The sweet fruit that is your Mercy O'Brien is mine, ripe for the picking. We both know you won't interfere, you can't."

Grinning, Zahra held her ground. "Can't, or won't?"

The *shaytan* arched an eyebrow. "You would break Jinn law for a human? Risk banishment from your own kind?" She shook her head. "I don't think so, little genie. Not even for a morsel as delicious as your Mercy."

With a defeated sigh, Zahra closed her eyes and lowered the dagger. The *shaytan* was right. The demon had proclaimed to Mercy what she was and what she intended to do. That Mercy thought the demon had been speaking metaphorically was irrelevant. Interfering with free will was forbidden by Jinn law. To interfere now, to stop the *shaytan* from seeking out Mercy, would be in direct violation of that law. Banishment would be the best Zahra could hope for if she acted in Mercy's defense.

"That's what I thought." The demon pushed the hand holding the dagger away with a single fingertip, side-stepping Zahra to make her way to the door. She paused, one hand on the handle, and glanced back at Zahra. "Oh, and, little genie?"

Her heart breaking, Zahra raised her head to stare back into the *shaytan*'s red eyes.

"Just in case you have any doubt...when I find your sweet fruit Mercy—and I will find her—I'm going to peel back the skin on that honeyed neck of hers and drink from her essence until there is nothing left but a lifeless husk."

Zahra shook her head sadly. *What choice do I have?* She grabbed the *shaytan* by the hair, wrapping her fist around it in a huge hank and hauled her backwards into the nearest stall.

Damn, what a night. Mercy rifled through her purse, searching for the keys to her apartment. The throbbing headache that she'd had since leaving the bar wasn't making the situation any better. Her purse slipped from her trembling hands. Mercy rested her head against the door and blew out a long breath.

"What the hell was I thinking?"

Seriously? Making out in the bathroom of a bar like a drunk teenager? As much as she'd like to blame the alcohol for what had happened, Mercy knew that it would be a lie. At least, partially. Some small part of her had realized what was happening, but simply didn't seem to care. She was just grateful that the blonde had walked in the restroom when she had, otherwise Mercy would've…*I don't even want to think about I would have been.*

Rubbing her eyes, Mercy sighed and shook her head. It was late and she was ready to end this day. She bent to retrieve her purse, when she heard the heavy tread of approaching footsteps and froze.

"Is everything all right?" A familiar voice asked from behind.

You've got to be kidding me. Mercy could barely believe her eyes. *I can't buy a break, can I?*

Straightening, she nodded at the blonde from the bar. "It is, thank you." *So, first I nearly have sex with a weird redhead and now this one follows me home.* Mercy hefted the purse on her shoulder, her mind running through its contents in case she needed a weapon against the woman standing only a few feet away.

"Okay, great." As if reading Mercy's mind, the blonde continued, "By the way, I'm not some crazy stalker or anything. I live in apartment 7B, two doors down."

"Oh, well…um, it's nice to meet you." Mercy smiled. "I've only just in moved in, so I really haven't had the chance to meet anyone in the building."

"No, that's okay. I'm new here myself," the blonde said. "I've recently lost my job and heard that Savannah is a nice place to make a fresh start."

"It is. I'm Mercy, by the way."

"Zahra." The blonde grinned and pointed to the ground by Mercy's feet. "I think you dropped your keys."

"Lord, I've been looking for them. Thanks."

"Of course. I'm sure it's been a long day." Mercy's cheeks flushed as she recalled the image of the blonde walking in on her in restroom. Once again, the blonde—Zahra—seemed to read her mind.

"And I don't want you to feel, um, awkward about, you know, that back at the bar."

Mercy wiped a hand over her eyes and shook her head. "Look, I realize that we're going to be neighbors, so I just want you to know that is so totally not like me. I don't know if I had too much to drink or—"

"Hey." Zahra placed a firm hand on Mercy's arm. "It's okay. Things happen. I mean, who hasn't gone a few rounds with a homicidal redhead in the restroom of a bar at some point? I know I have." She grinned ruefully.

Laughing, Mercy nodded. "I guess you're right."

"Exactly," Zahra said. "Well, it's getting late..."

"It is, isn't it? So, uh, have a good night."

With a small wave, Zahra continued down the hall past Mercy. Watching her make her way to her apartment, Mercy couldn't help but appreciate the curve of the Zahra's hips as she walked. A thought occurred to her. "Zahra?"

"Yes?"

"If you're free sometime, maybe we can get together and have a coffee or something."

"I think I would like that," Zahra said, smiling.

Nodding, Mercy stepped inside her apartment and closed the door behind her. Her living room was littered with moving boxes. Mercy resolved to finish unpacking first thing in the morning and start making her new apartment feel more like home. It had been one wreck of a day, but reflecting on her new neighbor two doors down, she decided it hadn't been a complete loss. As she moved down the hall toward her bedroom, Mercy smiled. Maybe it was just wishful thinking, but she felt like her luck was about to change for the better.

Ladies' Night

BY CHERI FULLER

I COULD FEEL THE BEAT pumping through my entire body. My eyes were closed and I just let myself feel the music. I was pretty optimistic about the evening. It was only our second date but Janet and I had chemistry. I opened my eyes and realized that my dance partner was nowhere to be found. I dropped my shoulder and pushed through the crowd and over to the bar. It was noticeably cooler and the drying sweat on my neck and chest sent chills down my spine.

I caught the eye of the young bartender. "Corona with lime?" She nodded and turned for the cooler on the back wall.

I half turned and leaned my back against the padded rail, scanning the dozen or so tables. Where the hell is Janet?

"That'll be $5.50."

Returning my attention to the bartender, I pulled a five and a couple of singles from my front pocket and laid them on the bar. I poked the lime slice into the bottle and slowly walked toward the back of the room, all the while looking for my date. I saw a small group of women surrounding the pool table, seemingly negotiating the terms for the next game, but no Janet.

My last chance was the restroom. Rounding the corner, I ran into a tall woman with a large Adam's apple coming out of the ladies' room. "Sounds like someone's getting lucky in there, sweetheart. You may want to give the other one a shot." She motioned to the men's room with a point of her chin.

I shrugged and continued on to my original destination. Pushing the door open, I was immediately hit by the glaring fluorescent lights and then by grunting coming from the large wheelchair accessible stall. Facing the mirror, I quickly took in my pale, disheveled reflection, and then focused on the two sets of legs in the large gap under the door behind me. The high-heeled boots belonging to the woman pressed against the wall looked very much like the ones Janet had worn with her tight jeans. The other woman wore stilettos and black hose. I didn't feel jealous – we'd only been out once before and there was no commitment – but it was tacky to simply abandon me on the dance floor to fuck some anonymous woman in the bathroom.

I could see that Janet was having a hard time standing, her boots were sliding out from under her and it seemed that the other woman was crouching and leaning in to keep her upright.

I set my beer on the counter, turned, and called out, "Janet? Is that you?"

There was a weak thud and a groan. I charged forward and yanked the door open, the sliding lock clattered to the ground. Standing before me was a wild-looking woman with blood running down her chin and dripping from her elongated canines. She dropped Janet, smiled, and said, "Well, there is a two drink minimum."

Centralia, 2013

BY MAY DAWNEY

READING, PENNSYLVANIA, FELT A LOT like home. Like Detroit, the city was big, impoverished, and still there were plenty of rich folk going about their business as if nothing was wrong. Rayha had been listening to their frustratingly benign banter in for the last twenty minutes or so as she sipped expensive coffee in the high-end bar she had agreed to meet her new client in. For once, the journey had been shorter than she had expected it to be; just an eight and a half hour drive instead of the nine she had envisioned. As such, she was early for her eleven a.m. appointment and sticking out like a sore thumb.

Because of the location, she had at least made an effort: her jeans were clean and she'd meticulously cleaned the blood off of her heavy leather jacket. She'd even done her dark hair up in a messy bun. Still, she was fresh off another case and she hadn't slept for at least forty-eight hours. The sunglasses that she had scrambled to find when the sun had come up hadn't come off and she was holding on to her tall black coffee—the second one—like a lifeline. She would have cursed Mrs. Williams for insisting on meeting as soon as possible but it wasn't as if Rayha got a good night's rest even on the best of days, anyway.

"Rayhana Kincaid?" Rayha was surprised to discover that Mrs. Williams was black, but not so much that she was obviously rich. If there was one thing Rayha had learned over the years, it was that all her clients picked meeting spots where they felt comfortable; they were about to let Rayha in on thoughts that—if spoken out loud to anyone other than someone who called herself an occultist—would brand them as nuts. They all needed to be somewhere they felt at home at, but far enough from their actual homes for these meetings to remain business interactions. Rayha had lost track of the number of bars, cafes, park benches and other assorted generic meeting spots she'd frequented over the last nine years.

"Rayha, please. Only my mother calls me Rayhana. Mrs. Williams?" She lifted herself up a little and offered the woman in her late forties a hand. With the other, she took off her sunglasses. She blinked against the glare and took in her client. Pencil skirt, blouse, and blazer. Jewellery that was expensive without being flashy: rich but not from rich upbringing.

"Indeed." Mrs. Williams shook her hand before she undid her shawl and took a seat. Rayha lowered herself as well and wrapped her hands around the mug again. Before the woman could change her mind about this appointment, Rayha got to the point.

"So, your daughter? Aisha? Tell me more."

Delilah Williams looked straight at her for a few moments, then leaned in over the table conspiratorially. "My Aisha...she's a good girl; bright, spirited. She takes after her father—he grew up with nothing, but he made it through high school, then college, and now he works as a prosecutor for the city. Aisha has always wanted to follow in his footsteps—she's always worked hard to be perfect for her father and myself."

"Mrs. Williams... I am sure your daughter is a wonderful girl, but that's not why I'm here, is it?"

Mrs. Williams hung her head and gathered her thoughts. It gave Rayha a moment to take in straightened hair, a slightly full figure, and hands that wrung together nervously. She only wore a wedding ring on her fingers.

"No, it is not. Five months ago, Aisha disappeared. We contacted the police that first evening and Darren, my husband, pulled some strings. They searched, but she just...vanished. I thought, *we* thought, that she was dead. It was—" Mrs. Williams faltered, but she didn't break down like Rayha had feared she would. Instead, she sat up and moist eyes focussed on her with great intensity. Rayha weathered the older woman's gaze stoically. Mrs. William's voice gained in strength when she spoke again. *Good on you,* Rayha thought.

"We got lucky; someone recognised her twenty-nine days after she went missing. She had been living in Centralia. That's a little—"

"I know what it is—a mining town to the north of here." It was also demon territory and most hunters wouldn't go near it for all the money in the world.

"Exactly. She must have lived there for weeks before she was caught stealing food from one of the few remaining residences. He called the police, who came to get her and took her to the nearest hospital—she was badly dehydrated and hadn't eaten in weeks. They had to keep her sedated because she...she—she tried to hurt herself and others and she wouldn't stop screaming. Four months ago, they moved her to the Spruce Pavilion here in Reading—it's an inpatient mental health treatment facility. They told us that Aisha's had a mental breakdown, that she's psychotic. Her healthcare worker asked us if she used to do drugs! Aisha didn't do drugs, not ever. She wouldn't! And none of the medication is helping her get better either; they have her tied down to the bed almost all the time now. She...she's getting worse. She used to at least acknowledge me when I came to visit but now—" Mrs. William's voice was rising, getting sharper in her desperation. They were drawing attention, and Rayha didn't like attention.

Quickly, she cut off the woman's speech. "And your husband?"

As expected, the question deflated the woman who was clearly on the brink of a mental breakdown herself. "He doesn't...he doesn't visit her. Not anymore. He can't see his little girl like that. He doesn't even go with her for the dialysis treatments she needs now. It's hard for me too, but I need to be there for her, you know?" Pleading eyes met hers.

Rayha nodded. She took another sip of her coffee. Clearly, this was a case of possession, but some things did not match up. Memory loss, dehydration, starvation—all normal. Lingering insanity? Far less common. Rare, even. "Yeah, I understand." She took a deep breath. "So, why call me?"

"Aisha has therapy. When she has a good day, she...they make her draw. They tried to make her talk, but she just rambles. She used to love to draw, even as a little girl." From the briefcase Mrs. Williams had placed on the floor, she pulled a stack of papers and handed them over. Rayha took a burning gulp of coffee before leafing through them. It seemed Aisha had a very limited repertoire no matter what colour the staff gave her: an arch, which seemed to hold double doors and a clearly demonic skull in the centre.

"There are hundreds more, all exactly the same. She keeps saying she has to open it, that it's her destiny. The doctors think she is just... delusional—that she is insane—but a mother knows her daughter. I believe her. I googled demon possession and gates, and eventually I found you. You lived so close by I...I had to try." Mrs. Williams was on the verge of tears. Her desperation was obvious. Sadly, most of the people who searched Rayha out were. They had tried everything science had to offer and had struck out. Well, this case seemed clear-cut enough: demon possession, some hell gate. Time to meet the patient and get to work. "I think I'm ready to see Aisha now."

Mrs. Williams examined her. Obviously, she tried to divine what Rayha was thinking. "So...you think you can help her?"

Rayha refused to be read. Instead, she handed the drawings back. "I think I need to see and examine Aisha to confirm or disprove a few theories. After that, I'll answer your question."

Mrs. Williams pursed her perfectly painted lips and nodded slowly. Rayha guessed Mrs. Williams wasn't used to being denied anything, and with her daughter's life at stake, she found it hard to swallow. "Alright."

Rayha drank the remainder of her coffee in one go, and winced as the heat ran down her throat. Mrs. Williams hurried to clear the drawings away and re-do her shawl as Rayha waited impatiently. She was relieved to pull the door of the bar closed behind her and disappear in the throng of nameless faces out today.

Reading Hospital was old, grand, and it stretched out for acres. Once more, she stood out like a sore thumb—rough around the edges and far too grim to feed into the fantasy of recovery. Rayha hated hospitals with a vengeance; even when she was fully closed off to the supernatural, the scent of antiseptics brought with it the feeling of death and despair. There were too many ghosts and demons in hospitals—especially in ones with as much history as this one. Shivers traversed her spine as she hurried along with Mrs. Williams, who guided her into the bowels of the building with the ease of someone who walks the same route day after day. Rayha kept her head down and one hand in her pocket. In the other, she carried her magic bag—a worn leather doctor's case filled with all the tools of the trade she thought she would need, and a few extra ones.

She came to a dead halt when they stepped into Spruce Pavilion. Almost everyone was a little bit psychic and could feel when a place had a bad vibe to it. Subconsciously, people tried to counter the feeling by going overboard with the decor. This place was a pastel nightmare. The main lounge area was decked out in wooden panelling. Everything was decorated for comfort and quietness; soft couches, round shapes... There were no hospital gowns to be found anywhere; it was all sweatpants, t-shirts, and sweaters. Soft colours—nothing black, nothing too bright.

Anxiety clawed up Rayha's spine and settled heavily at the base of her skull. She had seen the inside of plenty a mental ward as a teen and she only needed two seconds to know that if you went into this place with anything more than work stress or a mild depression, you weren't getting out. Oh, the staff was competent and the finances good, but this place reeked of the supernatural. Whatever was using this place as their personal McDonalds, they were getting their order supersized.

"Whatever happens today, do me a favour and get your daughter out of this place as soon as possible. You look like a woman who can afford to hire a nurse or two and keep her comfortable at home. I guarantee you that she is never, ever, getting healthy in this place," she told Mrs. Williams who had stopped a few paces off when Rayha had stopped walking. She set her jaw as she regarded her. Rayha met her eyes and shrugged. "I'm just saying."

Mrs. Williams opted not to comment. "She's this way. They had to sedate her again this morning, so I don't know how available she will be."

Rayha hummed in acknowledgment and slowed when Mrs. Williams did. Instead of opening the off-yellow door they had stopped in front, Mrs. Williams searched her face.

Rayha waited patiently for whatever was to come.

"The supernatural…you believe in that, right? You know it's real…?"

"I do. I've dealt with far too much of it not to. Why?"

"Nothing I just…I need someone to believe me." With trembling hands, Mrs. Williams opened the door and pushed it open, stepping aside so Rayha could enter.

The first thing Rayha noticed was that the lights were dimmed and the curtains closed. Everything in the room was tuned down, quiet. Aisha's bed was placed against the east wall, in the darkest corner. The rest of the room was bare; a chair that was probably only used by Delilah Williams, a desk that no one used at all, and carpeting that showed vacuum marks, showing how often it had been traversed lately.

"Okay, no. No, no. This is not good at all." She dropped her bag onto the desk and broke the lines left by the vacuum cleaner by waltzing over to the curtains and pulling them open with gusto.

"Wait! What are you doing? The doctors say she needs as little stimulation as possible; she could have another episode!" Mrs. Williams came up behind her and tried to pull the curtains shut again. Rayha turned and gripped the woman's wrist, meeting her eyes dead on.

"Delilah, I need you to trust me today. If you need me to explain my methods, I will, but believe me, the last thing your daughter needs right now is to be locked inside her own mind. The only thing there for her after what I believe she has been through, is madness. Now please, wait outside if you can't stand to watch this, but you have got to let me do my job." It was a stalemate for long moments as Mrs. Williams weighed her need to adhere to the advice of the medical professionals and to believe in some woman whom she had only just met and who could be insane enough to be locked in here with her daughter. Slowly her grip lessened and she released the curtains.

"Alright, but I'm staying."

"I am alright with that. If you want to help, turn on all the lamps and then help me get her bed in the centre of the room. We're going to need some room to work." Mrs. Williams nodded and strode through the room with renewed purpose. Rayha smiled as the African American woman closed the door and locked it from the inside. Appeased, Rayha pushed the curtains open again and fished her phone from her pocket. She unlocked it with a swift flick of her thumb and browsed to the music player. She searched her library and grinned. A second later, the first notes of The Who's 'Baba O'Riley' filled the room. She sacrilegiously skipped the first minute, then turned the volume all the way up.

As she placed the device next to Aisha's head, she took her first hard look at her real client. She was older than Rayha had expected her to be—roughly her own age. When Mrs. Williams had said on the phone that Aisha was still in college, Rayha had expected her to be in her early twenties. Aisha was at least twenty-eight, logical if Rayha accounted for law school. She was pale, skin over bones, and out cold. Her cheeks were concaved; she frowned despite being asleep, and twitched slightly. A half full bag of urine hung from the side of the bed, an IV dripped fluids into her arm, and she was being fed through a nasal tube. Rayha sighed and stroked the back of a bony hand for a moment. Aisha must have been beautiful before she had been taken—model beautiful. Now, she was a husk of herself—a husk like she had seen many others after being possessed for an extended period of time. Being locked in your own mind while someone else drove your body into the ground did that to you.

As the sounds of The Who's runaway synthesizer overtook the room, Rayha and Mrs. Williams rolled the bed to its centre. Then Rayha took the desk chair and placed it under the fire alarm. She opened the device and pried the battery from it. Stepping down, she regarded the fancy carpet as she pushed the chair out of the way.

"I'm going to have to wreck that," she announced. She scoffed at the salmon coloured monstrosity and Mrs. Williams followed her gaze down.

"The carpet? Why?"

"Right behind our plane of existence is TAX, part of the aetherial plane, a layer beyond this reality. This is where you go when you dream, and trained magi like me can enter it even while we are awake and take a look around. In the aetherial plane, it's very easy to spot those possessed or channelled through. I need an Enochian circle—an angel circle—to enter TAX. If this floor was stone or wood, I'd use chalk but now—" Rayha pulled a can of spray paint out of her bag. "We'll have to go with this."

"Can't we do this somewhere else? Somewhere with another type of flooring?"

"We can, but are you willing to tell the staff what we are doing and risk getting tossed out?"

Mrs. Williams looked at the door a moment. "No."

"Thought so. Now, may I?"

After a moment, Mrs. Williams nodded and Rayha got to work. She drew two circles around the bed, added a variety of symbols to the space between them, and then marked the four main cardinal directions with seals. She hadn't been exactly truthful with Mrs. Williams; yes, she needed a part of this ritual to open her eyes to the supernatural, but she didn't need the circle. She wasn't sure, however, what would come falling out if she started shaking this tree and she wasn't about to risk the patients and staff of the hospital by setting some demon loose in here. The circle would keep contained whatever came forth once she started prodding.

"Okay, all done. Now, I need you to step out of the circle and whatever happens—and I mean it, whatever happens, I have no idea what's going to take place here—you need to stay out of it. Stepping in without my permission will not only put Aisha's life in danger, but yours and mine as well, and everyone in this hospital. I need your word, Delilah, and if you don't think you can keep it, I need you to leave." Once more, Mrs. Williams struggled, but the decision was easier this time. Maybe a half of The Who album had mellowed her out—maybe Mrs. Williams just figured 'in for a penny, in for a pound'.

"I promise."

"Alright then. Keep everyone out of this room, stay quiet, and I'll get you some answers." She fetched her bag and put it at Aisha's feet, then leaned down and pulled a dagger from a hidden sheath in her boot. Mrs. Williams gasped. True to her word, though, she didn't interfere.

Back before she had met her angelic patron and he had given her angel juice to power her magic, Rayha had been a fairly decent Enochian magus. She'd already put together the full magic kit, could vibrate the names of an assortment of angels, watchers, and kings, and could penetrate fairly deeply into the other spheres of existence. Harut had been very amused with her efforts. After her initial annoyance at his mocking had waned, Rayha had realized she couldn't blame him; it took hours of ritual work for her to accomplish something he did with the snap of his fingers. 'Trained monkeys still cannot pass for men,' he had said. Harut's Grace had made things infinitely easier—and shorter. Still, there was rarely a time when she didn't feel like a tool when performing magic in front of the non-initiated. She raised her dagger to the north face of the circle.

"Nor-Molap-Sa-Lukal, oh mighty Taoagla, whose Word is Ambz. Come forth and take away my karma." The words reverberated through the air, and she felt them rumble on into the higher planes of existence. There was something unique about performing magic; a familiarity that tugged at her consciousness instantly. Ritual was ninety percent mental, ten percent supernatural; most of it served to prepare the mind for the journey. With practiced ease, she drew the appropriate sigil for the Guardian of the North into the air and moved to the east of the circle, toes skirting the inner line, reciting similar evocations and carving similar sigils for Iaiadia-Sa-Raas and Kikele-Ath-Babage, angels of desire and innocence. She moved another quarter, now ignoring Mrs. Williams who was in her field of vision. With every step, with every word, she felt her soul pull at her body, longing to journey deeper into the Fugue. She carved the last sigil into the air and pointed the blade towards the centre of the circle. "I rise above the Forces of Karma. I rise above the Forces of Desire. I rise above the Forces of Ignorance. I rise above the Forces of Restriction. Through the four radiant regions of TEX, I regain full consciousness throughout. I rise up! I rise up! I have gained mastery over TEX!"

Something clicked in her head and her eyes fell shut. Entering the Fugue was like breathing water, like touching fear, like seeing a dying animal's scream. It clawed at her spine, crawled up with razor sharp nails, and settled at the base of her skull. She opened her mind and was devoured by the darkness. She gasped and arched back. Her arms fell down and she leaned heavily on the footboard of the bed. Her heart pounded in her chest. Goosebumps crawled over her skin in waves. She pushed her face into the veil between the worlds and soaked in the rush. With a shudder, she linked with her aetherial body.

The world reknitted and became solid again. Swallowing heavily, Rayha opened her eyes. The angel sigils that had been invisible the physical plane hung before her in the air now, bright blue but fading quickly. Mrs. Williams was barely visible beyond the white veil that made up the circle and which burned like a magnesium fire. On each of the four cardinal corners she had called stood an angelic figure, wings spread out like a barrier, arms folded over their chests. They all had blue eyes, a strong nose and jaw, and a muscular body. As always, the sight of their bare forms unnerved Rayha a little. They were all carbon copies: created, not born. They didn't have primary or secondary reproductive organs, no body hair at all, no nipples or a belly button. None of them—as far has Rayha had experienced—had any identifiable features save for their name. For all intents and purposes, they did not have free will, nor personal experiences; everything they were was part of their hive mind. Even with their deformities and beastly appearances, seeing demons unnerved Rayha a lot less than seeing the angels did; at least demons had genitals, breasts where applicable, and a will of their own. They represented the worst of mankind—many of the older ones being half angel, half human or transformed humans—but at least she understood them. She could identify with demons. The angels were different; other. She disliked seeing them in the Fugue.

With a sigh, Rayha sheathed the dagger and crossed to the side of the bed for a supernatural inspection of the patient. Unlike the regular light blue aura of human life, Aisha's was a dull grey. It was weak and laced with streaks of red and black; demon colours. She reached out to open one of Aisha's eyes for a closer look.

"Aisha…"

The word echoed within the circle and stretched out; distorted, alluring. Rayha's head shot up.

"Just to verify, you didn't just say 'Aisha', did you?"

"No, why?"

Rayha cursed under her breath. "I know what's wrong with your daughter. Remember I told you about entering the aetherial plane? About how we do that in dreams? Well, when we do that, we don't really *travel* to TAX, we just look at it through the veil between our planes. When we do travel to it, that's what we call a nightmare. TAX is also where our soul goes when we get possessed because there is not enough room in the body for two souls. In Aisha's case, the demon isn't allowing her to leave TAX so she is caught in a continual nightmare, and she hasn't had a distraction from it for months now."

When Rayha turned to look at Mrs. Williams, her eyes were wide, and she had her hand in front of her mouth in shock. "How can we—can you help her? Can you get her back?"

"Yes, but I need something from her first—I need to know what happened to her. I'm going to summon an angel—my angel, you could say, although if you'd ask him, he'd tell you I'm his hunter." Rayha grinned as Mrs. Williams' eyes widened.

"You—you speak to angels? The Lord's angels?" Mrs. Williams crossed herself.

Rayha resisted the urge to shift her vision back to the unmoving angels still guarding the circle. "They prefer the Aramaic term 'Iyrin' instead of 'angel' and 'Elah' instead of 'Lord', but yes, I work for one of God's angels. His name is Harut and he's going to get Aisha to talk. She'll be safe, I promise. I want you to remember that it won't be her—not really. It'll be her voice you hear, but it won't be Aisha. Remember, do not step into the circle under any circumstance."

"I remember. Please, do it." The reverence in dark eyes had Rayha sigh inwardly. For Mrs. Williams' sake, she wished angels were even half as helpful as she was imagining them to be right now—and half as benevolent.

"Good. Okay, this is going to go quickly if Harut is willing to listen." She raised her arms up. "Harut, Iyr of sorcery, teacher and trickster of mankind, I pray to thee." A flash of lightning seen only in the Fugue, followed by the rustling of feathers. They surrounded Aisha's body like a cocoon as the wings stretched, then folded in. Harut's hands pressed against the side of Aisha's head as he kneeled behind her—through the bed. Material objects didn't transfer to the aetherial plane, or the other way around. Aisha's eyes blinked open, revealing bright blue instead of her natural hazel as Harut pressed his forehead against the top of her skull. She shuddered and Harut shook himself out.

"I am here," Aisha spoke in monotone. Again, Mrs. Williams gasped. She took a tentative step forward and reached out. Just in time, she remembered her promise and stopped. Her arm fell down, along with her tears. *As if she was seeing Elah in person*, Rayha thought bitterly. If only...

"Thank you for coming. I need your help. Go through her mind, tell me who took her body?"

"Agreed." Harut fell silent and Aisha's eyes stared up at the ceiling, motionlessly. She didn't blink, nor did her body move at all. This wasn't possession; Harut was channelling through her body. The only parts of her he could manipulate were her mouth and her eyes.

"I see fire and smoke. He took her here; he whispered until she opened to him. Now she is in the dark and she digs. She is not the first. He has taken others, worn them down until they fell. Many bones lie deep in the tunnels. She did not fall, she dug. She dug until she found the gate. He will not let her go. They call him 'Paqach'; He Who Opens."

The rolling of thunder resounded dully in the space as Harut disappeared. Aisha's eyes fell shut again. Mrs. Williams gasped loud enough for Rayha to realize she had heard the bang too, which was not a good sign for the black woman's sanity. She needed to hurry this along. Obviously Mrs. Williams had the same susceptibility to the supernatural as her daughter had. Her mobile phone cycled back to 'Baba O'Riley' and Rayha licked her lips. Rayha hated herself for the plan growing in the back of her mind.

"Delilah? Delilah? I need you inside of the circle now. Come here?" Mrs. Williams blinked and shook off the daze. She watched Rayha for a moment, hesitant, then circled the circle on high heels that dug deep into the carpet. Rayha was tired—bone tired. After this case, she was going to self-medicate until she passed out for a few hours.

With her dagger, Rayha cut a door counter-clockwise and sealed the opening once Mrs. Williams was inside. She sheathed the blade again. "New promise: whatever happens, you'll stay in the circle."

If any part of Delilah Williams' mind had still doubted Rayha, hearing Harut speak through her daughter had cured her entirely. She nodded without question, "Rayha...? Thank you. For the first time in months, I have hope my daughter will be alright."

Mrs. Williams' watery smile reminded Rayha of all the other parents, children, friends and other assorted loved ones who had done the same over the years. She was proud—and infinitely relieved—to be able to say that her balance still tipped towards the side of success, but the dark pages in her ledger would haunt her forever. She vowed to herself that Aisha wouldn't become one of those. Rayha was going to leave Reading behind with the knowledge that Aisha was home safe with her parents; that she would get the chance to become a brilliant prosecutor one day.

"It's my job," she answered. It was her standard answer when things became a little too personal.

As The Who filled every inch of the small space, Rayha shrugged off her heavy leather jacket to reveal a tattered The Clash-shirt and dark arms full of cutting scars and old burns. She felt Delilah's eyes on the marks for long moments, but the older woman declined to comment. Good.

"Okay, Aisha, hey…we haven't been formally introduced. My name is Rayha and I'm going to try to help you. By now, your mind should feel a little clearer, huh? I know that you are still very drowsy because the doctors gave you something to sleep, but people like us—who've gone through what we've been through—we don't like to sleep, do we? I know you can hear me, and you feel you mom, too, don't you?" She motioned for Delilah to take her daughter's hand, which she did—tightly.

"Ash? Ma's here, everything's okay, angel girl. Everything will be okay now."

Rayha smiled encouragingly and nodded. The dark skinned woman pressed her eye sockets against her shoulders to dry her tears; she obviously did not want to release the hand she had clasped in both of hers. The action left make-up stains on the expensive blouse, but Delilah didn't notice.

"You know, there are many ways to reach the power of God, and He's known by many names." As she talked, she opened her bag. "My mother calls Him Allāh, or Al-raḥmān, 'the Compassionate'. Harut calls Him Elah, which I have adopted because I talk about God more to Harut than to my mother. Elah's no longer here to guard the Earth, but there are others who have taken His place. The Orisha are some of those guardians, as are the angels. They can be petitioned for help, and I'm going to ask Babalú Ayé to help you today. He's the Orisha of healing, and he's kind-hearted and strong." Rayha took a statue of Babalú Ayé from her bag; a dark skinned man covered from head to ankles in a garb made of straw. She placed him near Aisha's head, then lit a tea light and placed it at the statue's feet in a copper bowl. She shook a hand full of coins from a small velvet pouch and placed it beside him.

Delilah watched her curiously, even more so when Rayha unwrapped a nice, thick Cuban cigar.

"Only the best for our special guest," Rayha commented when Mrs. Williams frowned. With a smirk, she clipped off the top and bud, and bent down to light it with the tea light on the bed. She sucked hard, relished the burn, and straightened out when the cigar looked to stay lit. She exhaled blissfully and reached out to press her hand lightly on a balmy forehead and brushed up over curly dark hair. Aisha whimpered, and Rayha smiled at Delilah, who immediately looked at her for confirmation that this was a good sign. It was.

"I'm pretty good at Enochian magic, but I'm a hack at Santeria. Because Harut, the angel I told you about, has put a bit of his Grace inside of me, most of the Orisha like me enough to indulge me, though. It's like a letter of recommendation from one holy species to another. Babalú Ayé will be willing to help." She sucked hard, gathered smoke and blew it onto the statue. She repeated the action twice more, head bobbing up and down with the The Who's 'The Song Is Over'. She tried to loosen her body to the music, inhaled deeply and puffing the smoke over Aisha's face, seeing her inhale sharply. Ashes fell onto the sheets.

"Okay, Delilah, I need you to get up on the bed and hold Aisha down. Keep her down no matter what. We'll use the restraints if we have to, but I think she has too many bad memories of those to help. A human touch is better—especially if it's her mom." Delilah nodded and let go of her daughter with hesitation. She undid the strap of her heels and put them next to the bed, then hoisted up her skirt, completely unperturbed to wrinkle her expensive clothing or look foolish in front of a near-stranger. Well, Delilah had just seen her wave a dagger around and vibrate angel names after spray-painting a circle onto the expensive carpet; Rayha figured they were even.

The feeling of kinship increased when Delilah straddled her daughter's legs and reached out to press her hands down on Aisha's wrists, to keep her arms trapped next to her body and Rayha realized she didn't think of Delilah as Mrs. Williams anymore. With a smile, she turned to Aisha.

"Aisha, I know you can still hear the demon who was inside of you. Well, Paqach has no business talking to you, so I'm going to ask Babalú Ayé to close your ears to him. That should make you feel a lot better. All you have to do is listen to the music. Can you hear it? Yeah, you can, can't you?" Smoke filled the entire room now, and once more, Rayha puffed out smoke in the direction of the statue and Aisha's head. "Hold her tightly, okay?"

Mrs. Williams nodded.

Rayna cleared her throat. "Oh blessed and Glorious Babalú Ayé, giver and taker of plagues, we call to you in prayer. We lay ourselves at your boiled feet and beg of you to grant us our heart's desire." Gently, she pressed Delilah's head down onto her daughter's chest. There was a spark in the air now, an electric charge that Rayha wondered if Delilah felt as well. Something powerful was listening, coming forward from the Fugue. She took another deep drag from the cigar and coughed the smoke into the air. Her lungs tightened, the smoke burned her throat and caused her eyes to water. Her feet moved rhythmically, her head and shoulders moved as she stomped on the spot, an instinctual call to dance rising up now the powerful Orisha drew closer.

"Show yourself to us, stomp the ground with us, and lay your hands upon this poor soul, tainted and broken. Take pity and come to us! We throw ourselves down at your feet. Close her ears, close her mind to the darkness, and once she hears only that which man is supposed to hear, wake her from the slumber she has been forced into. Give her back life!" Rayha was shouting now. *The Who* once more went crazy on the synthesizer. She groaned when the delicious flame of darkness that signalled the arrival of the Orisha traversed her spine.

A low vibration caused the floor to tremble, and in the smoke, a tall figure stepped forward into TAX. Just like the statue, Babalú Ayé was covered in straw, in a long cloak, bound together on top of his head, obscuring him from view. He had a staff in his hand. Every bit of skin Rayha could see was covered in boils. She shuddered with a respect she was never able to give to the angels. Unlike them, the Orisha were fully aware and fully in control of their own will. They were incredibly dangerous, and unlike with the angels, Rayha made sure not to put a single toe out of line when one of them was around. She bowed down.

Babalú Ayé hummed and reached out. The very air seemed to bend aside to allow him, and even without seeing the movement, Rayha knew what was happening. Aisha suddenly took a deep breath of air and strained up. Delilah attempted to keep her daughter contained. Rayha caught sight of wide-open eyes with blown out pupils and a gaping mouth with a lolling tongue; Aisha was being exorcized on the spot.

It was over as suddenly as it had begun. Aisha fell back and gasped, Delilah whimpered, and Babalú Ayé stepped back. Rayha didn't watch him leave. Instead, she extinguished the cigar into the candlewax and put the small flame out with it. The hairs on the back of her arms settled slowly, and Delilah sat up, instinctively realizing—feeling?—that they were alone once more. Rayha grinned at the rush of the close encounter, feeling the high. "Whew!"

Before Delilah could reply, Aisha woke up, once more showing how God damn powerful the Orisha really were.

"Mom...?" Her voice was soft and rough with disuse, but made it over the music that still blasted from crappy speakers. It instantly drew two sets of eyes down. Light brown eyes, dazed but bright, looked up at them—at Delilah. Delilah sobbed. She released Aisha's wrists and reached out to cup her daughter's cheek.

"Aisha...? Baby, is that you?" Delilah was out of breath, and emotion squeezed her throat shut, pitching her voice up. Rayha looked away embarrassed as Aisha surged up with a sob, wrapped her arms around her mother's neck and pulled her down. She allowed them a few moments to reconcile before she cleared her throat. From over her mother's shoulder, Aisha looked up.

"Rayha, right?"

Rayha nodded with a smile. "I knew you could hear me."

"Yeah...your voice was the only thing louder than—" Aisha swallowed and glanced away a moment. Trembling slightly, Mrs. Williams slid off her daughter and the bed. She took a renewed hold on Aisha's hand.

"Hey, no need to talk about that; just some questions about the now. Can you still hear the voice you've been hearing?"

Aisha shook her head.

"How badly do you want to go back to Centralia right now?"

"I don't! Not at all."

"How about open a hell gate and let loose some demon?"

Delilah regarded Rayha oddly, but seeing as her daughter was actually answering questions—and coherently so—she wasn't about to interfere.

"No. That...I never wanted that. He made me!"

Rayha grinned. "I know. Good. Very good. All right, that's step one. Aisha, wanna help destroy a hell gate?"

Before the young woman could reply, Delilah interfered. "A hell gate? No, she doesn't—she is back now, she's cured! She doesn't need to go back *there*."

Rayha sighed. It seemed Delilah's hesitance to trust Rayha had been restored now Aisha was awake. "We're half way to cured—at best. Paqach won't give up without a fight, and unfortunately, your daughter *did* uncover a hall gate while she was possessed. We need to find it and destroy it, and seeing as the only person who has actually seen it is Aisha, I need her to come with me—preferably before Paqach realizes she is out of his reach forever and finds another host to set in motion the end of the world."

Delilah stared at her with stubborn determination. Even with her hair dishevelled and her clothes a mess, she managed to exude an air of superiority. This time it was Aisha who interfered.

"Mom? It's okay. Rayha is right. I've seen what Paqach wants to release. He was so happy to be so close—so *hungry*. He needs to be stopped and if that means that we go to Centralia, then we go to Centralia." Aisha reached over herself to take her mother's hand and met her gaze. There was nothing but determination in hazel eyes.

Delilah sagged just a little. She nodded. "Alright then, I'll find a wheelchair and sign you out. And the carpet and the...the smoke; I'll explain it—somehow." She swallowed heavily and moved to step back.

"Delilah, stop. You're still in the circle. Let me dismiss it first before you hurt yourself." A note of fear touched Delilah's eyes as she came to a dead halt. At least the proceedings had convinced her that magic was real. *Muggles...*

Rayha made short work of the circle. In reverse order, she thanked and dismissed all four of the guardians and she watched as they all dropped one arm, placed their other fist against their chests, then turned and walked away. They faded into the Fugue before they'd finished a single step. All the while, Rayha felt two sets of eyes heavily upon her. She got through the ritual stoically and refused to feel like a tool. Instead, she braced herself. The circle fell and with it, what appeared to be a hot blade pierced the back of Rayha's skull. She hissed sharply and sagged forward, onto the headboard of the bed.

"Rayha!" Aisha called her name, but Rayha held up a trembling hand.

"I hate that part," she muttered as her soul settled heavily back into her body. "You can go, Delilah. I'm going to have to take a moment."

She kept her eyes closed as she sagged to the floor and cradled her forehead in her hands. Gravity she hadn't been aware of while in the circle now pulled at her limbs like lead weights. Her head was throbbing and she was parched. Her mouth tasted like ash and death. Her lungs hurt. Rayha pulled her knees up and waited for the dizziness and nausea to pass.

"You okay?" she heard after a while.

Rayha nodded carefully and met worried eyes. She straightened carefully. "Think so. How are you feeling?" She mirrored Aisha's smile and Aisha's brightened.

"I think I'm feeling as well as can be expected—which is to say, terrible? It's good to be awake, though…and lucid."

Rayha nodded. "I know. It's almost over." She blinked her eyes open again, and took in the young woman before her. If only things were almost over. She really wasn't looking forward to the next part. With a heavy heart, she glanced at the door. "Aisha, time to listen to me very carefully. I need to give you a few instructions before your mother comes back…"

An hour and a half later, Rayha pulled out of the hospital parking lot. Aisha lay flat on the backseat and Delilah Williams had taken a seat next to Rayha. Both looked worse for wear, and Rayha was avoiding her own reflection at all costs. Aisha nodded off on and off but shot up, fully awake, only minutes after. Rayha set her jaw, knowing full well that the other woman would most likely never sleep soundly again. For now, they had bigger worries: as Rayha had feared, Delilah started showing signs of possession about an hour into the oppressively silent drive. Small twitches of her hand and in her face, a mumbled word here or there, the sudden turning of her head. At least now Aisha wouldn't have to get out of the car. Rayha met sad brown eyes in the rear view mirror.

Half an hour later, it was Delilah who opened the door first and got out of the car when Route 61 stopped existing; it had been closed off years ago to keep people out of Centralia.

"Don't let her get hurt, please?" Aisha said softly as Rayha got out before Delilah could get too far.

She nodded. "I'll do what I can." She opened the trunk and got out her magic bag along with a length of rope and a flashlight. Even from here, she could feel the dark aura ahead—there were demons in Centralia, and she was carrying a bull's eye on her back with Harut's Grace in her veins. This trip might be the stupidest thing she had ever done—and she had done a good few stupid things in her life.

While non-initiated suspected that the cause of the fire that set ablaze the coal under the small town was a trash burning that hit a coal strip in a cave, Rayha knew better. In 1962, miners had dug their way to a door not unlike the one she was trying to keep closed—a portal into a prison for a demon that was too powerful to exorcize or kill. He had been locked away by Elah thousands of years ago, trapped and chained in the space between the material plane and the fugue to protect mankind. When he'd been set free, a battle for the survival of mankind had followed, and it had cost the lives of many good hunters and the retreat into the Heavens of many angels. During the battle, the demon had set the ground on fire with flames rising to over a thousand degrees Fahrenheit. Centralia still burned—it would burn for hundreds of years more—but the demon was dead.

Route 61 had taken a hit from the fires still creeping below the surface; it was concaved and cracked, and smoke billowed up from deep crevices. Delilah guided Rayha off the road before they even reached the town, and into the new-growth forest that had come up over the past fifty years. She didn't falter, didn't question her direction, and she didn't notice the woman a few paces behind her. What she did do, was mutter to her new best friend—the demon whispering into her ear. When they reached a well-hidden cave-like entrance into the rock face, Rayha followed Delilah down into the darkness and shone a flashlight ahead of them, even though the woman before her didn't seem to need light at all. With her other hand, she marked the wall with chalk, making sure they would be able to get out later.

Within minutes, it became hot. Natural tunnelling turned into manmade mine shafts. As they walked, more and more rubble littered the floor. The fires hadn't reached here yet—logical if there was a hell gate to repel them—but they were close, pressing against the edges of whatever kept them at bay. Rayha took off her jacket to better resist the heat and pulled her shirt over her nose and mouth against the wisps of potentially poisonous smoke.

They had to crawl through certain sections of collapsed or partly-dug tunnelling, and Delilah still had not looked back even once. They had to be close now. Rayha followed her patiently and reached into her bag for a set of heavy-duty leather cuffs, ordered straight off of a BDSM web shop: expensive, good quality, and meant to constrain without lasting damage. Pressing forward, she gently took a hold of Delilah's wrist. The woman hissed, but didn't resist when Rayha cuffed both wrists behind her back. The next time Delilah had to crawl, she slithered along the floor like an ineffective serpent and Rayha looked away, embarrassed.

The hell gate had been more impressive in Aisha's drawings. Looking at it after a long and monotonous journey, Rayha couldn't help think that the wood was old, and that the bright red of the doors had faded into a mute pastel. The demon seal was impressive, but Rayha had seen a few of them now and they just did not have the same impact that they used to have. The door cast a faint glow into the tunnel—strong enough not to have to use the flashlight anymore and too weak to show the details on the skeletons of former victims of the demon that lay scattered around. Delilah stepped right over the bones and headed for the door.

"Whoa, hey, none of that now," Rayha called out, and Delilah turned. Her eyes were bloodshot, and her clothes torn. Any semblance of upper class had been stripped from her as she stood hunched over, panting, spitting saliva. Delilah was not fully possessed yet, but Paqach wouldn't take long now they were at the gate. Down here, she could almost hear his whispers herself.

"I'm sorry I have to put you through this, Delilah. Aisha's too weak and I can't do it because I need to perform the exorcism. When I realized you were just as susceptible to demonic possession as your daughter, I knew Paqach would try to get you here instead. You are stronger, and Aisha gets fifty percent of her genes from you. She was chosen to open this gate, so there was a fifty-fifty shot you would do in a pinch."

Delilah growled and hunched further. She pulled at the cuffs to no avail. *Fuck.* Well, time to bait the monster. "Paqach, He Who Opens, show yourself. As a Guardian of Humanity, I summon thee in the name of Elah and all his Iyrin." The words vibrated off of the narrow tunnel walls.

Delilah spit and hissed. She stalked closer and Rayha backed off after setting down her bag.

She prepared the rope. "Come on, you pathetic waste of demon skin, come and get me. That's right, you have a nice host right there, now just get inside your meat suit. Come on, you little shit, don't just make *her* want to hurt me—*hurt me yourself!*"

It was enough. With an animalistic whine, Delilah threw her head back. Her arms rose to tension, but the cuffs held—for now. When pitch black eyes levelled on her, Rayha smirked.

"There you are, you half breed. Come and get me!"

Instantly, Delilah sagged through her knees and into a squat. Teeth showing, she leaped forward like a frog and crossed over fifteen feet in one, inhumanly far, standing jump. Her heavy body cannonballed into Rayha's and all the air was forced from her lungs as she fell, Delilah on top of her. Her head hit the floor hard, but she managed to remain conscious.

Delilah pushed down with a strength that was nowhere near what her body could sustain. Rayha had to hurry before she tore some muscles—or managed to sink her teeth into Rayha's neck. Grunting, she pushed the partly incapacitated woman off of her and struggled to straddle her. The demon whined and smacked Delilah's head into the floor below, howling in rage as Rayha struggled to get a rope around

116

the black woman's legs. She was out of breath and rapidly losing her strength. She needed to hurry—if the demon got the upper hand even once, she was dead and so was everyone around.

With a boot firmly planted against the woman's throat, she managed to wrap the rope around her legs and yanked them back. She turned the furious woman onto her front and secured the rope to the cuffs before she dropped her onto the cold rock and stood, then leaned against the hot wall as dizziness made the world tilt. Maybe that blow to the head had done some damage after all. From the ground, the demon's bright, black eyes looked up at her and Delilah's mouth opened wide to emit a piercing howl that was hell on Rayha's painful brain. She resisted the urge to kick Delilah in the face—it wouldn't shut up the demon, after all.

"Buddy, I am going to love exorcizing you," she spat. The holy water from a vial in her kit caused smoke to rise up from Delilah's skin, along with a loud howl of pain from the demon's throat. He tried to squirm away in Delilah's body, but Rayha stopped him with a booted foot.

"I exorcise thee, unclean spirit, in the name of Elah, the Father Almighty, and in the name of the power of the Holy Spirit, that thou depart from this creature of Elah, Delilah Williams, who our Lord hath designed to call unto His holy temple." She waved a large wooden cross over Delilah's howling body and tossed the last of the holy water onto her form. Again, she yowled loudly and smoke rose up. Both sunk into Rayha's brain like a dull knife.

"Through Elah, who shall come to judge the living and the dead, and the world by fire, I exercise thee, Paqach, He Who Opens. Go back to whatever hell hole you crawled out of and stay the fuck there!" Rayha was shouting now, just to get over the screeching sounds of the demon. Delilah would probably have to do without her voice for a while. Her body strained against the tight bindings and her head arched back dangerously far. She stayed like that for long moments, not breathing, not moving, just contorted in pain. Then she sagged to the floor and gasped before she passed out.

Rayha ran her hand over her own sweaty face and leaned forward with her hands on her knees. Exorcisms: always so anti-climactic. She dropped the religious paraphernalia and took a deep breath. Immediately, she coughed at the smoke in her lungs—smoke that was getting thicker, she now realized. Maybe it wasn't the door that had kept the fires at bay, but Paqach. That was both good news and bad; bad because that meant they were in immediate danger, but good because the problem of the door would solve itself soon enough.

"Delilah, hey. I need you to wake up now." Rayha fell to her knees and started to undo the ropes with trembling fingers, then rushed to pack her bag. She called out the other woman's name again, then rolled her onto her back and slapped her hard in the face. It worked—it usually did. Delilah blinked her bloodshot eyes open with a groan.

"Hey, welcome back," Rayha fought to keep her panic at bay. The fire usually spread only inches every year under the surface, but the destructive force seemed to have forgotten that rule. It was overtaking what it had been denied for years now, and at a pace that was worrying. Already, Rayha was sweating heavily from the released heat, and the smoke would soon obscure their vision, which would make getting out impossible. "I will explain everything that has happened soon but right now, I need you to trust me and not ask questions. Get up and walk. I need you to do that now, okay?"

Delilah blinked and groaned, then reached out with an uncoordinated hand. Rayha grabbed it and stood. She pulled Delilah up and supported her as the other woman nearly sagged through her knees. Rayha yanked at the heavy woman pressed into her side and Delilah took a step, then another. With her bag clutched into her one hand and a flashlight in the other, Rayha let Delilah lean on her heavily as they headed back the way they came. She forced Delilah to move, either by pulling her onwards or by shouting at her. Delilah didn't say a word; she was still completely out of it. Sweat dripped down her temples and down her neck. Her shredded clothes soaked through. Rayha searched the wall with her flashlight and followed the markings through the up sloping tunnels. The walls became hot to the touch.

Delilah grunted and put one bare foot in front of the other. Rayha didn't remember her losing her shoes. It didn't matter—nothing mattered but getting the fuck out of the tunnels. The first sign of daylight invigorated them both and it seemed to wake Delilah up a little. Rayha didn't have to drag her anymore. Instead, she dragged herself along as fast as her abused body could manage.

A high-pitched whine echoed through the tunnels and Rayha was sure that it was only audible in the Fugue; the door had given way under the fire and whatever the portal had trapped, was now trapped forever—much to its dismay. Delilah shuddered and moved a little faster at the sound.

The tunnels collapsed maybe twenty seconds after they cleared the mouth of the cave. Hot sand and rocks landed onto their collapsed bodies, and Rayha shielded her face. Delilah just blinked. A manic laugh welled up in Rayha's throat and refused to be contained. It shook her entire body as it tore from her throat. They were still alive. *Fucking hell!*

Delilah Williams was released from Reading Hospital two days later with a mild concussion and a torn rotator cuff. Her husband had meanwhile moved the care of his daughter to their home. Aisha was eating regularly and on her own again, and she was becoming more and more vibrant. Rayha knew, because despite prolonged and vehement protest, Aisha had managed to convince her to stay with them until her mother came back home—just in case something demonic took place. Rayha couldn't blame her, and Darren—who turned out to be a proud and reserved man—had agreed to pay her for her time. To be honest, Rayha had not hated living in the land of luxury for a while, especially after she'd drank herself into a stupor and had passed out for nearly six hours that first day. The nightmares had been terrible—unsurprisingly after everything that had happened—but she had felt far more rested by the time the morning had rolled around.

She had spent the rest of her days with Aisha, talking and learning more about the intelligent and funny woman she had rescued, and Rayha had watched her throughout the nights because Aisha seemed to sleep in longer intervals when Rayha was there. Rayha held her hand for long hours and had wished that she didn't know what the future would look like for the gentle woman in the bed whom she really started to like.

Fifty-six hours after Rayha had first met Delilah, she said goodbye to them on the porch of the modest but upscale Williams home. Darren and Delilah waved her off first. They expressed their gratitude and then stepped back to give the two young women some privacy as they said goodbye, well aware of the bond that had formed despite Rayha's obliviousness to the fact she had already let the other woman in.

"I'm going to miss having you around," Aisha confessed with a soft smile. "It was good to talk about everything that happened and well—"

"Don't go there, Ash. Trust me, I'm only good for you in small doses. Anything more and I become quite lethal, let me assure you." The words came out harsher than she had intended, and Aisha looked away as if stung. From a few paces away, Darren squinted at her, while Delilah pursed her lips. Rayha realized she didn't need to alienate these people; they had gone through enough and she was leaving anyway. The Williams family was safe. She took a deep breath, then fished her wallet out of the back pocket of her jeans.

"Here, take this. Maximilian Payne is a psychiatrist—a good one. He knows all about demons and such. He's a good friend of mine and you can trust him." She handed Aisha the card and smiled, hoping to make amends. When Aisha smiled back at her and took the card, Rayha stuffed her wallet and hands into her pockets, and glanced back at her car. She was delaying the inevitable, and she wasn't even sure why. There was just something in the way Aisha looked at her, and she remembered how Aisha slept more soundly when Rayha held her hand.

"Take care of yourself, okay? And each other. If you need me...well, your mom has my number." Aisha nodded tearfully and rushed forward to hug her. She was still bone thin and even in three sweaters, she was shivering. But she was alive. Soft curly hair tickled Rayha's face and she instinctively wrapped her hands around the young woman's body, pulling her close for long moments. Her heartrate sped up.

"Bye..."

"Bye, Ash..."

When Aisha pulled back, they exchanged soft smiles. Rayha felt the familiar pang of longing—of letting someone in—but she fought it. No matter what, Aisha Williams couldn't become another victim of her messed up life. She stuffed her hands into her pockets again and turned around. She willed herself not to look back at the family that was dangerously close to wiggling their way into her heart as she pulled

120

out of the driveway. Still, as she settled in for the long drive back to Detroit, Rayha found herself checking to make sure she had her phone on her—just in case Aisha tried to contact her. Rayha sighed at her own foolishness, but of all the possible outcomes this case could have had, this was by far the best one.

Ugly Things

BY EVE FRANCIS

KYLIE EYED THE GUY IN the jean jacket by the front hall of the animal shelter. He was lanky, with long brown hair and skinny legs inside his black jeans with holes in the knee. There was a patch for Social Distortion on the back of his jacket that had clearly been cut from an old band shirt and then repurposed to make a horrendous looking DIY aesthetic. When she leaned forward at her desk, and he still didn't take note of her, she called out, "Hey there. Looking to adopt an animal?"

"Oh! Hello. Didn't see you."

A lie. Kylie could tell from the way his mouth twisted slightly as he smiled. When he stepped closer, she could smell weed and alcohol from the night before—or maybe earlier in the week. Her sense of smell was never good with time; everything kind of came in at once and then scattered in her mind, building a composite picture of who someone was. This guy reeked of music and beer, of late nights and bad decisions that he spent the next day regretting. She could feel the sense of regret on him right now. He wasn't here to get a dog, but to apologize to a girlfriend. He wanted to give her puppies instead of flowers as a way to show commitment. Kylie knew that never worked out good for anyone involved—especially the dog.

"Can I see a piece of ID?" she asked and took out an adoption form.

The guy reached into his back pocket and took out a worn wallet, stuffed at the sides with cards and old receipts. He rooted around until he found a driver's license. "Good enough?"

Kylie's smile was fake as she nodded. Luckily, she had been doing this long enough to make sure no one knew her true emotions. She glanced down at his license; the man's name was Bertram Abernathy, which struck her as an old man's name though his license stated that he was only twenty-five.

"It says here you live on Summer St. Is that your current address?"

"Uh-yeah. Just down by the beach. Very nice. Good for a dog."

"And the building allows pets?"

"Um…"

Kylie cut him off before he could make up an excuse. "Most buildings there don't allow pets. I can't release a dog from here if I don't think it's going to a good home."

Bert's eyebrows furrowed as she slid his license back to him. "I'm a good home."

Kylie moved her eyes to the computer so she didn't scoff. "Of course. But I have to fill out forms or my own job is in trouble. Come back here tomorrow with the correct paperwork stating that you're allowed to have pets, or show me a clause in the lease. Until then, I can't release any animals to you. I'm sorry about that."

"You would really rather euthanize the dogs than let me take one? Just because of some form?"

Kylie flinched, but tried not to let Bert see. "I want all dogs to have good homes. But the standards still apply, or else we'll end up right back here again. All dogs deserve a home," she said, eyes on the computer. "But only with the right people."

"Fine, fine…" Bert trailed off, murmuring curses. He wasn't directing any of this specifically at her, Kylie knew. She could feel his anger fade out to embarrassment and shame. He picked up his phone from his left hand pocket and then began to type furiously. With him still standing this close, she could start to smell the faint hint of flowers and perfume. From his girlfriend, no doubt, who he was calling now to apologize the old fashion way instead of getting a dog involved.

"Wait. Tomorrow is Saturday, isn't it?" Bert asked.

Kylie glanced up from her computer. "Yes, it is."

"And you're not open are you?"

"No. I guess you'll have to wait until Monday, then."

Bert rolled his eyes and left. Kylie smirked. *Good riddance.* She glanced at the clock, noticed it was almost lunch, and wandered down the shelter's hallways.

"That dog is hideous."

Kylie glanced up, feeling the words like a bite mark. Steve stood in his blue-grey uniform, his eyes fixated on the small mutt in the corner. Animal control had picked it up a few weeks ago. The dog's fur was matted in clumps around her ears and under her jaw, and seemed impossible to remove though Kylie and other workers had tried to brush out the knots. The dog was fat too, and she had the habit of sitting up with her belly over her paws with her tongue hanging out of her mouth.

"I mean," Steve went on, "it looks like a fat, drowned rat. Are you sure it's a dog?"

Kylie approached the cage, ignoring Steve's remark. She stuck her fingers through the bars and the dog waddled over. "Hey, Trixie. How you doing?"

"You named her?" Steve let out a low, long whistle. "You know better than anyone here not to get attached to the animals."

Kylie rolled her eyes behind his back. He smelled of cigars—must have been to his best friend's bachelor party the night before—and carried with him a low-grade fever. Or hang over, maybe—Kylie couldn't quite tell. But she knew that in spite of his gruff words, he was harmless. It was Natasha, the other animal control worker with the red hair and wide smile, who Kylie hated. She enjoyed each time an animal was put down; Steve always felt awful. It was why he warned Kylie now that naming an animal was the first step on the road to heartbreak.

"I know," Kylie said. "But I like her. And yes, she's a dog. Not a rat."

"But what *type* of dog?"

"A special one," Kylie answered. She was never any good at figuring out mutts; that was a human classification system. All Kylie knew for sure was that she recognized and remembered Trixie from a long time ago. Maybe she was an ancestor, someone who had been bred with her kind. Kylie also liked Trixie because she felt like her on a day-to-day basis. Being a mutt herself—a human and werewolf who was also a mutt—she knew how deep a word like "ugly" could cut. Name calling and the pack standards of beauty were one of the main reasons why Kylie lived by herself now. A community would have made some aspects of her life a lot better (the loneliness, for one, would ease), but it wasn't worth the assault on her self-esteem.

"I like Trixie. She listens to me." When Kylie raised her hand in the air, Trixie's eyes followed. Kylie gave her a few small commands—sit, come, fetch—and the dog moved through them with only a little wheeze. Kylie glanced back at Steve. "See? Trixie came here already trained. She's a good dog."

"That's all you, dear. You're good with the dogs."

"I suppose it's why they hired me," Kylie said, her smile breaking. She glanced at Trixie again who waited for her next command. "But you can't write out the dog's role in all this. Trixie is pretty perfect."

"You just better hope someone else likes her, too." Steve glanced at her cage and noted how many weeks—days now—she had before she needed to be put down. He let out another long whistle. "You ever think about taking care of her? Adopting yourself?"

Kylie sighed and ran her fingers through her long dark hair. "Can't. My apartment doesn't allow dogs."

"Tough break."

"Yeah, it is." Kylie glanced down at the long row of cages and heard the dull hum of dogs that needed homes. She shook her head, blocking out the sound, and gave Steve one final wave.

"Good luck today," he said as he headed out the back door.

Yeah, she thought. *I'll need it.*

By the time Kylie wandered back to her desk, a woman was there waiting. Her hair was dark and freshly cut against her shoulders. She wore a large hoodie over what seemed to be a concert tee shirt for a local artist—Kylie could still smell the sweat of a mosh pit—and dark blue jeans. Her brown eyes lit up as soon as she spotted Kylie at the end of the hallway.

"Hi!" the woman greeted. "You work here?"

"I do, I do. Sorry I was gone. Just taking a tour around to see the dogs."

"Hey, if I had your job I'd be in the back all day, too."

As she stepped closer, Kylie smelled something else—the faint hint of sage and roses—as if the woman kept an indoor garden and many spice racks. That was a good sign, Kylie noted. Keeping a garden meant stability, permanency. "Are you looking to adopt today?"

The woman nodded and produced her ID right away.

"Have you done this before?" Kylie asked.

"Oh yeah, but a few years ago. I doubt you have a record of me in the system."

"You'd be surprised with what we still have."

Kylie smiled as the woman's name came up right away. *Jeanette Aucoin.* It sounded nice in Kylie's ear. "Is your address still current?"

"Yes."

Kylie nodded. It was a house on the beach. A house—not an apartment or shitty dilapidated area. Kylie knew the place; it was where packs used to roam, since no one really baulked when bunnies or squirrels went missing or turned up half-mauled.

"It says here you adopted a dog five years ago."

"Yes. He's gone now, so I wanted to come by and get another."

Kylie looked up. She didn't know how she had missed this before, but Jeanette's eyes had a hint of red around them. She smelled like tears. "I'm sorry for your loss. Come. Let's find a new dog for you."

"Thanks," Jeanette said, taking back her ID.

As they wandered around and looked into cages, Jeanette told Kylie a few stories about her old dog, whose name had been Brewster. "We—my girlfriend and I—got him after we had been to a keg party and decided to get married."

Kylie quickly glanced down at Jeanette's hand as she opened a door for her. There was no ring there now, so she anticipated that the marriage plans had been put off. Even if this was Florida, and gay marriage hadn't been legal back then, Kylie was used to a lot of her gay friends having their own ceremonies anyway and wearing the ring. On paper, they were roommates or "good friends" but it still mattered to make a promise in front of those they cared about.

126

"We broke up, obviously," Jeanette said after a pause. "Should know better than to take someone seriously who proposes drunk, you know? But that's neither here nor there."

Kylie was quiet, unsure of what to say. Jeanette's sudden confessing was still tinged with hope and promise, not desperation. Kylie gave her a smile and encouraged her to keep going.

"We did have the wedding, though," Jeanette added. "It was really nice. But it just never lasted much beyond that initial honeymoon phase. Oh, well. I got the house and the dog. So it really came out in my favor."

When Jeanette winked, Kylie blushed. The dogs around them paced and whined, demanding attention as they moved through. Jeanette stopped and bowed down by a cage, sticking her fingers close to the bars. A golden brown dog came over, licked her fingers, and then barked.

"Hey now," Kylie said. The dog lowered its head and then licked Jeanette again without question.

When Jeanette stood, she gave Kylie a nice smile. "You're good with them."

"It comes with the territory."

"No, not really. The guy we adopted from the last time was a mess. Pretty sure he hated his job."

"It can be hard. Being around animals that you know won't find as good of a home as they deserve. I can understand anyone else being bitter."

"But you're not?"

Kylie shook her head. "No. I'm not. Try not to be, anyway."

She was glad when Jeanette just nodded and continued to walk and look around. It would have been really hard to explain to Jeanette that even if the dogs didn't get a home, Kylie at least took comfort in making sure their final days were nice. It helped, she knew, when she could sense their fear and usually their last wishes. Besides a home, she could get them water or food or a toy—or even take them out for a last walk. She couldn't let her overwhelming sense of emotion get in the way, though. This was her job and she did it the best she could.

"Do you see any dogs you like?"

"All of them," Jeanette laughed. "But I can only really take one right now."

"Understandably. Should we keep looking?"

"Yes, definitely. I'll know when I've found the right dog."

As they continued to look around, Jeanette told Kylie that Brewster had been a golden retriever and Border Collie mix, saved from a puppy mill. "But I don't like pure breeds. So much has gone into fitting dogs into this unrealistic standard of what counts as a breed that it only ends up damaging them. So, even if I see a dog that's a pure breed here, I'll probably avoid it."

"Why?"

"Because I know that dog will find a home. Same with puppies in the pound. But a lot of other dogs are passed over because they don't fit with the family model."

"I understand. That's a good reason." Kylie bit her lip, wondering if she should take Jeanette down the row of the undesirables. The ugly dogs. The ones with missing limbs or who were just too old. The ones no one would adopt. Kylie was surprised when Jeanette turned down that hallway anyway.

"Here," she said. "These are what I want."

Kylie followed along as Jeanette went over and pet a couple of older dogs. She made cooing noises as she talked to them, and Kylie could tell how much all the dogs liked her. She had a warm and calming presence to her, but there was more than that, too. Kylie was usually extremely good at reading people, but she was stuck on Jeanette. Besides her indoor garden, a house on the beach, and a former wife, there was a blank spot that Jeanette didn't reveal, something she kept close to herself and couldn't confess. Usually, blank spots like that made Kylie nervous. *But the dogs like her,* Kylie reminded herself. *So Jeanette can't be bad at all.*

Kylie had just dropped down by a cage of a dog missing a leg, petting him as he licked her fingers, when she heard Jeanette shriek

"Oh my goodness! Who is this?"

Jeanette stood in front of Trixie's cage. The dog sat with her tongue out, her tail wagging next to Jeanette.

"Oh. That's Trixie."

"She has a name already?"

"Um. Yeah. But it's not official or anything; just a nickname some of the guys and me have been using."

"Nice. Bet it has a story," Jeanette said, scratching behind Trixie's ears. "She's so hideous."

Kylie blinked. She heard all the chants and calls people had shouted at her when she was younger and transforming. *Hideous girl! Ugly Thing! Get out, mutt. Don't come back.* Kylie shook away the memories, trying to keep her composure. She was about to show Jeanette out of the shelter when Jeanette added, "She is so ugly and I love her."

"Uhh—What?"

"I want to protect her." Jeanette stood up now, her eye fixated on Kylie. "I want to adopt Trixie. Give her a better home. Is that okay?"

"Yeah," Kylie said, smiling now. Jeanette was perfect person for her. "Let me go get the paperwork done."

Kylie had too much stuff. One of her major problems as a werewolf with a heightened sense of smell was that absolutely *everything* had meaning to her. Each article of clothing, each broken lamp, and each childhood toy had its own distinct aura and scent to it, because it had the ability to capture memories and keep them time locked in her mind.

When she arrived home after her shift, she opened up her door and was assaulted with memories. She waited until the first force of the smell had dissipated, then tried to maneuver the rest of the way through her two-bedroom apartment. Her front hall was stacked with old newspapers and magazines, some covered with cellophane and Christmas wrapping paper. Over by her couch and TV stand were several dozen blankets with different cross stitched patterns or Disney characters on them, along with pillows that were supposed to be purely decorative or made by someone else she had crossed paths with a long time ago.

Then there were her bedrooms. The room she slept in was filled with desks and vanities, broken mirrors, and lamps from each distinct decade—oil lamps, ballerina lamps, and even some lava lamps. She had a walk in closet filled with t-shirts of her favourite bands, faux-fur coats, along with bell-bottoms and a wedding dress her mother had worn. The other bedroom, the one she didn't sleep in, had been filled up with music equipment over the years. Guitar picks, amps, and old bass guitars with broken straps. She sometimes played the instruments, but her voice and fingers weren't what they used to be. She had stacks of vinyl LPs and a tabletop record player, stacks of CDs from her old life in New Market Indiana, and a couple tape decks that still worked. Out of all the rooms in her apartment, this was clearly her favourite; it was one of the few with a worn pathway to each item and a chair she could sit in. But even here, the mess and memories were overwhelming.

With a large sigh, Kylie moved from her kitchen—filled with stock and supplies—and grabbed a bite to eat before shuffling into her music room. When she could barely get her record player to play the old Carpenters album—she had decided she really, really wanted to hear 'Superstar' on the way home—she found she could only sit in silence.

"Okay," Kylie said aloud. "I cave."

For the rest of the night, she pulled out garbage bags and cardboard boxes and filled them up with stuff she could part with. Then, she found an old Sharpie and wrote YARD SALE in big block letters. She left the sign in the front hallway of her building and waited until morning.

Though it was a Saturday near the end of October and not exactly peak yard sale season, no one ever really cared in Florida. The warm weather all year round and the amount of retired people gave the place a 'land that time forgot' feeling to it. So long as there was a yard sale and most things were a quarter, Kylie knew that people would show up and root through her things. It was one of the few consistencies that Florida had that Kylie's home town in Indiana didn't, and one of the major reasons she had moved here when she was seventeen years old and just transformed into a werewolf.

As the sun peaked over the Florida skyline, Kylie pulled out one of her old lawn chairs from the back closet and a fishbowl full of change. Most landlords didn't care about the sales on their property, so long as you gave them a discount on what you were selling, and Kylie knew what her landlord liked by now. After laying down a tarp on the front lawn of her building, she dumped out boxes of extra cutlery, Tupperware, and some of the books she had burned through in one night. There were boxes of LPs she had duplicates of, some blankets, and a couple of those hideous lamps. Since she knew that most people wouldn't want the newspapers she had stacked high, she kept them for herself. By the time she had finished setting up, her apartment was liveable again. Not perfect, and she knew that she would only set it back to a hoarding space soon enough, but that was fine. So long as she could do this ritualistic purges every so often, Kylie knew she could survive.

The first car showed up just as Kylie sat down. She perched her sunglasses at the end of her nose and gave the old man and woman a big smile. "Good morning! Take what you like and make me a price."

The older couple had only taken a few dishes, but they were only the beginning. Halfway through the day more than half of Kylie's books were gone, most of the blankets, and nearly all of the dishes. The lamps no one seemed to be interested in at all, which Kylie was fine with. She was kind of attached to that ballerina one and the green lava lamp. A pink car pulled up alongside her building.

"How much for your chair?" a man asked Kylie.

"Um." She stood up and glanced down at the lawn chair. There was a rip in the linings, but that didn't seem to dissuade the man when she pointed it out. "Five dollars?" she said.

"Four?" he countered.

"Sold."

Kylie passed it off to him, pocketing his ones and quarters, before she turned to examine the pink car that had pulled up. The woman was now outside her vehicle, digging through some of the LPs. Kylie smelled sage and roses, and then panicked slightly as she saw the familiar coif of brown hair.

"I thought that was you," Jeanette said as she stood and spotted Kylie.

"Um." Kylie looked around, still awe-struck. She had anticipated never seeing Jeanette again. Maybe at a dog park or something else animal related. But here, going through her junk and seeing how she really lived, it was almost too much. "Hi. How are you?"

"Good. I was just out for a drive when I saw this. I'm glad I stopped."

"Really?" Kylie glanced down at Jeanette's arms, which held her extra copy of the Carpenter's album she had listened to last night.

"Yeah, really. How much is this?"

"Oh." Kylie glanced at the box that listed the LPs as two dollars each, then said, "One dollar."

"Are you sure? It's a good album."

"I have another."

"Okay. Sold." Jeanette reached into her pocket and pulled out a couple dollars. "Keep the change for now. I'm sure I'll find more."

Kylie nodded and added it to her fishbowl. She was about to sit down when she realized she had sold her chair. She wandered over to the remaining blankets, picked up a Disney princess one, and then folded it under her. Jeanette now had a couple more albums under her arm. Kylie spotted the first Run DMC, along with Simon and Garfunkel, Sting, and The Beastie Boys.

"Good choices," Kylie said. "Very eclectic."

"Thank you. I pride myself on diversity." Jeanette handed her a couple more dollars. "Do you want to know how Trixie is?"

"Oh. Um. Yeah, if you want to tell me."

"How about I show you?" Jeanette asked, then took out her phone. "Can I sit with you?"

Kylie shifted over on the blanket, chuckling a little. "So long as you don't mind a princess covering."

"Not at all." Jeanette sat next to her and scanned through her phone's photo album. The first image was one of Trixie in a bath, covered in soapsuds, and her tongue sticking out. Kylie laughed.

"Oh, she looks happy."

"She is. I like her." Jeanette showed another photo, and then another. Kylie's stomach balled in weird, nervous energy. *You just miss Trixie*, she told herself. *That's all this is.* But as Jeanette's fingers brushed hers on the princess bed sheet, she felt her heart skip another beat.

"How much for this?" Jeanette asked.

"The princess bedding? Oh, everyone is buying my seats today."

"I don't have to get it. I just thought it was neat." Jeanette's eyes scanned over to the ballerina lamp. "Oh! *That.* I think I want that."

Kylie narrowed her eyes. "You're not humouring me, right? Making fun of my terrible decor?"

"What? No!" Jeanette looked horrified. Kylie softened, realizing how much Jeanette really was.

"I'm sorry. I'm used to people telling me I have ugly things."

"Really? Sounds like you need new friends. The 1990s is the new vintage. So I also kind of want that lava lamp."

Kylie laughed, placing a hand over her mouth. Jeanette got up from the blanket and moved to go through some of the lamps, making eager noises under her breath.

"You're right," Kylie said.

"Hmm?"

"I did need new friends. So I don't have them anymore."

"Good." Jeanette smiled. "You don't need to keep people around who make you feel bad."

"Yeah, again, you're right." Kylie waited as Jeanette picked up a couple more lamps, eyeing them with a pleased expression, but not actually purchasing anything yet.

"So," Jeanette added moments later. "Do you want to hang out?"

"Um." Kylie looked at Jeanette's dark eyes and saw how sensitive—and serious she was. This was more than just a hang out, but a possible date. She glanced back at her yard sale and her fishbowl of cash.

"If you're not done yet, I can come back? Maybe take you for lunch."

"No, no." Kylie stood. Her yard sales were never about the money. She grabbed her fishbowl in her arms and then grabbed the yard sale sign. On the back of it she wrote *free to a good home* and placed it near the rest of her remaining collection in the grass.

"There. Now I'm good."

Jeanette grinned, eyeing the sign. "So I *can* have the lamp then? And maybe the bedding?"

"Yes!" Kylie said, smile wide. "Of course."

Jeanette drove them both for coffee around the corner. Jeanette got a tall green tea macchiato and Kylie stuck to what she liked best: black coffee and a scone with cranberries in it. They sat by the window, close to the Florida shoreline, and then lapsed into a comfortable silence. Kylie interpreted the quiet differently than most people. While she got used to a person's scent, aura, and personality through their clothing, her mind rearranged them into an abstract painting. Jeanette was a composite of blue and green, seashells and the sound of water with the smell of sage. She was human—there was no doubt about that, but there was also something else about her that nagged at Kylie.

"So why do you go to yard sales on Saturday mornings?"

"Truthfully, I was thinking I could find a Halloween costume."

"Oh." Kylie paused. "That is tomorrow, isn't it?"

"Yes. But I'm glad I came out today anyway. I didn't even realize it was you until I got out of the car. So I guess it's a sign of good fortune."

Kylie smiled, blushing slightly, and looked down at her coffee. "Did you find your costume?"

"Nah. But I like what I got more."

"A sheet and some records? You could go as the ghost of music people paid for."

"Hah." Jeanette laughed. "That's good—but I was thinking of going as a witch, actually. Pretty standard fare. And I have a new familiar, now. In Trixie."

Kylie smiled again. "You're not going to get her a costume, are you?"

Jeanette's jaw dropped, absolutely horrified. "I would never."

"Oh, thank goodness. Animals *hate* costumes." Kylie leaned forward and touched Jeanette's fingers, causing their eyes to meet. The touch didn't last much longer than a few seconds, but Kylie could feel the warmth from Jeanette's fingers linger long after.

Music began to play from the front of the coffee house. Kylie glanced over to see a guy with a goatee holding an acoustic guitar on his knee as he warmed up to play a small show. He was dressed like a hipster and smelled like black clove cigarettes; a Dashboard Confessional wannabe, Kylie knew, but she could also sense his sincerity as he continued to play.

"Where did you grow up?" Jeanette asked. "I don't think you're from around here."

"You can tell?" Kylie smirked. "I'm from Indiana. Moved here when I was seventeen."

"To be a rock star? An actress?"

Kylie furrowed her brow. She knew Florida had a pretty good punk and ska scene—it was part of the reason she considered living here out of all the states. When she first arrived, she had gone to at least a dozen shows, couch surfing, before she finally found her apartment and job. Besides the small music scene, Kylie also knew that Florida was weird. The headlines alone told her as much. When she was suddenly dealing with her fate as a werewolf—and a mutt on top of that—she had figured this would be the easiest place to blend in amongst the freaks and weirdoes. Florida didn't exactly strike up images of the wannabe rock star or aspiring actress.

"Why do you say those two?" Kylie asked.

"Because you're really pretty. I figured it would make sense to break away from a small town to do something different like that."

"Oh." Kylie took a sip of her coffee. "Um…"

"I'm sorry. I guess you hear that a lot, right?"

Kylie ran a hand through her hair awkwardly. "No, actually."

"Well, then let me tell you, Kylie: You're very pretty."

Kylie felt her cheeks blush. "Thanks. And you? Where are you from?"

"Salem, Massachusetts."

"Oh. Then I guess being a witch for Halloween would really fit."

"Yeah," Jeanette laughed easily. "It would."

Kylie brushed her fingers against Jeanette's again, seeing if she could sense something else. Occasionally, if she tried hard enough, she could see into people's past. She didn't like to do it that often because it was difficult to concentrate on that level. But maybe for Jeanette, Kylie could sense what that blank part she kept hidden really was. Maybe she could smell burning, the sensation of rope—or even a hint of magic. She had never met a real life witch before—a demon, yes, and lots of werewolves, but not a witch. When all Jeanette did was loop their hands together more, Kylie lost her vision. Jeanette's hand was just *nice* in hers.

As the music changed, Jeanette leaned forward and pressed a small kiss to Kylie's mouth. She tasted warm, like the coffee she had been drinking, but also safe. Kylie opened her mouth a little, and Jeanette pressed her tongue lightly against her bottom lip. She didn't linger too long; they were in public, and even Kylie felt her body become flushed with slight embarrassment.

135

"You should come by," Jeanette said. "I'm having a party tomorrow. What do you think?"

"Oh. On Halloween?" Though Kylie didn't want to, she broke their grasp to check her phone. She had a deep, dreadful feeling in the pit of her stomach as she flipped to her calendar complete with moon phase. *Right.* Tomorrow was the full moon—on Halloween. No wonder she had been feeling groggy and ugly lately. No matter how much anyone called her pretty or kissed her sweetly, Kylie was always going to have to deal with this.

"You don't have to dress up," Jeanette said. "I don't mind. You can come as a dog whisperer. I'm sure Trixie will appreciate it."

"Thanks... But maybe some other time? I actually have plans."

"Oh. Okay."

Kylie felt Jeanette's disappointment like a knife. She reached forward and took her hands again. "I *do* want to come, I really do. I just can't tomorrow. You understand?"

Jeanette's smile softened and she nodded. She traced her thumb around the skin of Kylie's hand. "Yes, I do."

Kylie believed her without question.

On Halloween night, Kylie transformed—but it was more violent than the past. Maybe she had forgotten to properly time her transformation, or she had had too much caffeine during the day. Love, also, was another reason she could be feeling her body revolt like an ulcer in the pit of her stomach. She was in her living room when she fell down, her claws scraping away at the newspaper she had painstaking stacked the day before. She moaned and groaned, and prayed that new neighbors didn't hear.

I was supposed to be in the woods, Kylie thought. *I should have been away from here. Why am I changing so soon?*

Kylie felt her spine and hips snap and shift inside her body until she was now a four-legged creature. The black hair on her head fell away and was replaced by thick, matted fur. Her hands and feet extended into paws as her belly dropped and became covered with fur. She could only claw at her apartment door as her thumbs became absorbed into her wolf form.

Come on, come on, she urged herself on, slowly holding her last shreds of human thought. *I need to get out. I need to get outside into the woods so I can eat rabbits and squirrels. Not people. I can't be seen. I can't...*

Just as the last change occurred, her door fell open. She bounded forward, all thoughts now lost in pure sensation and movements. When an old couple screamed at her, she bounced by them, using all of her energy to not smell the scent of meat. She ran down the stairwell and out into the lobby; Kylie knew she was caught. She had been seen. She could never come back to her apartment again and all of her toys and trinkets were now the state's property, like her first house in Indiana. She would become an urban myth, a thing of legend that could never be caught. *If* she ran fast enough.

"Hey! Call the police! Animal control! A rabid dog is on the loose."

A wolf, Kylie thought, still hearing her own human voice though it was now only a whisper in her head. *I'm a wolf.*

"What a vicious, ugly thing."

I'm pretty, Kylie thought again. *Jeanette said I'm pretty.*

Sirens sounded at the other end of the apartment building. Before they could catch up, Kylie was running as fast as she could towards the ocean and the night.

When Kylie heard the cries of kids, she didn't know what to do. Children? Out this late? It didn't make sense. Her body and senses overrode her human emotion. She was beast, and she was so, so hungry. Children were close by and easy prey. She wasn't fair in what she craved or desired; she was just an animal.

She turned away from the shoreline and the safety of the bushes. When she saw a child dressed in a white sheet, she knew exactly what she wanted.

The kid in the sheet screamed—a boy—and ran towards a house. He clawed at the door as Kylie circled. There were flames and orange light on the porch. *A jack-o-lantern,* some small part of her mind said. She smelled pumpkin and spice, sugar and candy and chocolate; the dog side of her mind was repelled by the chocolate. When the kid disappeared through the door, she knew it was pointless pursuing.

She turned back to the road and saw another small creature—this time a girl—dressed as a ballerina. A familiar sense inside of her recognized it as something desirable and began a chase.

"No!" the girl cried. "No! Someone help me."

"Vile creature!" another voice, an older one. The smell of cigars and gin.

"Ugly thing."

"Someone call the police!"

The voices all blurred together now, like the faces of the people who loomed close to her. Too close. Kylie felt their words like bullets, and then, when a gunshot sounded, Kylie paused in her tracks. The little girl was swooped up by a mother's arm, and Kylie knew not to fight. She could get rabbits by the shore; it didn't matter anymore.

But as she turned around, another gunshot sounded, and she felt a sharp pain in her back leg. *No. No.* Her human body revolted. Things were not supposed to happen this way. She was supposed to be in the woods; it wasn't her fault. She had been doing this for ten years and it had never happened this way before. She had just lost track of time... This was also Halloween. It was the moon—the moon made her. Kylie's leg screamed with pain. Each movement forward caused blood to spill until Kylie realized she wasn't moving at all, but slumped on the road. Her breathing changed, getting shallower and shallower.

"Get away," someone said. The voice was familiar but still distant. "Get away."

"We need to call animal control or kill it," the other voice said. Red panned across Kylie's vision. Anger and fear. The emotions twisted and she couldn't tell if she was afraid or if everyone else was.

"You already shot her in the lg. She's not going anywhere."

"Her? It's an *it*. An ugly thing."

"No." The familiar voice again. Walking closer to her now. "She's just a lost dog. I know what to do with her."

Kylie felt a hand around her neck, scratching it. She jerked away, only to smell roses and sage. She looked up into dark, familiar eyes. Green skin and a hat. A witch.

Jeanette. Kylie tried to growl and groan, but only felt another hand on her body and then she was being lifted.

"Everyone go back into your homes," Jeanette called. "I know what's going on. I have this from here."

Kylie wanted to cry out again, to warn Jeanette of what was going to happen next. Now injured and out of the moonlight, Kylie knew she's surely change back into her human form. Only she'd be naked and wounded, still covered in a thin layer of fur until the early morning. It had happened once before, when she had broken her leg after being hit by a car when she was twenty-three. She had almost died that night as she waited until morning before going to the hospital. She couldn't let something like this happen again, not with Jeanette. Not with...

"Shush," Jeanette said into Kylie's ear. "I have you now."

Jeanette started to hum. Kylie recognized the familiar lines of 'Superstar' before everything faded to black.

Kylie woke up hours later. She tried to move, only to hiss at the pain and recognize her own human voice. She looked down at her body and saw she was wrapped in the princess blanket from her yard sale. The ballerina lamp was on a desk across from her, and Trixie was on the floor by the couch she lay on. The dog waddled over then barked happily, which sounded more like a loud grunt.

"Trixie?" Kylie said. Her voice was groggy, still sounding a touch like a growl. Everything—from her fingertips to her eyelashes—throbbed in pain.

Kylie looked around the room and saw black out curtains that blocked all the light save for a thin sliver by the doorway. There were roses around her, in boxes by the window, and dried sage hanging above the rose boxes. Her heart thundered in her chest. She knew where she was—and she knew she was safe.

"Hi!" Jeanette said, walking into the room. "How are you doing?"

"I'm...in pain."

"I know." Jeanette sat down with her on the bed. She was dressed in normal clothing now, no witch's costume. When she touched Kylie's hand and she felt the magic under Jeanette's skin stronger than ever before. "You were shot last night. The buckshot was terrible, but I managed to get rid of all it in your leg. Luckily, it wasn't silver so you're fine. Just a little in pain. Here, take these."

Jeanette reached into her cardigan pocket and placed two capsules filled with green herbs in Kylie's hand, before passing her a mug of water. Kylie took both pills without question and then lay back down. Right away, she felt her stomach ease and her body relax. Jeanette ran a hand over her forehead, before moving over to the window and pulling back the curtains to let a little light inside.

"I can't go home," Kylie said. She placed her hands over her face. This was just like when she was seventeen all over again.

"Shush," Jeanette said, taking her hand again. "I know. I saw the reports on the news. Your apartment building had quite a scare."

Kylie let out another low cry.

"Don't worry. I know now. I know everything."

Kylie peaked out from behind her hands. Jeanette wasn't mad, sad, or even angry. When Kylie sensed Jeanette next to her, the composite picture she arranged had changed. Jeanette was still blue and green with seashells, but now she had a darker background, filled with glittering stars that represented her magic. She was a witch, for sure. But a witch that worked at collecting and healing ugly things that no one else would. Kylie heard Trixie grunt by their feet and laughed.

"I guess I belong here, huh?"

"You do. But not because you're ugly," Jeanette said, curling Kylie's hair over her ears. "But because you care and see beauty where others don't."

Kylie's smile faltered with sudden emotion. Jeanette reached forward and kissed her, as if trying to remove the sadness from her expression without words. Kylie fell into Jeanette's arms easily, pressing their bodies together in a warm hug. She heard the faint sound of The Carpenters from the next room and knew she was truly home.

Do You Remember?

BY MARY-ANNE O'MALLEY

I ROLLED MY EYES AT Nat as he pretended to gag at the sight of the vegetables I was chopping. Typical Nat, pretending to be disgusted by healthy food. I was making a blood stew for dinner for Abby and me. I wasn't going to force him to eat any of it; Nat knew that, he just liked being an ass sometimes. Okay, most of the time.

I glanced over at him, and he pretended to spew vomit across the floor. For extra effect, he added sound to his little act. He could be such a twelve-year-old sometimes. Most people think that because Nat is a demon, he is inherently evil, while in reality he's only inherently annoying. I chucked a piece of carrot at his head. He shrieked, then snapped his fingers and disappeared in a cloud of smoke. He loved doing his vanishing act.

Nat had been my best friend for over a hundred years. He was practically my brother. Our foster mother, Lady Sarah, had a fondness for supernatural creatures, and she had taken both of us into her care around the same time. I was a young, freshly turned vampire, and Nat had just escaped a brutal master.

Because demons weren't recognized as citizens under the law until the 1890s, up until that time, instead of having basic rights they were usually enslaved and abused. Nat had escaped just such a situation, and ended up in Sarah's large Belfast home with a dozen other non-human creatures. Why he chose me to torment for the next hundred years, I don't know. Even in the present day, it is rare for a vampire to have a demon as a best friend, as vampires and demons tend to move in distinctly separate social circles.

The existence of supernatural creatures, including vampires, has been known since before Jesus died on the cross. In fact, some people believe that vampires are descendants of the disciples who drank Jesus's blood in the form of communion wine. That's just silly superstition, though; vampires predate Christianity. For that matter, vampires predate humanity.

Vampires are not uncommon among supernatural creatures, but we are vastly outnumbered by mages and witches. Still, we are respected among all people, supernatural or otherwise. Vampires have superhuman speed and strength, as well as the power to heal rapidly, attributes that have saved my and Abby's lives on countless occasions. Nat also saved our lives a few times, something he never lets Abby forget.

I was slicing a potato when Nat reappeared in the kitchen. He grimaced.

"I had hoped that leaving Ireland meant never again having to smell another potato, but you damn Irish, you just love…"

I tuned him out as I began to wonder where Abby was. She was supposed to have gotten off work at the hospital three hours earlier, but wasn't home yet. I knew she was going to stop on the way home to pick up some paper towels, but that shouldn't have taken her three hours.

I felt an old familiar dread rising in my stomach, a cold, gripping feeling that had been a constant during the first few years of my relationship with Abby. It bubbled up my throat, and I closed my eyes against the fear—fear that something had happened to Abby, fear that someone saw us kiss or saw me hold her hand. Fear that Abby might be fighting for her life because she chose to love me and I chose to love her.

I pushed the fear away. This wasn't a traditional Catholic village in nineteen-twenties Spain or a Nazi-occupied town in nineteen-forties Germany. This was the liberal town of Portland, Oregon. No one was going to try to harm Abby here. I heard Nat turn on the TV on as I continued cutting vegetables. A few moments later, I heard Abby as she burst into the house.

"I FUCKING HATE FUCKING VAMPIRES!"

Abby slammed the door behind her and stomped into the living room, and I glanced at her from the kitchen doorway. Her black hair was disheveled, and her green eyes flashed with emotion. She looked different—almost frazzled, or maybe even nervous.

Nat quickly turned the TV off and went over to Abby. I rolled my eyes; I knew exactly what Nat would do next. His favorite pastime was teasing Abby. He'd been doing it for a hundred years, and I doubted he'd ever find it tiring.

"I hate to be the one to deliver this earth-shattering news, but *you* are, in fact, a vampire, Abigail," Nat chided in a mocking tone.

Abby's green eyes grew darker as she approached the pint-sized demon. At three feet tall, he should have known better than to mock a thousand year old vampire. But Nat had a terrible sense of humor that was based on intense ridicule and crippling sarcasm. At five feet ten inches, Abby towered over the tiny demon, and now she was glaring at him, her fists clenched.

"What did you say, Nat? I don't think I heard you," Abby said through gritted teeth.

"Maybe you should have your hearing checked, Abby. *You* are a vampire. But you're also very old vampire. Maybe you're going senile. It would explain the recent decline in your intellect and—"

"Why you little…"Abby roared at Nat as she lunged down at him.

He snapped his fingers and disappeared, then reappeared three feet behind Abby.

Abby hesitated when she realized Nate had disappeared. Behind her, Nat giggled, and Abby spun around and lunged for him again.

He snapped his fingers and disappeared, only to reappear behind her again.

I watched in amusement as Abby, a vampire with superhuman powers of agility and speed, chased a giggling demon around the room. After a few minutes, Abby got frustrated and determinedly dove toward the spot where Nat had just appeared. She caught the slippery little guy's arm and quickly hoisted him up until he was dangling three feet above the floor. Nat struggled in her grip. He couldn't vanish when anyone was touching him.

Abby glared at Nat, who didn't look too frightened even though he was dangling from the fist of an irate vampire. She gave him a shake. "You, little demon, need to be taught to respect a ten century old vampire who could literally consume you whole."

"I thought you hated vampires, so why should I respect them?" Nat retorted.

"I could crush your skull with my pinkie finger." Abby said, her eyes dark with anger.

"True. But you being terrifying doesn't necessarily mean I have to respect you," Nat said flippantly.

Abby's eyes darkened further, and her lips curled back as her fangs descended. She let out a vicious roar, a roar that was usually reserved for intimidating mobs of people. It was so loud and terrifying, I had seen it stop violent hordes in their tracks.

Nat didn't seem particularly impressed by it.

"Given that you vampires are composed mostly of blood, I find the large amount of saliva you seem to produce very disturbing." Nat made a show of wiping his face.

That goddamn demon was going for the Oscar for Condescending Assholery tonight.

"It's a good thing little pipsqueak demons like you don't have blood," Abby raised Nat up until they were eye to eye, "or you would soon be drained of it."

"Oh, we both know you prefer the blood of your tasty little blonde over there." Nat gestured in my direction.

Abby's eyes followed his movement, and her eyes found mine. Her eyes widened when she saw me. She apparently hadn't realized I'd been watching them from the kitchen.

I raised an eyebrow and gave her a brief wave. "Hey, babe."

"Oh umm... Hey, sweetheart. ...Ummm... How was your day?" Momentarily forgotten, Nat continued to dangle from Abby's hand.

"It was fine. Met a goblin. She was fucking weird. Met another goblin. He was even fucking weirder," I replied.

"Goblins are always strange little creatures."

"So, how was your day, babe? You seem a little out of sorts," I said, watching Nat struggling to get away.

He was now biting Abby's hand in hopes of freeing himself, but she didn't seem to notice. Vampires become more impervious to pain as they age.

"It was okay. A little stressful, I guess. Some stupid vampire hit me with his car, then told me to get over it because we were both vampires and I should cut him some slack. I mean, it didn't physically hurt, but I still don't enjoying being hit by large chunks of metal. He could have at least apologized," she said with a frown.

That was one the many things I loved about Abby. One moment she would be threatening bodily harm, and the next she would be frowning because her feelings were hurt. Feelings meant a lot to Abby. She had known vampires who forgot to feel as they aged. They became indifferent to the beauty of smile, the radiant sound of laughter, and the comfort of just holding someone's hand.

Abby was terrified that she would forget how to feel, and so she sometimes exaggerated her feelings. That was fine with me. I loved making her smile, holding her hand, and kissing the tip of her nose. In the right circumstances, a kiss on the tip of Abby's nose could make that thousand year old vampire blush like a schoolgirl.

"That driver was just an ass wipe, babe. Don't let him bother you. It's really not worth it."

My eyes skimmed the length of Abby's body until they met her gaze. I raised an eyebrow, and Abby dropped Nat, who snapped his fingers and disappeared before he even hit the floor. He didn't reappear anywhere else in the room, so he had probably gone home.

"You're right. I shouldn't let annoying stuff like that affect me. I shouldn't have gone off on Nat. He didn't really deserve it. I'm...I'm just a little jumpy today." Abby crossed the room and stopped a few inches in front of me, then gazed into my eyes.

I smiled. "Sweetheart, we both know Nat's an asshole who likes to rile people up. We also both know you could never really do him any permanent harm, because he's my best friend."

Abby sighed. "Why you ever befriended that little demon spawn is beyond me."

I studied her for a moment. Her demeanor was casual enough, but her left hand was behind her back, resting on the left cheek of her jean-clad ass. I had spent enough time looking at her ass to know that she usually didn't park her hand there.

"You okay, Abby? You seem a little tense."

"I'm fine. Just a long day." She quickly moved her hand from her ass and closely examined her fingernails.

"Speaking of your day, where were you? I thought you were getting off work early tonight.

She shrugged. "I had a few errands to run."

"Did they include picking up the paper towels we need?" I turned and went back over to the counter, and began to chop more carrots for the blood stew.

"I'm a thousand year old vampire. I don't dabble in trivial domestic pursuits," Abby retorted.

"In other words, you forgot." It was a statement, not a question, but I softened it by following up with a smile.

"Sorry. I'll get them tomorrow."

"At a thousand years old, I would expect you to have a better memory." I picked up another carrot and focused on my chopping.

I heard Abby's light footsteps as she approached me. She gently moved my long hair off my right shoulder and exposed the skin of my neck and collarbone which was not covered by my tank top. Her hands slid around my waist as she placed butterfly kisses one my neck. I set the knife down on the counter, and tilted my head to give her better access. She worked her way up my neck with light touches of her lips, her warm breath making me shiver.

"You know, I can still vividly remember the moment I first saw you, all those years ago. I don't think I could ever forget a single detail," Abby whispered, then she gently licked the shell of my ear.

I shuddered as her hands slipped under my top and her fingers splayed over my stomach. Almost a hundred years with Abby, and just her slightest touch could still send my pulse racing.

"You do?" I squeaked as her fingers started tracing the contours of my stomach. I could feel her lips move as Abby smiled against my neck.

"I fell in love from across the room. You looked like the horizon—a beauty I would chase forever, a beauty I would never tire of. Green eyes, blond hair, and a freckled smile captured my heart," Abby said in a whisper, her hot breath making me shiver yet again. "Do you remember when we first met?"

I closed my eyes and recalled that day almost a hundred years ago.

I chuckled politely as Sir McArthur made yet another terrible jest about England. Sir McArthur roared with laughter at his own joke. When he had composed himself, he took another gulp of his drink and then proceeded to tell me one of his endless supply of stories about a fox hunt. The more he drank, the more pronounced his Irish accent became.

Nat had promised me this would be an exciting night in the volatile capital, Dublin. I had attended the party with that understanding. In fact, it was a gathering of Irish rebels celebrating All Hallows Eve with a night of drinking and dance, and discussions about rebellion and revolution. Even Maude Gonne, the famous Irish Rebel vampire, was in attendance. Nat had come with me, but had already disappeared with his current love interest.

I had attended because I anticipated a night of adventure and action. Instead I had spent an interminable hour listening to this drunk mage McArthur make terrible jokes about England. Born in Ireland, I held no true love for England, but if he was going to insult the English, at least he could have the decency to do it well.

"...and the thhhe...damn Englishman...he...he...tried twice to shoot the fox...but buttttt...he missed and he theeeennnnnn he then fell off his horse...and landed on his backside in a creek. See...seeeeee the damn English can't...can't even shoooot a fox properly." McArthur threw his head back and roared with laughter.

I smiled politely and tried to think of an acceptable way to escape.

"Buttt us Irishmen... We...I can shoot any damn fox. I...I...cannnn shoot him dead." McArthur looked at me with bloodshot eyes.

"I don't doubt your skill," I replied, deliberately avoiding his eyes.

"I...I...have skills in other areas, tooooooo." He winked. "I know what woooomen like and —"

Mercifully, McArthur was interrupted by a voice coming from behind me.

"Hello, Lord McArthur. I'm so glad I found you. I just saw your wife, and she's looking for you. She seemed about ready to cast a seeking spell, so I'd go find her if I were you," the distinctly Irish voice said.

McArthur's eyes widened at the mention of his wife. He gave me a sheepish grin, said goodbye, kissed my hand for far too long, and then scurried off to find his wife.

After he'd departed, I turned around to look at the person who had saved me. My gaze met green eyes that were the color of a frosted field of grass in the early morning. The woman was stunning. Long dark hair and full lips complemented an angular facial structure with high cheekbones and a defined jaw line. An emerald dress which went very nicely with her eyes, showed off her hourglass figure. My eyes went back to her face just as she bit her lip and revealed perfect white teeth.

"I hope you don't mind that I got rid of McArthur. You didn't exactly seem to be enjoying his company," she said after a moment. Her voice had a rich Irish accent and a smooth, throaty tone that sent a shiver down my spine.

"I didn't need to be rescued. I could have handled it myself," I replied tartly.

One eyebrow rose in amusement, and the woman's lips twitched into a small smirk. "I wasn't rescuing you, I was rescuing him."

"Oh?"

"You seemed to be about ten seconds away from cutting off his member and sticking it down his throat. And while he does have terrible manners, terrible manners are not yet punishable by death," she observed, her green eyes flashing in amusement. "Especially not such a death."

"I wasn't planning on killing him. I was just considering a little non-lethal dismemberment. Nothing to be concerned about, really."

The woman actually laughed at that, a rich, throaty sound that sounded pleasantly in my ears.

"I've always enjoyed a good dismemberment myself. Glad I'm not the only vampire that doesn't mind reverting to medieval torture techniques," she said with a grin.

"How interesting," I replied neutrally. "You seem more like the type of vampire who would write sonnets about flowers and midmorning dew."

"I do find flowers quite beautiful, but dismemberment and torture are so much more exciting. However, if you want me to write a sonnet about you, I certainly won't say no," she said with a seductive smile.

I opened my mouth to reply, but was forestalled by the approach of Mr. Collins.

He bowed in our direction, and then addressed himself to me. "Miss Waters, I was wondering whether you might permit me the honor of the next dance."

I sighed as I realized the evening would most likely be filled with men asking me to dance and attempting to make their lives sound interesting. This Irish rebel party was turning out to be quite dull. My eyes left Mr. Collins and found frosted green eyes boring into mine.

"Mr. Collins, I would—", I began.

"Actually, Mr. Collins, Miss Waters has accepted a prior invitation," the handsome woman said as she stepped closer and slid an arm around my waist. Her touch was light but firm, almost possessive.

Mr. Collins studied us for a moment, looking at me, then the woman, then studying her arm around my waist.

"Ah, Miss Abigail Blake. Given your advanced age, I guess it makes sense that you would want to taste a different sort of novelty now and again." Mr. Collins' tone was mocking, almost insulting.

"Age has nothing to do with it. I just know a quality dish when I see one," the woman, Abigail Blake, replied.

My fists clenched at them cavalierly discussing me as if I was a pastry or a meat pie. I was not some dish for either of them to sample as they pleased.

"Be careful, Abigail. People are often inclined to react violently toward anything they consider 'different.' Beware your wandering eye." Mr. Collins punctuated his warning with a glare, then spun on his heel and strode away.

As soon as he was had disappeared into the throng, I turned and slapped Abigail Blake as hard as I could. I have no doubt she could have easily stopped me, but she didn't even make the attempt. I pulled my hand back to slap her again, but this time she caught my arm and held it up above my head. She was so much stronger than I. Vampires get stronger as they age.

"You don't get to strike me again." She took a step closer. "I allowed it once because I deserved it, but no more," Abigail said sternly.

Her eyes bored into mine, and I was acutely aware of our close proximity. Our faces were mere inches apart, and I could see a few small freckles on her nose. My gaze dropped to her lips. They were full, and set in a grim line. Maybe a taste wouldn't be entirely unpleasant.

149

The spell was broken when she released my arm. She didn't step back, though, and I could feel her breath mingle with mine.

"I'm not some object. I'm not a 'meal' or 'dish' that you can sample when it suits your pleasure," I said through gritted teeth.

Her eyes moved to my lips as I spoke, and they had turned a shade darker by the time I had finished.

"I…I know you are not an object, and I apologize for that exchange. Mr. Collins and I hold a mutual hatred for one another. The only thing he values in a woman is whether or not she will take him into her bed. And I just sunk to his level and treated you as an object. I felt shame the moment those words came out of my mouth. That is why I allowed you to hit me. I deserved it."

Her verdant eyes were still on my lips, and her warm breath still mingled with mine.

My gaze dropped to her lips, and I wondered what they would feel like if she kissed me. Would she be rough and aggressive, or gentle and sweet? They looked so soft, so inviting. My fingers twitched as I envisioned tracing her lips with them. And how would it feel to taste her with my tongue?

"Will you dance with me? Please?" Abigail urged softly.

I wanted to dance with her. I craved it. It wasn't rational, it wasn't reasonable, it probably wasn't smart; but at that moment, I wanted her more than anything, despite reason, despite rationality, despite tradition. Her smile, her little smirk, her laugh, her essence—all disarmed my caution and countermanded my common sense. I wanted her, and if she allowed it, I would have her.

"Yes."

She gently took my hand and led me from the room, through some passageways and up some stairs before stopping in a storage room of some sort. I could hear the music from the band coming up through the floorboards.

"I used to live on this estate, and I know my way around. We're directly above the ballroom, in the attic to be precise. Now, about that dance you promised me."

She stepped closer and held out her hand, and I willingly gave her mine. Our fingers intertwined, she led me to the center of the floor, then put her other hand on my waist whilst my free hand went to her shoulder.

Even twenty years earlier, when I was turned at age twenty-four, I had been to a fair number of dances and had danced with many men. I enjoyed the music, but was somewhat indifferent to the actual dancing. The concept of moving in a strict pattern with another person had never really been enjoyable for me. After being turned, I had danced a few times, but with the same indifference. Apparently I'd never had the right partner.

Dancing with Abigail was incredibly different. I reveled in the push and pull of the movement. My skin ached for contact when the steps pulled us apart. Pleasure radiated through my body when we were chest to chest and hand in hand. It was exquisite torture to move away from her and then count the seconds until we were pulled back together again. My body tingled everywhere her fingertips grazed over me. I could feel her trembling as we moved so close that our lips were inches apart. As I studied the contours of her collarbone and chest, I could see that her breathing was labored.

Desire pooled between my legs as we danced and danced, again and again. I barely knew this woman. I had met her less than two hours ago, but every touch, every brush of her fingertips, every look into her eyes made me burn with wanting her. Made me want to sample her skin and capture her full lower lip gently between my teeth.

"Please tell me your first name, Miss Waters," Abigail whispered as the steps brought us close.

My mouth went dry at the husky desire I heard in her voice, but I managed, "Caroline. Caroline Elizabeth Waters."

"As Mr. Collins indicated, my name is Abigail Blake. Please call me Abby."

We had stopped moving, and she had one arm around my waist whilst her free hand gently tucked an errant strand of hair behind my ear.

"Abby," I murmured, mostly to myself, as I lifted my hand and brushed my thumb over her lower lip. It was exquisitely soft, and I once again wondered what it would taste like.

She caught my hand and pressed a kiss against my palm. "Caroline?"

"Yes?"

"Will you accompany me home tonight?"

"Yes."

Her lips parted, and she smiled widely. She gently tugged me along as she led us out of the attic and down some stairs. Our hands were clasped together, and I found it impossible to look away from her. From the small swish of her hips as she walked in front of me to the curve of her chest and contours of her collarbones, she was mesmerizing, and I followed her in a daze of happy infatuation.

We waited beneath the portico outside as her chauffeur brought her Rolls Royce around. A servant handed us into the back seat and shut the car door behind us, and the air grew thick with tension. Once the automobile had begun moving, I glanced at her. Hunger was apparent in her eyes, and I whimpered as she unconsciously bit her lip. I had never felt such depths of desire. A fire was boiling my blood, and she seemed to be the only one capable of extinguishing it.

Abby leaned toward me until our lips were almost touching. "Caroline?"

"Yes?"

"May I kiss you?"

"Please."

Part of me expected her to be rough and demanding. Expected her to crush her lips to mine. Expected her mouth to deny us both oxygen. Expected teeth, sharp nips, and an unforgiving tongue. But she was gentle. Her lips grazed mine with the smallest of kisses, then she paused with our lips millimeters apart and our ragged breath mingling. Her hand cradled my face, and her thumb gently caressed my cheek.

She kissed me again, this time with a bit more pressure. Her lips moved slowly over mine, and my eyes fluttered closed. She tilted her head, and her nose brushed mine as the angle changed. Our lips met again, and this time I was past wanting gentle.

My hand slid around her neck, and I kissed her hard. I took her lip between my teeth and bit it, then soothed the small ache with my tongue. Her mouth opened and when our tongues met, pleasure pulsed though me. She pushed me against the back of the car, and our breasts rubbed together through our dresses. The slight friction made the ache between my legs grow stronger.

I moaned as her mouth left mine and left a trail of hot, wet kisses down my neck. Her kissing and sucking the sensitive skin made my breathing more erratic, and my fingernails clawed at her back. My desire was already dripping down my thighs when I felt the tip of her fangs graze over my neck. I sensed a question in the movement.

152

"Yes," I whispered.

I cried out as she broke the skin and started to gently suck. Slight pain and warm pleasure merged in euphoria as she tasted me, gently sucking at the puncture while I trembled helplessly. Her hand slid under my dress and along my inner thigh, and I moaned as her fingers skimmed across my center as she pushed my panties to one side. She paused again and waited for permission. I clung to her as I nodded my consent.

Her finger began to move in my wetness, teasing me mercilessly, stroking through my folds but ignoring the place where I most wanted her. Her free hand cupping my breast through the material of my dress, she rolled my erect nipple, twisting it and ratcheting up my desire all the more. I shivered at the sensations of her mouth on my neck, her hand on my breast, and her fingers teasing me.

"God...Abby...more. I need more." I felt her smile against my neck as I begged for my release.

She shifted her hand and touched my throbbing clit with her thumb while she slid two fingers deep inside me, and I cried out. The pleasure was blinding, excruciatingly delicious and torturously wonderful. I came instantly, the world exploding in a mist of pleasure and sensation. My thighs trapped her hand as my center contracted around her fingers.

When my orgasm subsided, I collapsed against her. Her mouth left my neck, her hand withdrew, and she wrapped strong arms around me. When she kissed me, I tasted my blood on her lips. She held me tightly as I recovered from her attentions.

"Thank you for letting me make love to you, Caroline," she whispered into my ear as her hand stroked my hair. I tried to think of something witty to say, but my mind was still recovering, so I just stated the truth.

"That was incredible."

"I'm almost a thousand years old, I ought to be incredible."

"No false modesty for you, huh?"

"No. I know just how incredible I am," she said with a smile that made my insides melt.

I didn't know it at that moment, but I would spend the next hundred years learning just how incredible she was.

I blinked twice as my thoughts returned to the present. Abby was pressed against my back, kissing my neck softly.

"Do you remember it, Caroline? Do you remember that day almost a hundred years ago?" Abby asked again.

I smiled. "Yes. I don't think I could ever forget it."

"You remember that we had to hide our relationship for so long. We were always running, because people couldn't accept us. No one cared that we were vampires, they just hated the idea that it was a woman who held my heart." Abby's hands tightened around me.

"I remember it all. I remember being terrified you wouldn't come home. I remember all the running. We ran so many times. I know you miss Ireland. I know you want to go back home."

"I do miss Ireland, sweetheart, but being with you is worth any amount of homesickness. Just being able to wrap you in my arms and kiss your neck makes all the running and everything and anything else worthwhile." She tickled my neck with gentle butterfly kisses.

"Being with you, Abby,…its…its…I'm so happy we have forever to be together."

"Forever. I love hearing you say that." Abby nuzzled against me. "Do you know what happened in Ireland today?"

"No. What happened?"

"They legalized gay marriage by popular vote."

"That's wonderful, Abby! That's amazing—"

One of her hands left my stomach, and I instantly missed the contact.

"It means I can marry you legally, Caroline. It means we can have an official 'forever.' Let me take you home, Caroline. Let me commit to you. Let me be your forever."

My breath caught in my throat as I realized where she was leading. She kissed my neck again, then held her closed fist in front of me and opened her hand. She was holding a gorgeous ring with a beautiful yet simple band and a brilliant diamond that was not too small but not ostentatiously large. It was perfect. Like Abby.

Abby's arm tightened around my waist as she whispered into my ear, "Caroline?"

"Yes?"

"Will you marry me?"

"Yes!"

The instant the word was out of my mouth, Abby spun me around and kissed me. It was hard, passionate, but not overly rough or aggressive. I kissed her back the same way, passionate and gentle, a kiss mean to convey love, not hunger.

After a moment she broke the kiss and reached for my hand. She took it, looked at me, then said, "Are you sure?"

"Yes! I'm sure. I love you, you senile idiot. The real question is whether you still want to marry me, since Nat will be my man of honor."

Abby sighed dramatically, then smiled. "If having Nat in our wedding means having you on my arm, my ring on your finger and a bigger smile on your face, then I'll give the damn demon his invitation personally," Abby replied.

"Good. Now give me the damn ring."

She laughed and slipped on the ring onto my finger before moving in for another kiss.

I could kiss Abby forever, and that's what I planned on doing.

Rowan

BY EMMA STERNER-RADLEY

ANNABELLE RAN PAST ANOTHER OF the peculiarly bent trees that was a landmark for her. In the dark, it was difficult to find her way, but she had run this path so many times that she had identified trees whose unique appearance stuck in her mind, and they were guiding her to her destination.

She was breathing rapidly, partly from the running and partly from fear. She was horribly afraid of the dark, so it was particularly cruel that she had to make this nocturnal trek every evening. She was running from her imagination, which was painting monsters on every tree and behind every bush. It was the middle of October and the trees had shed their leaves like tears, and she heard the leaves crunching under her feet as if they were the steps of some creature in pursuit. She cursed her own slowness. But it would be worth it. It was always worth it.

Soon she would be with the girl she loved, and here, in the dark of night, her parents couldn't stop her. Here, in the dark of night, she and her love were safe from people's prying eyes and free from the preacher's judgmental Bible quotations. Even on the eve of the 20th century, it was hard enough for a girl to love a girl, but to love a girl who wasn't human... That was so much worse.

Sweat trickled from her hair line, her lower back, and even her underarms. The autumn air and her fear of the darkness made it cold sweat, but that didn't ease her concern that she would not smell very nice when she reached her beloved.

As she waited for her parents to finally fall asleep, Annabelle had spent a lot of time getting ready. She had tied her chestnut brown hair with ribbons and put on her nice beige woollen dress, adding a cherry red cardigan on top for extra warmth. She had borrowed her mother's rouge, powder, and lipstick and applied it sparingly. She would have to remember to return them in the morning, before her mother could miss them.

It was ridiculous that she was forbidden the use of cosmetics. She was eighteen and should have her own make-up, but her father said no make-up for her until she had a husband. At least she was allowed to keep the bottle of rosewater her grandmother gave her each birthday. She had applied it a little too liberally, and hopefully the sweet rose scent would cover up the not-so-sweet smell of the cold sweat.

Wait! What was that! Was that a moving shadow on the ground next to her? Yes. Yes, those were footsteps! Yes, that was breathing. Yes, that was her heart beating so hard it hurt.

Annabelle didn't dare turn around. She tried her best to convince herself that it was just her imagination frightening her once more. The fine hairs on her neck and arms stood up, and she prayed a silent prayer that she would soon be at her destination, safe in her lover's arms.

Whatever horror was behind her moved closer, and she had the sudden feeling that it was smaller than she had first thought. Still, she ran faster, but so did her pursuer. Before long, it overtook her, and as the moon peered out between the clouds, brightening the dark night at that exact moment, Annabelle could make out that was actually... A large badger!

The poor thing scurried off to the right, probably running away from her. Oh, the tricks her fear played on her! She gave a breathless laugh, which came out as a wheeze and slowed her running. She must almost be there now, and she didn't want to pass out before she reached their trysting place.

Her legs ached, filled with lactic acid, no doubt. She had a bad stitch in her side, and her lungs felt as if she had inhaled ice. It didn't matter now, though, because in front of her was the rowan tree. The wind blew through the almost naked branches, loosening some of the lingering leaves and sending them trickling down towards her. Still breathing heavily, she kicked a few leaves out of her way with her low-heeled, lace-up black boots and walked up to the tree, suddenly feeling almost carefree.

Annabelle moved close enough to rest her hand on the bark. In the chilly autumn air, it felt almost warm to the touch. She felt a sudden ripple go through the bark against her palm. Gasping softly, she backed away with a smile.

Freeing itself from the rowan was a humanoid figure. Covered in bark and with moss on its legs, it emerged from the trunk of the tree with creaking noises and the low hum of a female voice. The hum vibrated through Annabelle's skin, and her heart felt as if it was pumping brandy through her veins.

When the creature was completely free from the tree, Annabelle watched as its bark-like skin slowly faded to the texture of human skin. It was brilliant white, like moonlight, and seemed to glimmer like a pearl in the dim light of the forest. Oh, how she longed to touch it! She breathed her lover's name. "Rowan."

The dryad smiled at her and extended her hand. Annabelle reached out, and their fingertips brushed. Rowan's delighted giggle filled the night with a clear, tinkling sound. It reminded Annabelle of a silver bell ringing and reverberating in a quiet room. She couldn't contain herself any longer. She ran to Rowan and clasped the otherworldly creature in an eager embrace, pressing their bodies together.

Rowan's melodic voice murmured, "You do not have a coat, my love. Are you not cold?"

"No. Last time I got too warm running here in my coat, so tonight I decided to make do with a cardigan. Anyway, you are one to speak. You are nude!" Annabelle nuzzled the warm, naked skin of the dryad's shoulder.

Rowan shifted back slightly and gave another of her beautiful but almost eerie laughs. "I am a wood nymph. I feel what my tree feels, and my rowan tree does not feel cold."

Annabelle looked down with a bashful smile. "Of course." She didn't dare to say out loud what she was thinking—that she was glad that no clothes hid Rowan's body from her eyes and her touch. She traced the line of one of Rowan's collar bones with reverent fingers, and smiled as the caress gave rise to goosebumps on the wood nymph's skin.

"You seem cold now, my dearest," Annabelle said with a mischievous smile.

The dryad took her hand and brought it to her lips. They felt soft but dry against her knuckles, where the first kiss landed. Rowan kissed her way up the palm to Annabelle's wrist before stopping. "How are you doing tonight, my love?" she asked.

"Better, now that I am with you." Annabelle moved in for a kiss from the warm lips, anticipating the taste of leaves and autumn spices she would find there.

The next morning was a Saturday. Annabelle wished it wasn't. Saturdays meant that her parents were home all day and would spend the day berating her for any little nit they could pick. These days they would usually focus on her constant state of fatigue, to the point that her mama had even talked about calling for a doctor. Annabelle could hardly tell them that she was tired because she was sneaking out at night, running far into the wild forest to seek out her supernatural lover and spend the night in her embrace, talking and making love until the darkness began to dissipate and the threat of sunrise loomed over them.

True to form, her father now looked at her over his teacup and muttered, "No one will ever want to marry you looking like that, girl. Your skin has a deathly pallor, and the darkness under your eyes is beginning to look like bruises!"

Annabelle stifled a yawn and in a studiedly polite voice murmured, "Does it matter, Papa? Anyway, we are too close to the mountains to find appropriate suitors for me. At least that is what Mama says."

Just then her mother entered the room and commented tersely, "Yes, it is. However, we should begin to travel into town and make a more concerted effort to find you a husband. We could visit my sister. She could introduce us to the right sort of people. But before we do that, you must start getting more sleep, and perhaps more iron. I will ask the cook to serve red meat tonight, and maybe you should have a drop of port before you go to sleep. We will get some roses into your cheeks, even if it kills me! I won't stand for you looking like that."

Annabelle nodded dejectedly. She hoped that the port wouldn't make her fall asleep, making her late for her nightly meeting with Rowan. She had been drunk the first time she met the dryad. It was her eighteenth birthday, and she had been feeling stifled in the house filled with her parents' acquaintances from church and a variety of distant relations. Her Uncle George had snuck her glass after glass of champagne, and Annabelle's head was swimming with the sweet alcohol. She went outside to clear her head, and in the distance she could see the forest that began at the edge of their vast back garden.

She didn't know why she had started walking towards the woods, but she suspected it was her intent to get away from her strict parents and the house full of inebriated adults, all telling her what she should do with her life now that she had turned eighteen.

Soon she was beyond the first trees, and still she didn't turn back. She supposed it had been the champagne which helped her battle through her fear of the dark and keep moving forward. She stumbled around for a long time, her head filled with thoughts of future husbands, possible missionary work, and all the other things people were telling her were vital to her now.

Eventually she had entered a clearing with a large rowan tree at the edge of it. Leaning against the tree and watching her with an amused smile was the most beautiful creature she had ever seen. The appearance was that of a young woman, but her skin and eyes could not have been those of a normal person. The skin shone and glimmered like human skin never did, and her eyes were a brilliant green that was almost yellow, and seemed to glow in the dark.

Thick auburn hair splayed over the young woman's shoulders, falling to cover her clearly naked breasts and ending at her navel. The thatch of hair between the girl's legs was the same striking colour. Annabelle remembered that detail clearly. She remembered noting the contrast between the dark auburn hair and the white, glittering skin. She also remembered the exotic creature giving a little chuckle when she caught Annabelle staring between her legs. Even in her champagne daze, Annabelle had the decency to feel horrible about having stared, and she mumbled a profuse apology.

"Do not fret, pretty thing. You may look. The forest has no secrets that it is not willing to share with a curious soul," the extraordinary creature said with a welcoming smile.

Annabelle dared to look up again, and gazed into the odd but beautiful eyes. She was caught. Caught in the air of charm, the sweetness and strangeness of the one who soon pronounced that she was a dryad. The word had sounded foreign to Annabelle's ears.

She had tried to shape the word in her mouth. "Dr...dryad?"

"Yes. Some prefer the term wood nymph. You humans typically believe that we are mythical, but as you can see, we are very real indeed. We are just rare, and very good at hiding. We live our lives tending to one tree, to which we are bound. We can be inside our tree or outside of it, but we cannot travel far from it. Most of my kind reside farther away from humans. Dryads tend to live in more dense forests which are located in more inhospitable parts of the world."

Annabelle looked around the glade and felt her body sway at the champagne still in her system. "Well, we are close to the mountains here, and there are not many houses this far out. I can see why you settled here."

The dryad laughed her tinkling laugh. "Oh, I didn't so much settle here as I grew here. My tree was growing in this clearing before your houses were built."

Annabelle's tipsy mind tried to catch up with the implications of that. "But...but our house was built twenty years ago!"

The dryad nodded. "By your way of counting time, my tree would be about sixty years old, I believe."

"Does that...make you sixty years old?" Annabelle asked, incredulous.

"I suppose so, yes. But time moves differently for us, sweet one. We spend a lot of time sleeping inside the tree, sharing its life force."

Annabelle blinked. "But you don't look older than me!"

The dryad laughed once more. "I was created looking like this." She gestured at herself. "My physical form doesn't age, only my tree ages. My soul is tied to the tree. If it gets hurt or dies, so do I. Otherwise I just continue my existence like this, seeing the seasons change and watching the forest evolve around me."

"Doesn't that get lonely?" Annabelle asked tentatively.

The dryad was quiet for a while as her gaze moved from Annabelle to the night sky, and then back to Annabelle.

"Yes. Yes, it does. That is why I decided not to hide when you came stumbling into this clearing. I thought that you looked like a person who could keep a secret, unlike most humans, who would either hurt me because they were frightened of me, or wish to use me to their advantage. I have seen humans before, and the trees all tell tales of how your kind use and destroy what is around you."

Annabelle frowned. "Not all of us."

The dryad glided closer to Annabelle, her motions slow and fluid, almost as if she wasn't subject to the same rules of gravity as humans. She reached up with long elegant fingers and brushed a stray strand of hair away from Annabelle's face. "No, I suppose not. You feel…different. Kind, curious, and…lost."

"Lost?" Annabelle echoed, trying to keep a drunken slur out of her speech.

"Yes, lost. As if you do not know what you are or what you are meant for."

Annabelle looked down at her feet. "I suppose I don't know those things. Do you?"

The dryad smirked mischievously. "You look to me like you were meant for kissing."

Annabelle had giggled nervously then. "I cannot kiss another girl, especially not a naked girl who is actually a tree, and a complete stranger as well! My father would never let me out of the house again."

"I cannot change that I am female, nor that I am a wood nymph. I can cover myself with leaves if you would like."

"No! I mean, no, please don't," Annabelle mumbled, blushing crimson.

The dryad tilted her head to eye Annabelle, and then gave a warm smile. "At least I am becoming less of a stranger. You are getting to know me right now."

"You would be less of a stranger if I knew your name. My name is Annabelle Fairlight. What do I call you? I can hardly call you 'dryad,' any more than you could call me 'human.'"

162

"Perhaps you could call me Rowan, as the tree to which I am bound is this majestic rowan tree." She caressed the bark of the tree beside her.

Annabelle was suddenly drawn from her memories of that first night by her father shaking her shoulder.

"Girl! Are you even listening to me? There you go again, daydreaming your time away like some penniless poet. It won't do, Annabelle. You must get yourself together!"

"Yes, Papa. I'm sorry," Annabelle replied, with yet another stifled yawn.

The day droned away in boring tasks like piano lessons, practising her needlework, and endless sermons from her mother on posture and poise. Luckily her mother went out on some errands and her father had locked himself away in his study, so Annabelle stole a much needed nap in her room in the afternoon.

As darkness began to fall, Annabelle felt herself coming alive. It was almost as if the daylight drained her and the falling night replenished her energy, feeding her soul the nutrients it needed. Annabelle felt as if she lived for her moments with Rowan. Those were the only times she felt alive and like herself—no more pretence, no holding her tongue to keep from saying the wrong thing, and no mind-numbing boredom.

As soon as the house fell quiet that night, she hurried to Rowan. She ran through the forest, again chased by her own fears, which were slightly calmed by the glass of port her mother had made her drink before bed. Oh how she wished she didn't have to meet her beloved in the dark forest. Starting every meeting frightened and out of breath wasn't ideal. But if that was the way it had to be, it was worth it.

This night she found Rowan already out of her tree, walking through the clearing, playing with her long, auburn hair. Annabelle ran to her and threw herself into the nymph's arms. Rowan clasped her close and buried her slim, slightly upturned nose in Annabelle's hair. Their lips met, and each put her longing and joy at seeing the other into the kiss. Annabelle felt more intoxicated by that kiss than she had from the port.

When their lips slowly parted company, Annabelle breathed, "I've missed you!"

Rowan tightened her grip around the young woman's slim waist and whispered, "And I, you."

Annabelle gave a gleeful laugh and grabbed Rowan as if to dance with her. Humming a waltz, she attempted to swing them around, but Rowan's feet didn't move. She stared at Annabelle's hand clasping her own in the air, and then peered up at the brunette's face as if she had lost her mind.

"Annabelle? What are you doing?"

"Dancing! I just suddenly felt like dancing! Don't you know how to waltz? Oh, how silly of me. Why would a dryad know how to waltz? Well, it is movement we humans do to music. I can show you, if you like."

"If you wish. May I enquire what the purpose of this 'waltz' is?" Rowan asked, her brow knitting.

"It's fun! And it is a jolly good way to be close to your partner's body," Annabelle added, a saucy gleam in her eye.

Rowan quirked an eyebrow and grinned. "I can think of better ways for our bodies to be close, my love. The moss is dry tonight, and not too cold. Lie down on it with me, and I'll show you."

Annabelle laughed and slapped Rowan's bare hip playfully. "Plenty of time for that later. Let me teach you how to dance. Don't worry, I'll lead."

She placed one hand around Rowan's waist and grabbed the dryad's hand with her other. "Good. Now watch my feet and count to three in your head. Like this."

Annabelle counted the three beats of the waltz out loud and moved her feet in time. She did it a few times until she saw Rowan's feet begin to follow her movements quite accurately. Given the dryad's fluid movements, she seemed a born dancer. Despite her inexperience, she soon followed Annabelle's lead as they waltzed around the clearing in the moonlight.

What a sight they were: Rosy-cheeked Annabelle in a warm, sage-coloured dress and a grey knitted cardigan, and pale Rowan, with her pearlescent skin and her auburn hair blowing freely in the wind. Both were laughing and stealing kisses whenever they did not have to watch their feet or the surrounding trees to keep from colliding with anything.

Annabelle tried to hum a waltz by Strauss, not recalling if it was Strauss the first or the second, but found that the giggling and kissing were making it difficult to focus. Her heart felt so light! Rowan's body seemed to meld with her own, almost the same way as when they made love, and the moment felt as perfect as a glittering diamond.

It was bound to happen, of course. Whirling around as they were, they were destined to misstep at some point. It turned out to be a rock under Annabelle's foot that initiated the fall. She tripped over it and began to tumble down, grabbing on to Rowan for support and unfortunately pulling the nymph down with her.

They landed in the moss, just as Rowan had earlier suggested they should. As they looked into each other's glittering eyes, they knew that they would soon be doing what Rowan had mentioned too. Annabelle was lying on top of the naked dryad, suddenly very aware of the woman's shape underneath her. Her blood sang with desire, and she leant down for a kiss. Her eyes closed, and her heart leapt with bliss. This was the pinnacle of happiness for both of them, and they savoured it as they lost themselves in delightful explorations.

The next morning Annabelle noticed a love bite, starkly dark on her pale breast. She stared at it, her fingers tracing the outline of the mark made by her lover. It felt odd, seeing something connected to Rowan while in her house and in the bright morning light. Their love was a hidden treasure that gleamed in moonlight, but now it had somehow reached out and touched the rest of her life with this little red mark.

Annabelle gave a happy sigh as she touched it reverently. This mark was so much more real than all of her mundane life. Rowan's beautiful mouth had made this, and now she would know that it rested under her clothes, close to her heart all day. She felt as if nothing her parents said or did could touch her today. Like a magical talisman, this mark would keep her safe and floating happily above their reproach and snide comments.

Another day passed in a haze of boredom and sleep deprivation, though Annabelle and Rowan did always rest a little while during their nights together. They would lie there talking and marvelling at each other's beauty, until Annabelle's yawns got more and more frequent. Rowan would tell her to rest for a spell, and after a few automatic refusals, Annabelle would succumb to a couple of hours of sleep. She never knew whether Rowan slept as well, but the dryad would wake her in plenty of time to return home before sunrise.

However, the two hour naps did little for her as the day moved on, and she wondered for the hundredth time if there wasn't a way for her and Rowan to be together without having to hide in the night. Soon winter would come, and then it would be difficult for them to meet outside. Rowan had promised her that when her parents passed away and Annabelle inherited the estate, then they could be together in the daytime, as long as Annabelle didn't have guests. But her parents were only in their mid-forties and would surely live a long time yet, so that had no bearing on their problem with meeting in the upcoming winter cold.

Annabelle sat reading a book which her mother had assured her would be good for her mind. Her eyes were in the book but her hand was on her chest, covering the mark hidden under her clothes, and her mind was in the forest. Was Rowan sleeping in her tree now? Or was she awake, waiting for her return and perhaps missing her? The day inched on at a snail's pace, and Annabelle saw it through with her hand frequently but discreetly seeking out the love bite on her breast. She heard her father and mother whispering about her behind her back, but ignored their worried voices murmuring thoughts on what might be wrong with their only child.

Blessed night finally arrived, and Annabelle ran through the forest to see Rowan, wondering to herself if this trek would ever cease to terrify her. She thought she heard steps behind her and wondered whether it was her imagination—another badger, or maybe a monster of some kind. She shook off her fear as well as she could and ran faster. When she reached the rowan tree, she saw her lover sitting high up in the tree, gently stroking an owl which was perched on the same branch with her.

"Hello up there! Come down here to me," Annabelle called up to the dryad, holding out her arms as if to catch her beloved in her descent.

In perfect control of her movements as always, Rowan lithely swung her body off the branch and landed with only a slight thud right in front of Annabelle, and then fell into the arms of her human lover. They kissed with an eagerness only a full day apart can bring, and Annabelle laid her head against Rowan's shoulder as she waited for her breathing to return to normal after her run.

"Did you miss me, my love?"

"As much as the flowers miss summer, dearest girl." Rowan planted a soft kiss on Annabelle's head.

Their lips met in another kiss, and Annabelle let her hands travel down Rowan's bare back while thinking about how the dryad's shimmering skin felt more like home than any building she had ever found herself in.

There was a noise in the bushes, and they both snapped around towards it. There was a shadow there, the shadow of a man. Rowan quickly stepped in front of Annabelle, shielding the young woman with her body. The man wasn't moving, and it was clear that he either hadn't been hiding or had just arrived. He had simply been standing there, and he must have seen them embrace and kiss. He took a step forward, and the moonlight illuminated his face. It was Annabelle's father.

His gaze locked on hers. "Annabelle, you will return home with me without delay!"

"Papa! What are you doing here?"

"Your mother said that she heard noises last night and believed you were sneaking out of the house. I promised her that if that was the case, I would follow you and see what it is you do all night to make you such a sleepwalker during the days. Now I see that you have been seduced by this vile...creature," he hissed, staring at Rowan.

Annabelle saw the fury in her father's eyes and realised that whatever discussion might arise out of this should be held when they were away from Rowan, or her father might attempt to harm the nymph.

Annabelle trembled with shock and fear. "Alright, Papa. I will come home with you now." She stepped away from Rowan, giving the dryad a look that was meant to comfort her but probably scared her even more.

"Are you certain, Annabelle?" Rowan whispered.

Annabelle nodded dejectedly.

"My daughter knows what is best for her." Edward Fairlight grabbed Annabelle's wrist and began to drag her away from the clearing.

Annabelle cast one last glance at Rowan as she was pulled away, and she saw her lover hold up her hand in a sad wave.

As she and her father trudged back to their home, he pummelled her with questions.

"What was that monster? Where does it live? How long has this been going on? Was this why you have shown no interest in young men?"

Through tears and sobs, Annabelle tried to answer the barrage of questions, and soon her father knew more about what a dryad was and what his daughter was doing consorting with one.

When they were home and the door closed behind them, her father gripped her shoulders and hissed, "Your mother is asleep, so I don't expect you to wake her. Go upstairs, wash your face, and go to bed. We will discuss your punishment tomorrow."

"A-are you not g-going to sleep?" Annabelle sobbed.

"No. Thanks to you, I am *not* going to sleep. Now leave my sight before I take my belt to you!"

Annabelle hurried up the stairs to her room. Too frightened, sad, and exhausted to do anything but cry, she decided to forego washing her face and getting into her shift. She thought she heard the front door open downstairs, and assumed her father had gone out to clear his mind or to walk off his anger. She laid on the bed with the pillow over her head to cover her sobs, and that was how she fell asleep.

The next morning, Annabelle took her time getting washed and dressed. She wanted to delay the moment when she would have to face her parents. When she finally got downstairs, she saw her father by the fireplace. He heard her approaching steps and turned to look at her. His face wore an odd look of grim satisfaction.

"Good morning, Annabelle."

"Good morning, Papa," she replied in a small voice, trying to ascertain the nature of her father's strange mood.

"It is a chilly morning. Luckily this fire I just lit is burning bright and fast. It seems that rowan wood burns well." He turned to look at Annabelle's mother, who was coming in from the kitchen and smiling proudly at her husband. They both turned their heads to look pointedly at Annabelle.

Her father's words hit Annabelle like a blow. *Rowan wood burns well.* Rowan's tree! He couldn't have!

In an instant she was out the front door, running toward the woods. She ran even faster than she ever had when she'd thought that all hell's devils and monsters were chasing her. Her heart pounded, and a voice in her head kept repeating, *Please say it's not true, please say Rowan is alright.*

The run to the clearing felt as if it took twice as long as usual, despite her fear giving wings to her feet. Her whole body ached and burned. When she finally arrived, her vision was blurred from running so fast and from unshed tears brimming in her eyes.

Soon the tears fell in abundance. All that was left of the rowan tree was a poorly chopped stump, scattered branches, and stray bits of wood. To Annabelle, it was a murder scene, and she fell to her knees by the stump. Rowan was tied to the health of her tree, and the tree had been hacked down and then burned at her father's hands.

Annabelle keened to the skies as she realised that the sound of the front door opening and closing that she had heard must have been her father going back to Rowan, armed with an axe. Annabelle's wails were like wind through shattered glass, but she was beyond caring about what anyone thought, should they hear her.

Her one solace, her one freedom, and the most remarkable creature to ever grace this earth…were gone. She felt like she had been chopped to bits as well, and through streaming tears she looked around, thinking to see huge stains of dried blood. But she knew that the life force shed by the tree and its nymph was the sap she could see spattered on the ground.

Annabelle clung to the butchered stump, and her tears soaked its surface. Her screams and wails were interrupted only by the occasional heart wrenching cry of "No!" and "Anything but this!"

Her father hadn't followed her. No one intruded upon her grief and pain. She cried herself dry and then lay there, huddled over the stump as if it was the only haven in a sea of uncertainty.

The sun was high in the sky when Annabelle finally become aware of her surroundings again. She knew she couldn't stay by the stump for the rest of her life. She had to find either a way to continue her life, or a way to end it. Perhaps, if there was a heaven, she could be with Rowan in the afterlife. If dryads had an afterlife.

Annabelle started at seeing an old woman standing on the other side of the clearing. She had not heard her arrive. But the old lady looked innocent enough, with a brown shawl covering her shoulders and her basket full of mushrooms.

"Sorry to frighten you, little one. I heard your weeping and came to see that all was well." The crone squinted closely at Annabelle.

"No. Nothing is well," Annabelle sobbed tiredly as she slowly sat up. Her joints creaked from having been hunched over the tree stump for so long.

"I can see that, lass. Why don't you tell an old woman what ails you. I might know a way to arrange things more to your liking."

"Highly unlikely, Madam," Annabelle scoffed. "My one true love has been killed by my own father."

The old woman peered at the tree stump. "You mean the wood nymph who lived in that there rowan tree?"

Annabelle stopped wiping her nose and looked straight at the old woman. "You knew her?"

"Well, I wouldn't say that. But I live in these woods, and I've come across her a few times. We would both keep a respectful distance, though. Fascinating critters, those nymphs, much better than people," she said with a nod.

"That is most certainly true," Annabelle whispered, as she picked up a small, broken branch.

The old woman set down her basket and hobbled over to Annabelle. She took the branch from trembling hands and scrutinized it closely.

"I'd venture to say that the nymph was ever so keen on you."

"Why do you say that?" Annabelle asked.

"Because this tree gave plenty of berries this year. More than it has in the last ten years, I'd say."

"Oh really?" Annabelle replied politely.

"Yes indeed. I kept a lot of the berries and dried them. Good red berries to ward off evil spirits and to keep a body hale and healthy."

Confused, Annabelle looked up with a sceptical look. "Ward off evil spirits?"

The woman handed the branch back to Annabelle. "Aye, dear girl. What else would an old woman living in the forest and knowing about nymphs be, if not a witch?"

Annabelle was a bit annoyed that someone would talk of such nonsense when she was so mired in grief. "Witches are just fairy tales."

The old woman straightened her decrepit back and peered directly into Annabelle's brown eyes. "Oh, and wood nymphs are not? I am as real as that pale girl you love, dearie!"

Annabelle was appropriately chastened. "Yes, of course. I'm sorry, I am not myself right now."

"Of course not, child. Oh, it makes me sad to see a lovely young thing like you so heartbroken." The witch wrung her hands. "Ah, but perhaps I can help you."

Annabelle saw the woman's face brighten. Trying not to to let hope take root in her heart, she asked timidly, "What do you mean?"

"As I said, the berries were bountiful this year. I used some of them in potions and ointments, but I saved the rest. I parched them carefully and put them in a jar. With a little magic, I could bring them back from their preserved state, and we could plant them. I am almost certain that if that tree grew again, your nymph would be brought back with it. This time we could make sure she was planted far away from humans, to keep her safe. This forest is huge. It grows all the way up to the Scottish border. We could plant it there."

Her eyes aching from crying, Annabelle stared at the witch, feeling burgeoning hope taking root and spreading its tendrils throughout her. In a quaking voice, she said, "Y-you could really make Rowan live again?"

The witch smiled. "I think so, lass."

"Do it! What can I do to help? Anything! Just plant her far away from my father, by the border as you suggested. If your legs are not up for the long walk, I'll do it. I'll do it even if it kills me!"

The witch looked at her pensively. "You do realise that you won't be able to visit her. She'll be too far away for you to sneak to her easily, and if your father follows you again… Well, best not, eh?"

Annabelle nodded gravely. "I…hadn't expected to. In fact, I don't know what I am going to do. I cannot remain living in my parents' house. I can't face Papa again, after what he did. He killed my one true love without a second thought, and Mama seemed proud of him for it! How can I even sit down to breakfast with them after that? I don't know what I am going to do, but that does not matter now. Please, help Rowan. Bring her back to life."

"Just to have you scurry off to drown yourself in the river, sweet child? I should think not! No, if I am to help you, I will complete the task properly, and that means reuniting the lovers. Let me think for a wee second here." She walked over to Annabelle and started to sit down on the tree stump.

Annabelle wanted to tell her not to sit on the remains of her beloved. She also wanted to point out that the unevenly chopped stump would not be comfortable. But this woman was her only hope of bringing Rowan back, so she kept quiet and sat there staring hopefully at the extraordinarily wizened face.

"Aye. I…think I might know of a way. But it is potentially dangerous, and it will mean you can never see your family or friends again. You must consider carefully before you decide."

"But I can be with Rowan?" Annabelle's eyes grew wide, and the tendrils of hope spread even further and wrapped around her pained heart.

"Yes, child. Just the two of you, for a very, very long time."

"Then no matter what it entails, my answer is yes. I shall miss my mama a little, and maybe one day I'll even miss Papa. But I was always a disappointment to them, and that led to them being a disappointment to me. Perhaps parting ways will make us all better people," Annabelle said in a quiet voice.

The witch was looking at her closely, maybe deciding whether it was determination she was seeing in Annabelle's eyes. Apparently convinced she spoke again.

"If that be so, I would say that we bind your soul to some sort of seed, nut, or berry of a tree, and plant it next to your ladylove."

Annabelle's breath caught in her chest, and wheezed, "You mean... *make me a dryad*? You can do that?"

"Aye, but it is not an easy task, child. It will be very painful as your soul is wrenched from your body, and there is always a small risk that it does not take."

Annabelle frowned. "Does not take?"

"Yes. There is a wee risk that your soul won't enter the thing to be planted. But then, if that is the case, it will just go back into your body, so I shouldn't worry so much about that." The witch patted Annabelle's shoulder.

"I want to do it! Whatever physical pain it might cause me will be better than facing a life without my Rowan."

The witch gave her another piercing look and then sombrely nodded. "Come along then, child. My hut is this way."

The hut smelled of herbs, smoke, and goat's milk. Annabelle stood next to the witch, who was looking at a collection of jars and bottles on a shelf.

In a croaking voice, the aged woman muttered, "Now, you will have to choose what kind of tree you wish to tie yourself to. Choose wisely. You might spend hundreds of years in it. You want it to be a strong kind of tree so you don't have to suffer in the face of blights or endure the risk of being blown over in high winds."

Annabelle chewed the inside of her cheek. She knew very little of trees and nature. "I...I'm not sure. My mama always says I have chestnut-coloured hair. Perhaps a chestnut tree?"

"Oh, child, I'm afraid I don't have any chestnuts, or even conkers. They just don't grow in these here woods. You'll want something which would typically flourish here. Then there would be a greater chance of it taking to the soil and growing properly."

Embarrassed, Annabelle shrugged. "Then I don't know. What kind of offshoots do you have?"

"Hmm. How about an oak? I know I have some acorns here. The witch who taught me said that wood nymphs are often found in oaks. Good hale and sturdy trees, they are. It will make a loyal, mighty and true companion to your ladylove's rowan tree. They're pretty, too. At least I think they are."

"Alright. Make me an oak." Annabelle smiled her first true smile of the day. She now realised that not only was there hope in her heart, there was also a curious excitement coursing through her. She had found a path to follow, and she was starting a new life. It wasn't being a missionary, finding a good husband, becoming some noble lady's companion, or even joining a convent; it was settling down with the woman she loved and spending hundreds of years learning about the nature around them and tending to their trees together. She giggled to herself as she thought that they might adopt some small bush or sapling to raise as their child. That engendered a question in her mind.

"May I enquire about something?" Annabelle dared to ask the witch, who was now busy arranging the ingredients for the ritual.

"Of course, child," the old woman replied absentmindedly as she placed a cluster of dried rowan berries and an acorn on the worn table in front of them.

"Why hasn't Rowan come back in any of the trees that were... sprouted from the berries through the years?"

The witch stopped what she was doing and thought about that for a moment. "You know, I've never seen anything grow from them there berries, but I think that might be because the tree had a guardian, its nymph. Perhaps it didn't have the same need to breed, to further its existence, because it was guarded. Or maybe it couldn't have other saplings, as that would have meant the nymph would have had to care for several trees. Anyway, the nymph is gone now, so the tree should want to breed to save its existence in these here woods."

Quite impressed by the wisdom of the answers, Annabelle swallowed down her questions regarding how a woman who lived in a hut in the forest understood so much and knew some quite big words. She had to focus on what was important, not on who this strange woman was.

"What if it doesn't? What if those berries are...barren somehow?" Frightened of the answer, Annabelle looked down at her hands rather than looking at the witch.

"Then I will feel it as I try to bring them back from their shrivelled state, child. And we will deal with that trouble if it arrives. Now, go get me a sharp knife from that drawer over there."

Annabelle obeyed, and readily found a long, sharp knife with a wooden handle inscribed with strange markings. As she looked at it, for the first time she felt some fear about the impending ritual.

When she returned to the table, the old woman was holding one hand over the cluster of berries and the other over the acorn. She was swaying as she murmured inaudibly. Soon Annabelle saw the desiccated items burst back into colour and fullness of life.

The witch turned to Annabelle and smiled widely, so wide that Annabelle could see that she was missing quite a few teeth.

"Well now, girl, if there isn't something live in these here berries, I'm a toadstool."

Annabelle's heart leapt with joy. *Rowan*. She was in those berries, and she could live again!

"Now for the tricky part, child. You have to be in here." The aged woman pointed to the acorn.

Annabelle's mouth seemed to go dry, and her muscles tensed in anticipation of what they might soon be feeling. She nervously licked her lips.

"You must trust me completely, lassie. I'll need your heartsblood on this here acorn. That means this knife will have to nick your heart to bring out a drop or two to place on the acorn."

Annabelle's eyes went wide, and she held her breath for a moment. "A cut? Straight into my heart? But surely that will kill me!"

"Sweet girl, I am 138 years old. I know how to preserve life. I will not let you die here today, not as long as you do what I say. I will give you something to drink which will dull your senses, but the extraction will still hurt and it will still be frightening. And, you must not move even a wee bit. If you move, the knife might damage your heart in ways I cannot mend, and if the transfer of your essence doesn't work, your soul would have to return to a dying body."

Annabelle swallowed thickly. Her heart was pounding so hard, it made her dizzy. "Alright. I will keep still," she replied in a faint voice.

"Good. You can still change your mind, lass. I will need a while to prepare the potion for you to drink and to get the herbs that together with your heartsblood will bind you to the acorn. Think on it for a while. Think on how your parents will find out that you are lost to them. I'll lower your empty body into the river a little further away from my hut, and it will soon float down the river and be found, I'm sure. Your parents will probably think you did away with yourself out of grief. That is a lot of guilt to place on their shoulders."

Annabelle thought about the smile on her mother's face and the satisfied twinkle in her father's eyes as he burned the logs of rowan tree, and replied darkly, "It is a just punishment."

The witch cast her another assessing glance and then nodded. "Still, take a moment to think on it as I prepare."

Annabelle did think about it. No matter how she pondered it, she knew that she had to do this. No other choice could ever bring her peace. She swallowed down her fear of that sharp knife entering her heart and the risk of death if she panicked and moved. She gave a mirthless laugh as she thought about how frightened she had been of running through the dark woods. How did that silly fear compare to what she was about to do? How did it compare to the fear of never seeing Rowan again? The forest would never scare her again. It would be her home, and she would be a part of it.

The witch handed her the potion. "Have you decided, child?"

Annabelle took the cup and emptied it in one long swig. The drink tasted bitter and stung her tongue. Only then did she nod, and that nod felt as binding as signing a contract or leaping off a cliff.

The old woman led her over to the large table. "Lie yourself down here."

A large beeswax candle was lit, and herbs placed over and around it soon filled the room with strangely scented smoke. As the old woman coated the sharp knife in crushed herbs and an oily liquid, Annabelle felt the potion begin to take control of her mind and body. Her movements felt sluggish, and soon she deliberately stopped moving.

At first her mind rebelled at the strange feeling of dizziness that was growing, but then it reminded her of the first time she saw Rowan, and how her head had been swimming with a champagne daze. The memory was sweet and calming. She closed her eyes and thought of Rowan—her hair, her eyes, her hands, her beautiful laugh, her sweet nature and her caring curiosity. Soon they could be together again, and that was all that mattered.

Annabelle didn't watch as the knife slipped inside her. She kept her eyes closed and drifted into a deep sleep, Rowan's name on her lips.

A chilly wind was blowing, and it ruffled her hair. No, not her hair...her branches! Annabelle's eyes flew open and saw nothing but forest around her. Her eyes felt strangely dry and she wanted to rub them, but as she managed to make her arm move to bring her hand up to her face, she noticed two things. First, her arm had to extricate itself from something to reach up, and second, when she did reach up, all she felt was smooth bark. She was in a tree! The reincarnation must have worked!

Slowly, she tried to free her body from the tree. When she finally took her first tentative step out from it, she could feel the damp moss and dirt under her naked foot. The second step came easier. Moving felt so much more fluid in her new form, and she understood why Rowan had always moved with such grace.

Rowan!

Where was she? Had it worked for her, too?

Annabelle looked around eagerly, and soon her eyes fell on a beautiful nymph lying atop the moss, watching her with a beatific smile on her elven features.

"Welcome out, Annabelle. And thank you for what you have done for us!"

The nymph easily stood and hurried over to wrap her arms around Annabelle's waist. It was then that Annabelle looked down and saw that she was as naked as Rowan, and that her skin glowed with the same pearlescent hue. Laughing happily, she embraced Rowan, naked skin against naked skin.

"It worked," Annabelle chirped.

"Yes, it did. We are now both dryads, and we are far away from your parents and other prying eyes. Since we were planted, I have only seen one human, and that is the witch who brought us here. I have spoken to the trees and made them promise to tell all growing things in this forest to treat that woman well. She will find that anything she needs will grow for her, and nothing in this forest will ever harm her."

Annabelle smiled and kissed Rowan. "I am so grateful to her, and so ashamed and horrified by what my father did to you."

"Do not think of that, my love. It happened in another existence. He is not part of our lives anymore, and he cannot hurt either of us ever again. Now it is just you and me and our trees. Take a look at your beautiful oak! It is as beautiful and as strong as you."

Annabelle turned to look at the tree from which she had emerged. "It *is* beautiful and…quite big! Shouldn't it be a mere sapling?"

Rowan ran her index finger over Annabelle's cheek and jaw. "Oh, my sweet, how long do you think you have been asleep?"

Annabelle tried to gauge how rested she felt. "I don't know. A night, perhaps?"

"Not even close, I'm afraid. Looking at our trees, I would guess that we have been sleeping and growing for somewhere around two dozen years."

"We have been asleep for twenty-four years?" Annabelle gasped.

"Yes. Time feels different to dryads. Besides, we needed time to take root, grow, and connect our beings to the trees. It might make more sense to you if you think of it as a pregnancy. I only awoke a few hours ago, when the aged witch touched my bark to see if I was alive. She felt the bark of your oak, too, and said that you were in there but not yet ready to come out. She asked me to say something to you when you emerged. She asked me to say 'happy birthday,' whatever that means."

Annabelle gave a quick laugh, then looked up at the tree again, biting her lower lip pensively. "Everything is so different. I feel so different."

Rowan looked worried, and her voice wavered as she said, "Does it feel wrong?"

Annabelle shook her head vehemently. "No. It feels…sort of…free."

"Free is what you are now. You're free, and loved, and safe," her beloved said with a reassuring smile.

Rowan took Annabelle's hands and held them tightly. Two sets of matching yellow-green eyes met, and Annabelle knew that she was one more thing than that. She was finally home.

ℌands-𝔉ree

BY CHERI FULLER

I USED TO BELIEVE THAT I would never voluntarily harm another person. I don't believe that anymore. The proof of my failing is dripping off my hands and into the growing puddle of blood at my feet.

I can hear the sirens. One of the people in the crowd must have called them; someone whose phone is not otherwise occupied with recording. This will certainly go viral and I'll be famous. Without my permission, my hands move to my hair and smooth it back. My wedding band gets caught on the clip with the butterfly that my sweet daughter picked out for me this morning.

Good Lord, what have I done?

I'm not fully to blame, of course. Surely he knew better than to be talking on the phone while driving. He pulled into my lane! I was right there, and he didn't even bother to look. He was certainly looking when I jerked the wheel and crashed into his front quarter panel. I definitely had his attention when I marched up to his open window, grabbed the phone out of his hand and smashed him in the face with it.

I only vaguely remember yelling at him while I hit him again and again. I was so angry. Now I'm more afraid than angry, but really, shouldn't everyone know the law by now? Didn't he deserve exactly what he got? What if I had been looking in the other direction when he pulled into my lane? What if my child had been with me and he had sideswiped us?

Oh, the look on his face when I pulled him from the car. I think he was in shock because he didn't put up a struggle. To be fair, I suppose I did surprise him, and he was probably light-headed from the repeated blows to his temple and forehead. Those phablets are much more sturdy and heavy than I had imagined. I may have to get one.

The police have arrived, and the crowd is parting to let them through. One of them, a handsome young man, has his hand on the butt of his gun but the other, an older woman, has hers out and is pointing it at me.

"Step away from him and keep your hands where we can see them," she says very calmly.

I look down at the rude man who couldn't follow the rules of the road and realize that he's looking at me. I meet his eyes and take a step back, raising my hands; I was taught to respect the law, unlike some people.

Suddenly I'm on the ground, the asphalt scraping my cheek, and my arms are yanked behind me. The cuffs are cold and pinch my wrists. I don't feel afraid anymore, instead, I feel proud. I stood up to someone who felt that his call was more important than the safety of those around him. I've performed a public service. And I'm going to be famous.

𝔖𝔱𝔦𝔩𝔩 𝔏𝔦𝔣𝔢

BY JESS LEA

CREAK-CREAK. CREAK-CREAK.

Lydia's eyes snapped open. Several words she would never dream of uttering aloud popped into her mind. She'd had another strange dream and woken up flushed and sweating, her thick auburn hair stuck to her neck.

Creak-creak. A rhythmic pressure upon the floorboards, wood rocking against wood: a squeak in one direction, a faint moan in the other. The same sound had woken her in the dead hours every night this week.

She flung off the bedclothes and lay glowering up at the ceiling, feeling the cold air playing over her skin. Mr Elphington didn't want servants burning candles all night, complaining about the waste, but Lydia chose to believe this didn't include her. The single, wispy flame gave her small room the feel of a cavern. Darkness hid the cracks that snaked across the plaster, the drifting cobwebs and speckles of mould too high for a housemaid's broom to reach – assuming any maid could be bothered to try. A governess's cell didn't warrant much upkeep.

The rest of the house was cleaner but no less decrepit. Lydia sat up, running a hand through her damp, tangled hair and adjusting her nightgown where it had slipped off her shoulder. She took a certain satisfaction from the knowledge that the Elphingtons' circumstances, like her own, had been much reduced.

Creak-creak. It wasn't the shabby lodgings or the pauper's salary that made her restless and miserable. Lydia was no stranger to privations.

When Father was alive, they'd run out of candles and had bread and milk for dinner more times than she cared to remember. What money they had went into the shop they ran together. Fossils and shells, corals and starfish, rare ferns and marine algae – treasures and trinkets for scientists, collectors, members of geological societies... The memory made her sigh. Father had no head for business and hoarded more items than he sold. His passion was discovery: scrambling up cliffs and down mine shafts, fossicking in canals, quarries and railway cuttings, picking his way along freezing windswept beaches at low tide like some great stooped bird... Lydia wiped her eyes. Dear old fellow. Far more concerned with the backbone of some queer lizard, pressed into clay thousands of years before – millions, Father insisted, no matter what God or decent people had to say about it – than with the strangeness of his own daughter: shy, unmarried at five-and-twenty, and surrounded by rocks. And what did social niceties matter, anyhow? Compared to the miracle of *life*, scuttling, thundering, and swimming across this earth in forms now vanished and unimaginable. Lydia had supplemented their meagre profits by illustrating books about seaweed, ammonites and fungi. Some of the books had drawn praise, although for the men who wrote them, of course. Life had been lean, but she had not thought herself unhappy. Not until Father died, and a month later a freak storm burst through the windows of their rickety shop and the flat above. Lydia had been out trying to close the sale of a fossil, a coal-shale fern in limestone, to a collector who described her to his friend as an odd little piece, *quite as dry and shrivelled as the relics she peddles*, before she was out of earshot. By the time she could struggle home in the downpour, there was little left to save.

Creak-creak. The sound caused her a surge of anger – a relief, after months of numbing sorrow. She had identified the sound now. It came from the nursery directly below: the movement of a rocking horse, tilting back and forth against a floorboard that groaned in protest. After each creak there would be a half-second's teetering silence, before the downward arc began again. The little monsters – did they never go to sleep?

Lydia would have been desolate as a governess no matter what. But this posting in the Elphingtons' household did nothing to soften the blow. The children – Lancelot with his spots, oozing nose, and tormenting of the neighbourhood cats; Maria with her ringlets, wide blue eyes, and sneak-thievery – were as good an argument for boarding schools or sterilization as Lydia could imagine. The boy leered at her and manipulated himself under the desk; the girl left pins on Lydia's chair, and they were both as good as illiterate. And then there were the parents. Mrs Elphington discoursed endlessly about her illnesses, in a breathless babble, which owed something to her injections of cocaine, prescribed by the nerve specialist who visited every week. Mr Elphington spent his mornings scowling over the household accounts and demanding economies to the servants' food, and his afternoons disposing of the money he'd saved, down at the racetrack. Meanwhile, the cook belonged to some evangelical sect, the valet's hands were shaky with drink by noon, and the housemaid read Lydia's letters. Possibly they had better qualities as well, but as a governess – belonging neither upstairs nor down – Lydia had little opportunity to find out. And little interest either.

The only one who intrigued her was a young woman in a dark serge dress and apron, with vivid golden-brown eyes and a splash of birthmark across one cheek. She passed Lydia in the corridor most days and met her eye, but never returned a greeting. Lydia took her for a lady's maid and, it would seem, a snob.

Creak-creak. Anger propelled her out of bed. Bad enough this family monopolised every minute of every day; she would be hanged if they would keep her awake at all night too. She would deal with those little brutes, and never mind what their neurasthenic fool of a mother had to say about it tomorrow. Lydia seized a candle and stormed out into the corridor.

A damp, chilly breeze found its way between the windowpanes and beneath the doors to go weaving around her bare ankles. The floorboards were rough; she heard scrabbling and flinched at the thought of rats.

Live creatures were not the only things causing Lydia to falter. This house was also a monument to Mrs Elphington's late father and his great passion: taxidermy. During her first few weeks here, Lydia had often found herself tripping over an elephant's foot wastebasket or recoiling from a preserved frog on a swing. The children had howled with laughter, of course. Probably it was thanks to them that some objects moved around behind her back. She was sure, for instance, that the crocodile's head had not hung on that wall yesterday.

Lydia had no squeamishness about bones, feathers or preserving agents, but the sad indignity of the creatures' fate troubled her, as did the gaze of their dusty glass eyes. On this floor, in grubby cabinets, there dwelt two sword-fighting toads, a pair of squirrels playing chess – one with his black knight poised above the board – and, most horribly, a litter of kittens in frilly dolls' clothes, taking tea. As Lydia passed them, the candlelight reflected leaping shapes in the glass cabinets, and the creatures' eyes gleamed.

Creak-creak. The sounds of the rocking horse were growing faster, more urgent, as she approached the nursery. Odd that she could hear no giggles or whispers. During the day she sometimes had to shriek at the children to be quiet.

How had she come to this? An angry, foolish drudge of a woman, a joke to those who bothered to notice her, resenting her life and brooding on what might have been? Lydia knew she could never have been rich, beautiful or admired, but she could have been – someone. Her hand grasped the nursery door. The creaks were growing frantic now, and so loud it was strange no one else had awoke to complain. *Creak-creak-creak.* She flung the door open.

A vivid shaft of moonlight illuminated the room and the drift of toys across the floor. Spinning tops, hoops, and rubber balls, defaced china dolls with their hair and eyelids torn off, lay scattered around the twin beds – where, it seemed, her charges slept peacefully.

The moonlight picked out the rocking horse itself. Once an elegant beast, its paint was chipped now and most of its mane was missing. A silver cobweb glistened between the horse's saddle and a stirrup. No one had ridden the horse for days. Lydia glanced back at the children; their faces were slack with sleep.

A shiver swept over her. She had a sense of being watched, but there was only the cluttered room and the moonlight.

Was she imagining things? Her skin was tingling and her pulse came quickly. In fact, her whole body felt strangely invigorated. Could the sound have come from the floor below? The old man's trophy room sat beneath the nursery.

The house was silent now. No more creaking. She should go back to bed; tomorrow was a busy day. She would spend the morning preparing the day's lesson, which the children would ignore. Then she would tidy the toys which would immediately be strewn across the floor again. Oh, and she would have to wrestle the children into their best clothes to visit their Aunt Charlotte, who smelled of mothballs and kept many small, snapping dogs which refused to be housetrained. That was one of the few experiences Lydia and the children hated equally.

Suddenly the thought of going sensibly back to bed seemed less appealing. Why prepare for tomorrow when tomorrow would be ghastly anyway? And there had been noises in the house. She was sure of it. Lydia made her way down the stairs, cringing at every loose floorboard, only to find the door to the trophy room ajar. A light was burning inside.

The corridor seemed to have grown colder. Lydia felt goosebumps rising along her arms and her nipples tightening beneath her nightgown, a sensation not wholly unpleasant. This room was never left unlocked. It distressed Mrs Elphington's nerves to see her beloved father's masterpieces, or so she said. Lydia suspected she was really afraid her husband would pawn the lot.

There was no sound save Lydia's own quick and shallow breathing. Should she call for help? Instead she pinched out the candle. The sting of the extinguished flame left her fingertips smarting. She edged sideways into the room. Another candle stood in the middle of the desk, burned halfway down.

Musty air tickled her nose; the room had not been thrown open for ages. The walls were lined with thick floral wallpaper now twenty years out of fashion. Before her stood a magnificent Bengal tiger, its black and golden body frozen in an endless, preposterous battle with a boa constrictor. Birds of prey hovered on the shelves with stuffed mice between their talons. A pair of Australian rock wallabies crouched with their snouts together, the female with long eyelashes gummed on, the male with his generative parts enlarged by the artist. Lydia blinked. It seemed a bizarre use of the old man's skills, although perhaps not much

185

stranger than anything else in here. She forced herself to look behind the settee and the fire screen, to pull back the curtains. She even opened the burnished oak cabinet, but found it full of nothing but shelves. She slid out the top drawer and found a tray of butterflies.

Lydia let out the breath she'd been holding, and felt a curious disappointment. The candle must have been left by a careless servant. And the noise – well, it must have been in her mind. Perhaps she was as nervous as Mrs Elphington aspired to be. Lydia swapped her extinguished candle for the burning one, and turned to go back upstairs.

She stepped back and felt softness against her heels. She realised she was standing on the edge of a lion-skin rug. Lydia bit her lip and tiptoed to one side; it seemed wrong, somehow, to tread on such a creature. Wrong to think of it being slaughtered and preserved for someone's amusement in the first place. It was a lioness; her jaws open in a wide, white snarl and her eyes a fierce shade of amber. They were beautiful. Lydia stared into them for a long moment. She might have stayed there for longer still, if it were not for a noise behind her, making her start. The squeak of door hinges.

Lydia whirled around, her heart thumping. The lady's maid stood in the doorway. She was framed by darkness, and still dressed in her dark serge and impeccable apron despite the hour. In the dim candlelight, the birthmark on her cheek melded with the other shadows. Lydia's hand flew to her mouth.

"Oh, I—" She flushed with embarrassment. "I heard a noise and I was just— I suppose this candle is yours?"

The young woman nodded but did not reply. She watched Lydia closely, making her all too aware of her tousled hair and the thinness of her rumpled nightgown. The cheap cotton pulled against her and she wondered if this woman could see the outline of her body through it; the peaks of her nipples, the dark triangle between her thighs. Her flush deepened.

"Well, I'd best go back to bed." She had to edge around the girl to escape. She smelled of night-jasmine flowers and Lydia briefly wondered if she had been out in the garden. As she hurried back upstairs not stopping to relight her candle, she could not cast off the sense that, for the first time in months or perhaps even years, someone had not found her invisible at all.

That night her sleep was troubled. A low growling reverberated through her dreams. Something was stalking her along the crumbling corridors, something that padded on silent paws, with eyes that shone yellow in the darkness. Slowly, it approached her room. The windows rattled; she rose to adjust them and found to her horror that she did not appear in the looking glass. Only the room behind her was reflected back. She groped and hammered at the glass, pressed her body against its icy sheen. Behind her the bedroom door shuddered as something pounded upon it, gouging at the wood. And then it wasn't the door to her room at all; it was a cabinet door, which trembled under each blow before bursting open to fill the air with a haze of butterflies.

Lydia woke, flushed and disoriented. Sunlight was pouring in; she had overslept and would face a scolding, if not a cut to her wages. And yet she lay on a moment, exploring the new sensitivity of her skin with startled fingers. Her nightdress was tangled above her waist and there was a curious slickness between her thighs. From where she lay, she could see the looking glass standing on the dresser reflecting the room as usual. In it she could see her brown eyes still heavy with sleep, and her lips swollen as if from kissing. And when the sunlight shifted it revealed strange cloudy shapes smeared across the mirror. The print of a hand, the butterfly press of a woman's lips, and below that, two neat, round little imprints – Lydia stifled a gasp at the thought they had been made by her own naked breasts.

She hurried out of bed to scrub the glass clean. But there was no way to erase what she found when she opened the door to her room; three deep groves in the wood, as if something had struck at the door with a great set of claws.

Lydia spent the day in a state of tremulous confusion. The children's fistfights and whining scarcely ruffled her; she was too busy listening for some other sound. Her skin was alert to every puff of breeze, every pinch of her ill-fitting boots and the chafing of her cuffs and stays. Each time she moved she seemed to hear the creak of her stiff bodice, the pins loosening in her hair, the whisk of her lace-edged drawers. As she gathered up the scattered animals from the children's Noah's Ark, her fingers lingered over the small, carved figure of a lioness. Lydia's tongue crept out to moisten her lips.

"Miss! Miss! Soft in the head!" A tin soldier flew through the air and narrowly missed her eye. The children hooted with laughter, and Lydia, without a second thought, raised a hand to cuff Lancelot's ears.

"Wretched girl!" A shriek from downstairs prevented the blow from landing. Lydia blinked and dropped her hand. The children gawped, not at their mother's wailing but at the look of anger on her own face.

"It's outrageous! With my nerves!" The cries continued. Lydia lost all interest in the children's misconduct, and rushed outside instead. She arrived in time to witness Polly the housemaid standing miserably on the lower landing, her acne blushing a deeper red as her mistress harangued her.

"How dare you put it there? I nearly fell! To say nothing of how it pains me, seeing my dear father's treasures tossed about. Little beasts like you have no sense of family..." In vain Polly protested that she had not put anything anywhere, and that she did not know how it had happened. Mrs Elphington was already staggering away to her sofa and her laudanum, while the valet, his face glowing red with exertion and rum, dragged the offending item from the top of the staircase back to the trophy room. Lydia shrunk back against the wall, her eyes widening. It was the lion skin rug.

That night her sleep was fitful and feverish. She flung off her blankets, and twined her bare limbs around the sheet. Her nightgown bunched above her waist and this time she let it stay there. The candle sputtered on the dresser, filling her head with dancing shapes and plumes of smoke.

She dreamt she was inside the trophy room again. Her back was against the wall and a sweaty friction was trickling between her shoulder blades. She could feel the wallpaper behind her, its raised floral pattern scouring her buttocks as some great weight moved against her, lifting her off her feet and forcefully moving her up and down. She could sense her body changing, her teeth growing and protruding, she narrowed her eyes and growled. Something nuzzled at her naked skin, filling her ears with its hot breath, licking her all over.

Her eyes snapped open. Her bedroom lay in darkness. Had a breeze blown the candle out? The bed was in chaos, the pillow across her knees, the sheets ensnaring her like a fisherman's net.

Why did her sleeping mind torment her so? Hadn't she had enough troubles to contend with? Was it not enough to be poor and stifled, alone in the world, must she go mad as well? All she asked was the strength to tolerate her lot in life, and to bear it with quiet dignity.

She ordered herself to stop this foolishness and to tidy the bed and go back to sleep. But no sooner did she lift herself onto one elbow than some invisible pressure toppled her back onto the mattress. The sheets, warm and damp, scented with her own sweat, twisted into ropes, snaking their way across her wrists and ankles. She gasped with shock and tried wriggling to one side and then the other, and found the pillow had somehow slid down and become caught between her legs. Struggling only seemed to make things worse. It caused the crisp cotton back and forth against her sex.

Lydia squirmed in astonishment but the linen restraints held her in place. Was she dreaming, still? The thought was reassuring. If she was dreaming, if this wasn't real, and perhaps it didn't matter if she didn't – stop? The pillow's shape felt plump and agreeably firm between her thighs, growing hotter and slippery as she moved. There seemed to be no avoiding it. If she clenched her thighs together, it meant clasping the pillow closer to her; if she parted her knees wide to avoid the contact, the position only made her body more vulnerable, more responsive. Every move of her hips elicited the lightest brush of cotton and was enough to send jolts of sensation through her. She bit her lip. What if she cried out loud? She could feel the thrumming pulse between her legs grow stronger— "It isn't fair – let me *go!*" The children's screeches woke her up.

The sheets lay in a harmless muddle at her feet. The pillow had been flung on the floor. Only her own body still flushed and throbbing with need, proved she had dreamt at all.

"'What's happening? Where's that lazy governess? Does no one think of me?" The children's howls were joined by that of their mother.

Lydia got shakily to her feet. Nothing prevented her; nothing tied her down or touched her skin. Perhaps nothing ever had. She had been freed from her hysterical dreams, and never had she hated the Elphingtons more.

Lydia promised herself she would keep away from the trophy room. Clearly she was suffering some grave disturbance of the mind, and should wary of making her symptoms worse. She would exercise prudence and not put herself in harm's way. This vow lasted until Sunday.

The Elphington family had set out for church together, and Lydia, pleading illness, had escaped. She ought to rest or read some improving tract; instead she found herself stealing downstairs and nudging open the trophy room door.

How had she missed the display of bee-birds during her last visit? There were at least a dozen of them, arranged around a single display tree, their delicate beaks poised in search of nectar, their plumage shimmering like jewels. But Lydia felt certain the exquisite little creatures had not been here last time. Had someone moved the display? The dust on the tree spoke of months of neglect, so she dropped her speculation.

With a quick peek over her shoulder, she opened the doors to the cabinet. One drawer held the old man's taxidermy tools. Balsa wood, cotton and clay, needles and tweezers, wax, oil paint and jars of glass eyes lay in orderly rows. Another drawer held smaller trophies: dried caterpillars, sea urchins and puffer-fish. She recognised a fossilized shark tooth. Had he collected ancient things too?

Touching the tooth brought back bittersweet memories of working with her father. Why must she hang on to knowledge she no longer had any use for? The same knowledge her father's contemporaries had mocked her for, anyhow? Surely it would be easier to forget. Her hand hovered over the final drawer, then she withdrew. She had been wrong to venture in here, wrong to stand dreaming of better times. She stepped back and closed the cabinet.

"Penny for your thoughts, dear?" Cook bustled past, as Lydia sat pushing her supper around her plate.

"Nothing worth repeating, Mrs Phillips." Lydia sighed, then added on impulse 'But tell me, who is the maid in the serge dress? I've never seen her at our meal times.'

Mrs Phillips grunted, only half listening, "Who, Polly?"

"No." Lydia tapped her cheek. "She has a birthmark here."

"You don't mean poor Susannah?" Mrs Phillips' eyes widened. "Fancy you hearing about her! No one's mentioned her in—well, ten years."

"What do you mean?" Lydia felt a chill scuttle down the back of her neck. Mrs Phillips sighed.

"She was an upstairs maid when I started here, but everyone knew her real job was assisting the old man." Mrs Phillips' mouth crinkled with distaste. "That hobby of his, hoarding dead things it never seemed healthy to me. But Susannah was an odd girl, always with her nose in some queer book about foreign countries and peculiar creatures, so he trained her up to help with it." Mrs Phillips sniffed. "And with a few other things, I daresay. I'd begun to wonder if she wasn't in a delicate condition. And then the accident happened."

"Accident?"

The cook sighed with some relish.

"Arsenic. They mix it with soap and lime, you know, to preserve the animals. The old man found her. A shameful business." Mrs Phillips raised her eyebrows. "Who can say what really happened to her?" She looked away. "Polly! I said I wanted this range black-leaded! Are you bone idle, girl, or just stupid?" Before Mrs Philips could turn back and resume the conversation, Lydia abandoned her supper and left.

For hours she sat before her mirror, her hands clasped, listening as the servants' footsteps dwindled, as traffic in the street faded, and the house settled down for the night. She stared at her reflection: her lips were bitten, her eyes wide. She must be going mad. She was seeing ghosts and claw-marks, hearing impossible noises, dreaming about... Lydia shook her head. She must pull herself together. It was hysteria, brought about by the strain of Father's death and her new reduced circumstances. Or perhaps it was her old circumstances that had driven her mad; perhaps women were unsuited to scientific study, after all. She sat upright, her spine rigid, until she could be certain the house was gone to bed. Then she changed into her nightgown, pulled back the bed covers – and realised with a gasp she would not be sleeping there tonight.

The bed was sodden, the sheets, mattress and pillow soaked through. Someone had done a thorough job of ruining them. Her nose twitched as she leaned in, recognising the chemical whiff of preserving agent. She remembered the bottles she had seen in the old man's cabinet.

The little vermin! Anger drove all other thoughts out of her head. This had to be Lancelot and Maria's handiwork. The thought of their laughter as they destroyed her meagre possessions filled Lydia with rage. She yanked the door open and stormed downstairs.

Reaching the nursery, she seized the door handle, gave it a vicious twist – and nearly sprained her wrist, for it would not turn. It was locked. Lydia had not known there was even a key.

Assuming the children were behind this too, she raised her fist and pounded on the door, and was surprised to get no answer. Looking around in bewilderment, she saw Mrs Elphington's bottle of laudanum sitting on a side table. Had the woman drugged her own children? Surely not. There was no sound from the direction of the parents' rooms either. Mounted on the wall sat a crocodiles head, and nestled between its long yellow teeth was the key.

She could unlock the nursery. She *should* unlock it. Instead she stepped away. The squirrels in their cabinet were frozen in their game of chess. But something was different. The black queen that had been held in the first squirrel's paw now sat squarely on the board, while the white king stood cornered. Lydia swallowed. Checkmate.

Lydia felt her body grow still. She could sense the goosebumps dancing across her skin and her heart pitter-pattering. If she could not sleep in her bedroom tonight, she would have to lie down somewhere else. Her legs shook only a little as she turned her back on the nursery and made her way again to the trophy room.

Inside everything seemed as usual. She stretched out on the settee, nestling as comfortably as she could against the silk cushions, which were now fraying and ticklish with dust. Lydia took one last glance at the arching falcons, the tiger's body entwined with the boa constrictor, the bee birds in their rainbow plumage and the lion's skin stretched across the floor. Then she blew out the candle.

It started faintly. A delicate, high-pitched whirring set the air whistling across her face and throat, and ruffled her hair. Lydia shut her eyes and thought of the bee birds, with their beaks like needles and blur of multi-coloured wings. She must not move, dared not raise an arm to seize one, for what would she find? A warm, living body, its tiny heart throbbing in the palm of her hand? Or nothing but air?

She jumped as something nudged against her wrist, but forced herself to hold her position, her arms lying above her head. Her breath coming fast, she waited as a cool weight began to slide across her forearms, passing over and around them and wrapping them in a thick, muscular, living grip. She felt it squeezing around her wrists in gentle warning, felt the sleek texture of snakeskin.

Lydia's body was stirring in response as it had done the night before, but now she was unafraid. Her hips twitched, her breasts tingled, her breath burst from her. She needed attention, some kind of contact, but was helpless now to touch herself. A pulse was fluttering between her thighs, and she heard herself cry out in relief when something surged forward to open them.

Claws like grappling hooks pinned her nightgown to the settee, and the silk cushions slithered beneath her. A weight was upon her, its dimensions clearer than they had been last night. She could feel it taking shape as she arched her body forward to meet it: powerful haunches, a brush of whiskers, a ribcage big enough to wrap herself around. The hide was growing warm and solid, filling out with sinew and muscle, and the drum of a living heart.

Her thighs were held wide apart now, her knees pushed almost to her chest. She could smell sweat, dark and pungent, and felt great hot puffs of breath as something nuzzled at her exposed belly, at the sensitive flesh beneath her hipbone. Her eyes screwed shut, Lydia pictured the transformation. The painted papier-mâché of the lioness's jaws softening into real gums, vivid-pink, ridged and wet. They sprouted teeth that caught the plump flesh of her thighs and held her tight. And all the while, the façade of turpentine, paint and clay was dissolving away to a real tongue. A tongue that was hot, moist and tantalisingly smooth. Not the harsh texture of a cat's tongue at all, but something different. Almost human. It flickered against her skin, before nuzzling a path up higher, towards her most intimate self.

The first touch was almost more than she could bear. Her wrists jerked instinctively in their restraints; she tried to swallow back her cries, before realising there was no need, no risk of discovery tonight. Locked doors and laudanum had seen to that. The thought should have shocked her; instead it caused her a helpless hiccup of laughter, which jolted her closer to the source of these new caresses. They were slow at first, rasping up one side of her sex and down the other. She was being tasted; she gasped and felt her body respond, seeping its wetness as if to offer up its sharpest flavours. The snake coiled around her arms stopped her from reaching down, made it impossible to discover if this was reality or just a dream. She no longer wished to know. Instead she was straining, her bare feet clawing at the cushions, her hips lifting of their own accord, until she felt that tongue on a place she, herself, had scarcely dared to touch before.

The sensation made her melt like candle-wax, forced her breath from her in sighs of pleasure. Her whole body was moving now, and the vigorous rhythm caused the settee to scrape backwards and forwards on its carved feet. It knocked against the cabinet, a sharp rapping that only partially drowned out Lydia's moans, which grew louder as her lover's tongue pressed against her. It parted her lips with one searing sweep, before pushing inside, higher and deeper. She wailed as she came undone, collapsing in a sweating heap. And became aware, gradually, that she was lying alone among the cushions.

Her wrists were free, her knees could close again, but still she held her position as long as her body could bear it, reluctant to let go. Save for her panting breaths, the room was silent. If she had dared to open her eyes at the height of her pleasure, would she have seen great golden irises looking back at her? But she had not been brave enough, and now she kept her eyes closed so that she would not have to see the darkness between her spread thighs, the lack of anything or anyone, save herself and her own imagination.

Certainly her movements must have been violent, for she could feel the edge of the cabinet door hard against her knuckles. The jerking of the settee must have forced it open. With a sigh, Lydia looked up, dragging herself into a seated position. The room was pale with moonlight.

The lion skin rug lay across the floor, apparently unmoved. The other creatures were back where they had always been. Only the cabinet looked out of order. Its doors lay ajar and its drawers were popped open. She rose slowly to her feet, still dazed and unsteady, and made her way to tidy up the cabinet. She gazed for a moment at the shadowy relics – the preserved beaks and claws, the condor feather and preserved eagles' eggs – before closing the drawers one by one.

Lydia hesitated over the final drawer, the one she had not looked at before. There was something in there. A dull, drab shimmer at the very back. She reached in and felt its weight. It was heavy, all knobbles and joints, and a cool texture like stone. Was it a skeleton? She traced her forefinger along it and drew back with a gasp.

Lydia pulled the drawer free and heaved it over to the windowsill to look at its contents in the full glow of the moonlight.

The light was poor, but she recognised the shape at once. She had seen this in books, and copied out every line for Father's records. How had this collector gotten hold of such a thing, and how had it remained a secret? If the Elphingtons had known, it would have been auctioned in a thrice.

With the greatest reverence she smoothed her hands over the paddle bones of a plesiosaurus, perfectly intact, and clearly from a good-sized specimen. Father had called them sea dragons. Lydia recalled pictures of a giant otherworldly creature with the round, squat body of a turtle and a long, snakelike neck rearing up out of the water, snapping its spiny jaws. A creature so improbable you could not imagine it existing at all, and yet here was the proof.

Lydia stood alone by the window, watched by dozens of glass eyes, and ran her fingertips over the fossilised shape of the bones. She imagined them flexing into life, sweeping their way through a wild, alien sea that had once covered this land and had long since drained away.

Lydia left the house at dawn. Nobody inside stirred. She had unlocked all the bedroom doors before leaving. She had no need to resent the Elphingtons any longer. It was a crisp grey morning, and the edges of the paving stones along with the leaves on the scrappy trees, seemed to stand out with a sharp kind of beauty.

She hugged her carpetbag to her. It was threadbare and shabby; no one would think to steal it, but still she held it close and smiled, thinking of its contents. Not a whole specimen, of course, the very idea of an intact plesiosaurus made her dizzy with envy, but a good portion. It would be enough to get her started in her profession, although it saddened her to think of letting such a splendid thing go. But there would be others, and she, Lydia, would be the one to find them.

She paused at the gate, glancing back towards the sleeping house. The dawn was touching the windows panes and making them shimmer. For a moment, Lydia could have sworn she saw a figure standing at the window of the trophy room. A young woman, perhaps, with a birthmark, a neat black dress, and the golden eyes of a lioness?

Then a cloud crossed the slowly rising sun, and the window darkened. Lydia nodded, turned away, and set off alone down the street.

Lunar Calling

BY KATE WELSHIRE

DEEP IN THE WOODS, TORI ran, the soles of her feet pounding on solid ground as she sprinted up the darkened path. The young woman drew to a halt, pausing to retie her dark, shoulder-length hair into a ponytail and catch her breath. She pulled out her phone and checked the time, eyes squinting at the bright light of the screen. She had ten minutes until curfew, and there was one turn left to get to the head of the worn walking trail.

The forest surrounding the school and dormitories was a popular jogging area, but was uncharacteristically quiet in the cool night air of spring when most of the residents were inside, getting ready for bed or cramming for a test.

The solo runner was about to continue up the trail when a low, shrill call pierced the tranquility and froze her in place, heart pounding. Identifying the noise as a howl fading into the distance, she was paralyzed, until a second, much closer howl echoed through the darkness. Without a glance at the path behind her, and before her mind could catch up with her feet, Tori broke into a full run. Her blood pulsing too loudly in her ears for her to listen for any more sounds, she fixed her focus solely on the light of her dormitory up ahead.

Only when she had hurtled up the steps and was standing on the front deck did she stare back into the woods, searching for any movement among the trees. The forest had returned to stillness. She checked her phone again and then hurried inside after one last look into the dark.

"You saw a wolf?" Cassie asked the next day at lunch in the crowded cafeteria. "I don't think that's possible, Tori."

Tori sighed and put down her fork. "No, I *heard* a wolf." She shrugged. "Maybe it was a coyote. Whatever, I heard some kind of wild animal out there."

"Are you sure? I didn't hear anything, and our room is on the side of the building that is by the edge of the woods."

"You were probably just too engrossed in talking to your boyfriend to hear anything else," Tori muttered.

"Hey, as far as you know, our conversation was perfectly innocent."

"No, I actually do know better than that. Why do you think I cleared out in the first place?" She shuddered with distaste at the exchange she might otherwise have been forced to overhear. "I could have been eaten by a wolf, and it would have been entirely your fault."

Cassie had the decency to look slightly abashed. "I can't help it! I spend months at a time in an all-girls school. I need some male companionship!"

"Stop right there. I've already heard much more about your 'male companionship' than I ever wanted to."

Ignoring Cassie's ineffectual protests, Tori continued eating. She had only just mentioned hearing the howling. When she had returned to their room the night before, she had been lost in her own thoughts, lying awake, watching the moonlight sifting in through the window and thinking about the shrill call.

She chewed slowly as she contemplated that eerie cry. "It sounded... almost lonely."

"Lonely?" Cassie snorted in disbelief. "Maybe you are the lonely one. Now you're making up woodland creatures to keep you company."

Tori would have gladly told her to shut up, but two of Cassie's basketball teammates, Summer and Lia, settled down opposite them at the table.

"What's going on?" Summer asked.

Atypically short for a basketball player, she was lovely girl who was generally pleasant and always greeted Tori, even though she was not in Summer's inner circle of friends, most of whom were athletic.

In contrast, Lia was tall, lithe, and exuded confidence even when she was standing still. Tori remembered the first day she had come to Kenawley two years earlier, sophomore year. She was like something straight out of a dream, and Tori was immediately captivated by her. She had impossibly long, dark hair, which went well with her dark hazel eyes, eyes that were currently looking completely disinterested in the conversation.

Tori shook herself out of her thoughts about Lia and feigned a sudden interest in the remaining food on her plate.

"Last night, Tori saw a wolf in the woods," Cassie announced.

"Cassie!" Tori hissed. She shot a glance at Summer and Lia, gauging their reactions. Summer looked alarmed, but Lia's expression remained blank. Embarrassed, Tori protested, "I didn't actually *see* one, I just heard something that sounded like one."

"Like a howl?" Summer raised an eyebrow. "That's strange. We have been using those woods for as long as we've been here and, as far as I know, no one has ever seen a wolf. They usually stay near their pack, in their own territory. Maybe it was the wind you heard."

Suddenly unsure, which made her grumpy, Tori shrugged, trying to appear detached.

"It could have been a wolf."

Tori's eyes snapped up in surprise at Lia's remark. Was Lia actually defending her?

When Lia first enrolled in Kenawley, Tori had hoped to get to know all about her, but Lia soon settled in, and her easy confidence and numerous abilities had people flocking around her. After that, Tori was just another one of her admirers. Mostly, Tori just tried not to look awkward in front of her. However, every now and then, there were brief moments when Lia was unexpectedly open with her. If Lia agreed that maybe Tori had heard a wolf, it might have been worth having to suffer her schoolmates' skepticism. She felt a small flare of hope until a slow, smug smirk appeared on Lia's face.

"Sure. A wolf could have been drawn all the way here because it sensed an easy prey was out in the woods all by herself in the middle of the night."

The day officially sucked.

Too busy with schoolwork to take a jog around the school, Tori pushed thoughts of the howling out of her mind until the weekend. On Friday night, she took advantage of the later curfew to sit at her desk in a pair of comfortable wind pants and work ahead on an essay. She had typed a few sentences, then stopped and gazed out the window facing the woods.

Suddenly determined, Tori stood, pulled on a hoodie, and fished her shoes out from under her bed.

"Where are you going?" Cassie asked from her prone position on her bed.

"Just out for a jog." She quickly pulled on her shoes to escape before any further questioning ensued.

"Don't get eaten by anything!" Cassie shouted as Tori slammed the door.

Tori took a deep breath and started on her normal trail, but she went more slowly than usual, concentrating on the sounds around her. She was just about to give up and head back to the dorm when she heard rustling leaves, which seemed to be getting louder as the sound got closer. Ignoring the instincts that were telling her to run, she crouched low beside a tree and waited. Despite the full moon, only flecks of light were filtering through the trees, but she could just make out the dark fur and tail of an animal that sprinted past.

Satisfied at knowing she was right, Tori grinned. She wasn't sure what led her to follow the trail the wolf had taken, except maybe the opportunity to take a picture to show Cassie, and at the same time to prove to Lia that she was not wolf prey. She briefly lamented the school's "no knives" policy, but decided that if she kept her distance, she would be fine.

"I just need one good look," she reasoned.

Her heart pounded with excitement and fear as she made her way deeper into the woods, especially when she lost the wolf's trail only a couple of minutes later. She could not hear any sounds that indicated the wolf was still in the vicinity. Eventually she stumbled out into a clearing that she recognized as being near a spring. Sometimes in the summer, students would take a hike out there, but no one was really interested in it during the cooler months.

Having failed to achieve her goal of getting a picture of the wolf, she gazed down from a ridge overlooking the pool of water below, resigned to at least catch sight of the beautiful spring. She realized with a start that she was not alone. The water rippled around a moonlit figure, but it was definitely not a wolf. She quickly knelt behind a large rock on the ledge and peered over it.

She watched the supple back of the naked woman as she swept deft fingers through dripping hair. Even though the profile of the woman was made more mysterious by being cast in shadow, Tori could tell that she was beautiful, every movement graceful as she bent to collect water in her hands. Glistening water droplets slid down the woman's smooth skin, to the swell of her hips.

Tori could not help the tiny gasp that escaped her lips. It was the slightest noise, but the woman quickly turned her head as if searching for the source. Tori crouched lower and scrambled away, embarrassed to have almost been caught staring openly.

For the second night that week, she was dashing through the woods back to her dorm. This time she did not stop at the front steps to look back into the woods; she kept going until her bedroom door closed behind her.

From her reclining position on her own bed, Carrie raised an unimpressed eyebrow at her. "What did you see this time, a ghost?"

Tori's titter bordered on hysteria. "Actually, maybe I did."

"You are such a weirdo. Want to talk about it? I won't spread the word around school. Much."

Still plastered against the door for support, Tori swallowed and shook her head. "Nope, I'm good." She was aware that she didn't quite sound convinced about her own mental state.

"You are a mess. Go get changed before you get dirt everywhere. I'm shutting off the light in twenty minutes." Carrie shook her head fondly and turned over.

Tori looked down at her muddy pants and groaned. She quickly picked up shower items and headed to the communal bathroom up the hall.

Cool water washing over her, she blushed as she remembered the shadows cast over perfect skin, creating a beautiful chiaroscuro.

She did not make it back to her room before Carrie turned the lights off.

The next few days, Tori's emotions vacillated between embarrassment and curiosity. She avoided the eyes of her schoolmates, afraid that the unknown woman might be enrolled at Kenawley and somehow knew it was Tori that had stumbled upon her at the spring. At the same time, she was struck with a deep longing to find out who it had been. Who would be out at night, all alone, bathing in the spring? There were not any residential areas for a few miles in any direction, and signs clearly marked the land as the property of Kenawley.

She had not meant to intrude on the woman in such a private moment. If she'd had greater presence of mind, she might have politely turned away. But she hadn't, and now she could not stop thinking about the nymph in the water.

To get her mind off of that night, she stopped by the mail office. There was nothing from her parents, but there was a letter from her sister. The note detailed the vacation plans she had for Spring Break in two weeks. She closed with, "I wish you weren't so far away. I'd love it if you could go with us."

Tori tossed the letter on her desk and sprawled out on her bed. The afternoon was free of classes, but now she was wishing it was not. She needed a distraction from the stress that her family dynamics always brought her, and nothing worked quite as well as the bizarre night forest happenings. She decided that if she went running during the day instead of at night, maybe she could avoid getting eaten and avoid seeing something that left her unable to concentrate. What she needed was a peaceful, therapeutic jog.

The sun was shining brightly in the clear day, so Tori meandered leisurely through the woods, kicking through piles of leaves and breathing in the fresh air. Without deliberately setting out with a particular destination in mind, she ended up at the clearing by the spring. She flushed at the image that flashed into her mind. Aware of the heat of her skin, she knelt beside the water and ran her hands through it.

"It's freezing!" she exclaimed in surprise. "How could she have...?"

She considered this realization as she wondered, not for the first time, if she had ever really seen or heard the things she thought she had while in these woods.

As if summoned by her thoughts, a dark shape moved into her peripheral vision. She turned and stumbled backwards in alarm, then fell into a sitting position, face to face with a dark, hazel-eyed wolf.

Instead of pouncing, as Tori expected, the wolf just stared. It was a long, tense, silent moment. In shock, Tori felt a scream trying to escape her throat, but she swallowed it down and met the wolf's stare. Eventually the wolf tilted its head, almost curiously, and snarled through bared teeth.

Tori scrambled to her feet and ran away from the pond, back into the woods. Judging by the nearness of the steps behind her, she knew that she could not outrun the surefooted animal, even with her track training. With a burst of speed, she lunged for a low hanging branch on a tree in front of her. Her hands gripping tightly, rough bark cutting into her skin, Tori pulled herself up, her feet scrabbling against the tree trunk for leverage.

She climbed to the next highest branch before looking back down to make sure the wolf could not magically climb trees. When the wolf placed its paws on the trunk of the tree but made no further effort to reach her, she finally let out a long breath and slumped with relief.

Tori snapped open her phone and called Cassie. She squeezed her eyes shut, hoping Cassie could notify school security or otherwise organize some kind of rescue party. When the phone went to voice mail, she remembered Cassie was in an afternoon class. Panting heavily, she pocketed her cellphone and rested her head against the tree.

The wolf circled the tree, excitedly wagging its tail. Any appearance of aggression was abandoned. It looked as if it wanted to play.

"You look like a dog. It's ridiculous." Despite being trapped in the woods by a wild animal, she laughed.

The wolf laid its jaw on its paws and gazed up at her as if helpless.

"Don't look at me like that. I'm not falling for it. Just two minutes ago, you were chasing me. I'm not coming down," she insisted sternly, and then paused to evaluate the merits of reasoning with a wolf.

The wolf continued to lie there, casting longing looks up at her and flicking its tail every now and then. It seemed content to wait, as if it was not in a hurry to run off to capture some other prey.

Tori resigned herself to just settling down to wait until Cassie checked her phone or the wolf got hungry and left.

"You know, I used to have a dog back home," she offered after a few minutes of listening to the quiet sounds of nature around them. The canine lifted its head again at the sound of her voice, as if indicating that it was listening intently. "I heard your call the other night. It sounded… lonely. Are you lonely? Where is your wolf pack? Do you have family you miss?"

The wolf let out a high-pitched, muted whine and pitifully lowered itself down to the ground.

Tori considered the intense, compelling eyes, which almost seemed to reflect an understanding.

"Can canines sense emotion? Well, sometimes I miss my family. Of course, I don't always." She held up a hand as if to forestall criticism. "Don't worry. They would say the same thing about me. This school is great, but sometimes I think my parents sent me here to get rid of me. I know they think they are giving me an educational opportunity, but they don't seem to care that I am so far away. I don't even get any letters from my parents. Maybe if they sent some chocolate to say they know I exist, or a green pen to show they remember my favorite color, I might feel less abandoned. You know?"

The wolf was still, not looking away from her eyes.

"Ugh, I must seem pathetic. I'm whining about family, and you probably wish you had yours right now."

She stopped her rant and checked her phone again. Then she idly kicked her feet against the bark while regarding the wolf with a long, evaluating stare. "You're not…going to eat me, are you?"

The wolf puffed out a breath, which could have been a sneeze but seemed oddly like indignation.

"This is utterly irrational," Tori berated herself.

Very slowly, she made her way down to the lower branch. When the wolf stood on all fours but made no aggressive move, Tori sat on the lowest limb and cautiously tested the animal by dangling one foot. When the wolf suddenly leapt, she almost drew back and kicked it, but it only licked her ankle happily.

"Gross! And you better not be seeing if I'm tasty enough to devour," she scolded. Disregarding that possibility, she continued to steadily lower herself until, with a deep breath, she jumped down the last couple of feet to the ground.

Before she could mount any preemptive defense, a large weight slammed into her, making her stumble back against the tree trunk. She mentally catalogued the state of her limbs and vital organs. Once she had determined that she was not about to be mauled, she slowly opened the eyes she had squeezed shut on the initial impact. Her gaze was met with a searching gaze from the wolf. Tori felt more trapped by those piercing hazel eyes than by the strong paws pressing against her.

Tori let out the breath she had been holding. "Are you really a wolf?"

The predator responded with a show of very sharp teeth.

Tori cautiously placed her hand on the sleek fur between its ears and assessed the broad skull. "Yeah, you're a wolf of some kind. You aren't feral, though. Did you escape from the zoo or something? Is that why no one has seen you before?"

Her musing was met with a low growl. "Okay, I get it. You are not a trained pet. I apologize if I insulted your ferocity."

The wolf dropped down to all fours and lingered by Tori's side.

After seeing the civility the animal showed by sniffing her feet and hand, Tori ventured a step closer to the wolf. "Did someone leave you here?"

She would have sworn that she saw understanding in the hazel eyes. Wolves were known for their cunning, but it seemed as if there was something almost empathetic between them. Before she could reflect on that odd sensation, she was jolted out of her contemplation by a vibration. She quickly grabbed her phone to silence it, casting a glance at the wolf to make sure it had not been spooked. She brought the cellphone up to her ear, keeping her eyes locked on the wolf.

"Hello?" she answered.

"Hey." Cassie's voice was tired. "Why did you call while I was in class? We all don't all get lazy afternoons."

Tori hesitated, considering her answer. She wondered how sane it would sound if she said she had just gotten a kind of hug from the feared predator that was currently waiting patiently, content to stand still by her side while she talked on the phone. What would people do if they knew about the wolf? Call Animal Control? The woods were used regularly for hiking outings, and the Kenawley administration would not want what they would perceive as a wild animal lurking around. It made her heart ache to think of the sprinter she had seen dashing through the trees being locked up.

Tori finally settled on a semi-plausible explanation. "It was nothing. I was just wondering where my Physics book went, but I found it."

"All right, whatever," Cassie said.

Cassie's voice smacked of the suspicion with which she had regarded Tori lately, but Tori was just glad that she had accept the flimsy excuse and let it go at that.

Tori hung up and dropped the phone back into her pocket. "I really have to go," she told the wolf reluctantly.

The wolf responded by gripping a piece of her shirt hem between its teeth.

A spike of residual fear coursed through Tori, but it faded in the face of what looked like pitiful pleading. "This is ridiculous. Why do I feel the need to apologize to a wolf? Look, maybe I'll come back later, but right now I have to go appear normal for my roommate because I feel a strange impulse to keep you a secret, okay?"

The wolf let the shirt fall from its teeth and stood down, but its sad eyes were still sending guilt vibes.

"Great. I'm glad we're in agreement."

Tori slowly walked backwards, toward the clearing by the pond. Once she was sure the wolf was not following her, she started jogging back to the dorm, wondering how she had gone from being chased by a sharp-toothed hunter to promising that same hunter that she would return.

She did not make it back to the pond the next day. After a long study session, all Tori could think about was a hot shower and a good night's sleep. When she got back to her dorm hall, she saw a small package in front of her door. It was a chocolate bar tied with a green ribbon.

Tori gaped in disbelief for a few seconds before picking it up and carrying it into her room. She held the package up for Cassie to see. "Did you see this outside our door?"

Cassie shook her head. "I didn't even hear anyone at the door. It's obviously for you, though."

"How can you tell?" Tori turned it over, looking for any writing.

"I don't like chocolate, you know that." Cassie waggled her eyebrows. "Are you sure you don't know who left it here? What have you really been doing out there in the woods, meeting a secret lover?"

Tori immediately withdrew into herself, which she realized would make Cassie even more suspicious. She could not help it, though. She was hiding a secret, but not the one that Cassie imagined. In order to mask her nervousness, she went to collect her toiletries. "I don't spend my time flirting with my vast social network like you do."

"I won't judge. It sounds pretty hot." Cassie grinned. "Does she go to this school? Because there are better secret make out places than the woods. The seventh row in the library, for example—"

"I don't want to know," Tori declared loudly, closing the door on Cassie's amused cackle.

In the days that followed, Tori was finding herself with way too much to think about in addition to the demands of school. She'd had some bizarre experiences, and they were distracting, to say the least. That was totally the excuse she decided to use for her poor performance in school activities.

In a session of basketball in PE, for instance, she felt responsible for her team losing. The opposing side included half of the members of the varsity basketball team, including one of the tallest eighteen-year-olds at the school, Lia. She was everywhere, blocking Tori's efforts at every turn. *Someone who is so tall should not be blessed with agility as well*, she griped.

Tori growled, frustrated when another of her passes was batted away. Spinning around to recover the ball, she lost her balance. She braced herself to crash to the court, but a strong arm caught her around her shoulders. She looked up from the hand tightly gripping her arm, and found herself looking into the hazel eyes of Lia herself. They were frozen in that pose for a few moments before she was tipped upright.

Balanced back on both feet, Tori was still disoriented, and not just from tripping. She covered her discomfort by clearing her throat. "Um, thanks," she mumbled, embarrassed and excited at the same time.

Tori fully expected Lia to gruffly wave her off with annoyance, but she just gazed at her quietly, as if searching for any sign of pain. Finally Lia's eyes moved back to Tori's face. She must have caught the surprise and awe in Tori's expression at the strength that Lia had displayed, because Lia's concern quickly morphed into a carefully indifferent glare. Then she grinned. "You should stick to running track. It does not require as much coordination."

Feeling Lia's capable and compact strength pressed against her was still fresh in her mind as Tori watched Lia's strong back stalk away. How had Lia moved quickly enough to keep her from falling? She sighed. Thoughts about Lia were only going to make her more confused.

She decided to seek out the one being who seemed content to listen to her without judgment. Her feet crunched through old leaves as she walked into the woods. "How pathetic is it that I'm running to a wolf with my problems?" she muttered.

She made a circuit around the area of the spring, where she had seen the wolf before, then sat on a large rock to enjoy the sunlight. She had already started to calm down from the events of the day when she heard a distant rustling coming from the path that led to the school. As the noise grew louder, she poised herself to bolt, should some frightening creature emerge. When the familiar sight of dark fur and a panting lupine face appeared, she relaxed.

When the wolf saw her, it leapt up onto the rock and nuzzled Tori, then lay down beside her as if it belonged there.

Tori laughed in delight. "Sure, just make yourself at home there." She pushed her hands through the surprisingly soft fur on the wolf's back. "You are so weird. You don't behave at all like a wolf."

As if affronted, the wolf huffed through its nose and then poked at her with its snout until Tori tipped backward off of the rock and landed on her back in the leaves. When it gently placed a paw on her sternum, Tori said, "Okay, I give up. You're perfect!" She struggled to sit up and then regarded her companion seriously. "It is strange to me that you seem to understand what I'm saying. I think my dog could read emotions. He always looked sympathetic when I was sad. Is it kind of like that?"

The wolf backed away from her until it was standing a few feet off.

"Don't be like that," Tori called. A quick search among the leaves yielded a long stick that she held up triumphantly. "We can play some more. Here, fetch!"

She threw the stick far into the woods, but the wolf made no attempt to rise to the challenge. It looked unimpressed.

"Even forest animals judge me," Tori muttered. She stood up and brushed stray bits of the ecosystem off her clothes. "All right, I get it. You're not a dog."

The wolf growled and crouched low.

Tori froze. "I thought we were past the stage of you wanting to eat me."

She instinctively stepped back, and the wolf moved forward, but stopped when Tori stopped. Realization slowly dawned on her, and she smiled. "Ah, you resent being treated like a dog, but you're still up for a chase, huh? I should warn you, I used to run track. Are you sure you're up for this?"

An excited bark was the only warning she received before the wolf was up and sprinting toward her. Tori broke into a run without chancing a look back. It was only a few minutes before the wolf overtook her, and she suspected that even then it was holding back. Panting, Tori took a rest, while the wolf was still full of energy. It circled her proudly.

"All right, you win," she agreed. "When I'm out here with you, you somehow make me forget my problems. Life has been so weird for me lately."

The first thing that came to mind was the unusual things that had been happening in the woods, both the bather at the spring and meeting her wolf companion, and the second was the confusing happenings back at school. She decided to settle on the least embarrassing one. She did not want to admit that she had spied on someone in a private moment, even to a wolf who might or might not understand everything she said.

"Right after I was talking to you about some of my favorite things, there was a package of chocolate left at my dorm. If my parents sent it, it would have been at the mail office. I know this is going to sound strange, even to you, but I can't help wondering if you had something to do with it."

The wolf stared back blankly, as if to say, "I'm a wolf. Does it look like I have a secret chocolate supplier?"

"No, I suppose not. Maybe you're just my lucky star." Tori smiled warmly and leaned over to pat her companion's back. "If you are, then I should come out here more often. I'm going to head back now, but, same time tomorrow?"

The wolf gently nudged her hand, and Tori took that as a pact between them. That was the start of it.

It became normal for Tori to sprint out into the woods and be greeted by the energetic wolf's demand that they go running. Sometimes schoolwork kept Tori from making it. Other times, she would wander around in the woods and not encounter the wolf at all, but looking for one another quickly became a routine.

Each time the wolf would push Tori to the limits of her strength, and Tori could feel her soreness turning into muscle. When the seniors gathered in PE to play soccer, Tori actually managed to push past Lia's defense to score a goal. She wanted to allow herself a moment of smug satisfaction, but when she turned to celebrate her victory, Lia actually looked a little proud of Tori. That left her even more bewildered, a confusion that was not eased by the flutters of other feelings for Lia that she tried not to think about.

Being with a companion who was equipped with sharp teeth also gave Tori the courage to venture deeper into the woods than she ever had before. One day, they were bounding through unfamiliar territory, and Tori managed to pull ahead. When the wolf let out a loud, urgent yelp, Tori glanced back, but by then she was already slipping downward toward a large pit. She blanched in horror as the solid ground disappeared. Her feet slipped out from underneath her on the way down the steep dirt slope, and she landed hard on her right side. As the shock wore off and pain flooded in, she winced and swore loudly.

Tori looked up to assess the situation. Apparently the drop was so steep that she had not seen it as she sped right up to the edge. She was falling in before she even knew it was there. It was not a deep pit, but it was closed in on all sides.

Above her, the wolf whined loudly as it pawed the rim.

"No, don't! I don't want you to fall too! I'll see if I can climb up," she called, trying to reassure the wolf before it got hurt while trying to help her.

Her hand braced against the wall of dirt, Tori struggled to get to her feet. A sharp pain in her right ankle made her grit her teeth to suppress any shouting or expletives that might alarm her concerned comrade. Despite Tori's efforts, the wolf must have been aware of her pain, because it lowered its head in contrition, as if taking the blame for making her run.

"I'm fine! It's not broken. It's just a little tender from the fall." She stretched her hand up to the lowest lip of the pit, but could not reach over the top. "I don't think I'll be able to get up with it aching like this, though."

Tori tested her foot against the mud to try to get some leverage, then hissed in pain as she put some weight on her ankle. She pulled her phone out of her pocket, where she kept it while she ran. When she flipped it open, she discovered that her screen was cracked, probably from her impact against the ground. She pressed some buttons, but there was no response from the phone.

She groaned loudly in dismay. "My parents will actually kill me. If I ever make it out of here." She looked up at the wolf, pacing above her. "Okay, now would be a good time to make use of your keen understanding. Can you go get help? I don't want you to get hurt, though. Just don't growl, okay? Most of those girls really wouldn't harm any living thing. Maybe if they think you're a dog, they'll follow you back to me. If you see any men in uniform, run away."

Tori's hopes soared as the wolf jerked its head up and abruptly sprinted away. Wondering if her trust was misplaced, she settled down in the dirt. There was nothing to do but wait. In the meantime, she inspected her wounds. There were a few bruises on her legs, and her ankle still hurt, but she had full motor control. She counted that as a win.

After a few minutes, Tori began to seriously doubt her decision. She had just sent her only protection out to get help like some inspirational 1940s movie, and now she was alone. She tried calling out for help, but the only response was the chirping of birds in the distance. She had just begun calculating how much time she would have before it became dark when she heard a familiar rustling of leaves coming closer.

Before she had time to worry about predatory wild animals, a familiar face appeared at the edge of the pit. After a moment of pure relief, Tori childishly muttered, "Great," as she saw who her rescuer was.

Lia raised an eyebrow. "I can leave, if you prefer."

"No, no!" Tori responded hastily. "Did a wolf find you?"

Clearly amused, Lia snorted, "Are you still prattling on about a wolf you supposedly saw? If there was a wolf near school, you would be hearing the screams all the way out here. Sorry, no epic rescue animal story here. I was taking a walk in the woods when I heard you shouting for help."

Trying not to feel betrayed by her lupine companion's failure to bring a rescue party, Tori shrugged. "Whatever. That wolf is still my lucky star. Do you think you can help me out? Maybe get a rope or something?"

Lia crouched down and Tori could see that her hair was ruffled and her hands and wrists were covered in dry mud, as if she had been digging around in the dirt.

"Do you think you can stand, or are you injured?" Lia asked.

"I think I'm okay." Tori managed to stand without displaying too much pain, putting most of her weight on her left foot.

Lia planted her feet in a solid stance in the dirt and grabbed a nearby bush to help anchor herself. She reached out her hand. "Can you hold up your arm for me?"

Tori did not even try to hold back her skepticism. "No offense to your massive sports-induced ego, but there is no way you are strong enough to pull me straight out like that."

Looking delighted that she was being challenged, Lia smirked. "Humor me?"

Tori reluctantly raised her arm, and Lia leaned into the pit to get a tight grip on her forearm. Tori grabbed her arm as well and felt a sheath of muscles shifting, then she was being pulled up, and into Lia's steadying embrace. Tori flailed a little in surprise, but Lia held her gently, purposely avoiding her right side.

"Whoa!" Tori exclaimed, too shocked to feel embarrassed. "How did you—?"

"I exercise. You should try it." Lia bent down to examine Tori's legs. "You say the ankle is not broken?"

Tori shook her head. "It doesn't even seem sprained, but it hurts a lot."

Once again, Tori felt herself being lifted off the ground. This time Lia scooped one arm under her legs and laid the other across Tori's back, and suddenly she was being carried back toward the school.

Tori clung to Lia's shoulders. "What are you doing?" she demanded uneasily.

"Would you rather walk?"

She swallowed her pride and admitted quietly, "No." She rested her chin on top of Lia's shoulder and watched the powerful back muscles flex as Lia walked, seemingly unhampered by the strain. "I know you're good at everything, but this is ridiculous. You don't look musclebound. How are you carrying me so easily?"

"Maybe you are just tiny."

"I'll take that as a compliment, thank you," Tori muttered back.

She could practically hear the grin in Lia's voice when she responded, "If you must. Do whatever helps you get by."

The rest of the trek back was mostly quiet. Tori kept scanning the woods to see if the wolf was anywhere near, and to keep herself from thinking about the feeling of being plastered up against Lia's chest. She hoped that the wolf was not putting itself in danger by trying to help her.

When they reached the campus, a few girls stopped and stared at them, and Tori curled tighter into Lia, trying to disappear. Lia chuckled, but made no attempt to embarrass her any further.

Lia carried her all the way to the nurse's station and deposited her on one of the beds. Tori fully expected her to make some snide remark and then leave, but Lia leaned against the wall as Tori explained that she had been out running and had tripped over a root or something, which had caused her to fall into the pit.

Eventually the nurse on duty turned to Lia with a smile. "Thank you for bringing her in. I think we've got it from here."

Lia opened her mouth as if to protest, but snapped it shut again without saying a word. She gave a curt nod and left.

The next day Tori and Lia met in the hall. Leaning on a crutch, Tori was limping slightly, and she stopped to rest when she saw Lia. She offered a short wave. Lia frowned and stoically made her way over to Tori's side.

Lia gestured to her bound ankle. "What did they say about it?"

"Oh, it's just strained. This is just a precaution for the next few days to make sure it doesn't get worse." Tori bit her lip nervously. "I know I made some uncalled for remarks yesterday, but I really do want to thank you for helping me. I don't know how I would have gotten out without you."

Lia nodded, uncharacteristically subdued. "Listen, maybe you should stop going into the forest."

Tori shook her head. "That's not gonna happen. I like it in the woods. It's a good place to think."

"If this wolf you say you've seen is as good as you seem to think she is, she would probably not want you to get hurt again, perhaps even more badly."

"She?"

Lia's lip curled. She was clearly amused about something. "Well, *if* there is a wolf, it is hanging around an all-girl's school, isn't it?"

After again admonishing Tori to stay away from the woods, Lia excused herself, leaving Tori awash in a conflicting swirl of emotions, chiefly interest and confusion, which was a state that was becoming quite common for her. It was obvious that until her ankle was sound again, she was not going to be able to go into the woods anyway. But she did want to find some way to be sure the wolf knew she was safe, and to explain why she would not be back at the spring for a while.

It seemed as though Cassie was part of the conspiracy to keep Tori away from the woods. When Tori went back to her dorm room after classes each day, Cassie watched her like a hawk. If she so much as reached for a book, Cassie cautioned her to be still. Tori was getting tired of the attention, and she was missing going into the woods.

Cassie's resolve was admirable, lasting all of four days before she announced, "I have to get out of here. Do you know how many party invitations I have had to decline? My social life is dying."

Not sharing in Cassie's grief over her self-inflicted confinement, Tori growled, "Then go already! I never asked you to stand sentry over me."

"Oh, hey, you should come with me! Partying will help you let loose and heal. Plus, that way we can hang out, *and* I can keep an eye on you."

Tori shuddered. "Oh, wow. That's just what I need, more supervision. No thanks. Where do you think I am going to go like this? I get tired just walking to the cafeteria."

Cassie had the decency to appear hesitant, but she was already heading to the door. "I better be the first person you call if you need something!"

"That depends on how intoxicated you are in an hour," Tori grumbled as the door closed behind Cassie.

Tori had not actually intended to leave the minute her guard was gone. She went out to sit on the porch and enjoy looking the woods. If by chance she was to see the wolf, she could at least say hi. Leaning on her crutch, she hobbled out into the cool night air, and a long, low howl immediately came to her, carried by the breeze.

Tori gasped. She had not heard that mournful sound since that night she had first become convinced that there was a wolf in the woods. The pangs she'd felt that night came back to her when she thought of the wolf out there alone, howling for family.

"I'll just go to the tree line so that she can see me," she reasoned, and she slowly descended the stairs, favoring her injured ankle.

When the howling continued in the distance as she struggled out to the trees, Tori ventured farther. Eventually, step by labored step, she was halfway down her regular trail without realizing it. Tiring from the necessity of favoring her right side, she leaned heavily on her crutch for support.

She was startled to suddenly see eyes reflecting the moonlight in the dimly lit clearing, then relaxed when she saw wolf paws step into the area. "Oh, you scared me," she said with a chuckle.

The wolf snarled.

Tori searched the wolf's eyes. They were much darker than the hazel eyes she was used to seeing. "You're not her!" she said in dismay.

There was no hint of understanding or empathy showing on the wolf's face as it stalked forward, clearly evaluating its prey.

Ignoring the pain, Tori planted her feet solidly on the ground and held the crutch in front of herself defensively.

The wolf lunged, but it was knocked from its course of attack by another dark shape that darted out from among the trees. The two fought, rolling around on the ground, snarling and snapping.

Frozen with fear, Tori watched anxiously as they bit and clawed until one caught the other's neck in its jaws. The subdued wolf immediately froze in submission. After a few moments of domination, the victor released the beaten wolf and growled loudly, and the loser scurried away into the woods.

The champion turned toward Tori and she tried to back away, but her ankle finally gave out and she stumbled. She flailed wildly to keep her balance as the wolf crept forward.

"No, please keep away."

The wolf's hazel eyes looked at Tori, then it bowed its head, as if to communicate docility, but Tori did not notice. She was still in a panic from the wolf attack, and wondered if perhaps the second wolf had come to her defense because it was guarding its own food supply. She jabbed her crutch toward the potential attacker.

The wolf curled into a ball and lay down.

Tori's ankle was throbbing with pain, and when she could no longer maintain her defensive stance, she dropped the makeshift weapon with a soft, defeated cry.

The wolf's head jerked up. She ground her canine teeth together and stretched out her front legs.

Watching the wolf intently, Tori was stunned to see the fur covered paws begin to lengthen into the separate digits of human hands. The fluffy fur receded up long arms, and an expanse of smooth skin shifted over a sturdy back. A mop of dark hair draped down over broad shoulders and covered the face, until it lifted to meet Tori's wide-eyed stare.

After a few ineffectual attempts to force the word from her throat, Tori finally shrieked, "Lia!" She tried in vain to form a coherent sentence.

"You...I... What?" Speech had fled in the face of having just watched a wolf transform into a schoolmate of hers, and the awareness that said schoolmate was kneeling before her, very naked aside from a few patches of dirt and a stray leaf. Tori choked.

Apparently not bothered either by being a wolf or being naked, Lia asked urgently, "Are you okay?"

"Yes?" Tori replied numbly. "Maybe? I'm not really sure. Have I passed out from pain and entered a state of hallucinating?"

Lia ducked her head in a rare display of shyness, took a deep breath, shrugged. "I am a werewolf."

A hysterical laugh escaped Tori's frozen throat. "Of course you are. That would explain the super strength and being perfect at everything."

"Explanations can come later. Right now, I need to get you back to your room."

"I'm all in favor of that, considering there is a feral wolf lurking around here somewhere."

Lia nodded and scooted closer to get her arms around Tori.

Tori coughed dryly and looked away. "Do you plan to walk back to school like that?" She pulled her hoodie off and held it out to Lia. "I'm begging you, put this on."

Lia raised an eyebrow, but took it and shrugged it over her shoulders. It barely reached her thighs. "I stashed my clothes nearby. I would have gone there first, but obviously I could not leave you. If it will make you feel better, we can stop and get them before we head back."

"Please," Tori croaked.

In the next breath, she was once again being effortlessly lifted into Lia's arms. Tori wrapped her arm loosely around Lia's neck and buried her face in her own hoodie. "It was you the whole time. You really did understand everything I said," she murmured, embarrassment flushing her cheeks at the realization. "How is this possible? Do you need a kiss to break some kind of curse?"

"Why? Are you offering?" Tori squeaked at the suggestion, and Lia laughed. "It is actually an inherited condition. My whole family is like this. It is not a curse."

"Sorry," Tori said quietly. "I didn't intend the question as an insult. Actually, I think I'm in shock."

"You don't have to say anything," she said tightly. "I know it's a lot to take in."

Tori fell silent, thinking that it was the first time she had ever heard Lia sound nervous. Did she think she would be rejected? Tori certainly had a lot of questions, but she was determined that she would at least listen to what Lia had to say. Lia was the same intelligent, independent woman she had come to know over the past two years.

Lia broke the silence. "Do you think you can stand for a minute if you lean against this tree?" When Tori nodded, Lia gingerly put her down and bent to pick up some garments that were tucked next to the trunk of the tree. In one fluid motion, she peeled off the hoodie and handed it back. "If you are cold, you should put this back on."

Tori quickly averted her eyes from the bare skin illuminated by the pale moonlight, and Lia smirked. "You can look. I know you already did once before, back at the spring."

"You— That was you?" Tori sputtered. "That was an accident! I didn't mean to!" Lia was humming happily as she tugged on her jeans. "How are you so comfortable with being totally exposed, anyway?"

Lia shrugged. "It is, quite literally, second nature to me. Sometimes it just feels more relaxed when I'm not wearing clothes." Fully dressed, she once again hoisted Tori into her arms.

When they reached the schoolyard, there were a few people around and so they did not speak. Lia took Tori straight to her dorm room. She didn't ask which dorm that was, but neither mentioned it. Fortunately, Cassie had not yet returned from the party. Lia gently set Tori on her bed, which Tori did point out, and settled beside her.

"I did not mean for this to happen," Lia said quietly. "I hoped you were going to stay out of the woods. You keep getting hurt because of me."

"I'm sorry. When I heard that lonesome howling, I had to let the wolf—well, you, I guess—know I was okay."

Lia tensed. "The first time, it was me that you heard. Tonight, it was the wolf that attacked you. Knowing you would hear the howling and that you would likely come to find me, I would not have called."

Tori studied her face, wondering how such smooth skin could twist into the sharp face of the wolf. "Was that a werewolf too?"

"He was just a wolf. Most likely he was a lone wolf drawn here by my own howling." She regarded Tori with an unwavering gaze. "You needn't fear seeing him again. I have established this as my territory. Now he knows better than to come back."

Overwhelmed by the intensity of the hazel eyes that were fixed on her, Tori swallowed hard. "No one seemed to think there was any possibility a wolf was roaming around school property, and yet you've been here for two years. How come no one has ever seen you before?"

"I am usually good at keeping my wolf under my skin. I just..." She looked around the room, taking her time as she formulated her answer. Finally she sighed and said, "It is hard for a wolf child to be separated from the pack. It is not natural. So, I finally gave in and let my wolf out for a run. It felt good to be out in the woods and bathing beneath the moonlight again. It made it a little bit easier to pretend that I was not so far away from my family."

Tori looked Lia with understanding. She was in a similar circumstance. "But if it's so hard, why come to a boarding school, of all places?"

"Control is an absolute necessity for werewolves. I have always wanted to be a lawyer, but my family was skeptical that I could achieve that goal because being a lawyer is so stressful. If I were to be stressed to the point that I lost control over my wolf nature, the consequences would be disastrous. I wanted to come here because it would give me an academic boost and also prove to my family that I can keep my wolf nature under control." Her laugh was self-deprecating. "So much for that goal."

"No, you do! I can tell," Tori assured her. When Lia did not look convinced, Tori said, "The first time we met in the woods, you kept yourself from attacking me. That took self-control."

"Actually, I wasn't ever going to attack you." She rubbed her neck in embarrassment at the admission. "My wolf likes to play with you."

Tori scowled slightly. "You mean I thought I was going to die at the claws of a wolf who really just wanted to see me run?"

"It worked, didn't it?" Instead of looking apologetic, Lia's smile twisted into a predatory grin as she leaned forward. "The truth is that I have never felt in control around you. That is why I have tried to stay away from you the past two years."

"Not in control?" Tori whispered. Her heart was beating rabbit fast, and if it what she had heard about canine hearing was true, she knew it was no secret how much she longed for more information.

Lia gently cupped Tori's jaw and studied her face. "I was always afraid…" When she found no resistance in Tori's eyes, Lia shifted her gaze along her jaw line to her ultimate goal. "…I'd do something like this." Lia tilted Tori's head up and slowly pressed her mouth to Tori's lips.

Tori's lips parted when Lia's tongue slipped between them, pressing in gently. Tori inhaled sharply and slid a hand up Lia's back and grasped her shirt, pulling her closer. Instead of responding eagerly, as Tori had hoped, Lia pulled away, leaving her dazed.

"Are you sure this okay?" Lia asked with concern.

She was the most tender Tori had ever seen her, and it made her want to throw away all caution and place herself completely in the control of the spirited feral hands. She glanced from Lia's open, vulnerable expression, to her lips.

Under the onslaught of the overwhelming energy of attraction pulling them together, they came together in a scramble of arms and teeth. Lia ended up with her hands in Tori's short hair, and Tori whined low in her throat and clung to Lia as the searching lips burned a path down Tori's exposed neck. Tori gasped, shivering as the blunt tips of teeth scraped against the delicate skin that stretched over rushing blood.

Suddenly Lia pulled back, wild eyes wide with lust. She pushed her hair back with nervous hands and flushed a deep red. "Wow," she breathed. "You are so not good for my self-control."

Tori subconsciously touched her neck, which felt abandoned, and contributed a blush of her own. "I've never seen you flustered before," she said in surprise.

"Your heart is beating so fast, it's intoxicating. How am I supposed to respond to that?" Lia murmured.

Instead of sharing the embarrassing realization that she wanted Lia to lose control and feel that ferocity for her, Tori said, "Other than staying away from me, which is out of the question, what would help you maintain control?"

"A pack structure is always grounding. That is what I always relied on before."

"Can humans be pack?"

"Yes, but pack is about immense trust and connection. I have friends here, but not that level of trust with any of them. None of them even knows about me."

Tori smiled. "Well, now one does."

Lia lifted her eyes; hope flaring in their hazel depths. "Do you want that, to be pack?"

"I think I could handle it. We seem to have a strong connection already." Tori tilted her chin mischievously. "We could always test that theory."

Tori kissed her firmly, and Lia pressed back. Tori yelped, and Lia pulled away, concern clear on her face.

Tori winced from the pain caused by jostling of the bed under her eager movement. "Sorry. My ankle still hurts a bit when I move it."

"We'll have to wait for that to heal, and then I'll just have to train you how to run without injuring yourself all the time." Lia curled up beside Tori on the bed and slung an arm around her. "Rest for now, okay?"

Tori's lopsided grin was unapologetically blissful, but for once, she was not worried about what Lia would think of her. She wasn't thinking about her anxiety over school or her family. Held in the wolf's embrace, she felt safe.

Lizzie Borden Took An Axe

BY R.G. EMANUELLE

> Lizzie Borden took an axe
> Gave her mother forty whacks
> When she saw what she had done
> She gave her father forty-one.

"Now, then, Miss Borden. I'd like to begin by going over the details of your case. If you would, please."

Miss Henry gestured with a graceful hand for me to begin. She closed the drawer of the tall walnut filing cabinet from which she had just extracted a folio and sat down. When she looked up, her blue-gray eyes startled me. I don't know what I was expecting. Something more cold and calculating, I suppose.

She appeared a serious woman, dressed in a smart dark gray suit with red buttons down the front, a red belt, and red trim at the bottom of her skirt. On her head was a prim little hat, the kind that ladies don't even bother removing, without so much as a feather in it. It was understated, but I got the feeling that it was purposely that way. Her red-tinted lips matched her suit's accents. Her eyes were warm, if a little wary, and her voice steady.

It was a hot summer day, just like that fateful morning two years before, but Miss Henry's office was cool, aired by an electric fan positioned on the window sill.

My own dress was only slightly less prim. As a Sunday school teacher, it had become my way to dress conservatively. However, I'd wanted to make a good impression on her, so I wore my navy blue silk, the best dress I had. Although with my slightly plump figure, I didn't think I'd look anywhere as good as Miss Henry did.

At my feet lay the canvas sack in which I carried my hatchet—a different one from the original. I took it with me everywhere I went now. Just in case.

Despite my nervousness and the importance of this meeting, I couldn't help enjoying the comfort of the upholstered wing chair, opposite her desk. I rubbed the rich leather with my forefinger. My father had been too frugal to indulge in such luxuries and they were still new pleasures for me. I was trying my best not to appear self-conscious. Someone who is self-conscious is looked upon suspiciously. I learned that the hard way.

A curio cabinet, the kind you see at the druggist's, stood against one wall of Miss Henry's office. Through its glass panels I could see several wooden boxes and a few large books. The boxes looked like teak, carved with intricate leaves, flowers, and birds. No doubt the locks on the cabinet had been employed.

With the folio open in front of her, Miss Henry folded her hands on top of the pages. She waited patiently for me to answer, although one delicate eyebrow twitched up. My stomach tightened, and I wished that Nance had come with me. I felt like some wild creature being studied in a laboratory, and a squeeze from Nance's delicate hand would have bolstered my self-confidence.

Up until then, I had professed my innocence, vehemently denying the abhorrent charges leveled against me. I cleared my throat before I spoke, in the hope of appearing casual. Then, I told Miss Henry my tale. It was the first time I'd ever spoken it aloud. And I hoped it would be my last.

My father brought home Mrs. Borden—my stepmother—when I was small, and I took an instant dislike to her. I couldn't have said at the time, or in the years that followed, what it was about her that brought on this feeling in me. Her dour, masculine face and thin wiry hair repelled me when I looked at her, and her hard, reproachful lips made her undesirable to speak with. I never understood what my father saw in her. I believe she tried to be a mother to me and Emma, my sister, but I always sensed a darkness in her that made me uneasy. I called her "Mother," having been conditioned to do so at an early age, but after a certain point, I could no longer abide calling her that. To me, she was Mrs. Borden.

Oh, she was mean and good for nothing. But there was something else. A feeling deep inside that something about her wasn't right. She often spoke to me as a mother would to her daughter, but she didn't fool me. Beneath that occasional pleasantness, there was something bad. Very bad.

She wasn't the nicest woman, but in the year of her death, her personality had worsened, and she'd become very cross with Emma and me. I'd overheard some people in town talking, saying that she was suited to my father since Father was not very well liked. It was true—he was quite discourteous to others and could be downright thoughtless and even cruel, like the time he fired three of his employees on Christmas Eve.

At first, I'd thought that perhaps Mrs. Borden had taken ill because, although her weight remained constant, she'd begun to look drawn and ashen, and maybe that was why she'd become so unpleasant.

I began to observe her, surreptitiously following her around, listening to her conversations, watching her every move. Whenever feasible, I followed her into town. I was a little concerned because of her appearance and wondered what her diet had become. But Emma and I had stopped taking meals with our parents some time before.

She acted erratically as well. She spent a lot of time locked in her room and I heard strange noises, particularly at night. There were scraping sounds and whistling. Not like someone whistling a tune, or like the wind whistling though vacant rooms. And there was an eerie feeling in the air, a disruptive tremor, a palpable sensation of evil.

I thus came to the conclusion that she was a witch.

Here, I stopped. Miss Henry nodded for me to continue. I did.

At the library, I learned all I could about witchcraft and it all began to make sense—the strange hours, her mysterious activities, and her behavior. I decided that her demeanor, her heightened cruelty, was a manifestation of her black heart. You can't be the Devil's bride and still be kind and compassionate.

I looked for signs of witchcraft everywhere. In her work room, I left nothing unexamined. I turned over every item in her room—her sewing box, her grooming case, the linen cabinet. I rummaged through her armoire and her drawers. Her dresses were old and the soles of her boots seemed worse for wear, but neither had secret spaces or hidden pockets. Nor did her hats, or her dressing gown, or her brooches. There were no potions, talismans, pentagrams, or magic books anywhere in the house.

Yet I was certain of my theory. Sometimes she would go out late at night, creep down the stairs, and go out the side entrance. She'd come back an hour or so later, tiptoe back upstairs, and disappear into her room. I knew because I began to sit up at night, waiting for her to leave. I wondered where she went and what she did at that hour but, unfortunately, following her at night wasn't possible. The subject of her nocturnal outings never came up in conversation. At least not that I heard.

Even her daytime outings were mysterious. She would go out two or three times a week, and tell Bridget—our maid—that she was going on an errand or to the shops, but she would come home with nothing more than what she had left with. Sometimes she would say she was going to call on someone, but whenever I met anyone we knew in town, they would always ask about my parents, claiming not to have seen either one of them in some time. So I wondered, whom was she calling on?

After her outings, she would rush upstairs, never stopping anywhere else in the house. I called her once as she did so. Without stopping, she said, "I'll be down shortly, Lizzie. I must go to my room first."

It was all very odd. Maybe not to someone outside of the family, but I knew better. Emma did, too. I could see it in her expression, but when I asked her once what she thought of Mrs. Borden's behavior, her face became like that of a frightened rabbit. She denied noticing anything and walked away. I never brought it up with her again. It was clear that it was completely up to me to address the situation.

And then, one night, everything changed. That night, I heard noises in the entry hall. With an iron bookend in my hand, I crept down the stairs, thinking it might be an intruder. There had been intrusions at some of the other homes in town and I thought we might be the current target of some fiend.

In fact, I did see someone moving about in the sitting room. At first, I saw only a shadow, and I stepped off the landing so I could angle my head to see better through the crack in the door. And that's when I saw her.

My stepmother, back from one of her nocturnal outings, stood by an end table, where she'd set down her hat. Her brown linen dress was slightly disheveled and the lace of one of her boots peeked out from the hem of her skirt. She'd lit one of the lamps and her shadow shone in a long swath from her feet out to the middle of the room. She turned toward me, unseeing, almost as if in a trance, and I had to clasp my hand to my mouth to keep from screaming.

Unlike the sickly pallor that had tainted her skin lately, her face was now flushed. Her lips, especially, were plump and bright red, and God help me, there were dark crimson smudges on either side of her mouth. The same crimson stained her chin.

My suspicions had proven correct—and incorrect. She wasn't human, that was certain. But she wasn't a witch. Dear God, my stepmother was a vampire.

Questions bombarded my mind. How long had she been this way? Did my father know about this? Did he approve? My father didn't seem to fear anything except intruders, but was he frightened by this? What was he planning on doing about it? Anything? Regardless of the answers, there was no question in my mind that I had to do something. How could I allow this abomination to continue living in my own house? It was up to me to destroy her.

I stopped again. Miss Henry's expression remained interested and strangely unperturbed. "Go on," she said.

I obliged.

Through casual asking, I discovered an occult shop on the outskirts of town, to which I paid a visit and had a conversation with the proprietor. From him I learned that shooting a vampire through the heart with a silver bullet would kill it, and he informed me from whom I could purchase some silver bullets. With one of my father's guns and some regular bullets, I went out into the woods every day for a week to practice shooting. Bottles on tree branches and stumps were my targets and I shot at them repeatedly for hours.

It was summer, and even in the canopy of the trees' foliage, the heat was stifling. No breeze wound through the maze of trunks, and the ground was dry and packed. By the end of each afternoon, my dress was soaked under my arms and my undergarments clung to my skin. My hair fell in wet clumps as sweat dripped down my face and neck.

But, despite my intense practice, I was a terrible shot. I couldn't hit anything. I came close a few times, grazing the side of a quinine bottle, but that was it. Perhaps in time, I would have learned to shoot, but I didn't have time, so I had to kill Mrs. Borden another way—with a stake through the heart, or cutting off her head. And I needed to be ready for the opportunity in whatever form it presented itself. So I spent another couple of weeks practicing with bladed weapons.

Whenever both Father and Mrs. Borden were out of the house, I made sure that Emma and Bridget were occupied as well. I locked myself in the basement and practiced wielding different weapons—a hoe, an axe, and a hatchet. I seemed to hit my targets most often with the hatchet.

"How did you manage to get Bridget out so often?" Miss Henry asked.

It felt like a pebble had lodged itself in my throat, and again I wondered if I should tell her the truth. This was not information I customarily shared. How could I? Then I decided that she would probably find out anyway.

"She thought I was giving her a little extra freedom because she… we…" I tried to swallow the pebble, make room for the words.

"You were intimate?"

My entire body became rigid, every muscle pulling into painful tightness. Had I said too much and jeopardized my situation?

Miss Henry's eyebrow went up again, only this time, I thought I saw a shadow of a smile at the edge of her mouth. But it wasn't a derisive smile such as I'd seen on a few other people who'd found out about my proclivities. It was more like a smile of…approval?

I nodded in affirmation, then proceeded to blurt out an explanation as quickly as I could. I cast my eyes down to the ruby carpet, decorated with what looked like little gold crosses.

"But she was fickle and spurned me for someone else. I had tried to make Bridget happy, but she was a spoiled, feckless thing who was destined to only break hearts without ever stopping to love them." I don't know why I told her all of this. Maybe because she seemed willing to listen without judgment.

I looked up. Her head was tilted and her eyes filled with interest. I had the urge to ask her why she was unmarried but decided it was best just to continue with my story. I cleared my throat and did so.

The day it happened, Mrs. Borden left a note saying that she was going to visit a sick friend. It was a lie. She had no friends. If anyone was sick, she was probably the one making them sick with her demonic, corrupt habit. Although it was daytime, I had no doubt that this was what she was doing.

It was still early in the morning. Father had left to go downtown and our houseguest, my Uncle John, had left as well. Mrs. Borden wasn't gone long before she returned. She rushed past me and made for the stairs, muttering something about changing the sheets in the guestroom.

As she climbed the steps, slowly, stiffly, as if in a trance, she said, "Bridget, please wash all the windows in the house."

Poor Bridget. To be given such a task on such a sweltering day seemed cruel. It was only 9:30 in the morning and it was already unbearable. The air was so thick and heavy, like a fog hovering just above the street. It wasn't the cruelty of the command that bothered me, though. It was more that she said it as if she wanted to say something normal. The veil of deception is more frightening than the mantle of truth.

From her expression, Bridget was distressed. I thought perhaps she would be sick. She had been sick the day before, as had Emma and I, and I thought perhaps the thought of washing windows turned Bridget's stomach. Slightly slumped, she trudged away to the utility room to get a bucket and rags.

But I had no time to come to her aid in the matter. Everyone else was out of the house—Emma was away—and Bridget was about to be occupied. Now was my chance.

While Mrs. Borden was in the guestroom, I went down to the basement, took one of the hatchets, and went back to the second floor, where I stood in front of the guestroom door. It was ajar and I peered in.

She stood facing the bed on one side so that I saw her profile. The shades were drawn but light filtered in from the sides. Her dress was neat but her hair was a bit tousled, a few strands springing erratically from her scalp. With her eyes closed and her face turned up slightly, she pressed her hands to her thighs. Once again, she had blood around her mouth. Obviously, she'd found a victim to satisfy her unholy urges.

Her face glowed with ecstasy, and I was overcome with revulsion. I flattened my hand against my stomach to quell the lurching.

With the hatchet hidden in the folds of my skirt, I entered. As I thought she would, she sensed me coming—smelled me, I suppose—for she opened her eyes, as if being awakened from a dream. Quickly, she turned away from me.

"Hello, Lizzie," she said, her voice tense yet far away, half-sleepy. Even with her back turned to me, I could tell that she had pulled out a handkerchief and was wiping her mouth. "What brings you up here? I didn't even know you were home."

My heart pounded and the roaring in my ears made her voice sound like she was speaking behind a window. I gripped the handle of the hatchet so hard that my knuckles began to ache. The worst thing that could happen at that moment was that I'd drop it.

I'd never known fear like that before and I worried that I would lose my nerve. I moved closer to her. The thing I had in my favor was that I'd taken her by surprise. She simply hadn't been expecting an attack from me. Why would she? I was her stepdaughter. I lived in the house. "I wanted to ask you—"

She turned to face me and that quick, I lifted the hatchet over my head and swung. I hit her in the head but I knew it wasn't good enough. I felt sick. I'd never done such a thing. I stunned her enough that I was able to get in a second blow. In a flash, she bared her fangs and her eyes turned a fierce ice blue—frigid and fiery at the same time. That cold penetrated my bones and turned my blood into ice, but I did not waver. I couldn't. I swung a third time.

She stopped the hatchet from hitting her again with her forearm and she pushed back with such force, that I flew back and landed on my posterior. Miraculously, I had not let go of the hatchet and when she threw herself down to pin me, I rolled over and scrambled to my feet. I'd read that vampires had unnatural strength and agility, but Mrs. Borden was a woman of some girth—a fact that obviously had not changed by her becoming a vampire—and clearly had to struggle to maneuver herself.

Before long, however, she was on her feet again. She wobbled a moment, probably because she was now bleeding profusely, though I knew she'd heal soon enough. I struck again and she fell to her knees. She seemed disoriented, so before she could regain her senses, I struck her head again. She twisted around and fell forward, and at last remained still. For some reason, I kept striking. My terror, loathing, and some insane, unnamable drive for justice made me strike over and over, until I was sure she would not rise again.

I sank to the floor, the hatchet in my lap, and stared at the now truly dead corpse of Mrs. Borden. My limbs trembled and my heart thrummed painfully in my chest. I decided that for good measure, I would cut off her head. Soaked through with sweat and still breathing heavily I rose and stepped close to her face, then crouched down and pressed the ruffle of her collar to get a clearer view of where to hit. I lifted my hatchet yet again and aimed for the imaginary line I'd drawn on the nape of her neck. But just as I was about to bring my weapon down on her, my father returned home, sooner than I had expected.

The sound of the clicking lock meant that Bridget had opened the front door and let him in. We always kept the doors locked because our home had been invaded once before and our things were stolen. Ever since then, my father insisted on securing the doors, even during the day, even when someone was home.

"Thank you," he said. "Where's Mrs. Borden?"

"Upstairs, changing sheets, sir," I heard Bridget say.

I remained quiet and waited for him to come upstairs. Their rooms were separated from Emma's and mine and the guestroom, and required a different staircase. I listened, and once I was sure that he was in his bedroom, I ran into my own room, changed my dress, and cleaned up.

Then I ran back down the stairs, where I would work out a plan.

I don't know what made me do this—I believe it was God's directive—I ran around to the other staircase and went up to my parents' bedroom. Just as it had been with the guestroom, the door was ajar and

I peeked in. It was brighter in there than it had been in the guestroom but that didn't matter. In an instant, the entire world stopped and I was pulled into a deep, dark hole. Frozen with terror, I forgot to breathe and I thought my heart would stop. No, it couldn't be true. I couldn't—wouldn't—believe my eyes. My father had those red blotches on his lips and chin and he stood in the same state of ecstasy as Mrs. Borden had.

My own father was one of the eternal damned.

I reeled back and prayed that he hadn't seen me, smelled me, or sensed me. Oh, my heart ached. Panic seized me. My hand trembled as I brought it to my damp brow.

I went back downstairs as quickly as I could and prepared handkerchiefs to iron. I put the ironing flats on the kitchen stove to heat, in case Bridget came in. This would be my alibi. It was just in time, too, for Father came downstairs a minute later. I stood mute as he entered the parlor and sat on the sofa. My world had stopped and I wept silently.

Leaving the flats on the stove, I followed him into the parlor. He looked normal in most ways, except for that gluttonous, Godforsaken flush in his cheeks.

"Hello, Father," I said.

"Hello, Lizzie."

"How are you feeling today?"

"Oh, fine. This heat is wearing on me, though."

Yes, the heat was probably causing him great discomfort. He looked pallid beneath the flush, and I didn't know if it was the heat causing him to look that way or if it was because he was one of the undead.

I tried not to cry. I had to be a woman. He was my father and, therefore, it was my duty and responsibility to dispatch him.

I paused my story and waited for Miss Henry to say something. She eyed me curiously and seemed to study me almost as an oddity as she turned an ornate letter opener in her hand. It appeared to be solid silver and I caught a glimpse of a ruby inlay in the handle.

"Please continue," she said, twisting the point of the knife against her forefinger.

Her gaze made my throat constrict. I noticed for the first time her warm brown eyes, like soft spring soil, and the small dimple in her chin.

I had the desire to turn the conversation to her, to find out what her life was like, but I was obliged to continue my story.

Father often chose the divan to lie down although I never understood it. It was an uncomfortable old thing, fraying at the edges. But for some reason, he liked to splay himself out on it, diagonally with his feet off the side. I offered to help him change into slippers, but he refused. Then he leaned back and closed his eyes. The heat must have truly had a profound effect on him because he was soon asleep.

To create a semblance of normalcy—and to give me an opportunity to plan my next move—I went into the kitchen and sprinkled water on the handkerchiefs to prepare them for ironing. But then Bridget came back in from cleaning the windows, and I needed her out of the way.

"Are you going out this afternoon?" I asked.

"No. Did you need something?" she asked me.

"Sargent's is having a sale on dress goods—cheap. Why don't you go?"

She looked up at me wanly, her hands red and raw looking from the window washing. She appeared pale and was sweating profusely, the previous day's illness obviously returning with a vengeance. After my trial, it was rumored that I had poisoned the milk, but truly I hadn't.

"No, thank you," she said. "My stomach still isn't right. I think I'll go upstairs and lie down a bit." She trudged up the stairs lethargically.

After she'd disappeared up the stairs, I waited a few moments, then went back to my room, where I'd left the hatchet. I wiped it and once again hid it in my skirts. Once downstairs, I peered into the parlor. Father was still asleep, lying back with his feet dangling off the side, just as I'd left him.

Step by cautious step, I approached him slowly, in case he awoke. As much as I'd read about vampires, Father and Mrs. Borden were the first ones I had actually, to my knowledge, encountered and I didn't really know what they were capable of. He didn't stir, so I moved closer, stopping every few steps to be sure he didn't awaken.

I stood over him for a moment, my cross hanging on my chest. He lay there in his reefer coat, the way he had hundreds of times before. His beard was fully white, so I surmised that his transformation was recent. The lids of his eyes were paper-thin so that I could see the veins crooking through them. But his face didn't give away his secret, and there was nothing in the way he slept that spoke of his evil doings.

I peered down at his harsh face, trying to see the person who had once been my father. I didn't know how long he had been a vampire, and despite public opinion of him, he had always been kind to Emma and me.

Doubt began to creep into my brain, making me believe that perhaps I'd seen incorrectly. I began to feel as if I were in a dream—a nightmare—and I was sleepwalking. I was sure I'd wake up soon. Then I looked down at him again.

As I observed his unnatural pallor, bilious anger and resentment rose up in me and I cursed the entire race of the undead. Why had they done this to my father? To me? Now I found myself in the position of having to take my own father's life.

Then I remembered that what I was about to take was not his life—that had already been taken—but his eternal damnation. I prayed that if I released his body from this curse, I'd release his soul from the Devil's grip so that it may ascend to Heaven to be with my mother. My real mother.

I walked around and stood behind his head and raised the hatchet. My arms trembled and sweat dripped down my forehead and into my eyes. My fingers stung from squeezing the wood. My strength threatened to waiver, so before I collapsed, I raised it higher and brought it down upon him, several times. Anger and resentment rose up in me and filled my arms with strength as I struck again and again until my arms burned with pain. I went back around to the front and looked down at his destroyed face, his eyeball split in two and his nose completely severed. He never stirred.

They told me later that I delivered ten or eleven blows. Nineteen to Mrs. Borden. The rhyme about me is wrong. Forty whacks. Can you imagine the stamina you would need to hit a body forty times? I was exhausted after Mrs. Borden; I don't know how I managed to dispatch Father. I guess it was my sense of obligation and family pride that drove me. And anger.

My stomach lurched and I thought I would be sick. What had I done? Killing the terrible thing upstairs was bad enough, but this was my father. But I had to do what needed to be done. I'd failed to cut off Mrs. Borden's head but I would cut off Father's. I straightened and took a deep breath.

I gripped the handle of the hatchet and with some difficulty, swung it over my shoulder. I stood there holding the hatchet aloft, my muscles burning, trying to take aim. After a few moments, my arms began to shake.

Just then, I heard movement upstairs. It was Bridget. I had thought that she was sound asleep, but now she was moving about. I'd run out of time.

Quickly, I ran down to the basement and thumped the head of the hatchet on the floor and hung onto the end of the handle. With one foot on the head, I brought my other foot down on the handle repeatedly, until it broke off. When it finally did, it was with such force, that I fell back and landed on my rear, once again. My hands were raw from the wood and now all scratched up as well. I looked at my right palm, searing with pain, and then looked down at the rest of myself. The blood on my dress had spread into big, dark splotches, so I had to get rid of it—the second one that day. Once again, I ran back up to my room and shoved both dresses behind my washstand and drew the curtain around it.

Exhausted now, my limbs trembling and my heart racing, I went back down and stood at the foot of the stairs, listening closely, holding my breath. I'd gone up and down so many times that my calves stung with pinpricks of pain. The thick air hung heavily around me and every part of me felt heavy. My breathing slowed and as soon as I found my voice, I called up to Bridget.

"Come down, quick! Father's dead! Somebody's come in and killed him!"

Bridget ran downstairs but I didn't allow her to enter the parlor. I may have been angry with her but I didn't think she deserved to witness the carnage. Instead, I sent her across the street to fetch Dr. Bowen.

What happened after that is a bit of a blur. Mrs. Bowen came running over and asked many questions and I answered as best as I could without incriminating myself. Later, at the inquisition, I had to recollect everything that I told her and the police when they came.

I believe that God commanded me to perform the divine service and saved me, because I was acquitted of all charges. I'm sure that in my turmoil, I contradicted myself here or there or said things I shouldn't have. But I got away with it. Because I was meant to. It was my mission, and duty to God. But where I had failed to perform the task properly, He saw to it that it was done, because the coroner's office removed their heads during their examinations.

When they pulled out my father's skull during the trial, I fainted. Everyone thought it was the shock of seeing Father's skull, but it was really because I was glad, and it was hot, my stays were too tight, and I was exhausted and relieved.

But it worked in my favor.

When the trial was over, I went to the coroner's office. It was late in the afternoon and there was only one man there working in the stifling office. When he walked in from the back room and saw me, his expression told me he was not pleased to see me. He stayed behind the desk and seemed to keep something in between us at all times—at first the desk, then as he moved around, the chair, and a coat rack.

I surmised that he had recognized me from the newspapers. "Eh, may I help you, madam?" he asked.

"I understand my parents' heads are still here," I said, smoothing the skirt of my mourning dress.

The man seemed to pale and his face stiffened, as if I had just confirmed something unpleasant for him.

"Um, yes, madam. They are."

"Well, I want my parents' bodies to be whole."

The man began shuffling papers on the desk, and he looked at the clock, ticking on a side table. "Madam, the day has been long and is quite over, I'm sorry, but I must go now."

I stepped closer to the desk and he jumped back, dropping the papers to the floor.

"Sir, all I want is to honor my parents."

"Yes, of course," he sputtered. "I'll see to it that the heads are placed in their coffins."

"When?"

"It is scheduled for day after next."

Sympathy from this man was crucial, so I softened my features as much as I could and forced water to my eyes. "Please, Mister—?"

"Latham."

"Mr. Latham. I must be there. My parents would have wanted it."

Mr. Latham stood frozen a moment, staring at me. He opened his mouth a few times before finally speaking. "Well, uh, if that is what you wish." His brows came together in confusion.

"I must see them one last time."

Mr. Latham picked up his papers from the floor and placed them in a heap on the desk, roughly pushing them together. "Em, I'm not sure you want to do that. I mean, seeing them may not be as easy as you think."

"Oh, no." I shook my head earnestly. "You mustn't exhume them."

Mr. Latham blinked. "Well, how else do you expect us to bury the heads with the bodies?" His face colored and he looked down at his feet regretfully. "I'm sorry, I didn't mean to be so blunt."

I played upon his belief that as a woman, the subject matter was too disturbing. It was a bit touching, as most people believed I was a cold-blooded murderer and afforded me absolutely no compassion. This man was treating me like a human being, even if he feared me.

"Mr. Latham," I said, my voice quivering. "Please, my parents were modest, private people. They would have hated exhumation. Can't something else be done?"

Mr. Latham looked up at me and shifted his weight to one foot. "Such as?"

I pretended to think, tapping my finger against my lips. Then, as sorrowfully as I could, I said, "Couldn't you just bury them at the foot of the graves?"

"Yes, I suppose we could do that."

"Oh, bless you." I sobbed a little. "Thank you. That would have pleased them." I moved a step closer to shake his hand, but he took a step back. I don't think he meant to be obvious about it. I pulled back and thanked him again and left.

And in that way, I knew that the creatures that had inhabited my parents' bodies would not find their heads and rise again.

"Well, it sounds like you are a dedicated young woman," Miss Henry said after I finished. She'd put down the letter opener. "You've proven your abilities and have managed to escape imprisonment. I think you'll make a fine addition to our group. I will inform the secretary to add Miss Lizzie Borden to the roster."

At the utterance of my name, my skin prickled. I'd always been glad my name was not Elizabeth. I abhorred that name. Although I did not think I would mind being called Eli or Beth once in a while.

"I prefer to be called Lizbeth now," I told her.

Miss Henry smiled and her eyes seemed to hold amusement and some amount of admiration.

"Very well. As you wish." She opened up the drawer of her desk and pulled out a small card. She dipped her pen into the ink well and wrote something on the card, after which she held it out for me. "Congratulations, Miss Borden. Welcome to our humble group."

I gripped the arms of the chair, afraid I would leap to my feet with excitement. For the first time in my life, I was speechless. It was probably because for the first time in my life, I felt like I was becoming a whole person, that my life would have purpose and meaning, and that I would be respected rather than feared because it was thought that I was a murderer. Many didn't know that I had taken evil out of their midst and quite possibly saved their lives, for God only knew which one of them might have been the next victim.

I stood up as calmly as I could, pulling my sack with me. "Thank you, Miss Henry. Thanks so very much. You don't know how much this means to me."

Miss Henry chuckled. "Oh, but I do. Many others have been in your shoes. I know the sense of relief and satisfaction that comes with vindication and purpose." She stood up as well, the little hat on her head more becoming now, somehow. She smiled and I noticed for the first time the dimples in her cheeks and how very attractive she was.

"You and your Nance can come to the orientation banquet for our new members."

I stared. How did she know about Nance? She must have seen the consternation on my face because she grinned and eyed me conspiratorially.

"Oh, yes. We know more about you than you think." Then she gave me a little wink before she came from behind her desk, signaling the end of our meeting. She stopped next to the curio cabinet and my gaze remained on a peacock, deeply etched into the side of one of the teak boxes. I could almost feel the grooves with my fingers.

"Ah, yes, Miss Borden," Miss Henry said. "You will receive one of those. All our members do. I assure you, our tools are of the finest quality.

For the first time that day, I smiled. She extended her hand and told me to return on the morrow. I shook her hand and nodded mutely, then exited the office. With the door closed behind me, I looked at the little card, a lovely cream-colored stock. In the upper left-hand corner was a logo of a cross, the bottom of which came to a sharp, elongated point. If someone were to find this card, they'd never know what sort of business it was associated with, for there was nothing else printed on it. In the center of the card, Miss Henry had written in a dainty script:

Miss Lizbeth Borden—Vampire Hunter

I smiled again, slipped the card into my reticule, and headed for home, a new spring in my step.

Floyd

BY CHERI FULLER

METRO RULE NUMBER ONE: DON'T make eye contact. My daily commutes were spent as though in my own closed off bubble, semi-aware of what went on around me. Wearing headphones helped with appearing disinterested in my fellow travelers. Sometimes I wore them without even having music playing; just the illusion of listening was enough to give the impression of obliviousness and unobtrusiveness.

"Nice day, isn't it?" said a deep voice that seemed to come from my right. I turned and looked at the woman sitting next to me. She was dozing with her head resting on the window.

"No, not over there." The voice was now on my left. My head snapped around to the other side only to see the crotch of a man standing in the aisle next to me. I looked up and watched him bop his head to the beat moving through his ear buds. He was entirely too young to be the owner of the rough voice I had heard.

"Not there, either, sweetheart." The voice was centered now. Centered and coming out of the small speakers that rested on my ears. I looked down at my phone to make sure I hadn't accidentally started the music player or audio book app. I hadn't.

"That's right, darlin', I'm talking to you – just to you."

I felt the muscles in my chest constricting and my face started tingling. I looked around again and there was no one paying any attention to me at all. I snatched the headphones off and tried to will myself to calm down.

"Yeah, that's not going to do any good. I'm in your head, sweetheart, and I'm not going anywhere. Not just yet, anyway."

Jesus! What the hell is happening? Am I going crazy?

"No, not crazy. And Jesus was a nice guy but he can't help you. He died a couple thousand years ago – and stayed that way. You may run into him, though.

"Anyway, I'm Floyd and it's my job to help you through the next few minutes and drop you off at the reception center."

The tinny speaker announced Silver Spring station and I jumped out of my seat and knocked solidly into the man in the aisle. I quickly, and too loudly, apologized and dashed for the door, shoving my way past the rest of the passengers.

"Just relax, it'll be over soon. I promise, there will be very little pain and then we'll get you settled in."

The door opened and I took a step forward to escape the car and when I looked up, I was staring into the barrel of a gun, and past that, the dark eyes of the woman holding it.

"This is it. Take a deep breath and-"

Floyd was right, the pain in my forehead lasted only a split second and then it was over.

He was also right about Jesus. He is a nice guy. A bit too talkative but very nice.

The Crocodile Eye

BY GILL MCKNIGHT

THE FINAL TURN OF THE drive would once have displayed the house in all its grandeur. Now the rot in the window sills and the flaking mortar were plainly visible. The lawns needed mowing, and the fir trees allowed to grow so close to the house they blocked the light, adding a green-tinged gloominess.

The cold lump of anxiety Claire had been carting about in her stomach since Euston station hardened. She fretted away all of last night on the Caledonian overnight express, finding no comfort in the deluxe sleeper compartment her parents had booked, despite their displeasure with her. She hadn't managed the kipper breakfast either. Instead, she watched the Cairngorm mountains roll by with her forehead pressed against the window.

Her great aunt refused to send a car to meet her at Inverness, organizing instead for her to board the local train over to Muir of Ord. Great aunt Nessa was famed in the family for her meanness. At Muir of Ord, Gowrie, with his clapped out Triumph 10 waited for her outside the station. His rattling cough and the elderly engine spluttered in competition with each other, with Gowrie's lungs beating the Triumph by a whisker.

The first abrupt surprise of the morning came when he piled her suitcase onto the passenger seat, leaving her to travel behind in the dickey seat. Claire didn't really mind, she would rather be distanced from his smoke stenched tweeds and phlegmy cough, and she suspected the chance to exchange barely a word appealed to him, too. It was merely her paranoia that read this as a slight. She rebuked herself for being silly and pushed the thought away. Nessa would never share a degradation with her servants, there was too much vainglory in the family name to sully it so. Gowrie knew nothing. He was old and indecent and didn't want to make small talk with a fancy young lassie just up from London. That was all it was.

The dickey seat had its advantages. Cold as it was, it afforded her the most fantastic views across the Beauly Firth, and out towards Black Isle on the way to Bog Fada and great aunt Nessa.

Claire looked for a knocker or bell pull on the formidable oak door, weathered by almost a century of Scottish weather and lack of maintenance. High above her, carved into the lintel, the family armorial sported the date of 1824, registering the house as ninety-nine years old. Earnan Gall, Nessa's father and parliamentarian, had built the house as a hunting retreat for the Glorious Twelfth. Nessa had chosen to withdraw here as a young lady, giving up on London life after the 'Incident'. Now Claire, hot on the heels of her own incident, stood on the moss-stained doorstep, unsure if this was the right place or time for the self-contemplation her parents hoped for.

She had no need of the lost doorknocker. The heavy door swung open, and Cromarty stood before her, brows knitted and a face like a thunder clap. The housekeeper had always been formidable. Claire remembered her from childhood holidays when her family had made the tortuous trip from London to sit in the mouldy old stately home for two weeks, while outside the rain poured incessantly.

"Good morning," she greeted the housekeeper.

"Mistress is waiting for you." Cromarty turned on her heel and walked away. Claire glanced at her suitcase, balanced on the edge of the stone steps where Gowrie had dumped it, before rattling off as fast as he could go. It was rude of the housekeeper not to bring it in for her. Again, anxiety gnawed. Was this whole visit to be shrouded in rebuke and reprimand?

"Miss?"

She started, caught off guard by a maid's sudden appearance at her elbow. A small smile played around the young woman's lips on seeing Claire jump.

"You startled me," she said, feeling her face glow.

A slyness entered the maid's eyes and she gestured towards the suitcase. "I'll take that up to your room." She brushed past and snatched the bag up as if it weighed nothing, although both Claire, and in turn Gowrie, had staggered under it. Without a further word she headed for the wide, gloomy staircase.

"Miss Claire?" Cromarty called from farther up the hallway. Her voice full of displeasure to find Claire still dithering by the door. "Your aunt will see you now before the doctor arrives." So, she had an allotted time in which to be welcomed, and not a minute more. Claire moved quickly after Cromarty and was led to the rear of the house where the rooms faced south and had the better morning light.

Great aunt Nessa was bundled in wool blankets, her armchair placed close to the blazing fire, despite the midmorning sunlight beaming through the closed French windows. She sat imperious in her own little cloud of dust. Her face was heavy and sour in its perpetual frown. Claire had never remembered her any other way, though the high cheekbones and aquiline nose echoed a former glory. Nessa always looked like she'd just had bad news from her broker.

"You should have been here an hour ago." Her greeting floated across threadbare carpets and heavy, out-moded furniture.

"I couldn't have arrived any sooner," Claire said, trying to inject a breeziness she wasn't feeling. What else could Nessa expect? By not collecting her from Inverness she had unnecessarily extended the journey. There was an awkward silence as Nessa squinted around the room, no doubt seeking for something civil to say. Her thin white fingers drifted to the huge amber pendant that hung from her neck to nestle in the blankets. It was as big as a duck egg. Exotica from Burma.

"How was the journey?" she finally asked. "I suppose your parents threw money away on a sleeper?" Her thin mouth twisted. Claire could hear Cromarty's disapproving sniff behind her.

"I was safe," she answered. Let the old spinster chew on that. What was wrong with a father wanting his child to travel securely? It was his money after all. It almost amused her to be defending him against these old curmudgeons, it showed the depth of his disappointment that she should be here at all.

"You were safe." Nessa flatly repeated the words with all the chill she seemed to find in the room. The inference was not lost on Claire. She was anything but safe. She was a calamity, shuffled off here until a decision on her future could be made.

Discordant chimes rang down the hall.

"There's the doctor." Cromarty moved to the door where she waited pointedly for Claire to follow. Nessa sank further into her swathe of musty blankets. Her cheeks hollowed as her jaw sagged in contemplation of the slew of maladies she would no doubt heap upon the physician.

Claire passed Dr. Graham in the hallway, he nodded curtly as he hurried by. A harassed man with a wealthy client, his job demanded due diligence with long patience. He didn't recognise her and she was unsurprised. They'd last met several years ago, the summer before the war ended, when Teddy had the endless nosebleeds. The mustard gas had eaten away his sinuses leaving abscesses and a constant trickle of yellow discharge. But at least he got to come home early, apparently he'd been one of the lucky ones.

"You're in the Blue room," Cromarty informed her. Claire could see she wanted to return to Nessa and the doctor.

"I know where it is," she said, having no wish to spend a moment more than necessary with Cromarty.

"Moira." A maid Claire remembered from her holiday visits appeared. "Show Miss Claire to her room." Cromarty moved briskly back to the morning room.

"Miss." Moira gestured awkwardly toward the staircase. Claire recalled the girl was a bit of a dullard. Nothing seemed to have changed. Moira still had that vacant, woebegone look of the permanently disenfranchised. She led Claire to a cold, depressing room lacking natural light courtesy of the firs outside. The ugly blue of the walls and soft furnishings did little to warm or welcome.

"I'll bring up your lunch tray, miss." Moira trudged off leaving Claire to regard the few books she had brought with her stacked neatly on her bedside table. A quick check in the armoire showed her things had been unpacked and put away. She didn't like anyone handling her things, even a maid. It seemed intrusive, and she tried not think about her underclothes tucked away in the top drawer by someone other than herself.

The topmost book, *The Enchanted April,* was part read, and she lifted it to take over to the window. But instead of opening it, she found herself standing perfectly still listening to the quiet tick of the mantelpiece clock. Far away, on the crystal blue horizon the soft, buttery summit of Ben Wyvis was visible through the slimmest of gaps through the trees. She might as well be gazing out through iron bars.

The tinkle of china warned her that the door was about to open. She turned expecting Moira with the lunch tray, but it was the other girl, instead.

"Do you want it over by the window, miss?" she asked, and there was that strange look in her eye again, as if she were secretly amused.

"Yes, please. Claire refused to be drawn into another round of self-inflicted martyrdom. Instead, she indicated the small desk set under the main window.

"Elizabeth von Armin," the maid said.

"Sorry?" Claire blinked stupidly.

The maid nodded at the book in her hands. "*The Enchanted April.* It's okay I suppose, but I preferred *Vera.*"

Claire's face coloured. She had barely started this book and had not read the other. Immediately she felt unreasonably guilty for not doing so. The maid hesitated, as if waiting for an answer.

"Yes. Well. Thank you." Claire indicated the door in what she hoped was a carefree dismissal. The maid's face fell slightly, though her eyes never lost their hard gleam. She had her hand on the door knob when out of pure curiosity Claire asked, "And your name is?"

"Ailsa, miss." She bobbed into a quick curtsy, that again felt too calculatingly perky not to be impertinent. Claire was unsure what to make of her. She turned her back, refusing to relax until she heard the door snap shut.

Lunch was cold mackerel and brown bread and butter, and a pot of strong tea. There was little she wanted to do after that than take a long walk around the forest and down into the glen.

Glen Fada was deep and narrow, necklaced by wide, barren bog land. Part way down the fir and rowan stopped in a tumble of landslips and knotted roots pointing skywards, and gorse and dogwood took over. It was a wild place, thriving with deer and rabbits. At the foot, a salmon river ran toward the Beauly Firth, and even the lazy, fat fish could not lure poachers in. It was an uneasy place to be, and the superstitious locals were deterred by the rumours surrounding it. People often got lost in the glen. There had always been stories of children swallowed by the bog, or stolen away by the Siths. When they were younger, Claire and Teddy had hunted high and low for the elusive fairies with no luck.

The greatest misfortune in living memory was actually Nessa's. Her fiancé, a young man fresh from making his fortune out of Burma, had drowned while fishing in the Fada river. It had been a long, hot summer of parties, and the obligatory hunting and fishing. Claire's father had been a boy at the time, but he remembered it clearly. Nessa had been inconsolable, her grief had shrouded her life for years to come. She refused point-blank to leave the house and return to London, not even for his funeral. No one could dissuade her, neither friends nor family. She had remained at Bog Fada ever since, alone, save for the few servants she retained.

Claire went to bed that night musing on the story, now a part of her family lore. Dinner had been another lonely affair, with Nessa too frail to leave her room and join her. A second tray had been sent up, this time hot mackerel with potatoes and neeps. Moira brought in the tray on this occasion. Ailsa was nowhere to be seen.

Claire read a bit, then prepared for bed. The bathroom was along the landing, near the stairs to the second floor where the servants slept. Bessie Smith singing *Baby Wouldn't You Please Come Home*, drifted down to her. Someone up there had a gramophone player. She was tempted to follow the music, but hesitated. Upstairs was not for the likes of her. Nor was it any of her business what Nessa's servants did after hours.

She returned to her room, tired after her journey and quickly fell into deep sleep.

The crying awoke her some time after two in the morning. At first she was unsure what had disturbed her, listening to the hiss of wind through the fir needles, she was about to give up and go back to sleep when it came again. A child's sob, deep and heart rending.

Claire was unaware of any children in the house. She lay and waited to see if the child's needs would be attended to. There was silence for a while, and then the cries came again, this time as a forlorn wailing. Fully awake, Claire pulled on her dressing gown, and stepped out onto the landing. The crying stopped. The weak night-light threw long shadows, and the skittering of moth wings against the tatty silk lampshade echoed her own shallow heartbeat. The landing was long, and though ill-lit she could see it was empty all way down to where it turned a corner. Claire tightened the belt on her robe, and nervously advanced. The crying took up again, closer this time, until she was certain the child stood just around the corner.

But there was no one there. The sob came again, farther up, pulling her onward. There was no lamp here. She reached for the wall switch but nothing happened. Her eyes grew accustomed to the gloom, and up ahead she saw the soft glow of a small white nightdress and long blond hair. A little girl, no more than a five years old Claire guessed, stood sobbing in the middle of the corridor.

"Hello?" she called softly, so as not to alarm her. The child looked back at her with wet, but relieved eyes. Claire approached her carefully, aware of her distress. "Hello," she repeated. "Why are you crying, are you lost?" She must belong to one of the servants, could Moira or Ailsa have a child?

"I can't find Archie." The little girl hiccuped.

"Who's Archie? Is he your brother?" Claire asked. She was not three yards from the child, reaching out her hand. "What's your name, little one?" The girl started, and swung her head around as if she had heard something. Then she turned and ran away so fast that she disappeared into the gloom in seconds.

"Wait," Claire called, but she was gone. Perplexed, Claire could do nothing but make her way, shivering, back to her room. She paused by the foot of the servant stairs vaguely aware of music still playing despite the lateness of the hour. A cold draught whistled from an ill-fitting window and reminded her of her warm bed and she returned to her room, confused by the night's events.

"There are no children in the house," Cromarty informed her the next morning. "None."

Claire fidgeted with her breakfast cutlery. "But—" There was no point in continuing the conversation. Cromarty squelched it with a frosty glare. She lifted the empty teapot and walked away.

Nessa kept no telephone in the house, so Claire walked down to the village to call her father from the phone box. The distance between them had softened him, he was kinder as they spoke. "How is the old girl?"

"She made me come all the way to Muir of Ord." They both laughed. Nessa's penny-pinching momentarily uniting them.

"Is she still wearing that ugly old pendant?" He harrumphed. "Abhorrent thing. I suppose it reminds her of whatshisname. Daft old trout, she should have got out of there years ago." This was his usual opinion of Nessa and her indentured bereavement to her drowned lover. "Worth a fortune, you know. It's been valued by Sotheby's. Must be the size, certainly ain't the aesthetics."

"I saw a child," Claire said, keeping him on the line a little longer. "A little girl. Last night. She was crying."

"Crying?" His attention was fading fast. She had chosen the wrong subject to engage him.

"But Cromarty told me there were no—"

"Last child I remember up there was Cromarty's own brat. Little ragtag of the thing."

"A girl? About four or five years old?"

"Yes. Girl. Got to have been about that age."

"And when was this?" Claire asked in genuine interest. She couldn't imagine Cromarty as a doting mother.

"Lord, I must have been about ten. It was around the time of the drowning. God awful year." He rang off soon after that, and Claire drifted back up the brae to the house, deep in thought.

She spent the afternoon in the library, after getting Moira to light a small fire. It was disgrace that the room was left so cold, it could hardly be good for the books. The real collection had been sold off years ago, much to her father's disgust. At least Nessa had realised her frugal ways were inducing mould, and mice, and other book destroyers, and had swelled her coffers considerably rather than let the pages rot. All that remained were reference books, the Austens, Eliots, and Miltons long gone. At first Claire sat with her own book but found she could not settle. Soon, she was roaming the shelves, tea cup in hand looking for anything to catch her idle eye. *Opuscula Mythologica Burma*. It had to be worthless to be on the shelves, but still, the old tooled leather and gilt embossing on the spine proved irresistible. Claire pulled it off the shelf and was surprised to see a faded inscription to Nessa from a Major J.R.R. Wiley. This was the dead fiancé, at least she guessed it so, knowing he'd been a Cavalry officer before becoming a successful gem trader in Mandalay. So, the book was not worthless after all then, at least not to Nessa. Claire was ashamed to disregard the old woman's tragedy so glibly.

The yellowed pages fell open where the back was cracked. Another reader had favoured these exact pages many, many times. The origin of 'The Crocodile Eye' lay before her. Claire realised she was reading the mythology around a particular pendant, which she had seen around Nessa's neck practically every day of her life. The amber stone was one of the largest to be found in the Hukawng valley. A rare specimen, cognac in colour, it was ancient and laced with legend. Inside, fossilized in minute detail, was a small black spider. A Heart spider, so called because of the tapered shape of its body. No other example existed, this specimen was over one hundred million years old. At some point in prehistory this little poisonous arachnid had been encased in pine sap for all eternity. The stone was priceless for this entombed creature alone. The moniker Crocodile Eye came from the cognac colouration with its streak of black. Claire had often seen the stone up close as a child, for her the cold malice the gem exuded leant more to the name than anything else.

"It's creepy ain't it?" The voice made her jump. Ailsa looked over her shoulder at the pages. Claire made to shut the covers but stopped herself at the last moment. She couldn't bare the smug look that slid over Ailsa's face.

"How so?" she asked instead, watching as Ailsa gathered up the tea things.

"Read on." She nodded at the book. "Read about the legends surrounding it. Nasty thing. I think the Burmese did well to be rid of it, though I suspect our bonny Major stole it."

"What a thing to say." Claire was surprised at this outspokenness. Ailsa was a curious creature, she most certainly didn't behave like a maid. She nodded at the book again.

"Read. You'll see what I mean."

Claire hesitated. Ailsa set the tray back down and took the book out of her hands and read aloud. "The Heart spider is so called as it was believed to burrow into the heart organ of its prey to lay its eggs, the living organ thus becoming a nest. When the young hatched by the thousands, they ate away the surrounding tissue to swarm from the breast of their host." Her voice was clipped and cool, and she did not hesitate over any of the words. She was intelligent and well-educated, but Claire already knew this. Ailsa flicked her a level look before continuing. "The Myanmar people believed the stone brought bad luck to those who touched it. Local legends state that the spirit of the Heart spider burrows into the heart of the owner and hatches out evil, offering anything the heart desires while slowly ingesting it until the owner dies an empty husk. Then another host must be found."

"How horrid." Claire frowned. She didn't sense that Ailsa was deliberately trying to disgust her. If anything Ailsa's face was as grim as hers.

"Imagine hanging that thing around your neck," she said. "Imagine giving it as a gift to the one you loved. He'd been chasing her for years, did you know that?" Claire didn't know. "Absolutely years. And then, when he gets her, he drowns." Ailsa snapped the book shut. Claire jumped.

Ailsa looked directly at Claire, who had no clue what to say. Once again, Ailsa looked disappointed with her. She set the book aside and lifted the tea tray.

"Was that you playing Bessie Smith?" Claire asked, far too quickly, and she flushed.

"Yes. I have a gramophone. You're welcome anytime you want to listen." Her eyes were bright again, slick with something Claire couldn't read. The pulse fluttered in her throat. Was Ailsa flirting with her? It was such an unusual thing for a maid to say to a houseguest, it couldn't be entirely innocent, could it?

250

That night the crying started again. Claire's sleep had been troubled, plagued by dreams of spiders, and children who looked like little voodoo dolls with amber eyes. She was on her feet immediately, reaching for her dressing gown, moving faster this time.

The girl was in the exact same place, sobbing dreadfully. "Are you looking for Archie, again?" Claire asked. She managed to get much closer this time. The child looked up at her, face filled with so much hope that Claire was determined to help her.

"He isn't talking to me," the child said, and looked to her left. There, in the gloom, Claire could just make out the shape of a boy. He was taller than the girl by about half a head, but still very young. And whereas the girl was in her nightgown, he wore grubby, ill-fitting clothes, like a village child.

"Archie?" Claire asked. Although he was small and non-threatening she felt curiously unsettled on seeing him. He emerged slowly from the shadows until she could make out his pale face and mop-top of dark hair. He had to be six, maybe seven years old. His arms were folded defensively across his thin chest, and his face was wet with tears, though he looked at her defiantly through his hurt. "Are you Archie?" she asked again.

He nodded glumly and slowly unwrapped his arms. Claire relaxed. She would find out who they belonged to and gently berate whichever servant allowed their children to roam the corridors this late at night. Cromarty was obviously lying to her, for whatever reason. Perhaps even covering for someone?

Archie outstretched his arms to her, imploring to be held as any small child might. Claire moved toward the hug, then stiffened, and her relief turned cold. The hands he reached out to her were bloodied stumps. Every finger and thumb had been severed off. Claire recoiled, and the boy opened his mouth, anger flooding his dirty little face, he squealed like an animal through the bloody cavern of his mouth. His tongue had also been removed. Claire made a noise, it was not a scream, she could not draw in enough air for that. It was a choking sound of horror and distaste; and the boy heard it and turned and fled.

Beside her the girl gave a wavering cry of grief and turned to Claire reaching for her like a babe to its mother. Claire saw that she, too, was missing half of her hands, severed across the palm, straight and clean, as if by a cleaver. She backed away from the child until her hip rattled against a table. The girl sobbed at the rejection, and ran after Archie, leaving Claire alone in the dark. Her chest ached with fright and cold sweat trickled between her breasts.

Claire stumbled back along the corridor to her room. On passing the servant stairs faint music drifted down from Ailsa's room, and without stopping to think Claire ran up to her.

Ailsa had cheap dark rum. It was cloying but Claire gulped it down greedily.

"No fingers, you say?" Ailsa looked mystified. "Yuck."

"The boy had no tongue." Claire took another gulp. Heat hammered through her and her legs felt liquid. She had no hope in standing for the next few minutes.

"I haven't been here that long, but I've heard the other servants talk about ghosts. Though Cromarty has been known to fire those who go on about it too much."

"Why would she do that?"

"To stop idle talk becoming hard fact, I suppose. You know what small villages are like, full of gossip and rumours."

Claire thought about this. "My father says Cromarty came here with her daughter when she first started."

"Moira told me her girl disappeared years ago. They say she wandered into the bog. A wee fella went the same way a few years before. Every so often the bog snares one." Ailsa shrugged the way one does in sharing the sympathy but not the experience.

"My ghosts were a boy and a girl."

"There's been more than two lost over the years." Ailsa refilled her glass, and took a generous measure for herself. The gramophone hissed as the needle bumped across the last grooves. Ailsa reached over to reset it and *Indiana Moon* filled the little garret room. Ailsa kept it cosily cluttered with all the paraphernalia necessary for a young modern. There were plenty of clothes, shoes, and perfume bottles. It reminded Claire of her friends flats back in Soho above the bars where they could dance until the small hours. She wondered what Ailsa did on her days off. There had to be somewhere to go and dance, she decided, looking at a dainty pair of pearl-strap shoes.

"Nice shoes." She gestured and rum sloshed down her front.

"Here." A cloth was pressed against the spill. "Do you dance much?"

Claire nodded, not trusting herself to speak. Her cheeks were flushed from the drink, and her earlier fright had unnerved her so much that she was far from sensible. She knew what the pressure on her breast was, and it was not to soak up the rum spill. She should never have come up here.

"With your girlfriends?" The question was insidious and knowing. The pressure on her breast was gently pushing her back on the bed until Ailsa lay over her. "Show me how you dance with your girlfriends." Her hand slithered along Claire's thighs up under her nightdress. Claire started upward but Ailsa kissed her, pressing her back down. She bruised Claire's lips forcing them apart and pushing her rum soaked tongue in. "Show me what your fancy London girls do. This is what we do up here, but then we're all rough Highlanders," she murmured into her mouth. Her fingers roughly probed the folds of Claire's sex. Blunt fingernails scratched at her labia. Claire squeezed her legs and eyes tight shut. The hand stilled.

"Look at me," Ailsa said, her voice thick and smoky. Claire opened her eyes. Ailsa looked down at her, her gaze hot and sly. "Open your legs."

Claire let her legs fall apart. Ailsa heaved off her to pull the nightdress all the way up to her waist. She examined her nakedness for several moments before declaring in a matter-of-fact voice, "You've a nice cunt. All trim and proper." She held Claire's gaze as she slid a finger into her as deep as it would go. "Tight, too." She pulled her finger out and in slowly, always watching Claire's face. When she swapped over to two, Claire gasped, and a small smile played on Ailsa's lips. "If you were the mistress here..." she moved her fingers in and out at a steady pump, "...I'd have you serve me tea every afternoon...naked...and I'd pour the cream and sugar all over your tits...and lick it off."

Claire's face flamed. She grunted. Grunted like a small animal. She could hear the wet slap of Ailsa's hand grinding against her. She spasmed when three fingers were roughly pushed into her, her cunt wet and eager to grab them.

"Tell me more." Claire's head fell back and she looked at the ceiling. "What if I were naughty?"

"I'd beat you. With the riding crops downstairs. Across your lovely, milky ass." Ailsa slapped her hard across the bottom. The sting was so sharp and unexpected, and thoroughly delicious that she came, feeling the deep ache bloom into dampness on her thighs and seep across Ailsa's palm. Ailsa disentangled her hand. "Of course," she said, lightly. "You'd have to be mistress." She raised her fingertips to her nose and inhaled.

It rained all the next day, trapping her in the house. She moved restlessly from room to room, edgy from the sex and her fright from last night, until she ended up back in the library.

"What do you know of the ghosts?" she asked Moira, out of the blue. She started as if Claire had poked with a sharp stick and sidled away. "Whatever's the matter, Moira? You don't believe in ghosts do you?" She laughed nervously, and saw from the ruddiness on Moira's cheeks that she did. "Well? Tell me." She knew she was bullying her, but she was bored and wanted to know.

"It's the lost children, miss," Moira said, sullenly. She lived in the village and would be well aware of the rumours Cromarty hoped to squash. "Since that twally got himself drowned there been seven bairns lost. They're nere allowed near the glen no more."

"Because of the bog?"

"Cos o' something, miss." Moira had scuttled close enough to the door to beat a quick retreat from any further questions.

Claire mulled over the curious answer, and looked to the shelf where the *Opuscula Mythologica Burma* was kept. It was not there. She frowned. Who would have taken it? Ailsa? Even thinking of her was enough to flush her thighs with warmth.

The empty slot on the shelf had been claimed by the lopsided tilt of a neighbouring book. Claire tilted her head to read the spine. It looked to be as old as the *Opuscula,* but a lot more battered. The title read, *Diabolism Alba.*

"Scottish witchcraft," Claire roughly translated. With shaking hands she drew it down from the shelf. Remembering the broken spine on the *Opuscula,* she allowed the book to fall open where it would. It opened at a page entitled, 'For the preservation of youth and beauty'. Another well-read passage, but what caught Claire's attention was the faint, irregular staining of the pages. She moved to the window to examine the brown marks better, until she was satisfied they were blood.

With a chill in her heart she sat down and read the nasty little piece. It concerned the dismemberment of children, detailing the best morsels of young flesh that, when anointed at particular phases of the moon, would grant longevity to those who feasted. Tiny fingers and tongues. Claire's stomach lurched. She took the book and left the library.

Ailsa was in the hallway with Cromarty. Her eyes narrowed as Claire approached, dropping to the book and back up at her. "Miss?" Ailsa said, and it came out as a question.

"Where is my aunt?" Claire asked Cromarty, ignoring Ailsa. She couldn't chance any weakness now, sexual or otherwise.

"She's resting." The answer was short and snappish.

"I asked where she was, not what she was doing." Claire's voice had become hard-edged. Her jaw was set so firmly she could feel the ache in her face muscles. A shadow of disquiet flickered in Cromarty's eyes. Ailsa didn't say a word, but watched with a cunning that missed nothing.

"She's in the morning room, if you must know." Cromarty refused to be cowed, but Claire didn't care. She was already moving toward the back of the house. "She's sleeping," Cromarty called after her. Claire ignored her.

Nessa wasn't sleeping. She was bundled in her blankets by the fire, reading the *Opuscula Mythologica Burma*. The heavy amber pendant lay clutched in her withered, age-spotted hand, her awkward caress almost a convulsion. The book lay open at the Crocodile Eye section. How often had she read it, Claire wondered.

"Did you forget this?" Claire held up the *Diabolism Alba*. "What a waste. All that pain, and you're old, and done, and dying, after all."

Nessa's face darkened. Her hard-as-flint eyes flashed nothing but hatred. "*You're* the waste, you walking disappointment."

Claire refused to be drawn. "What about Major Wiley? Did he really drown? Or is the answer in here somewhere?" She tapped the cracked leather cover.

"How should I know, you simpleton? It's not my book." This threw Claire, but she tried her best not to let it show. "Cromarty brought it with her." Nessa's face settled into a mask that Claire could only describe as undiluted evil. Cromarty had been her accomplice all these years. And her daughter, what about her own daughter? Claire was rigid with shock. Not that Nessa noticed, she was too caught up with her spite. "He got what he wished for— me. He had me, and then he died. It's what the Eye does."

She threw Claire a withering glance. "Did you really think I expected to live forever, stupid girl? I will live for as long as I want, and always be beautiful for my age." This was said with the hubris of an ill-informed old woman. Had she bothered with the London set she had been so quick to turn her back on, she would have realised how far removed she was from the modern measure of beauty.

Claire itched to tell her, but Nessa did not pause in her overspill of bile. "Am I to be accountable to a deviant such as you? Why, you are an unnatural, impudent, slattern, foisted onto me because no one else wants you to be seen! You have shamed your family name. You are unfit for the society you were born into. You have—"

Claire had heard enough. She strode over and tore the priceless pendant out of Nessa's hand. The chain broke away from the scrawny neck, scratching the flaps of loose skin. She refused to be left here to rot! She would sell the ugly thing, and run away to New York, or Paris, or wherever girls like her went.

Nessa cried out and struggled to rise from her chair. A corner of blanket slid from her knees into the fire and caught alight.

"No. No." Nessa flapped at the flames blooming on her lap. Driven by layers of dust and dry woollen fibre the blankets blazed up, swaddling Nessa in a fiery cocoon. Claire stood transfixed by the burning ball in front her. Nessa's screams brought Cromarty flying into the room with Ailsa at her heels. They halted in disbelief and bewilderment as to what to do. The screaming suddenly stopped, and Nessa, chair and all, toppled over and the carpet began to burn. Ailsa broke the horrified stupor that bound them by leaping forward and battering at the flames with a cushion. Cromarty quickly followed her lead and soon the flames died out.

What was left was repellent. Nessa's entire torso had been severely burned, leaving her head and lower limbs intact. Her face was wretched;

twisted into a grim rictus of unimaginable agony. Her chest cavity lay split open and seemed to stir with a thousand black specks that surged forward before dissipating into the air. All three women hastily stepped back, unnerved by the momentary slither of black.

"What was that?" Ailsa breathed. Her look ghoulish. "It looked like spiders. Tiny wee spiders. Thousands of them."

"Soot," Claire stated, her voice coming out stronger than she felt. "Only soot," she repeated. "She was seated far too close to the fire." There was a faint and deliberate accusation to her words. "There was nothing I could do."

Cromarty stirred, the blame not missing her. She looked at Claire with shock, her eyes travelling down to the pendant that hung over Claire's heart, then Cromarty paled and backed slowly out of the room.

"Inform the police," Claire called after her, "and Dr. Graham," she added as an afterthought. Her hand fell to the amber stone. She could not recall placing the pendant around her neck.

"We need to get out of here." Ailsa flapped away the acrid smoke layered about them. "It stinks," she said bluntly. She pulled open the French doors. They creaked as if they'd not been used for decades, and both women stepped out into the fresh air.

"I can copy her handwriting," Ailsa announced. Claire looked at her, confused. "Down to a tee," she explained further. Claire still could not follow her. Ailsa smiled. "A new will and testament by the morning." She grinned. "Unless you don't want to be mistress after all?" A faint flash of uncertainty crossed her face.

The amber in Claire's hand grew warm and heavy. If she had the house to sell she could keep the Crocodile Eye for herself, and still afford to travel. Maybe even with a maid? Of course, it meant her father would miss out on his rightful inheritance. Claire smiled. "Yes. I should like to be mistress."

In the early evening, a drizzly mist fell, and Claire walked to the head of the glen, glad to be free of the house and the endless questions from the professionals who managed sudden deaths such as Nessa's. Ailsa, now her housekeeper, was setting the morning room to rights after the body had been removed. Cromarty had disappeared.

Claire moved out from under the fir trees and emerged at the top end of Bog Fada. From there she could skirt the brackish waters and reach the head of the glen safely. She hesitated squinting into the mist that was blending into an early, cloud-covered dusk. Had she seen movement out on the bog? She stood and waited. Perhaps a deer was heading homewards? The mist shifted and for one short moment she thought she saw Cromarty. She was trudging through the bog, out into the heart of it, her long dress raised away from the mud that was already sucking at her ankles, ready to claim more and more of her with each step. On either side of her, walking over the same mud, but lightly, with no bother at all, were two young children. A girl and a boy.

Crash and Burn

BY CHERI FULLER

THE FRANTIC POUNDING ON THE door jerks you awake. Glancing at the clock, you groan when you see that you've only been asleep for an hour. The gin still weighs your brain down. You will the unexpected visitor to go away to no avail; the hammering continues, now joined by desperate yelling.

With a deep sigh, you swing your legs over the edge of the bed and snatch up the baseball bat kept next to the headboard. The polished wooden floor is icy under your bare feet and this only fuels your irritation. Oddly, you feel no fear, just annoyance at being disturbed. Out in the middle of nowhere, you shouldn't have to deal with people just showing up. There shouldn't be anyone around for miles, which is exactly why you bought the place. After the trial, all you wanted was peace and solitude.

The pounding hasn't let up at all and the yelling is getting more demanding. You check the peep hole. A blonde woman, her tear streaked face turned up to the porch light, is hitting the door with her open palms now.

"Ok! I'm opening the door! Please step back!"

As soon as the door is opened a sliver, the woman shoves her way in.

"My babies! My babies are trapped in the car! I can't get them out! You've got to help!"

There's something vaguely familiar about this woman but you can't place her.

She grabs your hand and pulls you out. She's hysterical and you have no time to think.

You're running now, the crying woman still holding your hand, pulling you through the woods. In the distance, you notice the glow of what seems like a large bonfire. The woman yanks on your arm and increases her speed, all the while crying and calling out to her children.

Moving at a full out run, you realize why the woman looks familiar. But she looks so different with her wild hair and face mottled by tears and fear. In court, she seemed nearly catatonic with grief and you tried to avoid looking at her at all. Your feelings of guilt and remorse and self-disgust had prevented you from doing more than begging for forgiveness and leniency.

It was shortly after reading the report of her suicide that you packed up and moved. Her suicide. You release her hand and fall to your knees and she stops running and turns to face you. Now you can see the bruises from the rope around her neck.

"My babies! What are you going to do to save them?!" She stomps toward you, her face morphed from terror and fear to rage. Your clothes are beginning to smoke and you feel your body temperature rise quickly. Looking down, you see the leaves you're kneeling on ignite but you can't make your body move. You look up and into the woman's eyes and, as your vision is overtaken by the rising flames, you say, "I'm sorry."

About The Authors

JOVE BELLE

Jove Belle lives in Vancouver, Washington with her family. Her books include *The Job*, *Uncommon Romance*, *Love and Devotion*, *Indelible*, *Chaps*, *Split the Aces*, and *Edge of Darkness*.

CONNECT WITH THIS AUTHOR:
Website: http://www.jovebelle.com

LILA BRUCE

Lila Bruce makes her home in the mountains of North Georgia, where the air is sweet and the summers are hot. Growing up in a military family, she traveled extensively as a child, living everywhere from Maine to Mississippi, Germany to Georgia, and a few parts in between. Lila loves to read and write contemporary lesbian romances and is a sucker for a happy ending.

When not writing, she spends her days adding to her ever-growing pack of basset hounds, consuming unhealthy amounts of coffee, and dreaming of the day she's able to leave her evil day job behind.

CONNECT WITH THIS AUTHOR:
Facebook: https://www.facebook.com/
profile.php?id=100008141147074
E-mail: authorlilabruce@gmail.com
Twitter: https://twitter.com/AuthorLilaBruce

CHERI CRYSTAL

Cheri Crystal is a healthcare professional by day and writes erotic romances by night. She is a native New Yorker who was born in Brooklyn and raised on Long Island. Recently, Cheri has crossed the pond to live in the United Kingdom with her loving wife. A day doesn't go by that she doesn't miss her three kids, technically adults, but thanks to Skype and lots of visits with her family, she enjoys living in England's southwest coast. Cheri began writing fiction in 2003 after reviewing for Lambda Book Report, *Just About Write*, *Independent Gay Writer*, and other e-zines. She is the author of *Attractions of the Heart*, a 2010 Golden Crown Literary Winner for lesbian erotica. In her spare time, she enjoys swimming, hiking, viewing wildlife, cooking, jigsaw puzzles, and spending quality time with family and friends.

CONNECT WITH THIS AUTHOR:
Website: http://www.chericrystal.com
Facebook: http://www.facebook.com/chericrystal

MAY DAWNEY

May Dawney is a twenty-nine year old fiction and fan-fiction writer. As a lesbian, almost all her work focusses on portraying lesbian relationships, either within an existing franchise or in a world of her own design. She has been writing for as long as she can remember, making comic books with her mom as a child, finding her voice through on-line roleplay, and honing her skills through fanfiction. She is relatively new to original fiction, but is quickly growing addicted to the freedom it offers.

May lives with her long-term partner, and their eighteen year old cat, in The Netherlands where she balances far too many projects for her own good—and she loves every single one of them.

CONNECT WITH THIS AUTHOR:
Website: http://maydawney.blogspot.com
E-mail: maydawney@gmail.com

R.G. Emanuelle

R.G. Emanuelle is a writer and editor living in New York City.

Her university degree in English and literature propelled her into publishing, where she spent 20 years as an editor, typesetter, and graphic designer. She is co-editor of *Skulls and Crossbones: Tales of Women Pirates*, and her short stories can be found in *Best Lesbian Erotica 2010; Lesbian Lust: Red Hot Erotica; Women in Uniform: Medics and Soldiers and Cops, Oh My!; Lesbian Cops: Erotic Investigations; Khimairal Ink; Read These Lips*, Volumes 4 and 5; and the online collection Oysters & Chocolate. When she was child, a neighbor called her a vampire because she only came out after dark, so it's fitting that her first novel, *Twice Bitten*, is about creatures of the night.

When she's not writing or editing, she can usually be found cooking or developing recipes, as she is also a culinary school graduate.

CONNECT WITH THIS AUTHOR:
Facebook: https://www.facebook.com/RGEmanuelle
Blog: http://www.rgemanuelle.com
E-mail: rgemanuelle@gmail.com
Twitter: https://twitter.com/RGEmanuelle

EVE FRANCIS

Eve Francis's short stories have appeared in Wilde Magazine, The Fieldstone Review, Iris New Fiction, MicroHorror, and The Human Echoes Podcast. Romance and horror are her favourite genres to write in because everyone has felt love or fear in some form or another. She lives in Canada, where she often sleeps late, spends too much time online, and repeatedly watches old horror movies and *Orange Is The New Black*.

CONNECT WITH THIS AUTHOR:
Website: http://evefrancis.wordpress.com
Tumblr: http://paintitback.tumblr.com

CHERI FULLER

Cheri Fuller is a book reviewer, podcaster, and freelance proofreader who tends to have more side-jobs and projects than time. Luckily, her family is very understanding. Or they're just happy to have a break from her. She chooses to believe the former.

Cheri lives in Wisconsin with her wife, young son, and two old dogs. When she's not working at her day job or doing something book related, she enjoys gaming, geocaching, and freaking people out with her short stories.

JESS LEA

Jess Lea lives in Melbourne, Australia, where she started out as an academic before working in the community sector. Historical fiction is her favourite obsession, especially for the way it lets us imagine the lives of women and people of unconventional genders and sexualities, so often left out of the official record. Jess spends her free time haunting the cafes of St Kilda, watching bad 60s horror films, and writing stories.

CONNECT WITH THIS AUTHOR:
E-mail: Jessleacontact@gmail.com

GILL McKNIGHT

Gill McKnight is Irish but spends as much time as possible in Lesbos, Greece, which she considers home. She can often be found traveling back and forth between Greece and Ireland in a rusty old camper van with her rusty wee dog. Gill enjoys writing, roses, and by necessity DIY.

CONNECT WITH THIS AUTHOR:
Website: www.gillmcknight.com

Mary-Anne O'Malley

Mary-Anne O'Malley was born and raised in the suburbs of North Carolina. Her childhood was spend on soccer fields, mountain bikes, and hiking trails. Summer held sunburn and scrapped knees while winter meant hot chocolate and Christmas trip shopping in the mountains. Hoping to graduate in 2017 she is an English major at UNC Chapel Hill with a creative writing minor. Life after graduation is mystery but she hopes to continue improving her writing skills.

Emma Sterner-Radley

Having spent far too much time hopping from subject to subject at university back in her native country of Sweden, Emma finally emerged with a degree in Library and Information Science.

Now she lives with her wife and two cats in England, there is no point in saying which city as they move about once a year. She spends her free time writing, reading, daydreaming, working out and watching whichever television show has the most lesbian subtext at the time.

Her tastes in most things usually leans towards the quirky and she loves genres like urban fantasy, magic realism and steampunk.

Emma Sterner-Radley is also a hopeless sap for any small chubby creature with tiny legs and can often be found making heart-eyes at things like guinea pigs, Dachshunds, wombats, marmots and human toddlers.

Tiana Tatanov

Tiana Tatanov is a debuting author from a small country in Western Europe. She has been writing short stories ever since she was seven years old and intends to keep doing so for as long as she can. Fanfiction introduced her to the wonderful world of erotica and she recently decided to take the plunge into professional writing. She strongly believes in the need for diversity in fiction, which she tries to reflect in her own work. Two of her short stories have been published in *Heart, Body, Soul: Erotica with Character* and *Between The Shores: Erotica with Consent*.

KATE WELSHIRE

Kate Welshire is a university student with an affinity for the absurd. She lives with her long term partner, which is a calico cat who judges all of Kate's life choices. Of which, day dreaming about fantastical phenomenon and sometimes spilling it onto a page is central. Her other interests include culture and language studies, art, looking at hipster photography, and consuming a worrisome amount of chocolate.

CONNECT WITH THIS AUTHOR:
katewelshire@hotmail.com
katewelshire.tumblr.com

Other Books From Ylva Publishing

www.ylva-publishing.com

The Secret of Sleepy Hollow

Andi Marquette

ISBN: 978-3-95533-518-2
Length: 166 pages (45,000 words)

Graduate student Abby Crane schedules a research trip over Halloween weekend for Sleepy Hollow, in search of material for her doctoral thesis and answers about her long-lost ancestor, Ichabod Crane. Local folklore says he disappeared at the hands of the ghostly headless horseman—or did he? With the help of the attractive Katie McClaren, Abby finds much more than she ever thought possible.

Caged Bird Rising

Nino Delia

ISBN: 978-3-95533-319-5
Length: 237 pages (62,000 words)

In a world dominated by men, it should be Robyn's greatest fortune that the handsome Hunter Wolfmounter sees her as the perfect fertile wife. But an encounter with a mysterious wolf changes her worldview. She flees into the woods, where she meets Gwen, who helps her to change—into one of the independent beasts she has always been warned about. But the men are hot on her trail.

Wicked Things

Jae & Astrid Ohletz (Ed.)

ISBN: 978-3-95533-273-0
Length: 355 pages (110,000 words)

Fourteen authors of lesbian fiction contributed otherworldly, thrilling and supernatural short stories that will keep you glued to your seat.

Sigil Fire

Erzabet Bishop

ISBN: 978-3-95533-171-9
Length: 131 pages (30,000 words)

Sonia is a succubus with one goal: stay off Hell's radar. But when succubi start to die she's drawn into battle between good and evil.

Fae is a blood witch turned vampire, running a tattoo parlor and trading her craft for blood. She notices that something isn't right on the streets of her city. The denizens of Hell are restless.

The killer has a target in sight, and Sonia might not survive.

Coming From Ylva Publishing

www.ylva-publishing.com

Driving Me Mad

L.T. Smith

For Rebecca Gibson, her journey to a work convention will be one she'll never forget. After driving around for four hours, Rebecca stops to ask for directions at an isolated house on the outskirts of Kirk Langley, Derbyshire.

Her initial meeting with the house's attractive owner, Annabel Howell, seems strange and unsettling, but at her hostess's insistence, Rebecca spends the night.

Plagued by nightmares, Rebecca senses that her dream world has blended with what she believes is reality. When she leaves the next day, her life has changed.

Can Rebecca solve a mystery that has been haunting a family for over sixty years? Will she find love along the way?

Or will the events drive her mad?

Ex-Wives of Dracula

Georgette Kaplan

What's worse than falling in love with a straight girl? Falling in love with a straight girl who drinks blood. And not even in a goth way.

High school senior Mindy Murphy, has been questioning her small town life forever and, more recently, her sexuality. Maybe it has something to do with her new friend, Lucia West. When they were kids they used to be besties, until Lucia grew a head taller and a cup size bigger. Now she's captain of the cheer team, winner of the Boyfriend Olympics, and voted least likely to remember Mindy at their high school reunion.

In short, possibly the worst person alive for Mindy to crush on. Especially after Lucia's bitten by a vampire. Now the only way to keep her alive is to get her blood, and the only way to cure her is to slay the vampire that turned her.

Who knows, maybe after they get this vampire business settled, Lucia can explain to Mindy why she kissed her.

Tales of the Grimoire – Book One

"Return Visit", "Ladies Night", "Hands-Free", "Floyd", and "Crash and Burn" © Cheri Fuller
"Rise & Shine" © Jove Belle
"Clitter Hill on Fur Tor" © Cheri Crystal
"Sugar and Allspice" © Tiana Tatanov
"A Lawyer, a succubus, and a blonde walk into a bar…" © Lila Bruce
"Centralia, 2013" © May Dawney
"Ugly Things" © Eve Francis
"Do You Remember?" © Mary-Anne O'Malley
"Rowan" © Emma Sterner-Radley
"Still Life" © Jess Lea
"Lunar Calling" © Kate Welshire
"Lizzie Borden Took An Axe" © R.G. Emanuelle
"The Crocodile Eye" © Gill McKnight

ISBN: 978-3-95533-428-4

Also available as e-book.

Published by Ylva Publishing, legal entity of Ylva Verlag, e.Kfr.

Ylva Verlag, e.Kfr.
Owner: Astrid Ohletz
Am Kirschgarten 2
65830 Kriftel
Germany

www.ylva-publishing.com

First edition: October 2015

Credits
Edited by Gill McKnight, Day Petersen, Astrid Ohletz
Cover Design & Printlayout by Streetlight Graphics

www.ingramcontent.com/pod-product-compliance
Lightning Source LLC
Chambersburg PA
CBHW031606240626

47153CB00002B/654